*O*f course she wanted to touch him, explore him. She could lose herself with a man as much fun as Walker—witty and warm, maybe even wise—but they wanted different things. She had a goal, a specific place where she wanted a relationship to end up. He seemed to prefer women who would hop on for the ride and not worry about where they were going or how long it was taking to get there. Kathryn used to be that sort of woman. A few years ago, Walker Hart would have been perfect dating material for her, but now her priorities had shifted. It irked her that people made her feel uncomfortable about her desire to hear the words, "Kathryn Lamb, will you marry me?"

Books published by The Ballantine Publishing Group
are available at quantity discounts on bulk purchases
for premium, educational, fund-raising, and special
sales use. For details, please call 1-800-733-3000.

MISS
MATCH

Leslie Carroll

IVY BOOKS • NEW YORK

An Ivy Book
Published by The Ballantine Publishing Group
Copyright © 2001 by Leslie Sara Carroll

www.ballantinebooks.com

ISBN 0-8041-1999-6

Manufactured in the United States of America

First Edition: April 2002

OPM   10   9   8   7   6   5   4   3   2   1

For my grandparents

Thanks to all the men I've ever known and to my native New York City for providing me with constant sources of inspiration; to my dear friend M. Z. Ribalow, and to my fabulous agent Irene Goodman who have believed with an unshakable faith in me and in my work every step of the way; to my wonderful editors Linda Marrow and Charlotte Herscher; to Ken Norwick for the most precious gift of time; to my parents Leda and Gerry Goldsmith and my sister Nicole Gruenstein; to The Playwrights Project of Healing Springs, North Carolina, for providing the most exquisite atmosphere in which to create; and finally, to Ronée Miller, Bill Richert, Tom Kleh, Renée Dodge, Susanne Ritt-Nichol, and Dennis Farrier—for being there when I needed a critical eye, a sympathetic ear, and a strong shoulder. You have all been remarkable cheerleaders. I am deeply grateful.

Chapter
1

"Turn front and face the camera, please, one-six-seven. And remove your hands from your hips."

Kathryn Lamb shook her mass of Titian-red curls. "No way. This is how the models do it. Makes them look like they weigh only ninety pounds instead of a hundred."

The disembodied voice spoke again. "Our clients won't be able to see you."

"Hey, pal, the camera adds ten pounds, you ought to know that. I'm giving you a slenderizing three-quarter profile. If I face front, your clients won't like what they see. Besides, I'm the one who's paying for this service. What happened to 'the customer is always right'?"

"I wouldn't want to date *you*," the voice grumbled under its breath.

"I heard that."

"Okay, Miss Lamb . . ."

"Ms., please."

"Whatever. You're the boss. Okay, *Ms.* Lamb, face the camera—well, *three-quarters* into it, and do your bit for humanity. You've got thirty seconds. Take a deep breath, relax, and when you're ready, nod your head, and I'll turn the camera on. When you see the red light, go for it."

"Is my lipstick okay?"

"Never better."

Kathryn inhaled, closed her hazel eyes for a second or two, exhaled, and gave the camera operator a firm nod, twisting her heart-shaped face toward him. "Hi, I'm Kathryn Lamb. I'm a high school drama teacher, and I love long walks on the beach, cozy fireside chats, and Welsh accents . . ." She doubled over in laughter.

"Houston, do we have a problem?"

"Sorry," Kathryn said, beginning to hiccup. "This is so corny. I've tried really hard to say something mean-ingful, but the bottom line is that I did this to get the nosy neighbor from hell to quit asking me prying questions about my social life . . . excuse me." She held her breath and tried to swallow, in order to chase the hiccups away, but the thought of trying to be serious and soulful while taking out a video personal ad sent her back into convul-sions of hysteria. "The bottom line is that I don't want to meet any guys for whom money is a reason for living, and I value humor . . ." Another hiccup. "Obviously. And intelligence. And I think a life without music is a sorry one. And I don't want any guys with last names like 'Quartermaine,' or first names like 'Dirk.' "

"Okay, Ms. Lamb, we're done."

"What???"

"That's it. Your thirty seconds."

"Are you one taco shy of a combination plate?"

"I beg your pardon."

"No do-overs?"

"This isn't gym class, Ms. Lamb. Didn't you read the fine print on the Six in the City application?"

"Who reads fine print? And I don't call what I just got,

'personal satisfaction,' which—according to your service's motto—is guaranteed."

"You'll have to talk to the manager about that. Just step through that door when you're ready. I'll label the tape, and then you'll have your personal interview and be on your merry way."

Kathryn grabbed her tapestry bag and fished for her embroidered blue velvet makeup kit, a special promotion from one of the major cosmetic companies. But it made her feel like a Tsarina, so she carried it everywhere. She checked her face in the Lancôme compact mirror, deciding that she could have used more lipstick after all, and should have repowdered her nose.

Why did I let some looney tune stranger talk me into doing this, she wondered. *I feel like such a moron.* At least she was out only half of the five hundred bucks it took to become included on the roster of eligible females at the Six in the City dating service. Kathryn's younger sister Eleanor, a former bank manager turned mommy, had agreed to foot the balance of the bill. An early thirty-fifth birthday present.

Kathryn knocked on the beveled glass door.

"Come in."

She entered the room just in time to catch a Nerf basketball in her tapestry bag.

"Which one of us gets the two points?" The speaker was a sandy-haired man, possibly in his late thirties, maybe early forties. Chiseled jaw with dimpled cleft, and pale green, almost sea-foam-colored eyes. *Whoa. If the five dates you guarantee me look like you, I'll get my money's worth,* Kathryn thought. He rose from his brown leather swivel chair and extended his hand. Big man, well over six feet—possibly even six foot three. "Hi, I'm Dirk Quartermaine. How're you doing?"

Kathryn paled about three shades.

"Just kidding. The name's Bear Hart. You were a lot of fun in there."

"That was *you*? You . . . !" She bit her lip to stifle the epithet that wanted to emerge. "That's not very fair!"

"I like to get to know my clients in every situation, so I can get a better handle on whom to match them up with."

"Are you Native American?"

"Only one-sixteenth. Why?"

"Your name is Bear Heart. What was your mother's?"

"Fond of Shopping." When Kathryn didn't wince at his sense of humor, he relaxed a bit deeper into his chair and smiled warmly. "My real name is Walker, which is actually my mother's mother's maiden name. 'Bear' comes from my college days when every woman I went out with eventually came to the realization that I was not marriage material, but a real teddy bear as a boyfriend. Which worked out okay with me, since marriage is an institution to which I never wanted to be committed."

I bet a lot of coeds cried on those big strong shoulders of yours. Kathryn kinda sorta wished she'd been one of them. Just to know what it felt like to bury her head against his . . . *better change the subject because he was already giving her erotic fantasies.*

"It's okay, Bear. I'm not into animal husbandry."

Walker laughed, a deep throaty sound. He seemed like a man who liked to grab life with both hands.

"Don't worry, I'm not part of the package."

That's a damn shame. "Oh, call me Kitty."

"*Kitty* Lamb? That's too cute."

"My kids started calling me that a few years ago. They thought it was cruel, but I thought it was funny, so the joke was on them, and it stuck."

"Kids?"

She chewed her lip, and gestured with her chin at the clipboard on his lap. "You read the book; you saw the film, Bear. I teach high school, remember."

"Oh, of course. Sorry." He leaned forward and stretched a long arm toward the coffee mug on the center of his desk, sending it teetering perilously toward a stack of manila envelopes. "Son of a b—! I'm usually much more on the ball than this. Nice save!" he added, referring to his client's lightning quick reflex.

Kathryn righted the cup and found a napkin on her side of the desk which she used to wipe up the single splotch of light-colored coffee that had made its way onto Bear's file folders.

"Nervous, Mr. Hart?" she asked sweetly. Actually, there was something sort of endearing about his near-miss with the "Go, Big Red!" mug.

"I don't think so. Preoccupied, I guess. Please don't get the impression I'm a klutz. I was actually a helluva running back once upon a time."

Walker was thinking of the damage her luscious curves were doing to that baby blue cashmere V neck she was wearing. He hadn't missed how tight her jeans were when she walked in, either. How she managed to sit on the photographer's stool and swivel around in them without cutting off her circulation had been something of a miracle.

Mr. Six in the City followed his newest client's eyes,

noting that they were almond shaped, sort of like a cat's, and with a bluish cast to them, although she'd listed their color as "hazel" in her profile. He decided it was better to think about something that didn't give him disconcertingly erotic thoughts about her; he could get lost in those eyes.

"I was also something of a ski bum in my misspent youth," he said energetically, bounding into safer emotional territory, "before I decided to settle down and get my MBA. But one of the best places to check out the ups and downs of business administration firsthand, especially in February, is, of course, as everyone knows—a ski lodge." He winked at Kathryn and noticed that she was trying unsuccessfully to suppress a smile.

"What happened?" she asked.

"Broke my leg in three places."

"Oops."

"Then I fractured my collarbone."

"Ouch."

"After the concussion, I finally gave up."

"Probably a wise decision."

Walker looked down at Kathryn's application. "Okay, Miss Kitty," he smiled. "You didn't put down your age."

"I was hoping you had a 'don't ask don't tell' policy here."

"Actually, I was just thinking that you barely look old enough to *attend* high school, let alone *teach* it."

"That was a nice save on *your* part, Bear . . . before you stuck your foot in your mouth *entirely*, I mean."

He found it sweet that she was blushing a little. "Is there anything you want to tell me that you didn't put down on your application?"

Kathryn ran a manicured hand through her coppery curls. "I don't know—I'm just looking to meet a nice guy, I guess. I was engaged to the fiancé from hell until the end of last year, and I'm ready to get back on the horse and do some serious dating. I *like* the idea of marriage, in principle, anyway. I want someone to come home to. I like how that feels, when it's working. It's just that it's never worked for very long for me. My job is not exactly a great place to meet people, except for the divorced dads . . . but that gets too weird. I did that once, and it sort of freaked me to get out of the shower in the morning and ride to school with my date and my student in the same car. Try giving a kid a grade when he knows what you did with his father the night before. Probably *heard* you, too. As far as I'm concerned, the other teachers—and obviously the students—are off-limits. But then, I like a guy who looks old enough to shave."

Walker reflexively stroked his jaw, ruminating on the tidbit Kitty had just dropped. Clearly, in the right company, the woman wasn't exactly shy. He blinked, which is what he always seemed to do when he couldn't quite focus because his train of thought had become derailed. It was sort of a mental "rewind."

"Okay. You said on the tape that you didn't want to meet men for whom money is their reason for living."

"Been there, done that, have the T-shirt. That was the fiancé, Lance. Rule number one: never date anyone named 'Lance,' let alone get engaged to one. Lance is what you're supposed to do to a boil."

"Why did you call off the engagement?"

Kathryn leaned back in her chair and gave Walker a sideways glance.

"I'm asking for purely professional reasons. For all I know, you could be one of those nut jobs who just toys with a man's affections and then dumps him once he's hooked."

"I'm not that kind of girl. The problem was that Lance and I were both in love with the same person: Lance. He was the only guy at his fifteenth high school reunion who wasn't follically challenged. And he was proud of it—to the nth degree. Lance couldn't pass a mirror without stopping to check himself out. And one Saturday last November, when he used the Barney's Christmas display window as a looking glass and actually said aloud '*Damn!* I look good!' I realized the relationship was doomed. Besides, do you have any idea what it's like to live with a man who buys more expensive conditioner than you do?"

"Actually, no, I don't." Walker gave his new client a warm smile. "Now, as our company's name—Six in the City—implies, we guarantee you five matches with different men, all of whom will be selected in accordance with your criteria. Five bachelors plus you, equals six. Each time we match you with a candidate, his name gets written on your card, which is kept in your file." Walker waved a white four-by-six-inch index card in the air.

"So, that's essentially a five-stud card," Kathryn deadpanned.

Walker maintained a poker face but his eyes fully conveyed the impression that he'd gotten her pun. "You can come in to the office and view their tapes, if you want to, after they phone you and identify themselves as a Six in the City client."

"Basically, that boils down to a hundred dollars per guy; and if they spend more than that on dinner, which is easy to do in Manhattan, then I actually come out ahead of the game."

"If you choose to look at it that way. I thought money was not a reason for living for you."

"It isn't. Just doing the math. Actually, only two point five of them need to drop a C-note. The other half are on my sister's nickel. By the way," Kathryn barreled on, "you are the one who coyly suggested that I talk to the manager about not getting any personal satisfaction from the videotape we just made. Well, I'm talking to you now. I don't think I got my money's worth in there Bear, and if it's all the same to you, I'd like a reshoot."

"Personally—sorry." Walker coughed when Kathryn rolled her eyes. "I've been running this service for a while now, and frankly, I think your tape is refreshing in its spontaneity. I'll make you a deal. If you don't derive any personal satisfaction from any of our five guaranteed fix-ups, I'll either refund your five hundred dollars or offer you a reshoot, gratis, and we'll start the whole process all over again. Care to shake on it?"

Walker stood up and offered Kathryn his hand. She leaned across the desk, took it, and was surprised at its warmth and how even such an inconsequential contact made her feel. She felt the blood rush to her head. He came around to her side of the desk unshod. She noticed that he was almost a foot taller than she was, and had maybe a pound or two of "cuddliness" around his mid-section, but she liked that. He looked great. Not perfect, but perfect was always under suspicion. Perfect meant they probably liked themselves more than they would ever like you. Lance had been perfect. "Slightly cuddly" meant that you could indulge in spaghetti and the occasional hot fudge sundae—heck, even a beer in his company, and not feel the need to convert just so you could go to confession. Kathryn was never a salad person, no matter how hard she tried. She looked like a woman, not a waif, which is why she'd been so self-conscious on camera. Oh, there were plenty of wolf whistles from the Neanderthals in the streets, but those weren't the kind of men she aspired to attract. Sooner or later she would have to face the fact that she did not have the wafer-thin looks of an elegant East Side matronette, although her kid sister kept trying to tell her that *real* men didn't find stick figures attractive. Kathryn tugged on the bottom of her pale blue sweater, to disguise what she thought was a tummy bulge.

She tried to divert Walker's gaze, which had followed her hands, from her midriff. "Cute socks," she offered. "What are those—dragons?"

"My mother sent them to me from Wales. She seems to have frozen my age at nineteen. When I was in college, I was into that sort of fantasy stuff. You know, dragons, druids. I used to be a big Tolkien fan."

"That's funny, so was I. My best friend in ninth grade, Melody Miller, used to have a basset hound named Bilbo—you know, from *The Hobbit*—and of course, because we had just learned what the word meant, we called the poor thing Dildo. I remember coming home from Melody's and telling my mother about Dildo and she washed my mouth out with soap. A green bar shaped like a brontosaurus."

"Creative woman."

"Apparently, It was a souvenir from the 1964–65 World's Fair in Flushing Meadow. She was saving it because, like those angled toothbrushes, it could reach back into every corner of your mouth."

"Do you mind if I pass judgment on your mother?"

"You could, but she'd one-up you. She's a civil court judge in Brooklyn."

Walker cleared his throat, then glanced back at Kathryn's Six in the City application. "I see here, under 'referred by whom,' you just wrote down 'a neighbor.' "

"Yup; our co-op's very own version of Gladys Kravitz. You know, that nosy neighbor on *Bewitched*? The woman who sent me to you lives in the penthouse and I run into her in the elevator from time to time. Very red hair—it's a color not found in Clairol, let alone nature. Wears all her Estée Lauder samples at once, along with various dangly, bangly, jangly accessories that are vaguely pre-Colombian, Pagan, and Pan-Asiatic. Sort of generic tribal. I've seen them in mail-order catalogues. And they usually clash with the pink designer cigarettes she smokes. I think she interprets "no smoking" signs as suggestions, rather than state law. Lots of flowy clothes in colors no redhead should wear—trust me. Lavender, fuchsia, persimmon. And don't let me forget her blood-red nail extensions. Kind of like a Hadassah sister gone Celtic."

Walker threw back his head and laughed in a full-throated burst of spontaneous recognition. At the same time, somewhere deep inside his head, a bell went off. *She's like me*, it seemed to tinkle, then the sound faded into the recesses of his mind.

"Oh, and take it from me. That woman's voice could cut corrugated."

The corners of Walker's mouth turned up ever so slightly. "And you trusted her referral of a matchmaking agency?"

"Put it this way, every time I see her, she launches into a litany of 'What's a nice girl like you doing sitting at home on a Saturday night? No boyfriend? So what's wrong with you that you wouldn't make some lucky man very happy?' She told me she owns a dating service. I should become a client; I'll meet the man of my dreams. I figured I'd shut her up by actually coming in and filling out an application. I don't see her—by the way—so my guess that she's a bit certifiable seems on the money. In any event, here I am. So she's certainly the pushiest woman on the planet."

Walker's smile broadened. "True. And she's more than a bit certifiable."

Kathryn felt a furrow breaking out on her brow. "How's that?"

His grin deepened into full Cheshire Cat mode. "I ought to know. She's my mother."

Whoops. Big Whoops.

If Kathryn had been any paler at that moment, the Egyptologists over at the Metropolitan Museum of Art would have rushed over with their mummification paraphernalia. "You . . . shit!" Her complexion flushed from white to rose. "Why did you let me go on like that?"

"I was enjoying it immensely. It isn't every day one hears one's mother so eloquently abused. Besides," he added, "I happen to agree with you."

It took several moments for Kathryn to recover her bearing. "But she said she *owned* this agency."

"She does indeed. I'm her designated hitter to manage it for her when she's out of town. Which she often is. On honeymoons. She's somewhat addicted to them. Been married at least six times that I can count, maybe seven, although one of them was a remarriage. Couldn't seem to keep her hands off of Cyril Haggerty."

Kathryn looked straight at Walker, not quite knowing what to make of him. "So what do you do when your mother isn't jetting off somewhere?"

"Ever watch CNN or the Financial News Network?"

Kathryn shook her head.

"*Wall Street Week* or *The McLaughlin Report*? C'mon, you must watch PBS. How could a high school drama teacher not be into some of that *Masterpiece Theatre* stuff?" He searched for a look of recognition in Kathryn's eyes. "I'm a guest on those financial shows from time to time. I just thought maybe you'd seen me."

"You mean while I was waiting for something less boring to come on TV?" Kathryn teased.

They both smiled.

"Exactly!" Walker exclaimed. "I'm a financial analyst. Not as exciting perhaps as trekking through an Amazonian rainforest in search of a rare species of wildlife, but I can't complain. I've made a pretty good living at it. Have you ever heard of *The Hart Monitor*?"

"Is that like a pacemaker?"

"More like a trendsetter." Walker grinned. "It's my own publication—a financial newsletter for people on Wall Street. Nowadays it practically prints itself; I could write my weekly column in my sleep and my staff takes care of the rest."

"No offense, but your weekly column would probably *put* me to sleep!" Kathryn quipped. "So how does being a financial analyst fit with matchmaking? It seems like an odd combination. What's the common denominator?"

Walker leaned back in his chair and folded his hands behind his head. "Either way, I'm speculating on futures."

Kathryn let out a warm laugh. She enjoyed his sense of humor. "*The Hart Monitor*," she said, letting the syllables roll over her tongue. "That's a very clever name for your newsletter."

"Many thanks. I have to admit it's much better than what I'd originally come up with, under the circumstances."

"Which is . . . ?"

"*Bear Market.*" He switched gears, knowing he'd hooked his audience. "By the way, you said you liked Welsh accents on your tape. Were you kidding?"

"Only partially. They have a lilt to them that's really sexy. Why?"

"Then you and my mother have a lot in common."

"Oh God, I hope not. I mean, I'm sorry—here I am going to town on your mother, for God's sake. You can't be that cavalier about her. That *is* the woman who gave birth to you."

Walker leaned back in his chair and changed the subject. "As a matter of fact, she went to Wales a couple of months ago on a whirlwind honeymoon with one of her own clients: a Frenchman at least twenty years her junior. Ludovic de Tournay. But she's always fancied Welshmen."

"Poor Ludovic."

"No. Poor Mom. Actually, it turned out that Ludo preferred Welshmen, too. But it all worked out. He found one named Rhys, and Mom found one who looked like Richard Burton in his *Camelot* days. So Rushie—my mother—got the marriage to Ludovic annulled and now she's living out her King Arthur fantasy with the Burton clone. She used to marry them all because she loved parties, but then she went through a spate where she decided she was getting too old for divorces. They depressed her too much. She just believes in happily ever after. Sort of like you, Kitty."

"That's a terrifying comparison. It's pretty interesting to me, though, that the apple didn't just fall far from the tree—it fell into another galaxy. She marries everyone and you don't want to marry anyone."

"Yup, that's me. 'A confirmed old bachelor, and likely to remain so,' my fair lady."

Cute, Kathryn thought. She smiled to herself.

"And if I hadn't been that way to start with, the matchmaking business would have done it to me," Walker continued. "All these people out there scrambling to make connections."

"So you figured you might as well cash in on our feeble attempts to live happily ever after?"

"No. I figured I wouldn't let the business my mother built with hope and love go into Chapter Eleven just because I'm a cynic."

"Bah, humbug to you, too."

"I didn't say I don't believe in love. I just don't believe in marriage. But this conversation isn't about me."

"Could've fooled me."

"You're the client. My ambition is to see that *you* find the man of your dreams and live happily ever after. Especially since I already cashed your checks. Would your sister be interested in deriving any pleasure from Six in the City?"

"I hope not, for her sake. Ellie's been married to a plastic surgeon for five years, has a marvelously precocious daughter who is two and a half going on thirty-five, and another kid on the way."

Kathryn shouldered her purse and extended her hand, mostly because she wanted to see if she would have the same sensation the second time around, when they shook hands. "Well, *Bear*," she said with a cocky grin, "I'm pretty skeptical that Six in the City can live up to its claims as advertised. But I'm the kind of woman who takes dares, so I'll see this through if only so I never have to hear your mother nag me again on the elevator."

"Don't worry, Kitty Lamb. I'm the kind of man who doesn't like to lose." He rose from his chair and went to meet her, but instead of rounding the curve of his desk top, he ended up trying to walk through it, halted mid-step by the thump of mahogany against flesh. "Ouch! Damn!"

"Does your thigh hurt?" Kathryn asked solicitously. She checked her impulse to reach out and tenderly touch the affected area through his chinos.

"I'm just a big doofus, that's all," Walker said. He was clearly embarrassed. "Pleasure to make your acquaintance, Ms. Lamb," he added, offering his right hand.

For some reason neither of them seemed eager to relinquish their mutual grip.

"Well," Kathryn said, slightly out of breath.

"Well," Walker responded, an awkward catch in his throat. "Keep me posted."

She turned on her heels and left his office with an oddly buoyant sort of confidence, her reddish curls bouncing across the center of her back, her backside swaying seductively in those impossibly tight jeans.

Walker felt a bit of constriction in his own trousers as he watched her leave. *Too bad she's here to find a husband,* he mused, as he stroked his jaw, realizing that he'd forgotten to shave that morning.

Kathryn considered looking back to catch another glimpse of Walker Hart, or even returning to his office on the pretext of having forgotten something, like an umbrella; but it wasn't raining, and she couldn't think of another excuse before the elevator arrived. *Curiouser and curiouser. Too bad* he *has no interest in a wife,* she thought ruefully, as she descended toward the street.

Chapter
2

Eleanor opened the door of her Park Avenue aerie, looking svelter four months pregnant than Kathryn felt after an entire morning on the treadmill. She wiped her hands on an Irish linen tea towel covered with chocolate stains.

"Hey, how's the jujube?" Kathryn asked her sister.

"Fine. Napping. These days I take the quiet when I can get it. Johanna announced yesterday that she lived in Paris. With Madeline."

"I wish her well. Did you know Johanna started calling me 'Aunt Kittycat'? I feel like something out of *Gone with the Wind* meets *Born Free*."

"I've stopped being surprised at what comes out of her mouth. The other day, we were passing the Empire State Building and she commented on how it looked like the Eiffel Tower. I guess she remembers the illustrations from the Madeline books." Eleanor rubbed her nearly flat stomach protectively, as they entered the kitchen. "They're fun. You should get one."

"It's not beyond the realm of possibility, you know. It's just that I'd rather have the husband first than go the turkey baster route."

"Ugh. If I never had morning sickness, you're about to give it to me." She filled a Williams-Sonoma copper kettle with water and put it on the electric range to boil. "No caffeine for me, but I'll make you coffee, if you want. Dan is addicted to Starbucks. We've got Kenya, French Roast, some 'girl coffee'—oh, it's Irish Mist— and we have Andes something . . ."

"No, herbal tea is fine. If you have something like orange cinnamon, I'll take it."

"Speaking of husbands first, how did it go at Six in the City?"

"So far, so good. The manager is major-league cute, by the way, but I stepped in it big time. That horrifying yenta that lives in the penthouse in my building—the one who told me she's the owner of the agency—well, the hunk is her *son*. It was a total case of open mouth, insert foot, swallow 'til you choke on stiletto, do not pass 'Go,' let him cash your five hundred dollars."

"Huh?" Eleanor removed two porcelain cups with matching saucers from her glassfront cabinets, carefully placing them on the counter.

"When he asked who referred me, I painted a colorful and not terribly flattering portrait of The Yenta. Then he ever so casually happened to mention that she's his mother. I am happy to report, though, that he seemed to take it rather well and doesn't hate me. But he does have five hundred of our dollars, so he doesn't have to like me. Just fix me up with five men who will."

"So while we're on the subject of stiletto swallowing, did you also tell him that you were willing to take your chances and skip the five guaranteed candidates for 'Mr. Kittycat,' in exchange for him?"

"He's neither on, nor in the market. The marriage market, I mean. Apparently, he writes about the *stock* market, when he's not pinch-hitting for The Yenta. He publishes something called *The Hart Monitor*."

Eleanor's jaw dropped to her chin. "Hold it . . . are you telling me you've just spent time in a dark room with no one else but Walker Hart? You'll be the envy of every single woman in New York! And probably more than half of the married ones."

"I certainly didn't feel like it. The upshot of our brief encounter in near darkness was that Walker—*Bear*—wouldn't grant me a reshoot of my video. What happened to 'the customer is always right'? Some big-shot businessman!" Kathryn said with a note of sarcasm.

"You have no idea who this guy is, do you?"

Kathryn shook her head.

"He's the poster boy for financial freedom. And I do mean 'poster boy.' I used to work with women who had his photo from *The Hart Monitor* tacked up in their cubicles—otherwise rational women—from temp secretaries to VPs. Not only is he 'major-league cute,' as you say, but he's a brilliant financial analyst. Wall Streeters consider *The Hart Monitor* their Bible." Eleanor's tone was becoming practically reverential. "He got his start back when he was in college. What made headlines was that he was an all-American footballer who began playing the stock market for kicks and ended up amassing an amazing, hugely successful portfolio. So, he was invited onto all these financial news shows to tell everyone how he did it and became something of a celebrity. He's still one of those 'usual suspects' they call in to wax rhapsodic about stocks and bonds."

"I suppose his being a hunk didn't hurt," Kathryn interjected.

"Then he started sharing his wealth of knowledge by publishing *The Hart Monitor*. Walker Hart's got the Midas touch. He emerged unscathed from Black Monday back in '87, saw that tech stocks were the wave of the future, and had the foresight to dump them before they all tanked. Before anyone else catches on, Walker Hart writes about all the latest trends and fluctuations in the market. And not just in the U.S. He's always ahead of the forecast on the European markets, the Nikkei Index . . ."

Kathryn held up her hand. "Okay, Ellie! I get it—he's a catch, personally and professionally. However, from my conversation with him, he has definitely been avoiding the hook for decades now."

"But," Eleanor sighed, ignoring her sister's comment, "all that was another lifetime ago . . . back in my unmarried yuppie days. Back when I wouldn't go out on dates on Friday nights because Walker Hart was putting in a guest appearance on *Wall Street Week*. What do you think of these, by the way?" Eleanor gestured to a Rube Goldberg-style contraption on her kitchen counter. Tucked into cages suspended from a makeshift metal rack were several water-cooler-style, conical, white paper cups filled with a dark batter.

Kathryn surveyed the rig. "Chocolate dunce caps?"

"*Brownie Points*. Like it?"

"Very clever. What gave you the idea?"

Eleanor smoothed the batter on the top of one of the cones and gingerly adjusted its position in the rack. "I always thought if Mrs. Fields could do it, so can I. Johanna asked me what I did before she was born. So I told her I invented things. And she asked what that meant. And somehow I got around to telling her some of the ideas I had before I had her. And I told her about Brownie Points. So she asked me to make some."

"And this is how you do it?"

"It's the best apparatus I've come up with so far. But it's a bit fragile. I'm afraid the entire structure will collapse like a house of cards when I try to move it into the oven." The mother of the year brought their tea to the table. "Honey?"

"Don't patronize me. I hate it when you do that. Only bra saleswomen old enough to be our mother ever call me 'honey.' "

"I was asking if you wanted honey in your *tea*. Boy, people would think *you're* the pregnant one. You're so touchy."

Kathryn dragged two Le Corbusier-style straight-backed chairs to the marble-topped table in Eleanor's breakfast nook. "Sorry. I've just been wondering if the whole video dating route was such a good idea in the first place."

"Isn't that the way it always is? The good ones are always taken."

"What good ones? I think I missed something, El."

"I mean the erstwhile manager of the matchmaking service, Mr. Hart."

"We actually don't know whether or not Bear is taken. He's just adamantly opposed to the idea of marriage. He even quoted Henry Higgins. You know—that 'I'm a confirmed old bachelor and likely to remain so' bit. But he made it very clear, verbally and physically, that he's definitely into women."

"Physically?" Eleanor's eyes lit up as she sipped her tea. "Have you ever dipped Pepperidge Farm Bordeaux cookies into hot tea? It's almost better than sex," she said with a wink. "Be right back."

"Well, you seem to be pretty successful with the sex part, so the cookies must be damn good."

Eleanor returned with the white bag of cookies. "Your train of thought may be easily derailed, but mine isn't. You said 'physically.' You know, I've grown so used to spending most of my waking hours with a two-year-old, that I positively *crave* adult girl-talk."

Kathryn placed her hands on either side of the teacup. "We shook hands, and I felt this warm red glow spread from my head to my toes and back again. And I'm sure he felt it, too, because he seemed distracted. So I tried a noble experiment and shook his hand again for no reason, except to re-cement the deal we'd just cemented, to see if I'd get the same sensation. And I did."

"So?"

"So it doesn't matter, because we sent me there to meet the guy who's gonna say 'I do'—and he doesn't. Bear could be the greatest, smartest, hunkiest guy in the world, but by his own admission he suffers from terminal FOC."

"Huh?"

Kathryn repeated her acronym. "FOC. Fear of Commitment. We've seen it before. An insidious disease that attacks the most desirable of the male species. Side effects are heartbreak and often anger in women who are residually affected by the affliction."

"Ummm." Eleanor delicately dipped a cookie in her steaming tea, then brought it to her mouth and let it melt. "So, at least you've been warned. Cross the boss off your list before anxiety about him ensues. When do you get your first call?"

"I have no idea. The men are supposed to call me and identify themselves as being clients of Six in the City."

Eleanor retrieved a lined yellow legal pad and a silver-plated Cross pen from one of the kitchen drawers. "When can you go shopping?"

"For what?"

"You dress like your students. We need to find you some serious dating clothes."

Kathryn tugged at her black leggings. "Any guy dating me for my wardrobe has got his priorities screwed up."

"Be that as it may, do you own anything in the category I just described?"

"I've got a couple of classic Little Black Dresses, and more pairs of heels than Imelda Marcos, but I don't exactly dress like that when I come over to visit you and Jo. I hate this neighborhood. I always feel like I have to pay to breathe the air, or that shopgirls are looking at me and thinking 'fraud' knowing I can't really afford to buy anything in their boutiques when I pop in to browse. I'm definitely a Greenwich Village type. Boxy high-rises make me crazy."

"Excuse me, but the last time I checked, you lived in one of the *few* boxy high-rises in the West Village."

"Because the last time *I* checked, schoolteachers couldn't afford one of those yummy, romantic townhouses with a garden. If I never saw glass and chrome again, I'd be a happy camper. There's a brownstone on Bedford Street that is so drop-dead gorgeous that I stand in front of it and stare every day on my way home. The residents are starting to think I'm a stalker."

Eleanor fiddled with the pen, then twisted it open and wrote "lingerie" on the legal pad.

Kathryn leaned over the table, her curls almost tumbling into the tea. "Lingerie? Isn't that a bit ambitious? I haven't even gotten the first phone call yet."

"Think of this as training lingerie. Practice wearing it; see how confident it makes you feel about *yourself*, then, when the time comes, you won't feel self-conscious about wearing it anymore. It'll be as much a part of your daily routine as that Tsarina bag you carry."

"Okay. Silk, satin, and lace. I'm certainly not opposed to the prospect. How does one do it on a Briarcliff salary?"

"Think of me as your fairy godsister."

"I'm not going to let you pay for my underwear."

"Happy early birthday, then."

"That's what I thought the dating service is. I distinctly remember you saying that you thought that's what I needed in order to get back on the horse after the Lance debacle and get on with my life." Kathryn took a swallow of her herbal tea and felt the liquid warming her throat. "I'm just not a hundred percent sure I trust the system, El. I still don't like the idea of these guys knowing where I live. I mean, they're total strangers. For all I know, they could be stalkers. I left my address blank on the application—although since I live in Bear's mother's high-rise, I guess that little secret's out, because *he* obviously knows the address—but these guys will still get my phone number. I'd feel safer if someone I trusted, like Bear, did the calling, but I guess he can't phone everyone to set up the dates, or he'd never get anything else done."

"So what's Bear's other problem, besides FOC?"

"The other potential problem? I think he's a bit of a klutz. Or accident prone."

"What?"

Kathryn nibbled the edge of her Bordeaux cookie. "Unless he was nervous about talking to me. But I can't fathom a reason why he would be, so I can only conclude that he's a bit—well, oafish. Cute, but clumsy. In the space of ten minutes, he practically knocked over his Cornell University coffee mug and then he walked into his desk when he got up to say good-bye. Spending time with him could be a health risk."

"Maybe he just thinks you're hot." Eleanor winked at her older sister. "Ever thought of that?" The sisters got up to clear the tea things. "How's school this year, by the way? I can't believe Barton is still the principal. You would have thought they'd have put him out to pasture decades ago."

"They should have. He's taken it into his head for me to assign the kids some stuffy old chestnut that they can't relate to and which bored the hell out of them, when the seniors really want to do a musical. I've got a soprano with glorious top notes at the ripe old age of sixteen and a half, and I want to be able to use her. She makes Charlotte Church sound like a rank amateur."

"So what musical do you want to do?"

"*She Loves Me*. It's an old musical, by the same guys who wrote *Fiddler on the Roof*, but my students don't know that. After reading the script about lonely-hearted pen pals who don't realize that they're actually coworkers who can't stand each other by day, my kids think it's a musical version of *You've Got Mail*."

"Isn't it?" Eleanor sighed and donned two enormous quilted oven mitts. "Want to check on the jujube while I try to get these into the oven?" She surveyed her gestating Brownie Points.

Kathryn tiptoed into Johanna's blue-and-white-striped bedroom. The toddler was curled up, thumb safely ensconced in mouth, on her "big girl bed," her arms around an enormous Winnie the Pooh and a well-loved rag doll version of Madeline. Kathryn fought the catch in her throat as she gazed at the sleeping child. Lately she had been feeling the first pangs ever of wanting one of her own.

"Ever since we've been calling her the jujube, she's taken to repeating it," Eleanor whispered over Kathryn's shoulder. "But it comes out like, 'ju-bee, ju-bee.' "

"Maybe she's just getting ready to play Hamlet," Kathryn joked. For some reason she didn't want her younger sister to see her choking back a tear. "You know, ju-bee or not ju-bee. That is the question."

"I thought of you the other day, when she was fussing over a toy I took away, and I told her she was making much ado about nothing. She actually stopped and got quiet."

"Well, at least we know she can take direction," Kathryn teased. "Which is more than I can say for *my* kids, who are more than a decade older than she is." Kathryn headed for Eleanor's hall closet, painted in *trompe l'oeil*, to look like part of the wall, and removed her brown velvet shrug.

"Call me when you want to do underwear," supermom said, as she kissed Kathryn good-bye. "Maybe we can get together and hit La Perla, then zip across town to Serendipity for the specialty of the house."

"Their frozen hot chocolate that comes in a bowl the size of a cauldron? Oh, that will help me keep my girlish figure. You've got a bun in the oven; you're *supposed* to indulge at ice cream parlors. I have neither the same excuse, nor the same luxury. Although I really love those kitschy toys they sell up front—and *they* don't have any calories." Kathryn retrieved her purse and started to head for the door. "Bye! Give the jujube a kiss from Aunt Kittycat when she wakes up." She rang for the elevator and sat down on the upholstered bench in the little hallway to wait for the elevator operator to bring the car to Eleanor's floor.

"Call me as soon as you hear from Bachelor Number One," Eleanor said from the doorway.

"And let me know how your culinary experiment turns out. In the meantime, I'll try not to think too much about Bear Hart. I swear, on the way over here on the crosstown bus, I was doing a 'sense memory,' trying to recreate how it felt both times we shook hands, and I did it to myself. I made myself feel the same way again."

"I'm sure your fellow travelers were entertained."

"I guess I could sort of store that sensation up, and replay it in my mind whenever I'm feeling glum."

"Or you could just load up on Godiva. Look, there's no reason you can't be Bear's friend, you know. Just keep focused on your priorities. But if you change your mind about him—or more to the point, if *he* changes *his*, remember: the way to a man's heart *is* through his stomach—"

"If you saw Bear in person, you'd see how true that is." Kathryn raised an eyebrow archly. "He does impress me as a man who doesn't forgo dessert."

"So bring him a Brownie Point."

The elevator ground to a halt at Eleanor's landing. "Now *that*," Kathryn said with a smile, "is a good suggestion."

Chapter
3

Walker stood at the full-story windows of his mother's penthouse, looking out at the view of the Hudson River. To the north, the sight wasn't too spectacular, although on a clear day he could see all the way up to the George Washington Bridge. That kind of vista made Rushie a very popular woman whenever the Op-Sail parade of tall ships cruised into New York Harbor on the Fourth of July. The first night Walker moved in to house-sit for his mother while she jetted off on yet another honeymoon, he realized that he also had a spectacular view of the Statue of Liberty to the south, in the immortal words of the Emma Lazarus poem, lifting "her lamp beside the golden door." From the wraparound terrace the city glittered, illuminated as though millions upon millions of stars had fallen from the heavens upon the townhouses and tenements beneath.

Maude Fixler herself, of Fixler & Crumb Realty, had sold Ruth Goldfarb Hart Haggerty Tobias Haggerty Aviles de Tournay Glendower the cooperative apartment, catering to Rushie's fantasies to own an urban aerie—in a neighborhood where she could indulge her bohemian sensibilities and still feel like a Jewish Nora

Charles. But almost as soon as the real estate closing was complete and Rushie had hired an interior designer, she was off on another trip to the altar. The major reason that Walker had agreed to watch over his mother's swanky, professionally decorated penthouse was to get his own jollies fancying himself a modern day Cole Porter.

The penthouse boasted only one piece of furniture that was his: the Steinway baby grand, which he had positioned on a carpeted platform at the far end of the living room so he could regale his friends with his renditions of Porter and Gershwin classics. The piano had cost him a bloody fortune to move from his sprawling acreage in suburban Connecticut—his welcome retreat from the frenetic singles bars along Second Avenue and the competitive, often arrogant men and women who inhabited the cutthroat world of dot-coms and blue chip companies that subscribed to *The Hart Monitor*. As long as he met his publishing deadlines he had the luxury of setting his own schedule, which meant that he could spend a generous amount of time in the pursuit of happiness if he so chose. Lately, he'd been thinking about becoming a country squire and taking up riding. He had plenty of land in which to stable and work his own horses. And it was nice to come home to a place where he could actually hear a bird sing every once in a while and, on a clear night, see more than the Big Dipper.

But when Rushie had summoned him to preside over her domain, he'd sublet the Connecticut property on a month-to-month lease to a United Nations foreign diplomat and his family. No one ever knew precisely how long Rushie would be gone whenever she gallivanted off on one of her honeymoon jaunts, but given her penchant for lengthy honeymoons, Walker could expect to house-sit for her in Manhattan for at least a couple of months. His mother hated to leave her new nest unattended for any length of time, especially since the roof had been leaking. For Walker, an open-ended subtenancy in Rushie's penthouse was far too long to be without his grand piano—his greatest source of solace. Besides, he hated the idea of a daily commute from Connecticut down to the Six in the City offices. So Mayflower Movers schlepped his Steinway, and Walker moved in to Rushie's penthouse.

He looked at the white south wall of the living room and frowned. Maude, in her Chanel suit and Bally spectator pumps, a blonde cross between a matriarch and a Machiavelli, had assured Rushie, with her realtor's take-no-prisoners manner, that the wall would be repainted before the new Mme. De Tournay left town. True to her word, Ms. Fixler had indeed seen to it that the brownish rivulets, the residual effects of a problem on the roof—since repaired—were duly painted over. But the network of rust-colored capillaries running down the wall was still there, no doubt about it. Walker had inspected the apartment the day he moved in and could have sworn he didn't remember seeing it.

He padded across the pale champagne-colored carpet and ran his hand along the wall. Bone dry. At least that was a plus. Walker turned around and surveyed the living room. Smiling to himself, he shook his head. His mother knew absolutely nothing about interior design, but felt it a moral imperative to be perceived of as an expert, hence the highly recommended professional decorator. And true to Rushie's form, she was nowhere to be found when it came time to actually make some decisions about colors, fabrics, mood, and style.

The decorator, Sven, who seemed to have no last name and who showed up at Rushie's penthouse wearing mulberry-colored skintight leather pants, was thrilled when he met Walker, whom Rushie had deputized to oversee her decorating. Attempting to size up his client's taste, Sven suggested that Rushie might go for an over-stuffed sofa upholstered by that "prince of chintz" Mario Buatta. Walker responded that he thought the man in question was the bullpen catcher for the Red Sox. Thus, Sven pegged him as a hopeless Martha Stewart surrogate. This gave Sven free reign.

So, beige, beige, beige, was the color of the carpet, al-though Sven had referred to it as "*brut champenoise*". Glass, chrome, and leather, with a few scattered animal prints were hauled in, arranged strictly according to Feng Shui, and the place now screamed "Rich Man-hattan Bachelor," rather than "Absentee Matchmaker." And it didn't feel like anybody's home.

Armed with his mother's mandate and on the advice of Joshua Leo, an old Cornell fraternity brother of Bear's who had inherited the Leo family art gallery in Soho, Walker purchased some works of art that Josh consid-ered "important," which meant that Walker could ex-pect them to appreciate in value. The collection included a bronze statuette of a nymphlike maiden arching her back toward the heavens, and an original Warhol litho, which didn't particularly excite him either, but at least it added a little color to the place. Sven, a card-carrying member of an animal rights group, refused to decorate any of his clients' homes with real skins; so the zebra on the floor was the best "faux" money could buy, and the cheetah toss pillows were equally politically correct.

Total cost was probably double the price of a weeklong
safari on the Serengeti.

Window treatments. He laughed to himself. Why did
his mother want Austrian shades, whatever they were?
Besides, why would anyone want to obstruct the view of
the river? The water was mesmerizing in any light. Who
was going to look in—some nut in New Jersey with a
telescope?

Walker picked up his black portable phone and dialed
a number.

"Leo Galleries. How may I help you."

"I'd like a Picasso and a six-pack delivered by nine P.M."

"Bear! How're you doing? I've got customers, can I
call you back?"

"Sure, Josh. I was bored and didn't like the idea of
watching *Monday Night Football* alone."

"No dates?"

"Don't want one."

"You don't want a *wife*. I've never known you not to
practice connubial comfort with a nonwifely candidate.
Gotta go, bro. See you at eight forty-five. Get some food
this time."

Walker slid the antenna down and placed the phone
on the smoked glass coffee table shaped sort of like a
water trap on the twelfth hole. He retrieved a stack of
take-out menus from a drawer in the kitchen and perused a couple. Chinese, Thai, Mexican, Ethiopian, Viet-
namese, Afghan, Italian, comfort food, pizza. A wealth
of choices and no recommendations to go on. He tossed
out the menus from restaurants that were more than
ten blocks away. No way take-out could get to your
door from over a half mile away and not be either soggy
or cold.

He peeked into the fridge, half expecting some food to have mysteriously appeared when he hadn't been looking, but there was only the bachelor's staple: a bottle of champagne. This one was Taittinger. Checking the freezer, he found a bottle of Stoli and a package of frozen egg rolls.

Walker never cooked for himself. Eating was a social experience as far as he was concerned, and therefore he did it only socially: when he was taking a woman on a date, or entertaining someone at home—usually Josh, who would come up to Connecticut on the commuter train—and *they* had guy meals, like pizza and beer.

He wasn't sure why he'd been feeling so restless lately. Maybe he was stuck in a rut. He certainly didn't dislike his lifestyle. He had more money than anyone had a right to wish for, though it wasn't the be-all and end-all, and the responsibilities of *The Hart Monitor* allowed him to set his own hours, therefore giving him the ability to manage—temporarily—his mother's abandoned business. There was never a shortage of women, but no one lately had really blown his circuits. Thank heaven he had eclectic interests. He was just as happy at a football game as he was at a concert. He liked his beer, and when he'd dated a woman named Talia, he'd even developed a taste for classical dance because she was in the corps of the New York City ballet. But Talia, even out of her pink satin pointe shoes, turned out to be extremely flighty and floaty. She was also a devout vegan who lectured him every time he ate a cheeseburger, wore clothing made exclusively of textiles where the fiber was grown organically—and to top it off, was more infatuated with herself than with him. What was it about dancers and mirrors?

The only thing that invariably restored his equilibrium after a particularly stressful workday was his music. Walker lifted the cover of the piano bench and flipped through the stacks of sheet music, drawing out a few selections. Then he fixed himself a Bombay Sapphire extra dry martini and placed it on the piano above his right hand.

It felt good to touch the keys again. He closed his eyes and let his hands roll over and over one another as he warmed up his fingers, getting used once again to the feel of the keyboard. His left hand felt a bit constricted, so he removed his gold signet ring. It had been his father's ring. He wore it because he had nothing else of his, and that was all the old man had passed on. Max Hart hadn't been much for possessions, and had walked out on the family when Walker was six years old, taking only a Gladstone-style overnight bag with him. Four years ago when the family learned of Max's death, all that was sent to Walker was the gold ring; a more substantial legacy than any of his childhood memories of the man.

Walker flipped the music stand into place, and arranged the sheet music on it, breaking into a passionate rendition of "Night and Day." Good thing his windows faced west. The only nice thing about being able to see New Jersey was that he had excellent views of the sunset as he played. Time must have flown because he couldn't figure out why he kept hearing an occasional strident buzz while he was playing through the score of *Red, Hot, and Blue*, until he realized it was the doorbell—and Josh—with two cold six-packs.

"Hey, bro!" Josh swung his elbow at Walker by way of a greeting and walked through the living room into the kitchenette. "Carlos downstairs said you were in, even though you weren't answering the intercom, so he let me up. Then you didn't answer the doorbell. These were cold when I entered the building," he admonished, indicating the twelve beer bottles in his hands. "But I heard the piano through the door, so I knew you were in here. You always seem to go off into LaLa land somewhere when you play."

Walker followed his friend into the kitchen. "Well, a life without music is a sorry one. Hey, you know I heard that today from someone else? A client."

Josh shoved the beers in the refrigerator. "We're gonna have to order in. I don't think you can make a meal out of Worcestershire sauce and vodka. And those eggrolls date from the Pleistecene era." He walked back out into the living room and sunk into an Italian leather armchair, immediately grabbing the opportunity to remove his tasseled loafers. "I hate these. I tailor my shoe wardrobe to whichever clients have appointments on a given day. We've got the loafer crowd, the combat-boot crowd, and the Timberland crowd."

Walker came out of the kitchen with two cold longnecks. "I didn't think the Timberland crowd bought art."

"*You're* not what you seem at first glance—why should everyone else be a stereotype?"

"Aren't you the guy who just pigeonholed art buyers into three categories of footwear?"

Josh changed the subject before he allowed his old college roommate to push him into an argument. Walker had been able to find the perfect ways to push Josh's defensive buttons for the past twenty years. This time, Josh refused to play. "So tell me about the client who has the same mantra you do."

"What?"

"Your 'life without music is a sorry one' litany. I agree with you, bro, but you mentioned that a client said the same thing this afternoon."

"Oh, yeah. This schoolteacher named Kitty Lamb . . ."

"Kitty Lamb? That is *too* cute."

"That's exactly what *I* said. Her real name is Kathryn. She came in because my mother nagged her into it."

"Does that mean she's not a serious client?"

"I'm not sure what it means. She admits that she came to Six in the City because she's really looking to get married, but she cracked herself up when she was making the video, because she thought that talking herself up while trying to be deep and meaningful was the corniest, funniest, most unnatural thing in the world."

"It is."

"But I thought she was adorable, and spontaneous and refreshing, so I just left the camera running when she started going off. She thought I would rewind the tape so she could start over again after she pulled herself together, but I had it all on video, so I told her that her thirty seconds were up, and that was it."

"You're kidding."

"Nope. And when she asked for a do-over, I wouldn't let her have one."

"That's unethical."

"*You're* telling me about unethical? Weren't you the one who hacked his way into the Cornell computers and changed all our grades? I remember the only reason they didn't expel you was because you cut a deal with them to reveal how you did it."

"That was my misspent youth. And you probably wouldn't have gotten accepted into a master's program if

I hadn't. Besides, Bear, this is your job right now. I can't believe you didn't allow her a retake. These poor stiffs pay ridiculous amounts of money for Six in the City. Why didn't you just rewind the videotape?"

"Honestly, I thought she was a breath of fresh air. Dishonestly? Or maybe subconsciously? Something weird happened to me in her presence. I know it's my job to fix her up, in the hope that she'll meet someone through Six in the City and live 'happily ever after,' but I sort of wanted to keep her for myself."

"In the twenty years I've known you, Bear, you have never wanted to enter the state of marital bliss any more than you've wanted to enter the state of New Jersey. That's completely unfair to Ms. Lamb. Poor Kitty."

"I did make a deal with her. I told her that if she was unhappy, or if she felt that her performance on the videotape in any way sabotaged her chances with the five guys we guarantee to fix her up with, that either we'd reshoot the tape and go through the cycle all over again, free of charge, or I'd refund her five hundred dollars. She seemed amenable. Finally. And don't worry, I told her that I'm not part of the package."

"And what did she say?"

"She said she wasn't into animal husbandry."

"I like her. Fix *me* up."

"You're engaged, bozo. And Lou is a great woman. I don't want you to do anything stupid, because I've been working on my best-man toast ever since senior year." Walker flipped the cap off his beer bottle. "She's got this heat that seems to come off her body."

"Who does?"

"Kathryn Lamb. When we shook hands to clinch the

deal, it felt as though someone had turned up the thermostat in my office. Then we shook hands again before she left. I think she was trying to see if the same thing would happen again. I'm glad she did it, because I was ready to try the same experiment. She also fills out a sweater like Lana Turner."

"You know what you're saying, don't you?"

Walker shot his friend one of his trademark "don't get me started" looks.

"Bear. Ask her out. It's patently obvious you want the woman."

"No I don't. It's patently obvious that she wants a husband, and it's patently obvious that I do not, I repeat, emphatically do not, want a wife. Ergo: I do not want Kitty Lamb."

"The Bear doth protest too much."

"My role—not my role, my *job*—is to find Ms. Lamb five clients who also want to get married, which is why they're registered with Six in the City. But I admit that I find Kitty attractive as all hell, and would love to check out what's under the blue cashmere sweater she was wearing this afternoon. Anyway, weren't you the guy who told me that marriage was the death of sex?"

Josh took another swig of Rolling Rock. "So I've heard. But even *I* am finally taking the plunge." He used a sock-clad foot to maneuver the remote control within his grasp. "I think if you're not going to ask the woman out, Bear, you should allow her a retake of her tape and give her an honest chance—since I'm sure you've already banked her bucks—to meet some truly eligible men."

"I'll think about it. Meanwhile, I'd rather watch Vinnie and the Jets. Just toss me the damn remote." Walker took a deep swig of his beer and looked over at

Josh, whose eyes were already glazed over watching the graphic image of two helmets colliding and exploding on contact. "Okay," he said to his distracted former roommate, "if it'll make you happy, I'll think about it."

Chapter
4

"Evening, Tito," Kathryn said, acknowledging the day doorman, as she strolled through her lobby two days later.

"*Buenos tardes, Señorita Lamb,*" the jovial gatekeeper responded.

Kathryn checked her watch. Good grief! Only four-thirty? She was so exhausted, it felt like she'd been slogging it out for days. The freshmen had been particularly belligerent that afternoon; openly, even hostilely, avowing that drama was kid stuff, sneering at the notion that make-believe could set you free. Tandy Newman had shown promise—proclaiming, when it was each student's turn to share a little bit about themselves, that she had theater people in her family. The kid had poise and polish, and was awfully precocious for a ninth grader.

Kathryn preferred to play theater games with them, to watch them interact with one another before they were burdened with a script. She also liked to see what their imaginations would produce without benefit of an already created character to explore. In order for these kids to let go, they would have to learn to first be comfortable with, then appreciate, and finally celebrate their own expressiveness. And the freshmen were at an awkward stage to begin with. She remembered the horrifying peer pressure *she'd* undergone at their age—stuffing her feet into clunky Frye boots that never quite broke in, fighting with her mother for the right to wear Levis to school like everyone else, instead of Danskin leggings. Kathryn smiled to herself as she looked down at her legs. Danskin leggings. Burgundy ones, and plum-colored suede boots that cross-laced up the center.

She loved her job, though. Her parents hadn't given it much credence, never letting her forget that a private schoolteacher's salary is lower than the average custodial worker's wages at a public school. Although, in their favor, they were glad that she had gotten the Briarcliff job. As far as they were concerned, if she did insist on wallowing in poverty, at least she wasn't doing it in a dicey neighborhood where the graduating seniors were almost her own age, and she would have to spend half her days busting up fights, instead of imparting actual knowledge to a bunch of overprivileged adolescents.

The only time she'd ever gotten a compliment from her father was when a parent had approached him after one of Kathryn's triumphs—she had coached and directed her seniors in a production of *Blithe Spirit*. The kid's father, Mr. Paredes, had told Mr. Lamb that he should be very proud of his daughter, because Evan had a lot of rage in him, and Ms. Lamb had taught him to focus and direct his energies more usefully and the boy had been a changed person for the past year. Because of Ms. Lamb, the kid had even decided to major in theater arts in college and had gotten himself accepted to a combination conservatory and liberal arts college out in Ohio.

Kathryn remembered her father saying to Mr. Paredes that a career in theater as opposed to one in, say, law, was not exactly something to crow over. Whereupon, Mr. Paredes explained that it was remarkable that his son had found any direction whatsoever, and had finally come across something he enjoyed doing, all thanks to his drama teacher. So, her own father decided to accept the compliment; he became suitably proud of his older daughter for almost two whole weeks.

It was amazing what memories could flood your mind while waiting for an elevator. Why did both of the damn things always seem to be stuck at the penthouse? If she didn't live on the ninth floor, Kathryn would have walked, but it was just high enough to be an exhausting trek. *Actually,* she thought, as she changed her mind and headed for the stairs, *I have to get myself in shape for the new lingerie.*

By the time she reached her front door, Kathryn was sure she had a charley horse from climbing all those steps. She unlocked all three locks and kicked the day's residue of Chinese menus inside the door, where they promptly slid halfway under her faded oriental throw rug. How did all those take-out places have time to leaflet everyone's apartment and still deliver any meals?

"Goddamn," Kathryn muttered to herself as she bent down to retrieve the menus, her purse sliding off her shoulder and thudding to the floor in the process. Her cordovan leather wallet, a cinnamon-colored combination lipstick/lipliner, a bottle of GAP spray cologne, a tortoiseshell hairclip, and a dog-eared copy of *Harry Potter and the Goblet of Fire* spilled out onto the floor. Actually, *Harry Potter* sort of thudded. The cylindrically packaged cosmetics, which she had forgotten to slip back inside the Tsarina bag when she freshened up after her last class, rolled somewhere under the sofa. She made an exasperated sputtering noise with her lips.

Kathryn threw herself on the wine-colored sofa and shoved a tapestry pillow under her head. One of her own needlepointed creations. "Just five minutes of rest, that's all I need," she said to herself. She immediately got up and turned on the CD player, slipping in the *She Loves Me* original soundtrack recording, then flopped back on the couch.

Then she popped back up, fixed herself a Harvey's Bristol Cream on the rocks with a twist, and resumed her supine position on the dark velvet sofa. A few minutes and several sips of sherry later, her attitude was adjusted enough to check her answering machine for messages. Actually, she had forgotten that her five Six in the City bachelors were going to start calling her. Will wonders never cease? The red light was blinking three times.

Message number one. "Hi, it's your sister. The jujube and I are thinking of going to the carousel before the weather gets too cold. Give us a call." And faintly in the background "Ju-bee, ju-bee. Izzat Aunt Kittycat?" followed by Eleanor asking Johanna, "Do you want to say hi to Aunt Kittycat?" and a distinct "No" from the tiny voice at the other end of the speakerphone.

Message number two. "Kathryn, it's Bear Hart over at Six in the City. Some of my male clients were in this afternoon checking out the new recruits, so to speak, and I know that a number of them saw your tape . . ."

Great.

". . . so you should be getting a call sooner rather than later from at least one of them. I think you'll be pleased with the results. As I said when we met, keep me posted on how things go. It helps me plan my marketing

strategy, and, obviously, we want to provide you with—
oops, there's my other line. Catch you later."

Kathryn's machine beeped, signaling the end of Walker's
message.

Message number three. "Hullo, Kathryn, my name's
Barnaby . . ."

Cool British accent. Way cool. Sort of Michael Caine-
ish with a bit more polish. Definitely London, though.

"I saw your tape over at Six in the City, and I'd really
like to meet you. I'm a musician, and I thought perhaps
we could go to a concert over the week-end."

That's how he pronounced it—with the emphasis on
the second syllable. "Week-*end*."

"You're welcome to take a gander at my tape, of
course, but if you don't get the chance to between now
and Saturday night, I've got dark hair, almost shoulder
length, nearly black in color, and my eyes are green. Oh,
and I'm 5'10", one hundred and sixty pounds."

Barnaby left his phone number, which Kathryn, with
nothing handy to write on, scribbled in the inside cover
of *Harry Potter*.

Her first call was to Eleanor. "Bachelor Number One
has phoned," she announced.

"And?"

"A musician named Barnaby, with an English accent
to die for."

"You always did go in for those." Eleanor's voice
shifted in tone. "Johanna, please don't pull the cord
while Mommy's trying to talk."

"What's today? Wednesday?"

"Last time I checked. Johanna, Mommy will be off the
phone in a minute."

"I'm going over to Six in the City to check out this

guy's tape before I phone him back. So far, so good, though. I mean it's Wednesday, and he called to ask me out for Saturday. That's a fair amount of lead time."

"If you are abiding by that *Rules* book, Kitty, I'm going to disown you and take back that insanely expensive lingerie we purchased."

"I actually did buy a copy a couple of years ago, just to check it out, and it was very useful."

"Please tell me you're joking."

"God's honest truth. I was reading it in the bathroom—"

"Appropriate," Eleanor interjected.

"—And I accidentally let the tub overflow while I was running a bubble bath, and there was water everywhere, so since it was the first thing handy—I'd be damned if I was going to ruin my new Fieldcrest towels—I ripped out the pages and they sopped up almost the entire sudsy mess."

"Ironic how a book on how to forestall the male of the species turns out to be the quicker picker-upper. So, let me know what Barnaby looks like. Call me as soon as you get back from the dating service. I've got to give Johanna some attention before she does something I'd prefer she didn't—like watch *Teletubbies*."

Kathryn checked her watch and thought it would be rude to wait too long to return Barnaby's call, and since Six in the City was open until seven P.M., she decided to go right over. It was a short walk from the apartment, anyway. She got down on her hands and knees, fished the cosmetics out from under the sofa, ignoring the couple of dust bunnies she'd promised herself to vacuum up last Sunday afternoon, and replenished her lipstick. Was she the only woman on the planet who seemed to "eat" lipstick? She could apply it and not do a damn thing with her mouth and by the time she had gotten out the door, the lipstick was all gone.

On the walk over to the dating service, Kathryn admitted to herself that she was rushing over there as much to pop in and say hello to Bear Hart, as she was to check out Barnaby's video. She hoped the boss-man would be around. And that he didn't have another attractive female client in his office.

Walker, in stockinged feet, answered the door himself. He broke into a broad grin when he saw Kathryn, and extended his paw. "Hey there, Kitty Lamb."

There it was again. That warmth when they shook hands. The warmth that spread all over her like a cozy fire in an Adirondack cabin on a snowy February weekend. Kathryn's gaze shifted from their joined hands up his torso to his pale eyes, and she drew in her breath. His collar was open, exposing a glimpse of honey-colored chest hair. "I came here to check out Barnaby's tape. He called me this afternoon."

Walker stroked his jaw. "Barnaby . . . ?"

"You've got more than one client with that name? You're limping by the way."

"I just stubbed my toe on the metal wastebasket. It hurts like a mother. I don't remember Barnaby seeing your tape."

"Well, I got a phone call from a guy identifying himself as 'Barnaby' with a British accent to cream over. Oh. Sorry. A British accent—and he said he's a musician, and wants to take me out on Saturday, so I want to see his video."

Kathryn felt as though she were watching a list of clients scroll past Walker's eyeballs. Finally, a look of recognition dawned on his face. "Oh, yeah. I know who you're talking about. Why don't you go inside to the screening room, and I'll get you set up. Want some coffee or anything?"

She was willing to prolong her visit as much as possible. "Are you having any?"

"I will if you will."

"Then I will. Black please."

"I've got a cappuccino machine," Walker said with a provocative look.

"I'm sure you do wonderful things with steamed milk. Sounds terrific. Hey, if I keep coming here and having cappuccino, which costs about three bucks in a restaurant, maybe I'll finally get my money's worth."

Walker seated Kathryn in a generously proportioned leather swivel chair, and retrieved a videotape. He turned on the VCR and handed Kathryn the remote.

"I wish I could bottle this moment," she said, and he looked at her quizzically. "A man handing me custody of a remote control. Shall I alert the media?" She started channel surfing on the TV just because she could. "Wow, such power," she crowed. "Now I know what a sexual thrill you men get out of wielding one of these things."

"Okay," Walker said curtly, rolling his eyes heavenward. "I get the point."

"Good. Now let me experience thirty private seconds with Barnaby, while you get the cappuccino." Kathryn felt awkward looking at a "husband prospect" with Walker in the room. She felt like she was somehow cheating on him, by even entertaining the notion of dating someone. It was ridiculous as well as absurd, but at least she admitted to herself that she had those feelings about Walker Hart. Of course, he had removed himself as a possible choice because he would be The Last Bachelor

Standing when the apocalypse eventually rocked Manhattan. And Kathryn had agreed to pursue this whole matchmaking scheme because she wanted to settle down, truly sick of the will-we-won't-we mating dance. She knew what she wanted: total romantic I-want-to-wake-up-in-your-arms-for-the-rest-of-my-natural-life commitment. But Walker Hart did not fit the mold. Yet, she felt so comfortable in his presence. They had spent only a few minutes in each other's company, but they had such an easy rapport. This was a guy she could go on talking to for hours on end, teasing him, baiting him. He was fun.

Walker slipped the ceramic cup under the steamed milk nozzle. *Kitty Lamb is a fun person to banter with,* he thought as he topped off the coffee cup. He really *had* been trying to remember which client Barnaby was; and after he did, his mind flew to comparisons with himself. The dark-haired client did have the kind of accent that made ordinarily sane women from New York swoon. Walker gave Kathryn her privacy, but secretly hoped that she would find something wrong with Barnaby just from viewing the tape. He'd never before felt this way about a client. Then he kicked himself for (a) potentially sabotaging his mother's business; and (b) still trying to keep Kitty in a compartment reserved for himself, even though the last thing he ever wanted to do was get hitched.

Barnaby was pretty impressive. He had a face the camera loved, and Kathryn was well aware that video flattered very few people. The musician had those smoldering, bad-boy, dangerous sort of looks, and a soft-looking mouth that curled into a sort of sneer. Kathryn played the tape a third consecutive time, this time listening with her eyes closed. *He could make the* yellow pages *sound good,* she thought. *I've had worse Saturday nights.*

Bachelor Number One's sex appeal almost eclipsed her thoughts of Bear Hart. In fact, she was fantasizing about showing the Brit her new lingerie, when the door to the screening room opened, and Bear popped his head in.

"Well . . . ?" he asked.

"He'll do," Kathryn heard herself say, self-consciously, tugging at the sleeves of her hunter green velvet tunic. Funny, how neither she nor Bear seemed genuinely enthusiastic. Barnaby was cute, but Bear was . . . well . . . Bear was unavailable, that's what he was. "Yes! I give Barnaby Street the thumbs-up," she said with self-conscious cheeriness.

"Well, then, I'll add his name to your file. And, Ms. Lamb? You're bound by your contract with Six in the City to let me know how the date went."

"How voyeuristic. Shall I hire a photographer? How down and dirty would you like me to get?" She grinned at him, and thought she saw his throat constrict.

"*What* my clients do on their dates is none of my business. General feedback though is a part of my marketing strategy. I need to track how many matches are successful, in terms of the date going well."

"So you have a 'good date' and a 'date from hell' category? Column A and column B?"

"Something like that. Both you and Barnaby will phone me sometime within a week after your first date, and let me know some basic stuff."

"Like . . . ?"

"Like: 'she was fun, but I wouldn't want to date her again'; 'she's a babe, and we're going out three more times this week'; 'she made Cruella D'Evil look like Mother Teresa on Prozac.' That sort of thing."

"Gotcha." Kathryn stood up and retied her right boot, which had somehow come unlaced.

"Don't you want your cappuccino?" Walker offered her the steaming mug of coffee.

Kathryn accepted the cup, which felt almost as warm as his touch had. She blew on the foam, watching it eddy across the top of the mug. "You sprinkled cinnamon on top," she noticed. "I'm impressed."

He nodded in the direction of the cup. "Actually, that's more or less the extent of my culinary expertise. The directions that come with the machine can be understood by a trained monkey, so I'm very proud to be in company with the higher primates."

"Oh, I'm sure you can find more things you have in common with the chimps," Kathryn teased.

Walker laughed. "The *cinnamon* was my own idea, though."

"Well, you certainly knew what to do with the nozzle," Kathryn said, making herself blush as she sipped the coffee through the foam.

"You look pretty in pink, Ms. Lamb."

"Sorry."

"Why?"

"If I'm going to blush at my own jokes, then maybe I shouldn't be making those kind of jokes in your presence." She handed back the mug. "You make a mean cappuccino, Mr. Hart."

They shook hands to say good-bye, and Kathryn felt that flush of heat spread through her again. She was sure that he felt it, too, this time, because he was screwing up his mouth, looking like he was about to say something;

then changed his mind before he opened his mouth, then
was about to say something different; then decided, for
whatever reason, to keep his own counsel.

"Good luck with Barnaby," he said flatly, trying to
sound enthusiastic.

"I'll make sure to get double prints so you can have
your own copies," Kathryn said slyly, giving him a
provocative parting pout. God, he was such fun to tease.
Too much fun.

Chapter
5

Anxious about having a total stranger come up to her apartment, Kathryn agreed to meet Barnaby downstairs in the lobby. As hunky and adorable as he looked on camera, if her date turned out to be a masher, at least Carlos, the night doorman, was there to protect her, although one of the reasons Kathryn was drawn to the swarthy-looking Barnaby was because he had an air of danger about him.

At ten P.M. on Saturday night, Carlos rang her on the intercom and announced her visitor. Kathryn threw a denim jacket over her velvet bodysuit and black leggings and tossed a brown leather saddlebag-style purse over her head and across her chest. She checked her image in the hall mirror—a wrought-iron fantasy creation of ivy and quince intertwined in an oval shape around the perimeter of the glass. She looked sort of like Morgaine Le Fay meets downtown rocker chick. Except that Kathryn's ears were the only body parts that were pierced. Satisfied with her appearance, she headed for the elevator.

Barnaby was waiting for her in the lobby, shifting his weight back and forth from leg to leg. She caught a glimpse of him in the mirrored pillars before he had the chance to see her. His purple-and-black vertical-striped jeans must have been spray painted on his body, making it hard for her to concentrate on his face.

Kathryn sort of swaggered over to him. She wasn't sure why. "Hi, I'm Kathryn."

"Barnaby Street." He extended his hand and pumped hers vigorously. "I've got another helmet for you on the bike, if you don't mind mussing that gorgeous hair." He moved his hand to scrunch her long curls as though they were some sort of experiment. "Kinky. I like that." He grinned. The British rock and roller turned to Carlos as though he were Mr. Lamb. "Don't worry, sir, I'll have her back by dawn." He grinned again, pleased with his joke. Kathryn noticed that he had remarkably good teeth for a Brit.

Barnaby turned and headed for his bike, which he had left by a Department of Transportation "No Parking— Loading Zone" sign just outside the high-rise. Kathryn smiled when she saw that the back of his well-worn leather bomber jacket was entirely covered with a peeling and cracking handpainted Union Jack.

Carlos pursed his lips, pointing with them in the direction of the departing rocker. It was Latino doorman-speak for "Keep your eye on him. He's very full of himself."

Kathryn shrugged. "It's a first date. He looked good on camera," she added, then walked out of the building into the street.

Barnaby handed Kathryn a shiny black helmet and adjusted the chinstrap for her. "Barnaby Street," she said, discovering something. "*That's* why your name sounded simultaneously strange and familiar. I take it you *want* people to think of Carnaby Street when they meet you."

"You're a smart bird," he said, chucking her on the chin. "My real name's Merton. But Merton Street sounds like where you go for haberdashery, and I needed a rocker name for when I'm gigging out, y'know?"

"Gotcha."

"And when I tell people my name's Barnaby Street, they all think they've heard of me."

Kathryn nodded. "Makes sense to me." She climbed on the bike, sliding her back against the sissy bar. The custom-tooled leather seat was pretty comfortable, actually, and the bar supported her lower back and added an extra measure of security, however psychological.

Barnaby hopped on the Honda and revved up the engine. Kathryn liked bikes. She loved the feeling of the wind all around her, combined with the element of danger involved. Aggressive New York motorists were legendary for hating motorcyclists, and she was riding for the first time with a stranger. "Where are we going?" she asked, as she wrapped her arms around his back. That felt good, hugging him to her chest. Sort of like safe sex, assuming a taxi didn't blindside them enroute to their destination.

"Hades."

"What?" Kathryn screamed into the wind.

"Hades. It's a club on East First Street."

Kathryn nodded her head into his back, acknowledging that she heard him. The ride across the winding Bleecker Street was exhilarating. Barnaby fully obeyed all the rules of the road, even stopping for red lights, but he had a tendency to floor it as soon as the light changed, and to brake at the last possible minute. Good thing she hadn't eaten any dinner. It was fun, though, she admitted.

They disembarked in front of Hades, Kathryn handed

back her helmet, and shook her head like a wet dog, then rescrunched her curls. "Helmet head," she said to her date, smiling apologetically, as Barnaby chained the bike next to several others parked on the sidewalk in front of the East Village nightclub.

"You're very game, Kate," he said, moving to one side to allow her to precede him into the club. She decided not to correct his choice of nickname. She'd always liked 'Kate' anyway. Besides, he might be tempted to get physical—and corny—later in the evening, and demand, "C'mon and kiss me, Kate," at which time she intended to award him undeserved points for originality and give in.

No wonder Barnaby had let her go inside first. It wasn't that he was a gentleman. He just didn't want to be the rottweiler's dinner. The dog was black as a moonless night in a mole hole and looked as hungry as a wolf pack during a famine, judging from the slobber dripping from its jaws. So far, the club was earning its name. A deadly black canine guarding its entry, and the interior was barely illuminated at all. The only lights in the place, apart from a votive candle or two on a couple of the tables, were some red and blue Lekos focused on a tiny stage at the far end of the room.

The din was unbearable. "So this is Hades," Kathryn yelled to her date.

"Great place, isn't it?" Barnaby grinned and steered her by the elbow, through the packed crowd at the bar. "Hey, mate," he said, punching the muscled tricep of a heavily tattooed man wearing a nose ring.

"Great to see you, man," Tattoo responded hazily. "Really great. Are you here for The Torykillers?"

"Yeh. I thought Kate here might enjoy them. She's really into music." Barnaby steered Kathryn toward the stoned man being held up by the bar. "This here is Kate. Kate, this is Mick."

"Hi, Mick," she yelled, blinking away his cigarette smoke. "Great to meet you. Really great." She regarded the man's body art. Mick's tricep bore a detailed depiction of a toothy dragon with a puppy caught in its blood-dripping jaws. "Nice tattoo. Interesting choice. Really interesting." She heard herself falling into their speech rhythms and vernacular. Actually, hearing herself do anything was a minor miracle. Her ears were already ringing from the industrial-strength blare of the band, and they had probably not been in Hades for upwards of two minutes.

Mick just nodded his head with the music. Kathryn figured it was his way of acknowledging her greeting.

"Do you know The Torykillers?" Barnaby asked as he steered Kathryn to one of the tiny tables.

"Not personally, no," she yelled.

"Super band from Birmingham. Really super. Have you heard of The Smiths? They were sort of a forerunner of this kind of music, back in the '80s."

"The Smiths? Oh, yeah, sure," Kathryn answered truthfully.

"Well, The Torykillers are a bit like them, but a lot less twee."

"Twee?"

"Something twee is a bit treacly. I guess you Yanks would say 'cutesy'."

Kathryn nodded in recognition. "Oh, I see. In that case, I had never thought of The Smiths as being twee. To me, Laura Ashley is twee."

"I don't know their music at all," Barnaby responded. "What are you drinking?"

"GT?"

"Any particular brand of gin?"

"Top shelf. Tanqueray is fine. Boodles is better. And ask them please not to go too light on the tonic. I'd rather have a shorter drink that I can actually consume without feeling like I'm drinking straight rubbing alcohol."

"Twist?"

"Please."

Barnaby muscled his way toward the bar. He got points for being solicitous about her choice of cocktail. He hadn't tried to change her mind and force beer on her, for instance. But this club?! And the band! And her date considered The Smiths too precious or cutesy. To Kathryn, their iconoclastic lyrics were cutting-edge, and their music was just melodic enough for her to keep listening. The Torykillers seemed totally tone-deaf to her, and with the volume on their speakers turned up past ten, the lyrics were almost indistinguishable from the sound of a 747 at takeoff if you were standing on the tarmac without earplugs. Kathryn picked out a few lines here and there.

> Eat my vomit, righteous bitch.
> Slit your wrists, but it's a waste of time.
> I was only joking when I said I loved you.
> Give a bloke a hit of cocaine.
> Foolish mule, dizzy cow,
> Believe me baby, it's over.
> I'm doing your granny's fanny,
> I'm screwing your granny's fanny.

Barnaby returned with her drink and Kathryn thirstily slurped down half of its contents. She realized right away that she was drinking her cocktail too quickly, as though the glass contained only tonic water.

"Great band, aren't they?"

"What?" Kathryn yelled, leaning in to Barnaby, cupping her ear forward, hoping it would help her understand his question.

"I said, great band. Alternative music."

"I always wanted to ask what that really meant."

"What *what* meant, Kate?"

"Alternative music. What is it alternative *to*?"

"Music!" He grinned.

Kathryn was trying to put a brave face on it. Such a glorious accent, and he had brought her to a venue where they couldn't hear themselves think, let alone hear each other talk. Maybe this was the rocker's idea of a good first date. Take her someplace where it's impossible to get to know each other.

Mick sidled up to the table, a cigarette drooping from the corner of his mouth. "Are you in on Tuesday, mate?"

"Yeh. I switched with Ian, since he's covering for me tonight."

Both men looked over in the direction of the bar. "Ian's making out like a fiend, though. Tuesday night tips are bollocks." Mick waved his hand toward the bartender and indicated that he should zip over another round of drinks to Barnaby's table.

"Yeh, but I've got Kate tonight, and that's better than bloody tips." Barnaby flashed a smile and his dark eyes glittered in the candlelight. With the day or two of stubble on his chin, he looked like a really sexy thug, and Kathryn tried to forget that she couldn't hear anything he said.

Mick appraised Kathryn, making her feel like a prime filet. The drinks arrived and she tackled her second gin and tonic, practically guzzling it. Since conversation was clearly not an option, she decided to focus on her drinks as her primary source of entertainment. By this time, she was beginning to feel pretty good, despite the din, and the current song, which seemed to go something like:

Suck it, dammit, suck it!
Don't make me have to make you,
But I can take you out back and show you who's boss
If you won't kneel for me.
Just like the Queen,
I can be mean and make your life hell.
So love me.
Love me tonight.
Give me head in the Tower of London.
So much power in the Tower of London.
Beheaded babies in the Tower of London.

Barnaby was talking animatedly with Mick. Because The Torykillers were wailing away in Kathryn's ears about fellatio and decapitated children, it was like watching a silent movie in a foreign language without the benefit of subtitles.

"Kate seems great. Really great, mate," Mick nodded, "but you're going to be needing the dosh for nasty little things like rent."

"Jax has been paying me under the table. Why should I pay taxes to the bloody U.S. government when I don't get anything from them?"

"How did it go with the immigration lawyer?" Mick asked, waving to Ian for a third round, as Barnaby tossed back the remains of his second drink. Since Kathryn couldn't hear what Mick and Barnaby were discussing anyway she turned her chair around to face the stage, pretending to look fascinated by getting a better look at the band.

Barnaby frowned. "My visa expires in December. He said there are enough rockers in this country as it is, and I probably wouldn't be granted one of those, y'know, genius visas, or whatever the immigrants get who are irreplaceable, or something. It was a real bummer, y'know, to hear him actually say, right to my face, that I'm nothing special. One of a million underemployed musicians. I mean, I almost had a record deal for The Lust Machine, but they pulled out at the last minute. So the lawyer advised me to get married if I want to stay in the country. It's my surest bet."

The drinks arrived and The Torykillers finally took a much-appreciated break; and for a few seconds before the stereo was cranked up, there was a deafening silence in which Kathryn heard Barnaby's last comment. Her eyes narrowed as she looked at her date. She wasn't soused enough to miss the meaning of what she had just heard; yet she was mellow enough not to let it truly sink in. She slurped her third gin and tonic, and was sure that she was levitating slightly. "Can I have another, please?" she asked Barnaby.

The sexy rock and roller semaphored Ian. "I'll pick 'em up myself after I pick up my mail," he called to the bartender, as he slid his chair away from the table and ambled in the direction of the men's room.

Well, it would make sense—if an immigration lawyer advised Barnaby aka Merton Street to find himself an American wife if he hoped to stay in the country—that he would register with a dating service, where he could have his pick of eligible women who were all looking to get married. It was possible that she was being too hard on him, and that he didn't want to go that route to stay in the United States regardless of the attorney's advice. Maybe he thought that was an unfair way to achieve what he wanted. On the other hand, she didn't know Barnaby from Adam, and maybe that *was* what he was looking for after all. She wanted a man to love and cherish, and who would do the same for her for all the rest of their days. He wanted a green card. There were women who would willingly enter into that kind of arrangement, but Kathryn wasn't one of them.

Barnaby returned to the table with their drinks. Kathryn consumed her fourth gin and tonic as though it were lemonade. The Torykillers started their next set, and were playing a song about masturbation, called "Arrested Development."

"Can we go, now?" Kathryn asked her date.

Barnaby flashed his lethal smile. "Sure, love. Any time you're ready."

"I'm ready now."

The British rocker rose and pulled out Kathryn's chair for her. His motives may not have been pure, but his manners were impeccable. They left Hades without paying. "It's one of the perks of being a bartender here," he whispered in her ear, as he steered her toward the door. Good thing his hand was on her back, because she was feeling a little wobbly.

"I was hoping we could have gotten something to eat in there," she told him, when they hit the sidewalk. "No wonder Cerberus over there looks so hungry. I feel for you, kiddo," she slurred, looking at the hellhound.

"We can stop for a burger or something if you like."

As much as she was really hungry, Kathryn started wondering what she was going to talk to this man about. She had learned enough in Hades to realize that she didn't want to go on a second date with Barnaby Street, so there was no point in prolonging the inevitable. "It's all right, Barnaby. Just take me home, please. It's been great. Really great." She realized she was still mimicking him and his friend, Mick the walking tattoo.

They boarded Barnaby's bike. Kathryn was too looped to feel as apprehensive as she normally would about riding back across town with a man who'd matched her drink for drink. Barnaby revved the engine and they shot up First Avenue.

A few blocks north, Barnaby pulled over to the curb.

"What's the matter?" Kathryn asked.

"D'ya mind if we take a little detour, Kate?" her date asked.

"I was sort of anxious to get home, but . . ."

"It won't take long. I want to take you to this fab T and P parlor on St. Marks."

"T and P?"

"Tattoo and piercing. You're really great, Kate," Barnaby said drunkenly. "I want something to remember this night."

"This place is brill," he pronounced, as they pulled up in front of the House of Pain on East Eighth Street. "I mean, they're open twenty-four hours!"

Kathryn followed the rocker into the tattoo and piercing parlor. "Nipples pierced while you wait," she said, reading a sign on the wall to herself. *What do they expect you to do? Leave them here while you catch a quick bite at Dallas BBQ?* She looked at the range of tattoo samples that lined the fluorescently lit walls.

"So, what do ya think, Kate? Tattoo or piercing?"

"Well . . . I think it's very . . . gracious of you to ask my opinion, but it's kind of a personal decision, don't you think?" The effects of the alcohol were beginning to make her nauseous, and she grabbed the back of an orange, molded plastic, waiting-room-style chair for support.

"Naw, Kate. You decide. After all, you might have to live with it."

"Well . . . tattoos are more *colorful*," Kathryn suggested.

"Right, then! Tattoo it is, Fluffy."

A huge Hell's Angel with a full red beard raised his bulk to his feet. "Where do you want this one, Barnaby?"

Barnaby stripped off his leather jacket and pulled his skintight T-shirt over his head. "Right over the heart, mate."

"Who's Emily?" Kathryn asked, feeling oddly propri-etary when she saw another woman's name stenciled in bright blue on Barnaby's right pec.

"Emily? Oh, right! Yeh, she's an ex-girlfriend, but it's more painful to get her name erased than to think about her every time I take off my shirt." Barnaby looked down at the right side of his chest. "Besides, I sort of like the idea of the symmetry thing, now that I'm getting one over here." He pointed to his left breast, just over the nipple.

"What do you want there?" Fluffy asked his client.

"It's a wee bit bourgeois, but I think a rose and a sword—no, maybe a heart and a sword. And just one word this time: *Kate*."

"What?" Kathryn asked, working overtime not to slur her speech.

"I said I wanted something to remember our date, Kate. Remember?"

Kathryn winced as Fluffy took out the tools of the trade. "But couldn't you have considered something . . . well, less . . . *permanent*?"

Barnaby, under the needle, looked at her like she was hopelessly middle class.

It was all Kathryn could do to keep all four gin and tonics down during the ride back to the West Village. At that late hour, the streets were deserted; and so Barnaby demonstrated the bike's engine capacity and used the narrow, curving avenues like the kind of test courses demonstrated in German automobile commercials, stopping only when the light was red. If there was nothing coming at them north or south, he only slowed down through the light. Lucky for them, no cops were in sight for the duration of the journey. He pulled up in front of her building and revved the engine one more time, in a display of testosterone poisoning.

"Hey, you! Shut up!" a voice called down from a five-floor walk-up across the street.

They both alit from the bike and Kathryn returned her helmet, which Barnaby attached, along with his own, to the sissy bar.

"Oh, you don't need to take off your helmet," Kathryn said drunkenly.

"I've heard of people doing it with their boots on, but if you want me to keep the helmet on . . ." He reached for it. "Kinky. I like it."

Kathryn put out her hand to stop him. "No, Barnaby.

That wasn't what I meant. I've had . . . a good time
tonight . . ."

"Super. So did I, Kate. It was really super." He touched
his chest where his new artwork had been installed.

"But I don't think we're really right for each other."

Barnaby looked crushed and confused. For a moment,
Kathryn felt sorry for him. He was incredibly good-
looking, but head-banging rock and all-night tattoo parlors were not her style, nor did she want to date a man
who barely made ends meet by working off the books at
a downtown club.

"I'm a Royalist," she said simply, and shrugged.

Barnaby looked at her, his hands on his hips. "So, let
me get this straight . . . you don't want to go out with me
again. Is that what you're saying?"

"In a nutshell, I'm afraid, Barnaby."

"But—" He pointed to his left breast. "I just got your
name tattooed over my heart, for fuck's sake!"

"I'm sorry," Kathryn replied. "It wasn't my idea,
remember?"

"Talk about painful memories! You're a ball buster,
Kate. And I thought you were top bollocks!"

Since her date was starting to bring out the big
guns, Kathryn realized she would have to sink to his level
to retaliate. "And I thought *you* were interested in a redhead, not a Green Card! Thanks for the date, Barnaby."

She turned and went inside her apartment building,
thinking of something Eleanor had once said about
someone as drunk as Kathryn was now: "He couldn't
even walk a straight curve." She heard the Honda's engine rev again, followed by the sound of Barnaby
flooring the gas and heading down the block. She sank
down onto one of the Naugahyde benches in the lobby.

"Are you okay, *chiquita*?" Carlos asked. "*Qué pasa?*"

"I'm just a little dizzy, that's all."

"I'm not supposed to leave the front desk, but if you need help getting upstairs, I can take you," the doorman said, wiping some Snapple from his mustache.

"No, thanks, Carlos. I'm all right. Just a little woozy. Four gin and tonics on an empty stomach."

Carlos looked sympathetic, then shook his head. "Drink *rum*," he said sagely. "Much better for you. *Cuba libre*, Bacardi, no problems."

"Yeah, right." Rum hangovers were just as bad. Maybe not for Carlos.

Kathryn made it to her bathroom just in time to collapse in front of the toilet. The room was spinning, and she could still hear the politically incorrect, sado-masochistic racket of The Torykillers in her head. She rid herself of the alcohol, then lay down on the cold tile floor, which felt good against her temples. She ran some cold water from the tap and drenched a lavender terry washcloth, putting it over her brow as she lay on the floor, feeling like the last time she had been given nitrous oxide at the dentist, except this time she was in more pain. She felt as though she were the size of a Lilliputian and had been splayed out on a record turntable, going around and around at about 45 rpm. If she'd had a "B" side, the song would be called "Don't Ever Do That Again."

What a waste the black net teddy from La Perla had been. When the room stopped spinning, Kathryn tugged off her boots and leggings, unsnapped her bodysuit, and carefully removed the Very Expensive Lingerie. It was so pretty and delicate—hand-embroidered tiny pink rosettes with green leaves against the black background. More like a leotard than a teddy because it hugged her hips instead of flaring out. One day, she vowed, someone would appreciate it. And her. It was the last thing she remembered before everything went as dark as Hades.

Chapter
6

"It wasn't the date *from* hell; it was the date *to* hell," Kathryn explained as she and Eleanor swung Johanna across the bridle path in Central Park. "One, two, three . . ."

"Whoops!" Johanna cried, finishing their cheer. "Again."

"We'll do it again on the way back home, okay," the toddler's mother consoled.

"Can we see the water, Aunt Kittycat?"

"Sure, jujube. Let's go see if anyone is sailing boats on the lake at Seventy-fourth Street." Kathryn turned to her sister. "Hey, speaking of sailing toy boats on that lake, have you read her *Stuart Little*, yet?"

"I think she's still a little young for the book. Dan and I bought the video though, but we have to prescreen it first. Hold it—what do you mean, date *to* hell?"

"Barnaby took me to an East Village rock club called Hades. With a drooling, snarling black rottweiler out front, I swear. My ears are still ringing."

"Did you do the orange juice and aspirin thing?"

"There isn't enough orange juice in Florida or aspirin at Mt. Sinai to cure this." Kathryn touched her head as though it were an eggshell. "I wore sunglasses to bed last night—I mean this morning—because the light hurt my eyes. Poor Carlos. He almost had to bodily deposit me on my doorstep, but I refused his kind offer of assistance."

"Carlos? I thought your date was named Barnaby." Eleanor looked puzzled. "I know my synapses were intact when I woke up, but I swear I missed something."

"Carlos is the night doorman. You know him. The one with the graying mustache who always says '*qué linda*' every time you come in and out of the building. He thinks you're hot."

"Oh, him." Eleanor blushed a little. "He's the one who always helps me with the stroller. So what happened with Barnaby?"

Kathryn gave Eleanor a play-by-play of the entire date, ending with her biggest regret of the evening. "The La Perla black net teddy seems to have been a casualty of the evening."

Eleanor's eyes widened—partly in shock and partly in angry disbelief. "I understand that he may have sounded like Michael Caine, but do you mean to tell me that after the evening you spent, you brought that man upstairs and allowed him to rip a three-hundred dollar piece of lingerie to shreds? Even the Cro-Magnon types should learn the finer points of undressing women."

"Barnaby didn't even make it as far as the lobby when he dropped me off. The only thing that got ripped off was my motorcycle helmet. No, I just sort of . . . well . . . passed out this morning. I vaguely remember getting undressed first; then I did laundry when I got up—because everything smelled like gin or worse—and I can't find the teddy. It's not in the apartment. I don't think it got in with the laundry, because believe me, I would handwash a three-hundred dollar piece of net in Woolite; but I went down to the laundry room anyway and looked, and it wasn't there. So I went back upstairs and had a good cry, which magnified my hangover."

Eleanor put a consoling arm around her sister. "These things have a way of turning up. It's probably under the bed. Maybe in your drunken stupor you actually put it away in a drawer."

Kathryn leaned her head on her younger sister's shoulder. "Thanks, 'Mom.' I just feel so guilty about losing it. One night I had it, and the next morning, there wasn't a trace of it."

Supermom lifted Kathryn's head and looked her in the eye. "We're talking about a piece of underwear here—not your virginity, for God's sake. Are you sniffling?"

Kathryn nodded.

Eleanor sighed. "You are so emotional."

"It's the way I'm built. I have a lot of Cancer in my chart . . . my moon and my rising sign. We cry at everything."

"Well, when you get back to the apartment and you still can't find it after a thorough search, if you're willing to submit to the mortification of letting people know what you wear under all that velvet, you could post some signs at the mailboxes and in the laundry room."

"How did you get to be the practical one?" Kathryn asked her.

"It was ever thus," Eleanor laughed. "Someone's got to do it. Capricorn Sun, Taurus Moon. I'm romantic, but I'm a grown-up."

"Is that supposed to imply that I'm *not*? By the way, how did the Brownie Points come out?"

"Crummy. In more ways than one. I think I have to develop a conical pan. Spraying Pam on the water cooler cups soaks them through and if you don't grease them, you can't get the Brownie Points out in one piece. So, it's back to the drawing board. It gives me a mission, though, which I am sorely lacking these days."

"So, you're living vicariously through mine?" Kathryn smiled.

"Something like that," Eleanor responded, looking guiltily at her two-year-old daughter.

Kathryn searched her entire apartment for the black teddy, including under the bed and beneath the sofa, which gave her an excuse to vacuum. Despite her hangover, the Electrolux wasn't nearly as loud as The Torykillers had been.

Unfortunately, even after a thorough quest, the Very Expensive Lingerie was nowhere to be found. Admitting defeat, Kathryn printed out some pretty signs on her laserjet and posted them at the locations she and Eleanor had discussed. It was highly embarrassing to admit losing a piece of rather racy underwear, but if it had gotten as far as the laundry room, she would rather have it back and endure the humiliation. She hadn't put her name on the sign. Just: "Lost. One black net teddy/ bodysuit with spaghetti straps, embroidered with tiny pink roses. Possibly left in laundry room. If found, please return to apartment 9B."

As she reentered her apartment, the phone was ringing, but Kathryn decided to screen her calls and let the answering machine pick up. Her outgoing message played, followed by the beep. A resonant baritone, with a raspy smoker's edge to it, started to speak. "This is Eddie Benson. I liked your tape. Would like to meet you. Since you're a drama teacher, I thought you might like to see a play. I can get theater tickets for something later in the week, if you're interested."

Eddie left his phone number, which Kathryn jotted down in her Arden edition of *The Taming of the Shrew*, since she happened to be re-reading it. She couldn't view his tape until sometime tomorrow, because Six in the City was off-duty on Sundays. Eddie sounded a bit gruff, but she liked the timbre of his voice.

Kathryn was finally beginning to recover from the hangover from hell. Lighting several aromatherapy candles, as opposed to switching on the lamps, seemed to help immeasurably. She flipped through her CD collection looking for the original cast recording of *Kiss Me, Kate*, to put herself in the mood while she reviewed *The Taming of the Shrew* for next week's class discussion. She was intending to bring up the musical version of the story anyway.

Brewing some tea took her mind off obsessing about the lost lingerie. Maybe it was an omen from the gods that she was going about this dating thing the wrong way. Well, only four more bachelors to go.

Listening to the clever *Kiss Me, Kate* score while she was waiting for the kettle to boil gave Kathryn an epiphany. Cole Porter. She had wanted to do a production of Porter's *Anything Goes* at Briarcliff for the past eight years. Maybe she could do that for the spring production and involve all four grades. Did the school have any crackerjack tap dancers?

While the kettle crowed away, Kathryn started singing "So in Love" at the top of her voice, along with the Lilli Vanessi character on the *Kiss Me, Kate* recording. Between the teakettle and her own soprano and Patricia Morrison warbling away on the CD, she didn't hear the doorbell until she turned off the gas on the range and brought her steaming cup of Darjeeling into the living room.

She placed the handcrafted mug on an embroidered coaster and left it on the secondhand mahogany coffee table, then danced over to the door, caught up in the jazzy rhythm of "Tom, Dick and Harry." She knew she should have asked who was there, but she was into the music; and besides, if it had been a caller from the outside, Tito would have buzzed her over the intercom.

She opened the door, still singing, "I'm a maid mad to marry, and would take double-quick, any Tom, Dick or Harry, any Tom, Harry or Dick. A dick-a-dick, a dick-a-dick . . ."

She went mute. Her face turned a whiter shade of pale. Then it fell. Standing in the doorway, wearing nothing but a pair of skimpy green running shorts and a grin, dangling a familiar piece of finest-quality mesh, was Walker Hart.

"I'm answering a personal ad. So, this must be yours," he said calmly.

"Oh dear God in Heaven," Kathryn whispered.

"Not quite," Walker replied. "I'm only staying in the penthouse."

"Please tell me you're joking," she said, trying to cover her mortification. "And give that back to me!" She made a grab for the teddy, but he swung it out of her reach.

"Aren't you going to invite me in?"

"Oh, my God, of course. Come in. Make yourself at home." As she led him into the living room, she reached for her teddy again and they played a brief game of cat and mouse until Kathryn went for Walker's midsection and started to tickle him. He immediately dropped his hands in order to fend her off, and she snatched the teddy out of his grasp, then skittered into the bedroom to deposit the flimsy garment on her bed.

"Well, well, someone is ticklish!" Kathryn called in from the bedroom.

She reentered the room and gasped when she saw Walker making himself at home by sinking into her sofa and resting his feet on a stack of *Victoria* magazines on the coffee table. "Does your mother let you do that at home?" she asked, adopting her best schoolmarm tone. As a defense mechanism for trying really hard not to stare *too* hard at his bare chest, it sucked. The man was built. Not buffed, but definitely built.

"You forget. I'm *in* my momma's house. She asked me to house-sit while she and daffy Dafydd The Welshman or whatever the hell husband number seven's name is, are happily honeymooning."

Kathryn was wondering why she hadn't noticed it before. Or maybe she had, and she was subconsciously trying not to. What had made her initially think that Walker had a few pounds of cuddliness on him? There were a few *ounces*, perhaps—just enough to make him appear eminently huggable, as opposed to too lean for a good snuggle. She had been so caught up in the surprise of seeing him half-naked on her doorstep, and then the ensuing embarrassment about the silly piece of lingerie, that she hadn't stopped to process the half-naked part. This glorious-looking man had invited himself, more or less, into her humble abode, and, shirtless, was now making himself very much at home, fiddling with her remote control. And then there were the well-toned thigh muscles. Kathryn was tempted to squeeze them, just to see if they were as firm as they looked.

"Were you running?" she asked Walker, trying to sound casual.

"Nope." He wiggled his toes at her. "I·just did my laundry and I don't have a thing to wear," he added, running a hand through his tousled blond hair in a paraphrased imitation of a TV commercial from some years back. "Anyway, why run when you can catch a great baseball game, or an old movie on TV?" Remote in hand, he flipped through the channels, finally settling on a *Star Trek* rerun. "Got anything to eat?"

"I don't permit any polyester in my house, which includes those mustard-colored unitards," she quipped, gesturing at the television. "So, if you get that sci-fi mumbo-jumbo off my set, I'll see what I can rustle up."

Kathryn went into the kitchen. "I was making some tea, before you came—and I've got some homemade gingersnaps."

"Sounds delightful."

Kathryn put a bunch of her decorated cookies out on a doily, and set it on an old Minton plate, a one-of-a-kind piece that she had found in one of the thrift stores along Third Avenue. She brought the plate out to the living room, and Walker stood up, hooking his thumbs in the elastic waistband of his emerald green running shorts.

"What . . . what are you doing?" she stammered, caught entirely off guard.

"You said you didn't permit any polyester in your apartment, so I thought I'd better remove these, to not risk offending my gracious hostess."

"Please don't do that," she insisted, waving her hand at him, dreadfully intrigued that he actually might undress. "I'll suffer the indignities to my sartorial sensibilities." If the man were truly gutsy and doffed the skimpy shorts, she might have to be anesthetized in order to keep away from him. "Besides," she added, offering him a cookie, "you were Flirting with Intent. Very bad form. We have sort of a doctor-patient, lawyer-client relationship thing here. You're supposed to be guiding me toward my destiny— which is, in paragraph four of my contract with Six in the City, allegedly to be provided in the form of five eligible bachelors, each of whom supposedly wants the same things I want out of life."

He nodded. " 'Flirting with Intent.' I like that. I plead 'no contest.' Sorry. It was unintentional."

" 'All is forgiven: come home.' Isn't that a funny phrase? My parents always used to say that to Ellie and me when we were kids and did something naughty."

" 'Come home'? Okay, then." He scrunched back down on her sofa, making himself comfy in the plushy velvet upholstery.

"You're doing it again." Kathryn shook her head and perched on the arm of the couch. Bear was certainly one of a kind. Yet there was something about him. He *was* very easy to be with. Just having him in the apartment, Kathryn felt a sense of security and stability she had never before experienced. The more she thought about it, the more she defined the feeling. This was *it*—the elusive sensation she wanted to capture and bottle so she could mete out a little bit of warmth for herself on those days when she was feeling lonely, or blue, or premenstrual.

Of course she wanted to touch him, explore him. In fact Kathryn was dying to find out what it would feel like to be given a Bear hug, but even if her wish were granted, she had enough self-awareness to realize that it would totally mess up her head. She could lose herself with a man as much fun as Walker—witty and warm, maybe even wise—but they wanted different things. She had a goal; a specific place where she wanted a relationship to end up. He seemed to prefer women who would hop on for the ride and not worry about where they were going or how long it was taking to get there. Kathryn used to be that sort of woman. A few years ago, Bear Hart would have been perfect dating material for her; but now, her priorities had shifted. It irked her that people made her feel uncomfortable about her desire to hear the words, "Kathryn Lamb, will you marry me?" which then might lead to a consideration of having children somewhere not too far down the line. Or not.

"Cookie!" he exclaimed, in perfect imitation of the fuzzy blue monster with the googly eyes from *Sesame Street*. He put two gingersnaps in his mouth at once and crunched until the crumbs spilled over his chin. "Hey, what are these, anyway?" Walker reached for one of the remaining cookies and examined it. "Is this a cat?" he asked, chomping away.

"I guess your mother was too busy matchmaking to teach you not to talk with your mouth full," Kathryn teased. The teacher-tone was her defense against letting her guard down too far with him. He already had the makings of a great friend, but that was as far as she could let it go. Just looking at his bare chest was raising her blood pressure and tempting her to consider rescinding her application to Six in the City in favor of a recreational romp with the boss. "Yes, they're cats. See?" She traced the shape along the perimeter of the cookie. "It's arching its back." She permitted one or two more indecent images to cross her mind.

"Cat cookies. Very feminine," Walker appraised, as he popped her demo-cookie into his mouth.

"I do that sort of thing," she said. "I make batches at different times of the year and cut out shapes that are right for the season. These are my personal favorites, though. I thought cats were *autumnal*."

"I thought they were autobiographical," Walker replied, patting the plump sofa cushion for her to join him. She gave him an odd look. "Kitty. Kitty*cat*. And I suppose you make lambs at Easter."

"Of course." She plopped down on the sofa and grabbed a cookie.

"I like the fact that you gave them green eyes. Like yours." He looked at her. "Wait a minute, weren't those green the last time I saw you?"

"They might have been. Depends on what I'm wearing."

"None of those weird E.T.-like contact lenses?"

Kathryn gestured at her book-lined walls. "Nope. Never needed 'em. I've read most of these without the aid of artificial stimulation. No, my eyes are probably brownish now because of this sweater," she said, referring to the cinnamon-colored velvet tunic she was wearing over her leggings. "And sometimes, they're blue."

"They were when you wore that light blue sweater, the day we met."

She nodded. "And other times," she added suggestively, smiling cryptically like the Mona Lisa. "But *then*, I've been told they turn almost indigo. It's an odd trick of nature. I've never actually seen them change that way— but . . . I've been told. It's been . . . a while . . . since they've been . . . that way." She shifted the subject, awkwardly. "Remember mood rings?"

"Those stones that changed color depending on your

body temperature? Black for cold; blue for hot. Sure. I actually owned one."

Kathryn looked surprised. "I did too. But I never knew a *guy* who had one." She had a feeling that Walker's natural warmth and passion rendered his mood ring perennially blue, but she steered away from commenting on it. Besides, this was the man to whom she had given five hundred somolians to professionally fix her up with the ephemeral "Mr. Right for Me." She realized she didn't particularly want him to leave her apartment. He'd ensconced himself on her comfy couch for all of ten minutes, and she was liking it. A lot more than she really wanted to.

She needed to create some distance between them. "I can't believe your mother is the schnook who bought the penthouse."

Walker blinked. "Why?" he asked cautiously.

Kathryn nibbled on a gingerbread cat's ear. "It seems there have always been problems with the flashing or the pointing, or something building contractors do to roofs to make sure they don't leak. For some reason, it acts like it's made of balsa wood. Apparently, even the slightest drizzle can cause a leak, if the wind is right—or wrong—and when the penthouse was a rental, it was up to the landlord to fix it at his expense. When the building converted from rental to co-ops, any problems with the ceiling leaking, or plaster peeling, or the walls staining, became the tenant's headache."

"So I guess that makes Rushie a prime candidate for Excedrin."

"Or you. You betcha. Had any problems yet?"

Walker didn't feel like admitting the truth. "I noticed some rusty stains on the wall a while back, so the building sent some workmen in and they seem to have cleaned it up. They certainly billed me for it. I didn't notice the discoloration the day I moved in," he added honestly. "Rushie is never around enough to bother with details like falling ceilings. When the going gets rough, the Rushie goes honeymooning. Besides, she's never liked asking the tough questions. She's deathly afraid of negativity—literally terrified that someone will disappoint her. Including me. Most especially me."

"She asked *me* plenty of tough questions. That's how I ended up enrolling with your dating service in the first place. Anyway," Kathryn added skeptically, "Maude Fixler could sell the Manhattan Bridge to the Topeka City Council."

"I'm sure it never occurred to Mom to ask about the structure of the masonry. And if it had, she would have been scared of what she might hear. Owning a penthouse to her is the pinnacle of Manhattan elegance. This is a woman who grew up in a basement apartment in Brooklyn."

"Well, I'm sure she's got an amazing view and immodestly large rooms for a modern high-rise, but I hope you or your mother knows a really good plumber who makes house calls. And a plasterer, and a painter, and that you guys don't hang anything of value on the walls. And that you don't have expensive deep-pile carpeting everywhere to soak up the damage like a thirsty camel."

"Yes to some of the above. There's some pricy stuff on the walls because Rushie wanted her home to look 'important,' and I know I overpaid for the plushy carpet. I also don't know any professional tradesmen."

"I'll bet you have clients who work with their hands."

"I never thought of that." Walker stroked his jaw,

something Kathryn noticed he did whenever he was just a touch perplexed, and didn't seem quite sure what to say next. He reached for another cookie, but his hand landed on the edge of the plate, popping the gingersnaps into the air. "I'm so sorry! I'll pick them up."

"It's okay," Kathryn said dismissively. "They've only been on the floor a little while." She retrieved two ginger cookies from the carpet and pretended to blow off some lint.

Walker looked embarrassed that Kathryn had tried to make light of his clumsiness, so he swiftly switched the subject of conversation. "Well, if I wake up in the middle of the night thinking I'm in third-class steerage on the Titanic, I'll come pounding on your door, requesting sanctuary," he said with a forced cheeriness.

"You'll get a dry blanket—if you're lucky, my grandmother's hand-knitted afghan—and a cup of hot soup. If it's really the middle of the night, you can find your own blanket and make your own soup. And by the way, you're doing it again."

"Doing what?"

"Flirting with Intent. You've already taken five hundred dollars of my hard-earned money. You're not allowed to consider breaking my heart."

"Right," he responded uncomfortably. "Kitty, I hope you know I would never break your heart. Not intentionally, anyway," he added, almost inaudibly.

"Bear?"

"Yeah?"

Kathryn bit her lip, then changed the subject. She was thinking about saying something along the lines of acknowledging their mutual attraction—putting it out there on the table—but decided not to pursue it any further. "So when do I get a tour of Xanadu?"

"Right now, if you want. But I warn you. Your apartment is sort of a study in scarlet, and Rushie's is more . . . well, you'll see it."

Kathryn grabbed her house keys and locked the door behind her. They took the elevator to the penthouse floor, and Walker unlocked his door. The first thing that caught Kathryn's eye was the view. The entire west wall of the living room, which was the first room she saw after he opened the door, was glass.

"After you, my lady." Walker gestured to Kathryn to precede him into the apartment. Kathryn didn't know what to make of it. She was blown away by the vista and by the gleaming ebony finish on the baby grand piano, which commanded the most prominent spot in the room, elevated on a carpeted platform. But the penthouse looked like it was inhabited by someone who'd had his soul excised at birth. Smoked glass and tubular chrome. Black leather, and boring beige wall-to-wall carpeting. It could have been a luxury suite at a five-star hotel. Expensively, but impersonally, furnished. The one reassuringly personal touch was a pair of oddly matched socks, lying on the floor at the edge of a coffee table shaped like something you'd find undergoing mitosis in a petri dish.

"Are you okay?" Walker asked, noticing that Kathryn seemed to be wincing.

"I'll be all right. I just think I'm allergic to this place." She was thinking that it was a good thing after all that Walker and she had such divergent tastes in interior design; otherwise, he'd be even easier to fall for. If they ever *were* to be a couple—which was never going to happen anyway—she could predict a lot of fights over aesthetics.

"I'm not insulted."

"You're not?"

"Nope. This isn't my taste either. My mother hired a Fifty-seventh Street decorator, and this was his high concept of Manhattan sophistication. Kind of soulless, huh?" He gestured to the piano and the empty cocktail glass perched upon it. "But I'm trying." He smiled. "It's the music—and the very dry martinis—that make it livable."

Kathryn nodded, willing to accept his explanation. Nothing about the Walker Hart she knew would have led her to believe that he preferred so much sinister-looking furniture in such boring colors.

Walker seated himself at his piano and ripped into a passionate composition that immediately caused eddies of emotion to cascade right through Kathryn's soul. She watched his long, tapered fingers expertly caressing the keys with varying degrees of intensity; now *pianissimo*, now *mezzo forte*, his body rhythmically swaying with the metre. Mesmerized, Kathryn found herself imagining what it might be like to feel those fingers playing her spine, her hairline, her . . .

"Do you like this?" Walker asked as he continued to play.

"Truth?"

"Bring it on."

"It's the most beautiful thing I've ever heard. And I'm not just saying that. It simply is. What is it? It sounds familiar."

"I doubt it, unless you've been listening inside my soul for the past dozen or so years. It's mine," Walker said modestly.

"It's yours?!"

"Yup." He continued to play the heart-wrenching ballad.

Kathryn swallowed hard so that he wouldn't catch the tear in the corner of her left eye that threatened to travel down her cheek.

Walker began to softly sing the lyrics. Without missing a beat, he handed Kathryn a typed sheet. "Here are the words, if you want to follow along."

"Is it okay if I look at these later? I just want to *feel* the song right now." Kathryn closed her eyes.

"Sure."

The ballad told the story of the bittersweet ending of a passionate love affair; yet it ended on a note of hope that the lovers could perhaps one day arrive at a reconciliation.

"It's gorgeous," an enraptured Kathryn murmured as the final chord died away. "It's amazing that you wrote this. You should write a Broadway show. Remember, 'a life without music is a sorry one.' How could you deprive the theatergoing public of your gifts? I'm not kidding. If the rest of your compositions are anything like this, not only will the show run for years, but Olympic hopefuls will be ice-skating to this ballad, Barbra Streisand will resume her recording career just to sing it and beat Neil Diamond to the punch. There's incredible passion in your work."

"You think it's easy to sit down and just write a Broadway show?" Walker laughed. "I've been tinkering with the same idea for more than a decade."

"If it was easy, it wouldn't be a challenge. Would it?" Their eyes locked.

Kathryn turned to look at a picture on the north wall of his living room, noticing that all the walls were painted the same shade of industrial linen white. "Who's this?" she asked looking at the canvas' sixteen repeated images painted in day-glo colors.

Walker looked at her, surprised. "Andy Warhol," he replied.

"I *know* it's a Warhol. I meant who's the subject of the painting?"

He joined her and looked at it blankly.

"At least it adds some color to the room," Kathryn said helpfully.

Walker continued to scrutinize the canvas. He moved closer to it, then backed away and squinted. "I have no idea who this is." He started to laugh. "I don't particularly like it either, but we're on the same page; I thought it brightened up the place. You do too, by the way. Immensely."

"Do what, Walker?"

"Brighten up the place."

Kathryn cocked her head sideways, slyly regarded him from the corner of her eye, and wagged her right index finger. "You're doing it again," she said.

Chapter
7

Kathryn stirred a soggy french fry—the remainder of her "comfort food" meal—around in a pool of ketchup, and looked up at her date. The fact that Eddie Benson had said very little on his Six in the City videotape had lent him an air of mystery, propelling Kathryn to accept his offer of dinner and an Off-Broadway play.

Unfortunately, laconic was turning out to be more boring than alluring. Eddie was nice enough, but a man of few words "offscreen" as well, which she hadn't realized until she tried to strike up a conversation after the theater, at the Runyonesque diner Little Willy's, on West Forty-seventh Street. It was kind of neat though, that Eddie had introduced her to Little Willy himself, who was anything but, by the way. The man had forearms like sides of Angus beef. Willy, not Eddie. Willy looked like he had some powerful friends he could call on if he couldn't take care of business himself.

Although . . . Eddie wasn't at all bad looking. He had a Baldwin-ish two-day growth of stubble on his chin—which could be sexy in the right light and at the right time of day—and his light brown hair kept falling into his deep-set eyes. Kathryn tried to guess his vocation. At least he didn't look like her stereotypical image of a dentist. Or an accountant.

"You aren't a dentist, are you?" she asked him suddenly.

"No."

Okay. Kathryn had never much enjoyed spending time with people where she felt compelled to keep the ball in the air. And this was a first date. Weren't people usually eager in these circumstances to find out as much about each other as possible, in order to make that big second date determination? Kathryn felt like she needed to ask a judge to issue Eddie a subpoena in order to get him to talk.

"On your tape, you said you were seeking some stability in your life." Since Eddie had been forthcoming about that topic, perhaps he might be tempted to expound upon it.

"Yeah. My mother was Italian, so food and hugs and Christmas were all pretty important in our house. And . . . my line of work, it's . . . well, it's unstable. So I'm looking for . . . stability. A little woman to come home to. Do you make sauce?"

Kathryn winced.

"It was a joke," he said, slapping the bottom of the Heinz bottle with the heel of his hand. "I already figured you're something of a feminist."

"Why do you say that?" asked Kathryn, amused. Well, at least he was talking about *something*.

"You would have been married by now if you just wanted to settle down. Make a couple, three kids. But you're not. So I would hazard a guess that your *career* is pretty important to you, too. Maybe it's been more important up until recently. Which is why you registered with a video dating service."

"Very good, Sherlock. I'm impressed," Kathryn replied. She took another sip of her vanilla coke, noticing that the juke box was playing Bob Dylan music. *God gave names to all the animals. In the beginning, in the beginning.* The lyric briefly made her think of Bear. She was trying unsuccessfully to think of a way to steer the conversation back to the subject of Eddie's life, as opposed to her own. Not that a person was defined by his or her occupation, but it did seem to be a primary avenue via which many single men identified themselves, especially if they were looking to commit to marriage. It was like flashing one's cash.

"So what *do* you do, Eddie?" She tried to make it sound as casual as possible. His bank account didn't interest her, but she was curious about his profession.

"This and that."

Helpful. "What makes you happy?"

"Knowing that I done my job. And that I done it well. Sorry. *Did,* English teacher-lady."

"It's okay. I'm only a *drama* teacher."

For the first time all evening, Eddie actually smiled. He had a crooked mouth, and Kathryn found his smile sexy. *He should do it more often,* she mused.

"I thought you would have liked the play, but you didn't seem to be into it. Sorry about that. My instincts are usually right about things."

"What makes you think I didn't like it, Eddie?"

"You kept sighing through it. And reading your program, even though it was so dark in there."

"Oh." He was right, actually, and it made Kathryn feel guilty. "Score one for you. And what made you think I *would* have liked that particular play?"

"Well, it's a woman writer. And you're a woman

drama teacher. Y'know, I thought it would be that sister thing."

"One sister is more than enough for me," Kathryn joked. "Can I be candid with you?"

"If you weren't, I wouldn't like it."

"Right. Okay. Well, the problem I always have with Kara Kimbrough's work is that she has no sense of humor. And she keeps thinking she's writing comedies."

He smiled again. "Good," he nodded, "I thought it was only me who thought it wasn't very funny."

"You didn't hear much laughing there tonight, did you?"

He finished chewing a huge mouthful of cheddar burger. "No. I didn't. Except for the four women in Birkenstocks down in the front row. I guess they were her friends."

"Or her sisters," Kathryn added wryly. "I'm glad we went to see it, though. Thank you."

"Why?"

"Critics have been talking Pulitzer Prize about it, so I was curious to see what the fuss was all about."

"Then I did do my job well." Eddie seemed pleased with himself. "See, it didn't have to be good, but somehow I knew that you would want to see it." He tapped his temple with his right forefinger. "Instincts."

There's a sort of raw charm to him, Kathryn thought. *If only he were more verbal . . . but maybe I'm not giving him enough of a chance.* She reached for the ketchup bottle and turned it upside down. Nothing came out.

"You gotta do what I did," Eddie said, stretching across the table to smack the bottom of the bottle. "Pardon the boarding house reach, as we used to say at home." He was very successful. His blow was so forceful that Kathryn's hand flinched and could no longer aim the bottle at the french fries. The condiment shot out in the opposite direction, landing in a huge crimson blotch on her black slipdress.

"Goddamn son of a bitch!" Kathryn hadn't meant to have such an uncensored reaction.

Eddie looked pathetically apologetic and handed Kathryn a fistful of napkins, which she used to scoop up the tomato puddle in her lap. She felt terrible for having blurted an expletive—only because in retrospect, it sounded like more of a reproach of Eddie's obvious good intentions than a spontaneous response to a fashion disaster. She dipped a wad of napkins into her glass of ice water and tried to remove the stain, but succeeded only in making the large, dark, damp spot even bigger.

"Ugh. It looks like blood," she said disgustedly.

"Send me the dry-cleaning bill. It was my fault."

"Thanks, Eddie." He was really nice. Too laconic for words, but a nice man.

"Well," he offered helpfully. "If people are looking at the stain on your dress, they're looking at the wrong thing. If you don't mind my saying so, you've got a very pretty face."

That was very sweet of him, actually.

Eddie leaned in for a kiss. Kathryn met him halfway across the Formica tabletop. She felt the slight stubble above his upper lip graze her own. He wasn't tentative, but he was a bit rough. Eddie practically bit her lip when he took her mouth, and Kathryn found herself not entirely disliking the sensation. It wasn't a bad kiss on the whole. Not stellar. Not earth-shattering. But not bad. Frankly, it was the best kiss she'd had all night.

"You smoke?"

Eddie grew a bit edgy. "Why?"

"You taste like you're a smoker, but you're trying to give it up." Kathryn watched his eyes, because his mouth wasn't moving. She was sure she was right. "And you've also got a lot going on in there . . ." she tapped her temple for emphasis. "But you're afraid to let people in. Maybe you're afraid you might get hurt. But if you hold yourself so tight, you won't be open to life's wonderful discoveries."

Instantly, Kathryn realized she might have gone too far, so she tried to lighten things up. "See, I can be a detective, too," she added gaily. As she kept her gaze fixed on his eyes, she caught the angry black cloud that crossed them. The cloud moved down his face and manifested itself in a twitch of his upper lip, which turned into a full-fledged scowl.

"Sorry. I hear it's a tough habit to quit. Smoking." The detective crack seemed to have made him touchy.

He waved his hand for the check. *I guess this date is over,* Kathryn thought. Their lethargic waitress ambled over to the table, did the addition while her lips moved and her charm bracelet jangled, then ripped the green-and-white page from her pad, slapping it face down on the table. "Pay the cashier when you're ready," she said apathetically, as though for the hundredth time that evening. Maybe it was.

As they headed out to the street, after giving Little Willy a personal good-bye in the form of a male fist-to-fist gesture, Eddie caught Kathryn looking down at the dark stain on the front of her slipdress. "I'd offer you my jacket, but . . ." he started to say, solicitously. "It's not that I'm not a gentleman, because I am." He seemed to be having trouble saying whatever it was he wanted to get out.

"I was just checking to see if you could see the stain in the dark—no, it's okay," Kathryn replied. "I'll throw it in a basin with some Woolite when I get home. And I do believe that for you, Eddie, chivalry is not dead."

"Actually, I became a . . . I always had a weakness for damsels in distress . . . and you do kind of have that Camelot look going with your hair and all." He smiled uneasily. "My mom used to say to me 'Who do you think you are, big guy? My knight in shining armor?' I was only seven years old the first time I 'rescued' her."

Kathryn laid her hand gently across Eddie's arm. "Let me guess," she said softly. "From abusive Italian father to abusive Irish husband—and he was a cop, to boot."

One corner of Eddie's mouth twitched slightly, and he looked down at Kathryn as if to say something, but thought better of it. But Kathryn hadn't missed that flicker of sadness and hurt—of childhood pain and memories long-buried in the momentary dilation of her date's dark eyes.

They started to walk east toward Eighth Avenue. It was a warm night, and the streets of Hell's Kitchen were populated with the usual denizens: pushers, prostitutes, and the occasional runaway, interspersed with pastel-clad, shiny-faced tourists with digital cameras, college students of both sexes in their requisite clunky black platform shoes, and unemployed actors trying to look, well, employed. The last two groups tended to distinguish themselves from the tourists by dressing like '70s refugees or in top-to-toe black, like Morticia Addams. Eddie volunteered to escort Kathryn home in the same manner via which he had come to fetch her: two buses.

"Sorry, these are new shoes," she apologized, since she was teetering a bit on her strappy sandals. "Imagine if I'd had a *drink* drink tonight—I mean alcoholic, as opposed to vanilla coke—I'd break my ankle in these."

Her words were nearly a self-fulfilling prophecy. They passed a phalanx of dented metal trash cans lined up in front of one of the faded red brick tenements on the block. With her right arm linked in the crook of Eddie's left one, and looking straight ahead toward the avenue, Kathryn didn't see the rut in the sidewalk. She stumbled and lost her footing, falling toward the row of garbage cans, unable to catch her balance before she landed on one hip on the ground between them.

As she tried to break her fall, a shot rang out, followed by another, and another.

"Stay down!" Eddie yelled, then threw his body on top of hers.

Another gunshot pinged off the metal trash can, inches from Eddie's ear. He grabbed Kathryn and rolled in the opposite direction, then pulled her by the wrist behind two more cans. A fifth bullet whizzed over their heads and lodged somewhere behind them.

"Jesus, Mary, and Joseph, Eddie, they're shooting at *you*!" Kathryn gasped.

That was about the time she realized why her date had been unable to offer her the use of his jacket to cover up the stain on her dress. He was wearing a holster. Eddie freed his arm and reached for his gun, returning fire at a shadowy figure in the window of a third-floor front apartment in a walk-up across the street.

In what seemed like a matter of a minute, the entire street was shut down from one avenue to the other by

police cars, their sirens blaring. A threatening voice commanded everyone on the block to stay put and not move,
under threat of being shot. Uniforms disembarked from
the squad cars and spread out over the block like a
SWAT team Kathryn had seen in an NBC movie of the
week. It seemed as though each officer had been assigned
a separate subculture to round up. Two blue uniforms
were chasing down stereotypical-looking drug dealers
who were trying to scuttle down the tenement steps into
sub-basements, clearly interpreting the warning over the
bullhorn as a mere suggestion. All parties were holding
their fire, as the street had become so crowded—between
the NYPD, the alleged perpetrators, and the curious bystanders who, applauding, probably thought the whole
hullabaloo was choreographed for an episode of *Law &
Order*.

Suddenly, Kathryn felt a tug on her arm. She was being
pulled away from Eddie by a short, squat, pug-nosed,
blonde officer. Her name tag said Swaggart. Emerging
from her hiding place, Kathryn almost turned her ankle
rising to her feet on her stilettos.

Officer Swaggart jerked Kathryn's arms behind her
back in one practiced, deft move and slipped the cuffs
on. It was surreal. "You have the right to remain silent.
Anything you say can be used against you in a court of
law. You have the right to an attorney. If you can't afford
an attorney, one will be provided to you . . ."

My God, she's Mirandizing me, Kathryn realized.
"Wait—do you think *I'm* a hooker?" she squealed,
barely finding her voice, as she was pushed head-first
into a squad car with other entrepreneurial ladies of
roughly the same age and unfortunately similar attire.

"Eddie, *say something*!" she yelled to him, trying to reach past her companions in the back seat.

Eddie was on the verge of a fistfight with a belligerent uniform. He reached into his jacket pocket, when the officer shoved his 9mm Glock in Eddie's face. "I was going for my *badge*, you overeager son of a bitch! Jesus! I suppose if I was black, I'd be dead by now!" Kathryn heard Eddie growl. He was livid, literally red in the face. "Detective Eddie Benson. Undercover. Vice. Midtown South, asshole!"

The rookie backed off, caught between embarrassment and confusion. Locked in the squad car, Kathryn watched the totally befuddled young cop try to fit the pieces together. "Hey, dickhead, you're so dumb I can smell the wood burning when you try to think," she shouted at him. The hookers in the backseat laughed. "You go, girl!" one of them exclaimed and made a loud, smacking kissy sound in Kathryn's direction. *Great, now we've all bonded,* Kathryn thought.

Eddie noted the rookie's name on the kid's rectangular badge, repeated it aloud, committing it to memory. Then Benson went ballistic. "Now let my *date* out of your goddamn car, you scumbag! Does your mother know you're out this late, Davis?" But as Eddie lunged toward the car, past Officer Davis, who was too green to be out on the street, the siren blipped, then blared and the squad car lurched away.

Chapter
8

How am I going to tell Ellie I was strip-searched and my date wasn't even there? Kathryn wondered, as she sat on a hard wooden bench at the Midtown North precinct on West Fifty-fourth Street, in a holding cell with industrious women of several ethnicities, varying shapes, and attitudes ranging from high dudgeon to white-hot fury to sullen indifference.

Well, at least I wore nice underwear. She shook her head, laughing silently. Not that the matron cared. In fact, the exorbitantly priced black lace teddy reinforced the prison matron's belief that Kathryn was lying about her line of work. She was on the wrong turf, that was all. "Uptown," "Brünnhilde" had snorted to herself when she saw the La Perla lingerie. Actually, the stalwart-looking Valkyrie prison matron was wrong. Kathryn was in an "honest profession," if you could call teaching anything to a bunch of randy adolescents "honest." Kathryn knew that a few high-end call girls lived in her *sister's* uptown high-rise. Maybe that's where Eleanor had gotten the notion to outfit her from La Perla.

"I never seen you before. Where you work, baby?" asked a RuPaul wannabe in a beehive wig the color of moonlight, "her" Adam's apple poorly concealed by a chiffon scarf in a garish leopard print.

"I'm uh . . . not in the Life," Kathryn replied.

"Oh, honey, we all say that from time to time," cooed the hooker. "But denial is not just a river in Egypt." The transvestite extended her large hand, manicured with inch-long nail extensions enameled in black and pewter. "The name's Liquid Silver," the hooker said. She ran her tongue over her glossed lips. "But my friends call me Lick." What's your name, sugar? You as sweet as pep'mint candy."

"Kathryn—Kitty."

"Kitty. Tha's nice."

"At least her name's not 'Pussy.' "

"Oh, shut your ugly face, Carmencita," Liquid Silver sassed back at Kathryn's detractor. "You *so* obvious, girl!" Lick turned back to Kathryn. "I like your hair, sugar. That nat'ral?"

"Yup."

"What you use?"

"Aveda. The shampoo and the conditioner that's specially formulated for redheads." Here she was trading beauty tips with a transvestite hooker. Well, at least Lick was more verbal than Eddie.

"I was a redhead last month for a spell. It was Buster's idea. My man." Liquid Silver sighed dramatically. "But it don't suit my nature. I'm not a fiery woman. I'm like . . . a cooler customer. Philadelphia mainline. That's where I was born." Lick primped a little. "Sides, I used to have a Barbie doll that had hair jus' like this and I wanted to grow up to look zackly like *her*."

"Well, I think it was a good choice. The platinum is

very striking," Kathryn said helpfully. "And it sets off your complexion beautifully."

Lick blushed under her mahogany skin. "Girl. You make my day." She shifted her butt on the hard bench. "I gotta move these bones, or I'm gonna get some spread-ugly looking ass. Who all wants to play a game?"

"I'm up for it," Kathryn said. It certainly would help pass the time. Who knew when she might be sprung. This could be fun. "Any other takers?"

"You know me, Lick," purred another transvestite hooker. "I can be *up* for anything. Tell you what," the streetwalker then said to Kathryn. "You pick the game and"—she pointed to herself—"Shemale Warrior Princess will go along for the ride."

"Okay. Who knows how to play charades?" Kathryn stood up and all of a sudden she found herself switching into drama teacher mode. "You get your butts off these hard benches and your imagination going at the same time."

She was a bit surprised to find a relatively enthusiastic audience. Kathryn explained the rules and demonstrated the pantomime shorthand for *movie*, *book*, *play*, and other subjects that would work for the game.

"They gonna wonder why it's so quiet in here," Lick laughed, "if I'm not supposed to talk. Hey, mama," she called to the prison matron, "wanna play, too?"

To Kathryn's shock, "Brünnhilde" sort of smiled and checked the corridor outside the holding cell to see if anyone might be watching who could write her up if they caught her fraternizing, as it were, with her charges.

"Okay, I got me a title!" Lick announced excitedly. "It's a movie! Oh, shit, I wasn't supposed to *say* it. Okay, you didn't hear that, ladies." She pantomimed the correct sign for *movie* and the game was underway.

"Five words!" called the matron, guessing correctly.

"Fourth word . . . a little word . . . uh . . ." Carmencita puzzled out.

Lick tapped her manicured talon on the tip of her nose, to indicate that Carmencita's correct guess was "on the nose," but the Latina just looked confused.

"I got it? Wait, what did I just say? Uh . . ."

Lick continued to touch her nose furiously.

"*A*," Kathryn reasoned. "The fourth word is *a*. Something something something *a* something?"

Liquid Silver nodded her assent to Kathryn. She then indicated she was going to dramatize the first word. She pretended to take out a pistol and fire it.

Random guesses flew from the cellmates. "Shoot?" "Kill?" "Assassinate the motherfucker so he don't walk no more?"

Lick made a "sort of" gesture with her hand. Then she pretended to shoot herself, writhed in mock pain, and fell to the floor in an agonizing, tortured heap.

"Die!" Kathryn called out.

Lick made the "okay" sign with her right thumb and index finger. She indicated she was moving right on to the second word, then grabbed her crotch as an illustration.

"Die snatch?"

"Shemale, sometimes you are so stupid, girl. Oops," Lick said, coquettishly putting her hand over her lips. "No talking," she added coyly. "Well shut my beautiful mouth." Lick then made a power gesture with her fist.

Blank stares from the cell. Then she pounded on the cinderblock wall and the wooden bench, trying to illustrate the second word of the film title. More confused faces. She returned to her crotch and began to graphically mime an erect penis.

"Ohhhh," Shemale cried, experiencing nothing short of an orgasmic epiphany. "Hard!"

Lick tapped her nose and jumped up and down triumphantly. Then she rapidly went through a series of pantomimes of shootings, stabbings, strangulations, stompings, and anything else she could think of.

"Die Hard with a Vengeance!" Kathryn yelled, maybe a little too loud. The matron gestured to indicate that someone was coming.

"*Coño*, you are too good at this, Kitty," Carmencita marveled. "I couldn't do this for shit. I was thinking about doing *Survivor* but I wouldn't have no idea how to get you all to guess it."

A world-weary sergeant poked his head in the door. "Kathryn Lamb?"

Kathryn looked up. "That's me."

"You can step outside, Ms. Lamb. You're free to go."

"You take care of yourself, girlfriend." Lick said, hugging Kathryn. "And any time you want to change your . . . circumstances, you just come 'round looking for Lick. Buster'll get you set up nice. Save on shoe leather, if you know what I mean," she whispered. "I can fix it so the men come crawling to you, sugar, 'stead of walking yo' cute l'il tootsies off looking for *them*."

"Thanks. I'll . . . keep that in mind," Kathryn said, hugging the statuesque transvestite. "And you keep yourself . . . okay?"

Eddie was standing outside the door, looking harried and sad.

"I'm sorry, Kathryn."

"You should be," she mustered, trying to make a joke

out of her predicament. It was impossible, given the circumstances. Good God, she'd been *jailed*.

"I shoulda told you I was a detective," he said, shuffling his feet. "But even if I had, it wouldn't have prevented us from getting caught in what went down tonight. Vice in Midtown North and Midtown South are working on a joint task force in Hell's Kitchen. The uniforms in North don't know me. Vice, undercover, we don't let too many people outside our department know what we do. A week or so ago, we got a report there's a snitch out there, and someone on the street tonight recognized me."

"I was *arrested*, Eddie."

He looked truly miserable. Kathryn somehow found herself feeling sorrier for *him* than she did for herself. "We got that taken care of," he said. "Don't worry about that. Swaggart didn't write anything down yet, so she won't be writing anything down, ever." He reached out to stroke her cheek. "Jesus, kiddo, I wish I could take you home, but I got some paperwork here to fill out, plus on account of what went down tonight, I gotta go back to my own precinct and take care of some business. I'm sorry I can't see you home." He lowered his voice and leaned in toward Kathryn's ear. "I'd like to take you out again sometime, though."

He looked like a basset hound. Kathryn couldn't blame him for what had happened that night, but she couldn't see herself dating an NYPD vice detective. "You're a very nice guy, Eddie," she began.

He shuffled his feet, and tossed his head a bit, giving her that "where have I heard that before?" look.

"It does sound that way, I admit, and I'm sorry," Kathryn continued. "But . . . well . . . your lifestyle is a bit action-packed for me." It was the truth, but not all of it. She couldn't envision herself carrying every conversation for the duration of a relationship. "Again, I'm sorry. You *are* a very nice guy."

He shook her hand. "I really liked being with you, Kathryn. I'm sorry, too." Eddie swallowed hard. "Well, I hope you enjoyed at least *part* of the evening."

"I'm having a hard time deciding whether it was the humorless lesbian comedy, the crossfire, or the strip search I liked best."

Eddie nodded his head. "I guess it was sort of a dud all around, huh?"

"No, Eddie. It really wasn't. The burger was *lovely*. And meeting Little Willy was an experience I will long remember. Thanks." Kathryn was feeling the need to change the subject. Any more pity for her date, and she'd be home making red sauce for his penne as soon as she was sprung from the pen. Which reminded her. "By the way, I get a phone call, don't I?"

The detective smacked his head the same way he'd hit the ketchup bottle. "Jesus, I'm sorry." He looked around. "You're not under arrest. You can make as many calls as you want. But I don't see an empty office; the place is crawling with cops."

"I guess you get that in a precinct."

Eddie laughed. "Yeah, right. You do." He gestured toward a grimy pay phone screwed into the gray-green station house wall, then fished for something in his pocket, handing her a quarter. "It's the least I can do," he said goofily.

"You're swell, Eddie."

The narc shuffled his feet again and looked down at the ground, changing the subject. "Ya know, if you ever get a parking ticket or something . . ."

"I appreciate the gesture," Kathryn said tensely, taking his hand, "but I don't drive."

"Well . . . if you ever get a car . . . I mean, look me up, sometime, ya know?"

Why do I feel guilty about this? Kathryn wondered. They shook hands again, and Eddie rounded a corner and disappeared into one of the tiny, overcrowded offices. Kathryn slipped the quarter into the pay phone, took a business card from the billfold of her wallet and dialed a number. *Be home,* she prayed. *Be home.* She sighed with relief when a voice answered on the other end, then immediately went into a tailspin of anxiety over what to say. She realized her hands were shaking.

"Bear? It's me, Kathryn. Are you busy?"

Chapter
9

"You're *where*?!" Kathryn heard him say. She tried *sotto voce* to explain her predicament until the disembodied voice of the operator warned her that her time was about to expire. Kathryn rattled off the address of the precinct and asked Walker to fetch her, then hung up, wondering if he would think her stupid for not just taking a cab or a subway home.

Wait a minute. Who the hell cares if he thinks I'm stupid? I was entitled to a phone call. It's really Bear who got me into this mess. Eddie was—is—his client. He owes me.

Twenty minutes later, Walker strode briskly into the station, took Kathryn's hand, and turned around without breaking his pace. "C'mon, let's go. Meter's running," he said as he steered her into a waiting taxi, then climbed in beside her. Kathryn spent the ride downtown recounting the evening's events to Walker, rattling them off at breakneck speed, as though she were calling the Preakness. "You *owe* me, Walker Hart," she kept repeating during their ride home. "You *owe* me."

Still, she had surprised herself by not crying yet. Kathryn managed to keep it together as they walked into their apartment building. "*Buenos noches, señor. Señorita,*"

Carlos said, tipping them a wink, which both Walker and Kathryn elected to ignore. "Evening, Carlos," they said, almost in tandem.

After they stepped into the elevator, Kathryn finally lost control. She started to tremble, then to cry, backing herself against the wall of the elevator. Walker came over to her and pulled her into his arms. Kathryn tried to wriggle away, but he held her tightly. "Shhh," he soothed, "It's okay." She accepted his permission to weep uncontrollably, shaking as he held her. "Of course you're a wreck, Kitty, you were almost killed. You're *supposed* to feel something."

Now she felt something. Something wonderful when she snuggled against his chest. Walker moved his hands from her back up to her shoulders and gave them a friendly squeeze. "Good God, you're in knots, woman. You're coming with me."

There it goes again. That magical, electrical shiver. "But this is my floor," she protested, as the elevator slowed to a stop on nine. "I feel gross. I need a shower or two or three."

"I'll take you home in a little while. First, you need some cognac and a massage."

Kathryn realized she was pretty content where she was, and gave up with no further struggle. "That's right neighborly of you, sir," she said, half crying, half laughing.

They arrived at the penthouse, and Walker reached for his keys and opened the door without letting go of Kitty. He led her to that dreadfully ugly, severe-looking black leather couch and seated her. "Be right back," he assured her, kicking off his shoes on the way to the liquor cabinet. He poured two fingers of Martell X.O. into a snifter and handed it to Kathryn. She took a grateful sip. "Better?" he asked solicitously. She nodded. He patted her knee. "Good." He padded toward the bedroom. "Be right out."

Kathryn buried her nose in the glass and inhaled its rich aroma, then swirled the amber liquid around, watching the "legs" slowly trickle down the insides of the glass. She could hear Walker singing from the bedroom, while he seemed to be making all sorts of thudding noises with paraphernalia in there. "If you're ever in a jam, here I am. If you're ever in a mess, S.O.S. If you ever feel so happy, you land in jail, I'm your bail. That's friendship, friendship, just a perfect blendship. When other friendships have been forgot, ours will still be hot ... Ka-yadda, yadda, yadda, ching, ching, ching . . ."

"You always know just what to sing," Kathryn called in to him.

"Just a major Cole Porter fan," he grinned defensively, lugging a large padded object into the living room.

"What the hell is that?"

"My massage table."

"Hold it. You weren't kidding."

"Of course I wasn't kidding. Did you think I was bringing a defenseless woman—not to mention a *client* of mine—who has just been shot at, falsely arrested, then jailed, up to my apartment for the purposes of seduction?"

The thought crossed my mind, Kathryn contemplated, crossing her legs.

Although the thought did cross my mind, Walker mused.

"I'm not letting you touch my back," Kathryn said, placing her drink on the amoeba-shaped coffee table, using last month's copy of *Sports Illustrated* for a coaster.

"Why not? I'm licensed."

"Bull puckey."

Walker sighed, then took her hand. "Come with me," he insisted, attempting to steer her toward the bedroom.

Kathryn planted her feet like a recalcitrant six-year-old.

"Cut it out, Kitty. I'm not going to throw you on the bed like a Neanderthal. I'm going to show you my accreditation."

"Keep it in your pants."

"You know damn well what I mean." He brought her into his bedroom and pulled open a drawer of his black lacquered bureau. His sock drawer. Walker withdrew a diploma-sized sheet of paper from the bottom of the drawer, nudging aside the balls of paired socks with dragons, clocks, and images of Betty Boop woven into the fabric. "See. One hundred percent legitimate," he said, poking at the official document with his index finger.

But Kathryn wasn't paying attention. She was silently cursing herself for wondering if the queen-sized mattress was very firm, and how anyone could possibly sleep in a bedroom with white walls, except for the one with the large pastel-toned litho that looked like it used to hang in a Marriott. No doubt one of Sven's choices. And it probably cost a fortune, but you'd never know it. Plus, not a book in sight. How different from her own inner sanctum that was cluttered with dog-eared volumes of everything from Shakespeare to Sheldon, depending on her mood.

"Kitty?"

"Sorry—I was thinking—this bedroom doesn't look very . . . lived in. I'm almost ready to check the nightstand for a Gideon's Bible." *What was that?* She realized she was sort of pleased that it didn't look "lived in." *Where did that come from?*

"Wrong pew." Walker grinned. "So, now that you know I'm not going to send you to the emergency room, and that I know what I'm doing, let me give you a massage. You're right, I owe you. So let this be a start."

"I'm not getting undressed."

Walker appeared to be getting exasperated. "Fine. It just won't be very effective. Not as effective as it would if you did. I won't look. I'm a professional. Once a body is on the table, it just becomes meat to me."

"That's gross. Have you ever considered pathology instead of matchmaking?"

Walker took out a bedsheet and a couple of large fluffy terrycloth towels from his linen closet and started to set up the table. "Do you prefer the head cradle, or not?" he asked, spreading the sheet over the leather-covered collapsible table.

"With," Kathryn responded, still not moving toward the table. "How did you end up a certified masseur?"

"In college. Before I discovered the stock market, I worked my way through school that way. I was raised in a single-parent household and the money was always iffy, depending on business. So I developed a skill that people will always need and are willing to pay good money for. I still have private clients every once in a while, just for fun. My friends, mostly. I'll give them or a family member of theirs a massage as a birthday or holiday gift."

"Then you're rusty," Kathryn pronounced, finishing her cognac. "You should give them shares of AOL instead."

Walker moved to refill her glass. "I gave my most recent massage two weeks ago. Fine with me if you don't want to take me up on my offer."

Kathryn recalled that Eleanor had once accused her of being a "massage slut," the kind of woman who would do damn near anything to get a back rub. The cognac was beginning to have its customary relaxing effect. Kathryn's legs and arms were bare anyway, and the slip-dress was pretty much history, if the stain wouldn't come out. So, what the hell. She slid out of the flimsy shift and unbuckled her sandals, leaving her feeling extremely vulnerable in the black lace teddy.

She pretended not to catch Walker's admiring look, as he watched her undress out of the corner of his eye. He seemed amused that her defenses had given way to his hedonistic offer. "Well, I'm glad the dryer didn't eat it," he said, pointing his chin at her fragile undergarment.

"Oh, hell," she gasped, grabbing one of the beach-size towels. She wasn't wearing a bra underneath the teddy, either.

"I'm not saying this to tease you, Kitty, but if I massage you in that net thing, it's actually going to hurt. Kneading that fabric into you will make your back smart a bit."

She hesitated. "Go into the bedroom."

He did as he was bid, and she slipped out of the teddy, leaving her underpants on, then hopped up on the massage table and covered herself from shoulder to toe with the towel.

"Can I come back yet?" he asked from the other room.

"All clear."

He had changed into a T-shirt that said "You're the Top" baring his muscular forearms, and came out of the bedroom with a small bottle of lotion, which he rested on that butt-ugly coffee table. Then he turned a dimmer switch on the wall and lowered the light so that it was no brighter than a candleglow and lit a stick of ambergris incense, leaving it to burn in a glass ashtray.

"Roll over, I'll start on your back."

Kathryn clutched the towel to her body as she rolled onto her stomach. She heard him squeeze some lotion into his hand and rub his hands together. It smelled luscious. "What is that?"

"It's jasmine massage lotion. I buy it in Chinatown."

She briefly started to relax when he placed his strong hands at intervals along her back, feeling for tension and assessing her alignment before beginning to do any deep muscle work. When he began to apply more pressure, slowly moving his hands up the length of her back along either side of her spine, Kathryn began to have her doubts about going through with the massage.

"Uh, oh." She bounced up from her prone position, covering her torso with the towel clutched in her fist. This was more than she could handle at the moment. Her being nearly naked. Walker touching her so exquisitely that any second now, all her resolve, all her attempts at willpower, restraint, dignity, would dissolve into a puddle and any uncertainty she might harbor about the appropriateness of this situation would entirely be overcome by the intense desire to allow him to do anything to, with, and for her body.

"What's the matter, Kitty?"

"No can do," she responded simply. "Where are my clothes?"

"I was only trying to make you feel better."

"I know, Bear. That's why no can do." She noticed that he was trying to keep his face placid, not to reflect his disappointment.

"Well, you still need to relax. Here, let me pour you another." He took Kathryn's snifter and refilled it, then handed it back to her. "And we'll try another cure for frazzled nerves."

"What?" Kathryn asked, turning away from him and getting dressed.

"Music. Let me just get this out of the way . . ." He folded up the massage table and lugged it into the corner of the room, then moved to the stereo and perused his CD collection. "Just the ticket, I think," he said, retrieving an album. "A timeless old standard. And more soothing under the circumstances than what I *have* been listening to lately."

"Which is?"

"The Torykillers."

Kathryn registered a look of utter shock—something between unbelieving and appalled.

"Just kidding! A feeble attempt at humor that fell way short of the mark. Ms. Lamb, may I have this dance?" Walker extended his hand, which Kathryn took somewhat reluctantly. The rich strains of Kern's "Only Make Believe" began to play and he enveloped her into his arms and began to slow dance with her, holding her tenderly.

It felt delicious. "I have a question for you, Bear," Kathryn said, after a weighted pause.

"Shoot."

"Bad word choice given the recent events of the evening, don't you think?" They both smiled. "No . . . I was just thinking about something. Did you get good grades in school?"

"It's rather a funny time to ask a question like that. Why? Am I being graded now? There isn't going to be a quiz at the end of the period, is there?"

"No, Bear. I was just thinking about something . . ."

"You said that already."

"But you didn't answer my question."

"I did okay in school. Besides, no one asks you for your transcripts when you're pushing forty."

"You're an exceptionally graceful dancer," Kathryn purred. "Not at all a klutz. You haven't steered me into the coffee table once."

"I'm a musician. I chalk it up to good rhythm. I was also a varsity athlete, if you recall. Your point is, Ms. Lamb?"

"My point is . . . that . . . since you walk into stuff sometimes, and tend to knock things over . . . that maybe you might need glasses."

Walker set his jaw and guided her through an intricate ballroom step. "I've never needed them before."

"I'm just saying . . ."

"No way. Besides, they'll make me look old. Or geeky."

"Not unless you get geeky frames," Kathryn replied simply. She gave him an inadvertent squeeze. After all, she had just intended to make a gentle inquiry and ended up fairly flattening his ego. "Besides, I don't think anything could make you look like a dweeb." She rested her head on his chest and allowed him to gently partner her around the room.

"Feel any better?" he asked, halfway through the

song. She nodded into his shoulder. "All part of Six in the City's patented personal satisfaction customer service guarantee."

Walker's hands still smelled of jasmine. Kathryn found herself working to keep her equilibrium. "After tonight's fiasco, you still owe me a replacement date, you know. A dance with you does not a date with an eligible bachelor make." She gazed at the ceiling to avoid making direct eye contact with him.

"Don't worry about it," Walker replied evenly. "I'll make sure you get excellent prospects steered your way. Not that the two matches you've met through Six in the City are sub-par in the humanity department, necessarily, but I'll give you a 'freebie.' Six guys for the price of five."

Kathryn's eyes were still focused upwards. "Um . . . don't look now, but did that leak get worse since the last time I was up here?" she asked her host, indicating the brown streak running down the corner of the wall at the far end of the living room. "You should talk to the landlord."

"My mother? The woman who flees in a crisis? Or gets married in one."

The song ended and Kathryn was still enfolded in Walker's arms. "Better now?"

"Yes," Kathryn replied, her eyes shining—from the cognac, *of course*—as she leaned her head against him. He was so much taller than she was. The top of her head came to just below his collarbone. "Thank you. I'll try not to get arrested again. If word gets out, it could be bad for business." She looked up into his pale green eyes, and he bent forward to reach her mouth.

"Ahhhhh-choo!" Kathryn's sneeze involuntarily jerked

her head away and Walker's mouth landed on her cheek. They looked at each other awkwardly.

"*Gesundheit,*" he said, after a pause.

"Well, I guess that's . . . good night, then," she said briskly. "I'll see you on the elevator or something. Or in your office. Thanks for the cognac. And the dance."

"I'll let you out," Walker said self-consciously, as he walked her to the door. "Sorry for the . . . everything."

Kathryn rang for the elevator and leaned against the wall of the hallway outside the penthouse. *Well, I sure screwed that one up,* she thought.

Inside his mother's aerie, Walker poured himself another cognac and sat on his leather couch, cradling the goblet in his hands to warm it up. Bad, bad Bear to try to cross the professional boundary with Kathryn. She was his client. What had he been thinking? That the woman was positively irresistible, *that's* what. And he'd nearly let his libido get the better of him. "You screwed that one up, big time, bro," he said aloud to himself. "Big time."

Chapter 10

"I felt like I was back at my first seventh-grade dance," Walker confessed to Josh over his second pint of Bass Ale at the North Star tavern in the too-trendy South Street Seaport. "Dork City."

"Bear ... I'm playing devil's advocate here. This is where you tell me to shut my yap; this is the woman of your dreams, and just because you pulled a Clark Kent when you tried to kiss her for the first time, it doesn't mean you were right all along about your conviction to remain a bachelor for the rest of your life."

"Phooey." Walker motioned to the bartender, an Irishman who looked fresh off the boat, and ordered another round.

Josh popped a beer nut in his mouth. "I was thinking about you and the subject of risk taking. Remember when you came back to the city after grad school and you were first flirting with the idea of starting up a financial newsletter?"

"That's not all I was flirting with." Walker launched into a chorus of "To All the Girls I've Loved Before." Several patrons turned their heads and an attractive blonde got off her bar stool and applauded. Walker held his beer glass aloft and brought it down in front of his chest with a theatrical sweeping gesture, as he took a bow.

"So where are all those women, now, bro?"

"Married. Except for the ones who are divorced."

"And what does that tell you?"

"That they all wanted to get married and/or make babies, which is why *I* didn't belong in the charming little domestic picture. How many times has Rushie been married? Are we up to a baker's dozen yet?"

"It still sounds weird to me when you call your mother by her first name."

"What do you call *your* mother, Josh?"

"Mommy."

Walker snorted into his third pint. "I've lost track of all the times my 'mommy' has been married. And I've long since stopped keeping a scorecard of her paramours. Suffice it to say, I've never seen a happy marriage."

"See, I take that as a challenge, bro," Josh said, raising his glass at his old roommate. "Don't forget, you're talking to an engaged man. I'd be a fool to let Lou get away."

"I seem to remember that *I* was the one who first told you that."

"Look, I love being with the woman. She's a treasure to sleep with and a pleasure to awaken beside, and she wants to spend every day of the rest of her life with me, although God knows why. So I finally decided that if I kept putting off the inevitable, she'd finally get sick of my being afraid to discuss the *M* word and go find someone who would, even if that someone wasn't me and didn't fulfill her in the same way. And this is not just idle speculation because I actually *know* someone that happened to. Peter Gordon Weinberg dated this girl for what—six, maybe seven years; she keeps pressing him to commit, he doesn't, so she smells the coffee, dumps him and boom! The next guy she dates, they're engaged within eight months. I didn't want to see that happening with Lou."

"You become a lot more voluble in vino, my friend," Walker said.

"Beer, Bear."

"Josh, I've been spending six days a week helping sorry souls try to achieve that elusive human connection known as connubial bliss. And I've probably met more deluded—and delusional—people than I ever want to see in a lifetime. I see how desperately they try to find 'The One' who will solve all their problems and enable them to live happily ever after in a penthouse in the sky. And most of it is castles in the air. It's sad. Marriage isn't going to solve those problems. In my experience of it, it *creates* them."

"That's your *mother's* experience of it." Josh slid the bowl of nuts between the two of them. "When the hell are you going to stop living your mother's life? She is not you; you are not her. It's fucked up, man. Stop using it as an excuse. You have free will. Choices. I think you ought to ask Kathryn out. You know, I should wear a wire when I'm out with you, because ever since she walked into Six in the City, you mention her name far more often than any other person in every conversation we have."

"Maybe that's because you always ask me how it's going with her."

Josh chewed on his lip and stared into his beer. "It only proves that the woman is on your mind. You've eaten her ginger cats—which in itself is borderline erotic, given the not-so-subtle implications here—and almost became intimate with some of her major muscle groups. I'd say that things have progressed pretty rapidly for someone who doesn't want to get involved with a woman who envisions a *chuppah* instead of a pair of house seats when you mention 'two on the aisle.' "

"She could have her wedding canopy *and* her Broadway show if I took her to a revival of *Fiddler on the Roof*," Walker said dryly. "I'm not saying that she couldn't be a good friend, Josh. She's pretty terrific. But she came to Six in the City in the first place because she's goal oriented, and I'm not casting my net in that direction."

Josh gave Walker a good hard look, then shook his head. " 'A confirmed old bachelor and likely to remain so.' Henry Higgins ended up a lonely man, my friend."

"So what do you think that was all about?" Eleanor said, following a slurp of Serendipity's delectable frozen hot chocolate. She slid the enormous bowl-like goblet across the marble tabletop to her young daughter, who had been staring, fascinated, at the bright colors in the old-fashioned ice cream parlor's stained glass panels and giggling flirtatiously with the perky waiters.

Johanna immediately began to blow bubbles with the straw, creating an incandescent brown froth. She smiled, very pleased with herself when Eleanor shot her a disapproving frown. The toddler giggled, then took a proper sip with the straw. "Drink it like a person," she scolded, obviously parroting something her mother must have told her more than once.

"I'm not sure what it was all about, frankly. If I hadn't

sneezed, I guess he would have made it to first base. By that point, I certainly wouldn't have minded if he'd kissed me, and I would have kissed back. I mean, he's terrific looking, and after the night I had, I wasn't exactly focusing on the ramifications of where things would have gone if we'd actually kissed. My feeling is that it was probably not such a good idea to begin with, and the sneeze was just a lucky break that got me out of having to deal with it either way." Kathryn reached for the goblet of frozen hot chocolate and took a generous gulp of the icy concoction.

"It confused me, though, Ellie. I mean, the first thing that popped into my head when I got back to my place was, 'does he come on to all his clients?' Which made me feel really sleazy, so I stood under a hot shower for half an hour. And then I thought 'if he's interested in me as a date, then he ought to say something and not just try to make a move.' Especially after he's been saying six ways from Sunday how he's not only uninterested in marriage, he's downright anti-the-establishment. And then I thought 'well, maybe it was a tense moment all around and he was just going with the flow and I'm making a big deal out of nothing and I probably should just let go of it . . .'"

"And stop obsessing," the sisters said in unison.

"You are just about the most obsessive person I have ever met," Eleanor said. "You really know how to worry something to death."

"Geez, and I thought it was astrological. You're more goal oriented than I was," Kathryn told her younger sister. "You wanted to go to grad school, you went. You wanted to marry a doctor, you did. You wanted kids, you made them. Sometimes I feel like I'm sort of floating through life. Other times, I feel like I'm cruising. Most times, I just feel like a hamster on a wheel."

Eleanor slid the glass bowl toward herself and took another drink. "I think that you should either make this guy your mission or forget about him and get on with the next four bachelors he's supposed to fix you up with. Don't get distracted. Keep your eyes on the prize."

"My turn." Kathryn leaned over and sipped the frozen hot chocolate. "So 'although I can't dismiss the memory of his kiss,' I guess we're in agreement that 'he's not for me.' "

"Well, from the way he protests personal involvement in the institution of marriage, he sounds about as convertible as a hearse."

"That's a weird metaphor, kid." Kathryn took another sip.

"His mother must really have done a number on him. And if he didn't have a father or a father-figure around too often when he was growing up, it's no wonder he's got a sour view of the sacrament." Eleanor reached over to wipe a thick chocolaty dribble from Johanna's chin that threatened to make a giant splotch on the toddler's pink gingham T-shirt. "But Walker seems like good *friend* material. And it's always nice to have a man around the co-op to phone, in case there's a waterbug to be killed, or a lightbulb you can't reach that needs to be replaced."

"After Barnaby and Eddie, I'm losing faith in his matchmaking abilities."

Johanna, who had been busy creating an animated discussion between two spoons while her mother and aunt were conversing, began to bang the utensils on the table. The din achieved the desired effect and the adults turned to look at her.

"I have to take her home for her nap," Eleanor said, as she asked for the check. "I'll get this."

"I'll leave the tip," Kathryn offered. "He's let the three of us sit here for ages sharing the same frozen hot chocolate, and we still didn't manage to finish it."

Johanna reached for the bowl with her chubby little hands. "Take home," she announced.

"Yes, jujube, we're taking you home. We just have to pay our check first," Eleanor told her, taking out her reading glasses.

The tiny fingers inched across the table, forcing the two-year-old to stretch her arm, followed by half her torso, toward the bowl. "No. Choc-o-late home," Johanna corrected her mother.

"Can we get this to go?" Kathryn asked, as the waiter came over to collect their money. "You've gained another fan," she added, gesturing toward her niece, who with single-minded determination, continued to reach for the enormous bowl of chocolate soup. "Well, she inherited *your* focus and drive, El," Kathryn commented to her sister.

They parted company on the sidewalk outside the famous ice cream parlor, after Kathryn obliged Johanna, who wanted "Aunt Kittycat kiss."

"I'll call you as soon as I hear from Bachelor Number Three," Kathryn promised her sister.

"Your horoscope said you were going to get lucky today," Eleanor said. "So maybe the man of your dreams will be on the other end of the phone when you get home.

It's funny, but ever since I've been home with the jujube, I've made a habit of buying the *New York Post* every day, so I can read the horoscopes, along with the gossip in Liz Smith's column. It's such an un-MBA thing to do. And I even got a subscription to *Vogue*."

"Well, you were always allowed to read more than the NASDAQ report, you know."

"I know," Eleanor said with a sheepish shrug, "but I always felt like I had to be such a grown-up when I was in the corporate world. Banking and me . . . we weren't a good match for one another, as it were. To tell you the truth, I *always* preferred Dr. Seuss to stock quotes."

"Who wouldn't?" Kathryn said with a laugh, as she headed off to the subway.

"Ahhhhhhhhgh!" Kathryn screamed into the phone forty-three minutes later. "I can't believe who called me. It's gotta be a hoax, but I played his message a dozen times, and it sounds like his voice. I even tossed a cassette tape into my portable player so I could make a copy of his message."

"What are you talking about?" Eleanor asked, catching her sister's infectious enthusiasm.

"Bachelor Number Three is a V.F.A.!"

"A what?"

"V.F.A.—Very Famous Actor. I'll divulge his name when you get here. Do you want me to play you his message now, or do you want to hear it in twenty minutes when you zip your butt down here to help me figure out what to wear to Nebuchadnezzar this Saturday night?"

"You're lucky Dan's home early for once in a blue moon," Eleanor said. "I'll hop in a cab. I don't zip when I'm in my second trimester."

Twenty-two and a half minutes later, Eleanor and Kathryn were replaying the incoming phone message, analyzing the caller's voice over and over, like amateur espionage operators.

"It definitely sounds like him," Eleanor said, running a hand through her hair. "Whoa!"

Kathryn noticed her sister was blushing. "I had a senior last year who could do a wicked imitation of his cadences, though. He could be playing a practical joke."

"It's him," Eleanor said, shaking her head. "Wow! Dan loved him in *Don't Shoot the Messenger*."

"He doesn't usually make my kind of movies, although he wasn't half-bad in that remake of *Scaramouche* last year. I don't know what accent he was doing, but he certainly didn't lack charisma. He was bizarrely cast in the updated *Lorna Doone*, though. The producers probably thought his name would sell tickets, or bring in teenage audiences, because the classics are not Rick Byron's forte. My favorite picture of his is *Avenging Angel*. That's the one where you see his butt—you know, in the scene where they attach the wings."

"I think that was a stunt butt," Eleanor said ruefully. "The skin tones didn't exactly match. Believe me, I checked. In fact I wore out that part of the video pressing *rewind*."

"There's a very easy answer to our conundrum," Kathryn mused.

"About whether that was or was not Ricky-poo's butt?"

"No—about whether that really was him, or my former student Aaron Rabinowitz calling me from his college dorm room with a crackerjack vocal impersonation. We call Six in the City and see if he's a client."

"You dial while I look through your closet," Eleanor said. "Nebuchadnezzar would be a perfect place to wear the best-fitting little black dress you own. The shorter the better."

"What is this mania for naming trendy Soho watering holes after ancient kings?" Kathryn called to her sister, who could be heard rummaging through a rack of clothes. She picked up the phone and rang the dating service.

"They *want* you to confuse one with the other, I suppose," Eleanor called back. "You're going to ruin this dress if you keep it on a wire hanger. This one, too. Nebuchadnezzar . . . Balthazar . . . I read in Liz Smith's column that the guy who owns Balthazar wants to open up restaurants named for the other two Magi, Gaspar and Melchior." She emerged from the bedroom holding two little black dresses against her torso. "Which one of these looks better on you?"

"The V neck." Kathryn's tone of voice changed. "Yes, I'll hold," she told Walker at the other end of the phone.

Eleanor tossed the dress with the plunging neckline over the back of the velvet sofa. "This is stunning," she noted, fingering the fabric. She checked out the label. "French. Good for you! This is a whole lot more sophisticated than your usual attire."

"No thanks for the compliment. That dress was my spring splurge. I found it at this wonderful boutique on the Upper West Side. I think it's called Broadway Studio or something. Everything is European and makes me look very thin. Any time I want to treat myself, I head up there. Unfortunately for my Visa bill, I'll look for any excuse to treat myself. Did you ever wear Vertigo clothing? Their pants make your tush look great!"

Eleanor shook her head and returned to more pressing business. "Those black sandals you wore to meet Eddie will be perfect with this, unless they got trashed during your stint in the pen. Besides, it doesn't matter if you can't walk in them—you'll probably be traveling by limo. I'm surprised you don't get vertigo from the heel height."

Kathryn held up the dress. "The lycra in the fabric does wonders for holding in everything I would rather hide. And the three-quarter sleeves cover the parts of my arms that I always hated. No amount of gym classes has ever managed to make these as firm as I would like them," she said, poking at the underside of her left upper arm.

Eleanor studied the dress and placed Kathryn's stiletto sandals on the floor, creating an imaginary Kathryn out of dress and accessories. "Hmmm. You're not a gen-Xer, so I wouldn't wear one of those little Y necklaces that were so 'in' a while back."

Kathryn nodded in agreement. "Too Jennifer Aniston."

"I suggest real gold—an unusual piece. I'll look through my stuff and try to find the artsiest thing Dan ever gave me. If you're going for a dramatic necklace, then don't wear earrings. But if you have some cool ones—like that Greek goddess-style pair you got at the Sag Harbor crafts fair last May, and you opt to go for those, then skip the necklace."

"This really feels like Cinderella, you know. Especially with you playing Fairy Godmother."

"I prefer to think of myself as the Fashion Police," Eleanor countered, and excused herself to use the bathroom, leaving Kathryn still on hold with the phone cradled to her ear.

A few minutes later, when Eleanor emerged, Kathryn gave her the good news. "Well, I just learned from Bear that our V.F.A. is on the level. Although I have no idea why he registered with a dating service—unless he finally wants to meet some women who look like real people for a change—he really *is* a client of Six in the City. And he claims he's a Rhodes Scholar, even though he spelled it wrong on his application. But the man's dossier checked out."

"Wow. That's all I can say . . . wow." Eleanor gave Kathryn an excited hug, before getting ready to leave. "I told you, your horoscope said this was a lucky day for you. If *this* one works out, you have to promise me tickets to the Oscars!"

"I'll have my people call your people." Kathryn kissed her sister good-bye, then buzzed Tito over the intercom to tell him that her sister was on the way downstairs and needed a cab to take her back uptown to Park Avenue. She had scarcely replaced the receiver in its wall cradle when a clap of thunder rattled the curios in her china cabinet, and the heavens opened.

Kathryn went to the window, pulled back the drapes and watched the rain come down in sheets. She craned her neck and looked up at the murky gray-green sky. "Okay, God," she said, "I know you need to make the grass grow and all that . . . but can you do me a teeny favor, if it's not too much trouble? I have a mega-important date coming up, and I really don't want to stress about having a bad hair day when the time comes. It's bad enough you had to give me such curly hair. So, can you please, pretty please, make the rain stop by Saturday night?"

A bolt of autumn lightning zigzagged toward the

pavement, barely missing a metal lamp post across the street.

"Hey, God?" Kathryn called out. "Was that a 'yes' or a 'no'?"

Chapter
11

Kathryn had been spending the past few days wondering when—or whether—the rain was ever going to end. But at least the deluge gave the weatherpersons on television an excuse to finally stop discussing the drought, which had been threatening throughout the summer to severely hamper New York City's water supply. The reservoirs upstate were now brimming, thanks to unceasing rainstorms of near-biblical proportions.

Weather, *shmeather*. Paramount to Kathryn, however, was whether she would still be able to wear her black strappy sandals on her date with the V.F.A. to Nebuchadnezzar, or if she should consider setting a trend in thigh-high rubber Wellingtons. If it could guarantee her a photo in the Sunday Styles section of *The New York Times*, just a single page flip away from the "Vows" column, it might be worth it.

But form before function, style over substance, had its place—especially where hot dates were concerned. So at 8:30 on Saturday evening, she had just smoothed the sheerest of black nylons over her freshly shaved legs and was fighting with the buckle on the linguini-thin strap of one of the sandals, when her doorbell rang with a frantic insistence.

She limped, one shoe off, one shoe on, over to the door and peeped through the keyhole, frowned—scrunching up her brow, then undid the two Medeco locks and the safety chain.

"Bear! What are you doing here?" Kathryn noticed he had a khaki-colored duffel bag slung over his shoulder.

"I was sort of wondering . . . hoping, in fact . . . that there'd be room at the inn?" He caught a whiff of her perfume and noticed that her hair wasn't quite as unruly as it usually was. Some professional had tamed her wild red curls almost into submission, but her hair was still striking enough to dramatically set off the deep jewel-toned silk kimono she was wearing: a color somewhere between emerald and teal.

"What are you talking about?" she asked suspiciously, as she allowed him to follow her into the living room.

"Chicken Little was right."

"Oh, Jesus, Walker."

"First the ceiling started to fall—there's pieces of plaster in the far corner, where that brown stain was—still is, actually. Then the toilets started to gurgle—but that happened two days ago. Now it looks like water has seeped into the ceiling in the bedroom. It looks like aliens have ominously taken up residence just under the paint. I covered everything I could with hefty bags, and called plumbers and roofers two days ago to get estimates, but everyone told me that they can't do anything until it stops raining."

"Judging from the forecast, we seem to be due for about thirty-six more days and nights," Kathryn commiserated.

"Are you . . . busy?" Walker asked.

"No, I always limp around half-shod. I'm getting ready to go out on a date, Bear. Rick Byron is coming to collect me in his chariot in half an hour. He's taking me to Nebuchadnezzar."

She started hunting for her other sandal. "I've got to thank you for this one." She pursed her lips and blew him a kiss. "Mwhanh!"

"Look, Kitty, I've got nowhere else to go. Not at the last minute like this. My apartment is in a shambles. I need to camp out somewhere until I can get the ceilings bled, or whatever it is they do with them, then replastered and repainted. Can I please bunk with you?" He affected his most pathetic drowned cocker spaniel, please-take-me-in expression.

"Bunk? Bear, I'm not going to be here—I've got a *date*—one that you are sending me on, theoretically. And to be honest, I'm not entirely comfortable leaving a stranger—okay, a near-stranger—in my apartment alone. I'm just not."

"I promise not to cramp your lifestyle," he said, kicking off his shoes. "I'll be like a house sitter. I'll water your plants. I'll change your lightbulbs. Hell, I'll even do your laundry. You won't even know I'm here," he said, sinking onto her sofa and stretching his legs across the couch's length.

Kathryn looked at Walker, who seemed to have settled himself in for the night. "I guess I'd be Cruella D'Evil to refuse you." She gave an exasperated sigh. "This is *temporary*. I mean it," she said, in her best schoolmarmish tone. "I want your solemn oath that you will not butt into my personal or social life. I already have a mother, I never wanted a roommate, and despite your characterization of your past relationships with all your women friends, I do not need a big brother-pal-shoulder to cry on. Have we got that straight?"

Walker grinned and nodded his head. Kathryn could swear he almost panted like a happy doggie.

"Then we have a deal." She went over to shake his hand. The rush of warmth reminded her of the first time they had shaken hands—when she came into Six in the City to make that stupid videotape—and she thought about how she had orchestrated another handshake just to see if she would undergo the same powerful physical sensation a second time. He held her gaze when they clasped hands, and for the tiniest split second, Kathryn regretted that she would be leaving the house for the evening to keep company with a man other than Walker Hart. Then she reminded herself that, hell—he was more Fairy Godmother than Prince Charming in her Cinderella scenario.

He ran his index finger across the top of her hand, after they shook hands. His touch sent a tingle up Kathryn's arm.

Walker noticed how soft her skin was, and felt a shiver course through his body. He withdrew his hand, recognizing that anything further—even a second such light, fingertip caress, would sully their bargain. He needed a place to crash, and he had convinced himself that he did not have designs on the woman. Besides, he thought, he had ruined a few damn good friendships that way. Pushing for sex, when they should have remained platonic friends. The sex was the monkey wrench that, pardoning the expression, screwed everything up.

"I . . . need to finish getting dressed," Kathryn said, looking at the top of her right hand where Walker had so gently caressed her. "Our V.F.A. will be here in twenty minutes." She disappeared into her bedroom.

While Kathryn was putting the last-minute touches on

her appearance, Walker made himself comfortable on
her couch, fiddling with the remote control, unable to
decide whether he wanted to watch the Mets or sit
through *Thunderball* on American Movie Classics. He
settled for channel-zapping between the two.

Kathryn emerged in a form-fitting black minidress
with a plunging neckline. Her straightened hair was
pulled off her face and she was wearing spectacular gold
earrings that looked to Walker as though they might
have been handcrafted for Helen of Troy. She carried a
little black velvet bag on a silken drawstring. Kathryn
opened her front-hall closet and withdrew a black velvet
devoré scarf, which she draped across her shoulders like
an evening shawl.

"Wow," Walker breathed. "All I can say is . . . wow."

"That's funny. That's just what my sister said when
she found out I was going to Nebuchadnezzar tonight
with Rick Byron, 'Hollywood's Reigning Hunk,' according to the September ninth issue of *People*."

"You look . . . spectacular," he said, truly taken with
the whole package before him. The movie star didn't
know how lucky he was. As far as Walker was concerned, it was Kathryn who was really the catch. "Don't
stay out too late," he teased.

"Hey, Bear. We have an agreement. Not only that, it's
thanks to *you* that I'm going on this date."

"Right. Very true." Walker decided his reaction was
simply proprietary. Josh of course, would have immediately labeled it for what it more likely was—jealousy.
"Have fun, then. Don't do anything I wouldn't do."

The wind chimes jangled a sweet response as Kathryn
closed the front door behind her.

*   *   *

Kathryn tipped Carlos a wave and walked out into the night straight into a black Mercedes stretch limo that was waiting for her at the curb. Rick, sitting in a rich Corinthian leather-upholstered back seat the size of Kathryn's kitchen, shook her hand and politely introduced himself. Kathryn laughed, realizing that his introduction was the proper and polite thing to do, but *of course* she knew who he was. He looked a little bit thinner than she remembered from seeing him on the silver screen, then reminded herself that the camera adds ten pounds. Although she noticed that no camera really did justice to his remarkable physiognomy. But what was this mania movie stars all seemed to have for highly lacquered—but untouchable—hair that was supposed to look as effortlessly tousled as though they had just emerged from a roll in the hay?

His attire, though expensive—probably Armani—was nothing to look at: black blazer with a black, maybe charcoal gray cashmere T-shirt, and black trousers, so she concentrated on studying the actor's face, from the fabled jawline to the blue eyes, which looked somehow bluer on film.

He offered Kathryn some Roederer Cristal Brut, which she readily accepted. Drinking prohibitively expensive champagne in a limousine with a bona fide film star didn't happen every Saturday night ... although, if things went well, who knew? She twirled the delicate glass stem in her manicured hand. "These are lovely," she said, admiring the crystal champagne flute. "Lalique?"

"Maybe," Rick shrugged. "My manager rents my limos. It's whatever they stock them with. I just know it's expensive."

The champagne had an immediate emboldening effect

on Kathryn. In fact, just thinking about her current circumstances was giving her a high. "So, Rick, does your manager arrange your dates for you, too?"

Rick gave her a playful shot in the arm and smiled. The killer grin she had seen on the cover of *G.Q.* and *Esquire* and *Vanity Fair*. "Low blow, Kathryn. Low blow."

"You can call me Kitty."

"Kitty." He tried the word out on his tongue a couple of times. "Can I call you 'Miss Kitty'? It sort of reminds me of *Gunsmoke*." He leaned back against the buttery soft black leather seat, and gave her a long look. "I could see you running a saloon—or a bordello somewhere on the frontiers of civilization. Do you . . . ride?" His eyes slowly roamed from her face down the length of her body, lingering on her full breasts, which were more or less on display in the Little Black Dress. If anyone else had looked at her like that, she would have splashed the champagne in his face or dumped it in his crotch. But when Rick Byron—*the* Rick Byron—did it, she became intoxicated, even empowered, and considered the look the ultimate compliment. After all, he was used to dating professional bodies; models and actresses who could afford to spend four hours a day with a personal trainer.

"Yeah," he reiterated huskily. "Definitely a bordello."

The chauffeur opened the door for them when they reached Nebuchadnezzar. The V.F.A. slipped his arm proprietarily over Kathryn's shoulder and escorted her into the trendy nightspot.

"Evening Mr. Rick. *Va bene?*" asked an impeccably tailored and groomed dark-haired man at an ebony lectern near the coat check. He bestowed two air kisses in the direction of the actor's cheeks.

"Very well, thanks, Fabrizio," the celebrity replied.

"I'd like you to meet Miss Kitty Lamb, a very special friend of mine."

Kathryn received a set of air kisses from the European gentleman. "*Bellissima,*" he said softly, approvingly. Then he turned toward the actor. "Chantal will show you to your table." He gestured in the direction of a statuesque black woman who had the same type of delicate, chiseled features as the East African model, Iman. Kathryn instantly felt inferior to the waitstaff.

Chantal seated them at a cozy leather banquette in the far corner of the room, where like pashas they could survey the other patrons. A bottle of Cristal appeared on the table before Chantal's swaying hips were halfway back to the front of the restaurant.

"Fabrizio must make good tips. He's quite a sartorial specimen for a *maître d'*," Kathryn observed, tongue slightly in cheek.

"He's the owner," Rick corrected.

"Oops," Kathryn said, as the actor filled her champagne flute. "He looks so young. And so *good*. I mean, he could be a movie star, too."

"Stranger things have happened," the actor said, clinking his glass with Kathryn's. "Steven Seagal started out as a personal trainer and martial arts instructor. Bottoms up."

"Cheers," Kathryn replied, and clinked glasses again. She was trying not to be nervous, but she felt like any minute she was in danger of putting her foot in her mouth. Maybe she had done so already. "Is Fabrizio Italian?" she asked, finding it easier to discuss the owner than figuring out the right thing to say to her date. She would feel like a goof if she praised his most recent role, or something.

Maybe he hated the picture. Then again, she had never known an actor who could resist a compliment.

"He's Monégasque—Fabrizio. His family is distantly related to the Grimaldis. Prince Albert comes in here all the time."

"Oh," said Kathryn, duly impressed.

"Oh, there's Gwyneth and Jake Paltrow," the actor said, gesturing to a sister and brother pairing of Hollywood royalty. "He's a terrific filmmaker," Rick said, nodding his head confidently. "And his sister's not a bad little actress."

"I'd say she comes by it pretty honestly. Blythe's just about the best there is."

"You know Gwyneth's mother?" The star actually seemed impressed by something Kathryn had contributed to the conversation.

"Brush with greatness," she confessed. "I did three months of summer stock at the Williamstown Theatre Festival with her—but that was a lifetime ago. I taught Gwyneth how to do needlepoint, so that she wouldn't get bored hanging around backstage."

"Should I wave them over?"

"NO! Sorry—I have to admit I already feel way out of my league here. I feel like you're going slumming this evening with Alice in Wonderland on mushrooms. The air in here is so rarefied."

A drop-dead gorgeous movie star wearing tight black jeans walked past their table. "Antonio," Rick called. The man turned around and gave the V.F.A. a handshake. "How's it going, *amigo*?" Antonio queried, looking at Kathryn the whole time. She felt like she'd died and gone to stud heaven.

"Antonio, this is Kitty Lamb," her date said, noticing

that the handsome Latin actor had been checking her out. "Kitty, Antonio Banderas. Hey, give Melanie a kiss for me."

Antonio nodded, and then gave Kathryn her own nod. "Very nice to meet you," he acknowledged, then headed off to the men's room.

Dinner lived up to its reputation for a restaurant acclaimed as much for its glittering clientele as for its food. Kathryn supposed such powerful movers and shakers wouldn't tolerate anything substandard, especially the food, which is why they all flocked to Nebuchadnezzar in the first place. Kathryn's *demi canard de barbarie à l'orange sanguine*—half a duckling with a *glacé* made from blood oranges—was truly terrific. The service, too, was discreet and the staff seemed to know what their regular customers liked to order. Kathryn spied cocktails and bottles of wine and champagne being brought to tables before they were ordered.

Of course, another one of the biggest selling points about the chic watering hole was that it was *dark*. Couples were nuzzling in other dimly lit corners—in fact the restaurant seemed to have been designed to have more than four corners. Kathryn felt a little bit like she was in the back row of a darkened cinema. She was light-headed from all the Cristal, but it was a delicious, tingly sensation. There certainly was a vast difference between the finest champagne and the merely drinkable stuff. She feared she'd been spoiled for life.

Her date was murmuring in her ear, regaling her with insider Hollywood gossip—who was gay, about to get divorced, go bankrupt, dropping first names as though he expected her to know each reference as personally as he did.

"So, you're a drama teacher?" he asked, finally getting around to discussing more mundane topics, like what *she* was doing with her life.

"Yeah, I teach up at Briarcliff, in Riverdale. Lots of private school brats whose parents are politicians and Broadway producers. You probably wouldn't have heard of it. Although it is one of New York's best prep schools." *Wait a minute,* Kathryn scolded herself. *I shouldn't apologize for what I do.*

"Hey! Why are you beating yourself up there, Miss Kitty? My mom was a Social Studies teacher back in Canton. I can't think of a nobler profession. Even though she was the toughest grader in the school and all my friends hated her guts."

"Thanks." Kathryn pretended to go for the cell phone in her little black velvet bag. "Would you mind telling that to my father? The noble profession part, I mean."

"I'll go you one better," Rick countered. "I'd love to come up one afternoon and talk to your kids. Just a real informal thing, not a big all-school assembly or anything. Just shoot the breeze with one of your classes. They're acting students, right?"

"My God . . . that would be super!" Kathryn answered, barely containing her glee. *What a coup.* That would be a pretty feather in her cap, sure as shootin' put her in better with Barton, who seemed to have it in for her lately. Maybe she could even wangle a raise for scoring that maneuver. Maybe Barton would think there was more where that came from. Did they grant tenure at Briarcliff? "Yeah . . . *Rick* . . . that would truly be terrific. I'd—*they'd* love it."

A very pretty young man sidled up to their table while they were in the middle of dessert. He had dyed blond hair and wore earrings in each ear. "Did you know that if Cameron Diaz married James Cameron, she'd be Cameron Cameron?" He laughed at his own joke. "Hi, Rick, do you think you'll be dropping by Lox, Cock, and Bagel later?"

Kathryn had heard the name before, and was trying to place it when her date identified the establishment for her. "It's an after-hours gay club on West Street where they serve a free Sunday brunch to the Saturday night crowd. They have the best house band in the city, though, which is why the straights all love to go dancing there." He ran his hand through Kathryn's kinky coppery corkscrew mane—which hadn't remained tame for more than five minutes in the wet weather. It was a reminder to the inquisitive blond club-hopper that the film star played on Kathryn's team. "It's up to Miss Kitty," he said mildly. "Nice to see you again, Hermès."

Hermès swished away from their banquette and Rick rolled his eyes. "Do you feel like going dancing later?"

"Can we play it by ear?" Kathryn asked him.

Rick brought his lips to Kathryn's ear and nuzzled her. Then, masked by her cascading hair, he stuck his tongue in her ear, and she almost jumped out of her skin. It was an amazingly erotic, and entirely unexpected, gesture. "That's a very good idea," he whispered, his breath suddenly cool, drying the wetness in her ear. "By the way, you smell *wonderful*." He gave her "goddess" earring a tiny push that sent it swinging like a little golden pendulum; then he turned her face toward his, tipping her chin to him, and kissed her full and warm on the mouth. His hands journeyed from her long, thick hair across her shoulders, caressing her back, and down to her gently rounded hips.

Kathryn responded entirely, aware for the briefest of moments of a flash going off somewhere in their vicinity. At the very least, she'd have something to tell her grandchildren—if she ever found a husband. No wonder there were so many offscreen and backstage romances among costars. With just one kiss, she could readily believe herself instantly in love with her date. He certainly made her feel like the only woman who mattered to him in the entire solar system.

The kiss seemed to go on and on. It was easy to see why her date was considered Hollywood's Reigning Hunk. He sure could put his mouth where his money was. Or something like that. *Wow.* When Rick finally pulled away to come up for air, he rearranged Kathryn's dress, the left shoulder of which had slipped perilously low. "We can go dancing at Lox, Cock, and Bagel . . ." he murmured, once more nuzzling the nape of her neck, ". . . or we can go back to my hotel room."

Chapter
12

He's not quite as tall as he looks on film, Kathryn thought when she finally got a real chance to stand beside the star as they walked into the plush lobby of the Plaza Hotel. Her mind had been so overwhelmed when she first arrived at Nebuchadnezzar, she hadn't realized that he was under six feet—although just about everyone was taller than Kathryn.

Heads swiveled when the actor poked his head into the smoky bar off the Oak Room. They were immediately ushered to a table by a fawning *maître d'*, who practically tripped over his flat feet to call a captain to alert a waiter that the V.F.A. and his date wished to order two Irish coffees. The actor had proposed a nightcap before they went upstairs. Kathryn needed her courage bolstered anyway—she could scarcely believe what she was contemplating doing—although, she reasoned, wouldn't just about *any* woman, presented with such an opportunity, embrace it with—at the very least—open arms?

Irish whiskey co-mingled with champagne in Kathryn's bloodstream. She downed her tumbler of ice water, and asked her date if he minded if she drank his as well. When he excused himself to visit the men's room, Kathryn sneaked into her purse for a couple of Excedrin, convincing herself that it was the cigarette and cigar smoke that was causing her headache, rather than the overabundance of champagne followed by the alcoholic nightcap. And when the film star re-joined her, he ordered a bottle of Cristal brought up to his room.

"I have a suite here when I'm in New York," he told her. "It's cheaper than having an apartment in the long run."

"So how much time do you find yourself spending in Gotham City?" Kathryn asked, enunciating each word. She realized she had begun to slur a bit.

"I prefer New York to L.A.," he replied. "So I try to get involved with projects here as often as I can. My next picture is going into preproduction now, and it's going to be shot here—I convinced Miramax not to go to Toronto—so I should be here for at least the next three months or so."

"Sounds great," Kathryn enthused. "What is it?"

"Ahh . . . well . . ." Rick fingered an amulet that hung around his neck. "It's bad luck to talk about a project before it starts filming," he said. "I've had really bad karma with that kind of stuff in the past." He noticed her interest in his necklace. "This is from my grandmother," he said. "To keep away the evil eye. She's Greek—believes in that sort of thing—and who's to say it's b.s.?"

He looked over at Kathryn and saw that she looked a little disappointed at his reluctance to talk about the film. He hadn't meant her to think he was treating her as though she were some nosy journalist from *Entertainment Tonight*. "Oh, it's not you, Miss Kitty," the actor said, scruffing the back of her neck. "It's the karma thing." He waved to the captain, who brought over a heavy brown leather portfolio. Rick scribbled his name in huge letters, and scrawled in a room number. *No ego problems there*, Kathryn thought, as she observed the size of his signature. The captain would probably take the autograph home for his wife—or sell it on e-Bay.

She felt herself getting increasingly anxious during the ride up in the private elevator to an exclusive floor. The movie star opened the door with a passkey that resembled a credit card. Kathryn took in the sight before her. Versailles meets sleep-away camp. The elegance of the baroque décor, in shades of gold, crimson, and cream, was undercut by overgarments and underclothes tossed everywhere. Clearly, the man was accustomed to having either a mother or a maid or a manager pick up after him. Left to his own devices, he seemed to let everything fall where it may. On the floor lay an open cardboard pizza box, a congealed wedge or two with the odd crust sitting inside, decorated with a carelessly tossed pair of navy cotton men's briefs. Kathryn had to admit to herself that the atmosphere was a little bit of a turn-off, and she wondered what she had expected instead. Perhaps his lack of domestic discipline reflected the kind of spontaneous, kinetic personality that made his performances so offbeat and appealing. She refused to believe that he might just be a slob.

The champagne had arrived in the suite before they did, and was chilling in a huge freestanding silver urn. A silver tray with two crystal flutes and two of the Plaza's unmistakable pale pink linen napkins sat on the desk.

Rick popped the cork with the flair of an expert. "That's the way to do it," he informed Kathryn, referring to his technique in opening the sparkling wine. "Like a satisfied woman," he added, referring to the soft, sighing sound made when the cork parted company with the bottle. "I learned that from the *sommelier* at Duke's in London." He filled their glasses and brought Kathryn hers, as she perched on the edge of the bed since most of the other sitting areas in the room were occupied by laundry—either dirty or clean.

"And speaking of satisfied women . . ." The actor relieved her of the champagne glass after she had taken only a couple of sips, placing both flutes back on the silver tray. He slipped his hand along her back, sliding the little black dress down past her shoulders and over her breasts, pushing her back onto the bed. "I've been waiting all night to see these," he murmured, taking one of her nipples into his mouth, sucking with a practiced intensity. Then he deftly switched off the chinoiserie lamp on the mahogany night table.

Lulled into a highly relaxed state by all the champagne, Kathryn twined her legs around Rick, responding to his insistent passion. *It's a fantasy come true.* He slid his hand up her leg, but in a flash of intrusive reality, she pushed it away and sat up.

"What?" he asked, confused.

"I can't afford to have these ripped to shreds," Kathryn whispered, and rolled her sheer pantyhose down her legs. Then she removed her sandals, followed by the nylons, and placed them on the floor by the edge of the bed, where she'd be sure not to miss them later.

"Come here, Miss Kitty," Rick beckoned, supine, his arms outstretched toward her. She climbed back onto the mattress and he pulled her on top of him, wriggling her out of the tight little cocktail dress. In a matter of a minute, she was completely undressed, naked and vulnerable on the rented bed of a famous movie star.

"There's something unequal about this equation," she whispered, as she tugged on the lapels of his sportcoat. She watched as he complied with her unspoken directive to get starkers, tossing his jacket, T-shirt, pants, and underwear around the room. He seemed proud of his body, which was lean and hard; muscular, but not over-developed. He slid on top of her, covering her mouth with his own.

Kathryn felt more like Alice in Wonderland than ever. She was aware of his kiss—although terrific—tasting of champagne and coffee, and allowed herself to succumb entirely to the pilgrimage his lips were taking across her body, down her breasts and stomach, between her thighs, tickling and teasing. If he continued to do that, she would dissolve into a giant erotic puddle on the spot. *I am lying here with* . . . She stopped in midreverie as he moved to mount her.

"Wait!" She whispered a command, which halted him as he hovered above her.

"What?"

Her voice was husky. "Do you have a condom?"

He relaxed his body on top of hers, his erection suddenly, surprisingly, gone limp.

"Why?"

"I shouldn't think you'd have to ask," Kathryn said softly. "I can't think of a delicate way to put this—but we really don't know much about each other. I don't know where you've been, so to speak. Except what I've read in *People*. Besides, I didn't exactly anticipate this, so I didn't throw my diaphragm in my purse when I left the house."

"Oh, you won't have to worry about getting pregnant.

I'll pull out in time." He tried to read the inscrutable expression on her face. "Don't worry, you can trust me—I've gotten very good at that."

"I appreciate the sentiment, Rick," Kathryn continued to say in a whisper. "But . . . this is a very awkward thing for me to discuss right now. I just . . . don't feel entirely comfortable about going where we're going without a condom." *There, I said it,* she thought, wondering whether she was blushing.

"I never wear them."

Kathryn lay on her back, silent, contemplating the choices before her. Either way, it looked like a lose-lose situation from her vantage point. She could risk losing perhaps her only opportunity to have wild sex with this internationally renowned movie star who seemed to really know his way around a woman's body, or she could risk losing it all in a single unprotected act. She cursed herself for feeling like a prude. She thanked her lucky stars for all the times she figured luck and the odds were on her side, and had ended up fine and healthy.

But . . . even through the champagne haze . . . as amazing as Rick's touch was, the moment felt wrong. And—hey—what was so wrong about wearing a condom? And what was so wrong about her insistence that he comply? To compound matters, her head had just started to ache with a slightly dull thud.

With no small degree of effort, she raised herself from the mattress, and stroked his tanned back. "I'm sorry," she confessed, almost choking back a tear. "I really want to be with you, but if you don't want to wear a condom, then we're at sort of an impasse here."

The actor seemed hurt, almost bewildered, like a third grader who's been told he doesn't know how to "play nice" when all along, that's what he thinks he's been doing. So he did what children do, which is lash out. "You really *are* a schoolteacher," he said sullenly.

Kathryn sat on the edge of the bed and ruffled his hair. "Believe me, Rick," she said quietly, "no one is unhappier about this than I am." She reached for her stockings and slid them back over her legs, then fought to buckle her stiletto sandals in the dark. After she finished getting dressed, she went over to the actor and gave him a hug. He remained on the bed, naked, in exactly the position she'd left him.

"I'd give you cab fare to get home, but I don't carry cash," Rick said, more embarrassed than arrogant. "My manager arranges everything, and usually all I need to do is sign for something. You'll need more than five dollars to get back to your place, and I don't have it." He looked worried, desperately afraid that he would lose her approval. "Please don't tell anybody about this. I don't want them to think badly of me."

"Do you mean not tell anyone that you lost the chance to get laid tonight because you wouldn't wear a condom, or that you didn't even have the carfare to send me home in a taxi?" She retrieved her purse from the desk and stood by the bed.

"Both," he admitted softly. He sat up and drew her to him by her hands. Her arms slipped around his shoulders and he buried his face between her breasts. "You're very warm," he murmured. Then, perhaps suddenly overcome by all the liquor he'd consumed over the course of the evening, he let go of her, stretched his body along the length of the mattress and rolled over. "Thank you, Miss Kitty," he burbled almost inaudibly. "It's been . . . enlightening."

Kathryn leaned over and kissed him on the forehead. His skin was slightly damp. "Goodnight, Rick. And thank you. Thank you very much."

"I'll call you," he mumbled, just before he passed out completely.

Arrgh! Kathryn realized she should have checked her appearance before she left Rick's suite. She didn't exactly look disheveled, but her makeup had been kissed off, and she should have brushed her hair. She caught her reflection in the mirror that hung between the elevators and tried to do a quick salvage job. At least her clothes were perfectly intact, but all that champagne, plus the Irish coffee, plus, having spent the past several minutes on her back while the room started spinning, did not bode well for exiting the posh Plaza with dignity. Kathryn managed, somehow, to hold her head high despite the smug look from the private elevator operator who no doubt assumed that she had just consummated a transaction with one of Hollywood's most eligible hunks. Not only that, the elevator jockey had probably concluded that since she hadn't stayed the night, she'd been a rental. *If he only knew the truth,* she snickered to herself. *One day, I'll congratulate myself for having been such an adult about this. But not tonight.*

Kathryn inhaled the night air, which had grown cooler since she'd entered the hotel. She loved the special, crisp, late-summer into early-autumn quality that New York seemed to take on toward the end of September. There was something surprisingly clean about it. It always reminded her of apple picking.

She hailed a taxi, which, owing to the lateness of the hour, whisked her to her door in a matter of minutes.

Sometimes you could get lucky with the lights along Fifth Avenue. Kathryn kept both windows open in the back of the cab, and by the time she got to her apartment building, felt infinitely better.

"*Muñeca*, is everything okay?" Carlos asked, much concerned, as she strode through the lobby, getting her second wind.

"Why wouldn't it be?" she responded, adding "Goodnight, Carlos," as she breezed into a waiting elevator and sped up to her apartment.

She fished for her keys in the black velvet reticule and opened her door. Good God—she had forgotten that Walker was in her apartment! His head jerked toward the door as she opened it. There he was, sitting on her wine-colored sofa, plying himself with black coffee, wearing the look of a furious parent whose adolescent daughter has overstayed her curfew. The television was blaring an old black-and-white *Hogan's Heroes* rerun.

"Turn that damn thing off!" Kathryn snapped.

Walker gave her a "how dare you cross me, young lady" kind of look, and at that moment, Eleanor emerged from the kitchen with a mug of steaming herbal tea in one hand and a bowl of microwaved popcorn in the other.

"What the hell are *you* doing here?"

"She was worried about you," Walker replied calmly.

"She's *pregnant*—or can't you tell? And she's got a toddler at home! You got her out of bed in the middle of the night because *you* were alarmed. How dare you! We made a deal, you and I, just a few hours ago—or can't you remember back that far? Instead of quietly minding your own business—as I so distinctly heard you promise—you butted in to my life at the first opportunity, and drew my pregnant baby sister into your paranoid fantasies in the bargain."

"Actually, I couldn't sleep, and I enjoyed the chance to meet your new roommate," Eleanor said, smiling sweetly. "He's very nice—except that he's got lousy taste in reruns."

"Bear! Go to your room!" Kathryn said throwing wide her arm and pointing toward the bedroom. Eleanor arched a questioning eyebrow. "Well, *we* could go in there and make him stay out here, but I need some orange juice and a snack," Kathryn told her sister. "You—out!" Kathryn gestured dramatically toward the bedroom. Walker obliged, trying to look as pitiable as possible. "And close the door."

Kathryn then motioned to her sister to join her in the kitchen. The two women leaned against the counters, while Kathryn decided what to eat at that late hour. "I can't believe he phoned you," Kathryn said, shaking her head and looking at the list of emergency phone numbers stuck to the refrigerator with a Royal Shakespeare Company magnet shaped like the Bard's head.

"So what happened?" Eleanor asked. "He was sure you'd be home at around one or two A.M. at the latest, and when you weren't back by three, he'd convinced himself that you were going to stay with Rick all night, and he went through about a half-dozen stages of emotions, like the Kübler-Ross model—anger, denial, depression, acceptance—whatever they are. Actually, he never made it to acceptance. A pathetic resignation is all he achieved."

"He's got a helluva lot of nerve, dragging you out in the middle of the night. He's a grown-up, for Christ's sake. And let's not forget his role in all this: he's the *matchmaker*. And he wouldn't even have known how late I was out if he hadn't insisted on crashing here because his ceilings are leaking and collapsing. I suppose in his twisted guy-logic, he's found a way to blame me for that as well! How does everything somehow end up being my fault?"

"Actually," Eleanor admitted, "I *am* really tired—finally. But I figured I would stay until you got home, so I could hear firsthand how the date went."

"Rick's not a bad guy. Although I'm not entirely sure I'd exactly consider him a grown-up. Then again, I'm not entirely sure I *want* a man who's a grown-up. Ahhhhgh. I don't know what I want. Especially after too much champagne." Kathryn lowered her voice to make sure that Walker wasn't listening. It was awfully quiet in the bedroom. "Truthfully," she whispered to her sister, "things were going very well . . . and I do mean *very*."

"So?"

"The man is well built, I'll give him credit for that."

"So?"

"And there I was thinking, my God, look who's on top of me right now, ready, willing, and able to do the deed. It was an absolute blue dream come true."

"Are you saying that wasn't a stunt-butt in *Avenging Angel*?"

"I can't say for sure, since the room was dark, but he certainly didn't *need* a body double."

"So?" Eleanor said excitedly, extracting a fluffy popcorn kernel from the bowl and popping it into her mouth.

"I stopped him."

Eleanor held the kernel on her tongue, as though her action was suspended in midair. "Why?"

"He wouldn't wear a condom."

Eleanor swallowed the popcorn and gave a little cough. "Well . . . well . . . I don't know what to . . . I . . . you did the right thing, I suppose."

"I've been agonizing over it," Kathryn confessed. "I mean there I was—we were right at the point of doing it, and I had this flash—I don't know where 'it's' been, so to speak. And who is he to take my health—my life, maybe, so cavalierly? And who am *I* to take such risks? And I thought about all the times I never cared, and I wondered if one day, my number would be up. And I just had a funny feeling about it all of a sudden. So I pulled the plug."

"Wow," Eleanor breathed. "All I can say is wow."

"He loved the way I look," Kathryn said wistfully. "And the way I smell. Oh, well," she sighed. She gave her younger sister a hug. "For God's sake, go home and get some sleep. I certainly need to. The champagne was very expensive, but I expect quite a hangover as soon as the booze wears off. Right now, I think I'm still drunk."

Kathryn escorted her sister to the door, and kissed her goodnight. Then she tiptoed to the bedroom and quietly opened the door. The room was dark and still. But not quiet. Face down on her queen-sized mattress, was all six-plus feet of Walker Hart—sound asleep and snoring.

Chapter
13

Kathryn debated whether or not to wake the slumbering Walker. She smiled to herself. His inert bulky form certainly did resemble a hibernating bear. None of the options available were optimal. She could try to shove him over—he was sleeping on the diagonal—and climb into bed beside him, which was inadvisable at best. Still, she was exhausted and was really looking forward to crashing on her own mattress. The velvet sofa was plushy and comfortable, but the morning light seeped in early, and that meant that she'd be able to get only an hour of sleep before the living room would become flooded with light, whether or not it was still raining.

Opting for prudence over comfort, she retrieved an old and much beloved quilt—one that she had helped her grandmother make when she was eight or nine years old—and tossed her needlepointed pillows onto the armchair so she wouldn't ruin her own artwork by scrunching her cheek against them. After a few moments, she fell asleep—or rather, passed out. But forty-five minutes later, when rosy-fingered dawn invaded her slumber, she was awakened by a half dozen gremlins who seemed to be chopping away at her brain with tiny metal pickaxes. Kathryn went into the kitchen, washed down a fistful of

aspirin with a glass of orange juice, ran a checkered dish-
towel under the cold water, then returned to the couch
and applied the compress to her pounding temples. A
half hour later, the gremlins appeared to have taken a
coffee break, but the morning light, now brighter, seemed
blinding.

She opened the door to the bedroom. Walker was no
longer in full possession of the mattress, having adjusted
his position at some point during the past couple of
hours. Kathryn really needed the sleep, so as gingerly as
possible, and still wearing her underwear, she edged herself onto the bed and lay down facing the wall, as far as
possible from the snoozing mass of maleness beside her.

Some time later, Kathryn awoke on her side pinned to
the bed by a large, heavy arm slung over her, attached to
a large warm hand that was cupping her breast. She
closed her eyes, murmured "yum," and inched her back
toward Walker's torso. When reality checked in, she
opened her eyes, surveyed the foreign hand and arm,
tried to extricate herself from its weight, gave up, and
closed her eyes again. Her new "roommate" was still
asleep, shirtless, in spooning position, breathing somewhat noisily beside her. Feeling wicked, and enjoying his
masculine scent, she snuggled against him and felt his
erection, prominent against the small hollow of her
back. Kathryn wondered if he was just pretending to
sleep, trying to see how much he could get away with, or
if he was dreaming about someone—an old girlfriend or
a centerfold, probably. She also considered that he might
be completely cognizant of his surroundings, using the
opportunity to indulge his attraction for her.

Kathryn was perfectly aware of the powerful chem-
istry between them. She'd accused him several times of

Flirting with Intent, and he hadn't corrected her, acknowledging his guilt in that regard.

Feeling safe, snuggled in the protection of Walker's warmth, Kathryn allowed herself to fall into a deep sleep. The next thing she knew, she was being actively cuddled by the man beside her—and it didn't feel like an accident.

Walker kissed the back of her neck, nuzzling up into her hairline, which sent delicious little tingles of electricity down her spine. He nudged her shoulder, and she turned to face him, as he drew her close. Kathryn's hands traced the blond-brown hair on his chest, which grew in perfect, soft symmetry. Walker reached up to stroke her face, tracing her eyebrows, then running his thumb along the full swell of her lips. He leaned in to kiss her, and Kathryn was anxious that her breath might still smell like stale booze. Or worse—morning breath. Not very romantic. Whatever the case, Walker didn't seem to mind. *Oh, God, wait a minute.* They were kissing. Bear's kiss was filled with need, longing, insistence, and Kathryn responded fully. He had a way of erasing her self-consciousness when he embraced her.

He pulled away and studied her face as if he was going to paint it. "Just what I imagined," he murmured, kissing her nose. "You do look beautiful in the morning."

"That's because I'm still wearing my makeup from last night," Kathryn joked. "MAC stays on forever." They laughed, and Walker drew her tighter to him.

"I could get used to this, kiddo," he said, stroking her hair.

Kathryn reached up to touch his cheek. Even needing a shave, he was remarkably sexy. "Don't," she replied. "Please . . . don't. I'll be very honest . . . I can't do this.

I . . . don't have the same kind of . . . resilience you guys have."

• "Why are you lumping me in with your opinion of every guy on the planet?" he asked her softly. "You think we *all* operate on that martian John Gray's rubber bands?"

"If you break my heart, I'll never get over it . . . and probably never forgive you. I still haven't forgiven you for dragging my sister out of the house in the middle of the night and breaking your promise not to butt into my life."

Walker defended himself. "I was worried about you. Can't a man worry? It's a crazy world out there."

"Bear, I was out with one of your clients. I assume you have a way of screening people. I'll bet you checked the three character references I wrote on *my* Six in the City application."

He issued a nonverbal, noncommittal grunt.

"It's none of your business anyway. Other than that finding me a husband is your business—literally. Trying to keep me away from one is counterproductive for you, personally and financially."

Walker ran his hand contemplatively along his jaw.

"Yes, you need a shave," she noted. "And you know something? I can sense this: you seem just a teeny-weensy bit pleased that my first encounters with the three men you've fixed me up with have not led to a second date with any of them."

"Maybe I'm just an idiot." He rolled onto his back and stared up at the ceiling.

"I don't know you well enough to agree."

"I want to make love with you, Kathryn," Walker said, still staring into the space above his head.

A silvery shiver ran through her spine. Kathryn rolled over and propped herself on her elbows. "You know what?"

"What?"

"I want to make love with you, too. Desperately. I admit it. And I've been fantasizing about it since the interview in your office. But, unlucky you, perhaps for the first time in my life . . ." She remembered the incident at the Plaza from just a few hours ago. "Perhaps for the *second* time in my life," she continued softly, "I am going to deny myself what might possibly be an earth-shattering sexual experience."

Walker noticed her grammatical correction. "Were you referring to last night as the first time?"

"None of your business," Kathryn replied. It was her turn to stare at the white ceiling above them.

"Do you want to tell me what happened?"

"Absolutely not."

"He didn't hurt you, did he?"

Kathryn looked at Walker like he was insane. "Of course not." She grew quiet again. "He wouldn't wear a condom. Okay? Are you happy now? You know all the gory details." Disgusted, she rolled away from him onto her side. "Oh, that's right," she added, "I'm *supposed* to let you know how it went. For your 'marketing strategy.'"

Walker stopped himself from giving her what he would have intended to be a sympathetic caress on the back. He was jealous, whether or not he had a right to be. And he *was* pleased that things hadn't been consummated between Kathryn and Rick. Although Walker had never really loved the work, for the first time since his mother had left him to manage her matchmaking business—however temporarily—he truly hated his job.

"If I really wanted you," he began, addressing her back. "Hypothetically . . . I would do just about whatever it takes to make love to you."

Kathryn remained facing the wall. "In your case, it would take a lot more than agreeing to wear a condom."

"What the hell is that supposed to mean, Kitty?"

"One assumes that Rick—like all of the bachelors in Six in the City's stable—has enrolled with a dating service because he is ready, willing, and able to make a commitment to a woman." She rolled over to look Walker in the eye. "A commitment to a committed relationship, which could eventually lead to connubial bliss. You gleefully admit that you don't fit the profile." She gave him a long look and spontaneously, lightly ran her fingers over his chest. *What kind of mixed messages am I sending here,* she wondered. *Damn!*

Walker stopped her progress, placing a warm hand over hers, clasping it over his heart, holding it there.

"I feel like we're on a carousel here," she said quietly. "Over and over, up and down we go with each other, covering the same territory and never getting anywhere. But do we want to get anywhere?"

"I want to make love with you," he said evenly.

"I'll cherish the thought," she replied, wanting more than anything to jump on top of him right then and there and show him just how much she desired him. "Believe me. But—and take this as a compliment—it will probably make me fall in love with you."

He glanced over at her. She tried to read his expression. "I told you; I can't afford the emotional price, Bear."

"Brunch?" he asked, as though they hadn't been discussing anything weightier than who was a weaker actress: Pamela Anderson or Carmen Electra. "I love Sunday brunch with *The New York Times*. Have you got any bacon?"

She was grateful for the change of subject. "I always have bacon," Kathryn replied, throwing on a New Orleans Saints jersey that fit her like a minidress. She continued the conversation while she went to retrieve the morning paper from the hallway outside her apartment. "Except for when the movie *Babe* came out. Then I felt really guilty about eating pork for about three months." Kathryn returned to the bedroom where the half-clad Walker was still stretched out on her bed and deposited the sports section on his flat stomach. "Here. I figured you might want this."

Maybe I could get used to this, Walker mused. "Let's eat first," he said, swinging his legs over the edge of the bed. He was wearing longish Calvin Klein briefs that defined the contours of his upper thighs. Walker followed her into the kitchen and grabbed the package of bacon from the inside door of the refrigerator. "Got a frying pan?"

Kathryn gestured to a heavy black cast iron skillet on top of the range. "I thought you told me you couldn't cook," she said.

"I don't. I just like to fry bacon," he grinned. "There's something about the smell. Very domestic." Walker laid six strips of bacon across the bottom of the skillet. "The house I grew up in was very rarely a home."

"Sorry." Kathryn flipped the switch on her coffee maker, then removed two eggs, a stick of salted butter, and a quart of milk from the refrigerator. "How do you feel about pancakes? I've got an old family recipe that I haven't been able to make in ages, because . . . well, you can't really cook pancakes for yourself."

Walker was relieved by this remark, which he interpreted to mean that Kathryn usually woke up alone.

Kathryn pointed a couple feet above her head. "Ooh! You're tall—could you grab that little pitcher for me? Do you take cream in your coffee?"

He nodded in the affirmative, then reached up into her kitchen cabinet for the delicate creamer, which was sandwiched among several vases of varying shapes and sizes.

"Hey! Watch it—please!" Kathryn called out, as his groping toppled a cobalt decanter, nearly sending it flying off the high shelf. "Jeez—you can be a menace in the kitchen, didja know that? A real bull in a china shop!"

Walker looked pained.

"Oh, God, I'm sorry . . . it's . . . I should have said 'Bear in a china shop.' No, I shouldn't have said anything. I'm sorry. Just . . . forget it."

He retrieved a red stepstool from behind the refrigerator and ascended so he could safely reach the creamer. Kathryn found herself watching his muscled rear, the contours of which were displayed to exceptional advantage in his form-fitting underwear. She felt even guiltier for having berated him.

He handed her the little pitcher. "I'll . . . check on the bacon," he said evenly.

Kathryn felt worse. He wasn't trying to bust up her stuff on purpose. But he could be so clumsy, sometimes. This time, was his lack of coordination just a casualty of male ego? Not realizing the shelf was higher than he'd thought?

They regarded each other tensely for a moment.

Kathryn changed the subject. "Yup. That's what I grew up with. Pancakes on Sunday mornings. And football all afternoon. In the fall, anyway," Kathryn said.

"Good," he replied. "Then you'll feel right at home." He went for the remote control and immediately turned on the television, locating the one P.M. NFL game.

"I *am* home," Kathryn reminded him. "*You're* the visiting team, remember? Besides, in my house, if there's a baseball playoff game on TV, no NFL on weekends until after the World Series." She whipped up the pancake batter in the blender, turned off the machine and tossed in a shot of brandy. Walker raised his eyebrows, impressed.

Kathryn looked across the kitchen, watching him tend to the frying bacon strips with extra tender loving care. For an instant, she wanted to sneak up behind him and put her arms around his waist. There it was again—that feeling of security, in the best possible sense—that she derived from his presence, even if he *was* a bit of a klutz.

Walker drained the bacon and lay the crisp strips on a double thickness of paper toweling to soak up any excess grease. Then he handily lifted the heavy iron skillet and drained the fat into an empty Redpack tomato puree can—without spilling a drop—while Kathryn heated the bottle of pure Vermont maple syrup in the microwave. She laughed. "*This* sort of technology, we didn't have when we were growing up. I remember when my father bought my mother a dishwasher as an anniversary gift, and it was a big deal."

"If your mother is anything like you, Kathryn, it

was probably a big deal because it was an unromantic present."

"Did you learn your sleuthing skills from Detective Eddie Benson, Midtown South Vice Squad? You're good."

He scruffed the back of her neck, and despite brief thoughts to the contrary, lifted her thick mane of hair and kissed her soft, bare skin. "Look at this place," he said, pointing his chin in the direction of her living room. "Anyone can see that you live for romance. Scarves over the lamps, your own needlework on display, home-baked cookies, Pre-Raphaelite prints on your wall . . . and just about the only time I've seen you when you weren't wearing velvet, you were wearing silk. Or lace. You're barely of this century."

Kathryn served the stacks of paper-thin pancakes and decanted the warm maple syrup into a small pewter cruet. "I have jams and jellies, if you prefer," she offered, gesturing to the refrigerator. "Apricot, and something with Chambord in it. Either damson plum or wild black cherry . . . I can't remember which."

"No, this is fine . . . this is *great*," Walker responded, leaning over his plate to inhale the sweet, warm aroma of the pancakes. He brought their plates over to the coffee table and set them down, using the "Automobiles" and "Help Wanted" sections of the Sunday *Times* as placemats.

"Oops, I almost forgot. Ready for coffee?" Kathryn asked.

"You betcha," Walker said, tasting the pancakes. "These are *delicious*." He closed his eyes, to taste them better. "What about a splash of brandy in the coffee, too? Since this is a special occasion."

"With the cream? Oh, what the hell, it'll taste like Bailey's. What are we celebrating?" Kathryn questioned, as she poured some brandy into each of two handmade ceramic mugs.

"Our first Sunday brunch together. I never had a neighbor I could spend Sunday brunch with before." He took the coffee mugs from Kathryn and set them down by the plates, then nestled himself in a corner of the sofa.

Kathryn sat on the opposite end of the couch and leaned over to the coffee table to retrieve her plate, which she set in her lap. "It's either this or sit on the floor and pretend it's a Japanese restaurant," she said. "Otherwise, the pancakes won't survive the journey from the plate to my mouth without half the forkful landing on my shirt."

Walker lifted her legs, swinging them across the sofa and onto his lap. He gave her toes a playful squeeze. She reached over for the remote control and gleefully played with the mechanism until she located a National League game. "That's my girl," Walker said appreciatively.

She tasted the brunch, crunching on a strip of bacon. "Good job, 'roomie,'" she said between bites, appraising the doneness of the meat. "This is damn near perfect."

His warm hand rubbed one of her calf muscles affectionately as he glanced over at her, then glued his eyes to the baseball game. "Yup. It damn near is."

Kathryn couldn't remember the last time she had so much fun doing next to nothing on a Sunday afternoon. By the time the Mets had lost to Atlanta, 10–7, her hangover was all but gone, the weather outside looked spectacular, and she was feeling just a tinge of cabin fever. "C'mon, let's go out somewhere," she urged Walker, jumping to her feet.

"I'm so comfy," he half protested.

"We need some sunshine. Let's go, big guy. Who says the best things in life can't be free?"

"Most people." Walker rose from the couch reluctantly. "Where exactly did you have in mind?"

"Central Park. We can toss a frisbee or something in the Sheep Meadow. On second thought, we can't. I suck at that. I'll probably hit someone's labrador retriever in the head and suffer bad karma for the rest of my life."

"I'll help you with your aim. Sit tight, I'll be right back."

Walker left Kathryn's apartment, and reappeared a few minutes later with two very well-worn catcher's mitts and a softball. "Okay, put some shoes on and let's go. And not those spike heels you usually wear."

"I thought athletes were supposed to wear cleats on the field," Kathryn teased. "So instead of several, I have just *one* on each foot, that's all." She bounced into the bedroom feeling extraordinarily peppy and returned wearing a tank top, tight jeans, a pair of white leather Keds, and carrying a large canvas tote into which she deposited the sports gear and her purse. She pulled a pair of sunglasses from the bag and slipped them on her head to hold her hair away from her face. "Ready when you are, sports fan," she said to Walker and led him out of the apartment.

"You're not as bad at this as I thought you'd be," Walker said, tossing Kathryn the softball.

She caught it deftly in her mitt. "Thanks a whole helluva lot. I appreciate your confidence in me," she called to him. She sent the ball sailing slightly past his reach. "Of course, my problem is consistency. I knew I shouldn't have blown off spring training."

"Okay. Get ready for a fast ball high inside the strike zone," Walker yelled. The next pitch he hurled was probably intended to have been shoulder level, but given their vast height difference, it was zooming way over Kathryn's head. She jogged backwards into the sunlight, waving away anyone trying to cut across her path. The softball thudded into her glove.

"Great catch!!" he yelled.

"Thanks! I know I'm a great catch!" she called back, deliberately twisting the meaning of his words. "It's just that you haven't figured it out yet," she muttered to herself. She looked at her watch, then shouted "Bear? We've been doing this for almost half an hour. It's really fun, but I'm beginning to get tired. The last time I had such a good cardiovascular workout was when I ran for a crosstown bus. Can we get a lemonade or something?"

He approached her, took the ball and mitt from her hands and dumped them in the canvas bag. "Wimp." He put his arm around her shoulder affectionately. "Let's go get you watered and fed."

"What am I now, a horse?"

They took a shady west-east path that meandered along the perimeter of the softball fields where a few amateur teams sponsored by local merchants were in the midst of heated competition. "Here's a good place to stop," Kathryn said, indicating the little café to their left. "Urban rustic. Isn't it cute?" She collapsed into a metal patio chair.

"One lemonade coming up," Walker said.

"Pink."

"One *pink* lemonade coming right up. Anything else besides 'girl lemonade'?"

Kathryn shook her head.

Walker went to purchase their drinks and returned with Kathryn's pink lemonade and a chilled Heineken for himself. He raised his bottle to her plastic cup. "Cheers."

"Bottoms up." Kathryn felt so dehydrated, the lemonade was half gone after one extensive gulp. "Much better," she sighed, leaning back in her chair. She heard the strains of a calliope, muted, in the distance. "Raindrops keep falling on my head," she sang softly, moving her body in time to the music.

Walker looked confused. "What are you singing?"

"What does it sound like? Don't tell me you don't know a Burt Bacharach song when you hear one. Or that you've never seen *Butch Cassidy and the Sundance Kid*. Can't you hear the music? It's from the carousel." She took another long sip of lemonade, put the cup back on the table in front of them and sat up excitedly. "Can we go on it? It's only a few yards away."

Walker pulled a face. "You want me to go on the carousel with you?"

"Which word didn't you understand?"

"Guys don't 'do' carousels. That's a chick thing. There are two things guys don't do. We don't eat ice cream cones and we don't ride on carousels."

Kathryn started to laugh. "You're so full of it. Gee, I had no idea that certain activities were gender-specific. And I have too seen a man eating an ice cream cone."

"Where?" Walker challenged. "Provincetown?"

"Right in our own neighborhood. Right outside the Magnolia Bakery on Bleecker Street as a matter of fact."

"That's precisely my point."

"Phooey on you." Kathryn pretended to pout. "Pleeeease. I just spent the last half hour doing a '*guy* thing'—playing catch with you."

"Okay, okay. You twisted my arm," Walker said, rising to his feet.

"Oh, goody." Kathryn took his hand. "I'm not just trying to get you to humor me; this is really important. I want to share with you my all-time favorite place in the city."

They arrived at the carousel, purchased their tickets, and waited behind the rope for the ride already in progress to stop. As soon as they were admitted, Walker went for the horse directly in front of him, tossed the canvas tote around its neck, and self-consciously mounted.

"Don't you want to look around first before you decide on a horse?" Kathryn asked him. "Each one has its own distinct personality, you know."

"I'm on a children's ride with a woman who anthropomorphizes wooden ponies," Walker said, shaking his head. He looked over at Kathryn who was swinging her leg over the spirited black bronco directly in front of his reddish stallion. "Besides, how do you know I didn't give my choice any forethought? I like this big fella; he reminds me of some of the most famous racehorses that ever existed. He's the same color as Point Given, Man O' War, and 'Big Red' Secretariat. In fact, I think I'll call him 'Big Red.' After all, I'm a Cornellian. That's our team nickname." He delivered a resounding smack to his steed's oaken flanks. "Go, Big Red! Giddyap!"

Kathryn turned back to look at him. "Well, well, somebody's getting into it," she teased. "And take that thing off his neck," she said, pointing at the canvas tote. "It looks like a feedbag. What kind of a racehorse wears a feedbag during competition?"

"A hungry one." Walker reached over and unhooked the bag. He deposited it on the wooden platform that formed the carousel's turntable. "I'm glad you're in front of me because I can't wait to watch your cute little butt when you post."

Kathryn immediately dismounted. "You don't *post* on a carousel horse, silly. It's a very smooth ride. Besides, you don't deserve the satisfaction of seeing my buns in the air, anyway." She climbed astride the slightly smaller horse to Walker's left, and grinned at him. "But just in case, I prefer to ride next to you than in front of you." She looked down at her horse. "I don't think I've ever ridden a mare on this carousel. I always go for the big horses on the outside. This one must be a filly; it's a lot smaller than yours."

"You can name it 'Little Red,' then. It suits you."

"You're a piece of work, Walker Hart, you know that?"

The operator collected their tickets, then went to sit in the center of the circle where he threw the switch that set the carousel in motion. The calliope was playing another old 1960's standard, "Georgy Girl," the title song from the film that made Lynn Redgrave a household name in America.

"They're playing your song," Walker remarked.

"That?"

"Yeah, Georgy Girl was a feisty redhead. Hey, there,

Georgy Girl . . . walking down the street so fancy free . . ."
he sang.

"I am nothing like Georgy Girl," Kathryn protested.
"She may have been feisty, but she was also an ugly
duckling! Is that what you think of me? Besides, wasn't
she 'always window shopping but never stopping to
buy'? I have the *opposite* problem, I'm afraid. Just look
at my Visa bill."

Walker was checking out the brightly painted circus
animals and acrobats carved on the central core of the
carousel. Kathryn pointed out a monkey wearing a mint-
green jacket and bellboy's cap. "He used to have a cigarette stuck in his mouth," she told her companion. "Back
in the days before political correctness and the wide-
spread knowledge about the dangers of lung cancer."

"There's no brass ring," Walker noticed. "What kind
of carousel doesn't have a brass ring?"

"It's never had one. Not in my lifetime, anyway,"
Kathryn replied. "Although it might have at some point.
The merry-go-round has been here since 1908."

"Totally bogus," Walker said, shaking his head.
"You're supposed to reach out and try to grab the brass
ring every time your horse passes it."

"I'll be sure to pass on your complaint in an angry
letter to the Parks Department." She reached out for his
hand as the ride began to pick up speed. "C'mon, you
curmudgeon. Admit you're having fun."

He squeezed her hand. "First, homemade pancakes
and the sports section; then a game of catch with my surprisingly athletic new roommate, followed by an ice-cold
imported beer and the opportunity to discover your
great sense of innate rhythm when you ride a horse—and

don't accuse me again of Flirting with Intent—am I having fun yet?" He swung their joined hands back and forth as the carousel reached its maximum speed. "Hell, Kitty, it's a walk in the park!"

Chapter
14

"Okay, who wants to tell me something about *The Taming of the Shrew*?" Kathryn asked her ninth-grade drama class.

"It's universal," Andrew Sherwood said laconically.

"Good. Why?" Kathryn urged.

"The play deals with stuff that happens every day," offered Tandy Newman.

"Strolling players always come across a nobleman willing to offer them solid food and a comfy bed in exchange for putting on a play that suits the nobleman's fancy?" Kathryn asked, playing devil's advocate.

"It happens in *Hamlet*," Tandy said smugly.

"*Touché*, girl. It certainly does. What else happens every day? Servants railroad innocent travelers into pretending to be the wealthy father of their moonstruck young masters?" It was more fun to teach Socratically than didactically. Kathryn loved to rattle her students' cages. Coax those young minds into some creative thinking.

"Doesn't that happen in other Shakespeare comedies, too?" Tandy asked.

"Similar things, yes, but we're talking about *Shrew* as

tackling issues that happen 'every day'—not just within the realm of Shakespeare's plays."

"Men and women," Chloe Harris mumbled. "Men, especially."

"What about men and women, Chloe?"

"You can't live with them, and killing them gets you ten to twenty." The class snickered.

Andrew jumped in defensively. "What about women? You guys always want it both ways!"

"What do you mean by that, Andrew?" Kathryn asked.

"Well, you want us to be really take-charge and tough, and then when we're not, you think we're wusses, but when we really *do* take charge, you get all pissed at us and scream feminism and stuff."

"Well, like you all want us to be independent, because you say you don't want a woman who just hangs on you and gets all clingy, but then when we get a life, guys get jealous or needy." Chloe was obviously girding herself for mental combat.

"I've known you since second grade and you never cut me any slack, Chloe," Andrew griped.

"Oh grow up! When we were little, Ms. Lamb, he used to sit behind me and try to tie my hair in knots, just to get my attention."

"That's 'cause you annoyed me," Andrew said defensively.

"If I really annoyed you, you wouldn't deal with me at all. You were just trying to get my attention," Chloe rebuked.

"Well, it worked, didn't it?"

"They've been dating since sixth grade," one of their classmates informed Kathryn.

Chloe shot the snitch a dirty look. "The play does remind me a little of *us*, though. I mean, men and women trying to work it out—getting in each other's way sometimes, and driving each other crazy, but in the end, we really need each other, and we both—I mean men and women, not Andrew and me—need to learn how to compromise and see beyond our own point of view on something, in order to get along."

"The battle of the sexes," Tandy interjected.

"Good. All of you. Good insights. What other themes are universal in this play?" Kathryn asked her class.

"I think," Lisette Mars said, splitting the end of one of her strands of long blond hair, "like Chloe said, there's the concept that men and women have to come together and learn how to overcome the obstacles between them in order to band together, sort of, but there's more than just that . . . because they have to do battle against a bigger obstacle that they both share?" It was more of a question than a suggestion.

"Like what, for instance? Any thoughts on this?"

There was a collective chuckle. "Parents," Andrew said definitively. The class groaned in commiseration.

"Siblings," Tandy added. Several of the ninth graders nodded their heads affirmatively.

"There's the big picture," Chloe offered. "I mean, in the play, Kate doesn't want to get married because her father wants to *force* her to marry a guy he picks for her. And they're all losers and geeks. And Petruchio's been traveling for a while and he *does* want to get married and finally settle down, but in the beginning, with Kate, it's on a bet. But he doesn't have anyone else in the world, and Kate's home life sucks—I mean look at the way her father treats her—and basically they're just two people who both want to be loved."

"And isn't that the way of the world?" Kathryn sighed. She smiled, and glanced at the clock on the wall. "Let's pick this up next time. We'll put a couple of scenes up on their feet and see what happens when we set things in motion. Again—good work, guys."

The class shuffled out of the room and Kathryn shoved her notepad and her *Taming of the Shrew* script into her tapestry shoulder bag. Despite their recent spat, she was sort of looking forward to seeing Walker when she got home. Smiling to herself, she recalled Andrew Sherwood's astute comment during class about the universality of Shakespeare's classic battle of the sexes. It was little wonder that the story had endured for more than four hundred years, when she, for one, seemed to be living it lately.

She telephoned her answering machine to see if there were any messages, and as she heard her own outgoing message play, thought about the argument she'd had with Walker that morning. He'd wanted her to re-record her message to indicate that he was reachable at that number as well. She had reminded him, rather forcefully, that she was expecting phone calls from at least two more Six in the City bachelors, who might get very confused, or at least turned off if they thought she was living with a guy—especially *this* guy. Imagine a prospective mate phoning to ask her out, and hearing on the answering machine that she was shacking up with the manager of the dating service!

Walker also claimed to be cranky because he hadn't been able to play his piano in a week—"I thought we agreed that 'a life without music is a sorry one,' " he'd said—so she banished him to the penthouse. Although the rain itself had finally stopped, Walker claimed that the weather conditions were still unfavorable for repairing the roof and ceiling, at least according to the contractors. Half the time Kathryn enjoyed his semipermanent presence in her apartment, but there were certainly occasions when she felt he was cramping her style. Maybe she wasn't as ready for this marriage thing as she thought she was.

When she got home, he was still out, so she decided to relax, throw on some show tunes, and do some baking. She'd put two trays of ginger cookies in the oven before she realized she'd been making heart shapes.

The doorbell rang, and with floury hands she went over to check the peephole.

"Hi, honey, I'm home!" Walker crowed. His voice echoed down the long carpeted hallway outside the apartment. She opened the door with a dusty white hand. Her roommate brought his right hand out from behind his back and offered her a wrapped bouquet of yellow roses. He gave her a kiss on the forehead.

"Yellow: for friendship. And dinner's on me, tonight." He waved a menu he had retrieved from the doorstep. "Did you ever try their pizza? Maybe we should get two pizzas," Walker said, as he followed Kathryn into the kitchen. "Josh is coming over from the gallery tonight. We usually get together for *Monday Night Football.*"

He was invading her space again, breaking their bargain. "Nice of you to ask first," Kathryn said sourly. "Are these a preliminary peace offering?" she questioned. "You know where the vases are . . . could you pull one down for me, please?"

Walker reached over Kathryn's head to the cabinet high above the sink. "This is a nice one," he said, as he stretched his arm toward an etched glass pitcher. "I didn't think you'd mind," he continued. "After all, we had such a good time together yesterday, and you said you grew up watching football. Besides, Josh wants to meet you. He's my oldest friend. He can bring his fiancée if you want another woman to talk to."

"That's really not the issue," Kathryn said quietly. "It just shows a total lack of sensitivity. This is my apartment, remember? You're a guest. What if I just wanted to lie around on the sofa with no makeup on—God forbid—and flip through catalogues all evening? What if *I* wanted to invite someone over? What if I wanted to rent a movie? What if I just don't feel like being a hostess? I had a long day at work, and—"

"Son of a bitch!" Walker exclaimed as the etched glass pitcher went crashing seven feet to the tiled kitchen floor. He regarded Kathryn's pale expression as she stared at the clear broken shards around her feet.

"You clumsy . . . !" she said, her eyes tearing up. She shook her head in disbelief. "Goddamnit! If it isn't one thing, it's another with you . . ."

"I am so sorry, Kathryn. One minute, I thought I had the handle in my hand, and the next thing I knew . . . I missed it and the other one knocked into it and I couldn't catch it in time, and . . ." He placed his big, warm hand on her shaking shoulder.

He hadn't done it deliberately or maliciously. He was just a menace around anything delicate or fragile. Coffee mugs. Crystal vases. Her heart. Kathryn took a deep breath and mentally counted to ten. "Well, maybe it was its time," she sniffled. "I mean, it wasn't new or anything. I got it in college at one of those traveling crafts fairs that come 'round every Christmas. You know—they make the rounds of regional Renaissance Faires all summer and college campuses in the fall and winter. They've got a built-in market, what with students cramming for exams and no time to Christmas shop before they come home for the holidays." She picked up each glass fragment lovingly and placed it in a brown paper trash bag. "See, this was the tree of life . . . or maybe it was supposed to be a pear tree . . . although I don't see any partridges nesting there." Kathryn showed Walker a ragged bit of glass with a blossoming branch exquisitely etched upon it.

He looked miserable. "I know how you feel, if that's any consolation. My Cornell 'Go, Big Red!' mug that I nearly busted the day we met has been with me since the day I made running back. It's a souvenir from an important chunk of *my* life, so I'd be pretty pissed if it broke. *Shit*. I feel like the poster child for 'No good deed goes unpunished,' " he said morosely.

"I'm not blaming you, Bear."

"You called me clumsy."

"It just blurted out. I'm sorry. It was the first thing that popped out of my mouth . . . look, I'm a little tense right now, and I lashed out. I mean here you are, taking over my house, running roughshod over my express directives to stay out of my life if I let you camp out down here, inviting your friends over to watch my TV . . . and I'm sure you got me the roses with the best of intentions— although I really like snapdragons, if you have a need to know my favorite flower—and then a vase I've cherished for over fifteen years breaks into a gazillion pieces . . . it's too much!"

"You won't have to do anything when Josh comes over. I'll take care of ordering and cleaning up."

"Walker, I'm really tired. I've had a long day, and this is my space."

"Didn't your mommy teach you about sharing?" He gave a childlike pout. "I'll even give you a foot massage." He dilated his pupils and gave her his best spaniel-like gaze.

Kathryn shook her head, smiling in spite of herself. "Oh, boy. If we're going to make this arrangement work, no matter how temporary it is—and it *is* temporary— please don't present me with any more *faits accompli*. It does something to my stomach and it makes me . . . I don't know . . . *bristle*. No 'done deals' from now on. Got it?"

Bear extended his paw. "Sorry. Shake?"

She shook his hand and caught the mischievous glint in his eye. He knew as well as she did what happened to her insides when they shook hands, and he had tricked her into falling for it. How could something as innocuous as a handshake send her nerves into an electric tailspin? In an effort to put some physical distance between them, she retreated to the relative safety of the kitchen to fix herself a cup of tea.

At 8:45, Josh Leo rang the bell with a six-pack in hand and Walker escorted him to the velvet couch. Josh seemed pleasant enough—perhaps more grounded than his old school chum. "I like this place," he said, appraising the atmosphere of Kathryn's apartment. "Very cozy. Like a nest. Bear could use some warmth in his life."

"Then I take it you're well acquainted with his other temporary arrangement?" Kathryn asked, as Walker began to lift the tangerine-and-rose-colored chiffon scarves off her lampshades.

"Hey, hey, hey! Put those back, please! What were we just talking about?!" When Kathryn glared at him, he carefully replaced the lengths of delicate silk.

"I'm the one who's responsible for any color he's got in that place," Josh said, looking at Kathryn's bright scarves. "Unlike the woman who actually owns it, that apartment has no personality whatsoever."

"Sure it does," Walker said defensively, secretly agreeing with Josh. "It has Sven-the-expensive-decorator's personality. If Rushie were left on her own, the place would look like Marrakesh meets Stonehenge, only with plastic slipcovers over the monoliths."

Kathryn switched into hostess mode, despite her earlier protestations, and brought out a plate of the heart-shaped cookies. Josh looked at the flowered porcelain plate and the paper doily, then at the shape of the cookies, then at Kathryn. He seemed to be asking her a question.

"Don't go there, Josh," Kathryn said, as their guest bit into a heart. "It wasn't a conscious decision." She took a cookie and nibbled at the point. "Not bad," she said, assessing its texture and taste. She moved Walker's yellow roses from the coffee table, where they sat in an amethyst-colored glass cruet, to a small end table, then picked up her book and settled comfortably into the cushions of the couch, ignoring the game completely.

"What are you reading?" Josh asked solicitously.

"The love letters of Mark Twain and his wife, Livy. It's great! See, it masquerades as autobiography," she said dryly, "but it's *clearly* fiction, because *he* was the one pursuing Olivia, and no man actively seeks commitment unless he's a creature of feminine fantasy. According to the letters, Twain was the one who wanted to marry

Olivia before he ever met her—he saw a miniature of her—a portrait that her younger brother was carrying, and was smitten from the get-go."

Walker looked up from his longneck. "Didn't it take a lot of persuading of both Olivia and her father that Mark Twain wasn't the undeserving, unreliable scum of the earth, gambling scrivener they thought he was?" He blasted Kathryn with a self-satisfied multiwatt smile. "You're not the only one who's read a book, Miss Kitty," he said and toggled off the "mute" button on the remote. The Titans were already toppling the Jets to the tune of three-zip.

The phone rang during the first quarter and Kathryn went to answer it.

"Kathryn Lamb?" The voice on the other end was a bit high-pitched, but pleasant sounding.

"Speaking."

"This is Glen Pinsky. I saw your tape at Six in the City. And I read your profile."

"Hi. How *are* you?" Kathryn asked warmly.

Walker looked up from the television screen. He watched her curiously.

"You're a drama teacher?" Glen asked.

"I sure am."

"I'm an English teacher at Trinity. Medieval and Renaissance. We cover Chaucer, Shakespeare, Marlowe."

"Sounds great. Can I enroll?" Kathryn was giggling nervously. She glanced in Walker's direction, caught him anxiously watching her, and then turned her back on him, cradling the phone to her ear as she faced the kitchen. She thought she heard him growl.

"I'm not very good at this," Glen said.

"You're doing fine so far," Kathryn encouraged.

"I have to admit, I'm painfully shy. Literature has always been my escape."

"Well, that's better than drugs." Kathryn laughed again. This time, she was sure she heard a growl emanate from the direction of the sofa, followed by the aggressive *thunk* of a bottle of beer hitting the coaster on the coffee table.

"Can we meet for coffee first, and see how things go?"

"Of course we can. Can I make a suggestion, though?"

"Oh, yes. Yes of course, Kathryn. I didn't mean to bulldoze you. But, in case I can change your mind, there's a Caravaggio exhibit at the Metropolitan Museum. Maybe we could meet there and see the show, and then repair to their café by the fountain for coffee afterwards."

"Oh. That would be *very* . . ." Caravaggio? He was a painter. Italian Renaissance? Or was that Canareggio? She always got the two confused. "Well, Glen, why not?" she heard herself say. It had been ages since she'd visited the Metropolitan. She was always planning to hit the new exhibits, but somehow never actually made it to the museum, despite her good intentions to be culturally well rounded. And it was a complete one-eighty from being shuttled down to Hades. At least on paper Glen seemed to have more in common with her than Barnaby Street had, despite the allure of the rocker's great English accent.

"When did you have in mind?" Kathryn asked.

"The museum is open late on Fridays, I think. Maybe we can meet there after work. Or is Friday night too *important*?"

"Well, Friday night is 'date night.' So what better

night to go out on a date? I'll be the one with the red carnation in my lapel," she joked.

"Oh, I know what you look like. I saw your tape, remember? You look like one of the engravings in Tennyson's *Idylls of the King*."

What? Well, he was an English teacher. "Thank you, Glen. I'll take that as a compliment. I suppose you . . . teach that work, which is why you have such a familiarity with it."

There was a silence on the other end of the phone. "I must confess I've always thought the women in the engravings were, well *hot*, to use an expression. Victorian Vargas girls. Was that too forward?" Glen asked meekly.

Uh . . . wait. Did this guy think of nineteenth-century engravings like most guys of her generation regarded Betty and Veronica? "Not at all," Kathryn replied, shaking her head, even though they were on the phone. She was not about to let the two men watching football in her living room—especially Walker—get a whiff of how odd she feared Glen Pinsky might be. Maybe he just wasn't comfortable on the phone. He seemed a bit anxious, even desperate to try to impress her. In person, he might improve. "Not at all. See you Friday at around six-thirty. Have a good week. Bye." She hung up the phone and raced to her computer, firing up the Internet.

Caravaggio, she queried and pulled up dozens of interesting Web sites, more than half of which were in Italian. Eliminating those, within a few minutes she had managed to locate a site that had photos of some of the painter's masterworks. Brooding, dark, violent canvases they were. Classic subjects like the "Martyrdom of St. Matthew" and "The Sacrifice of Isaac" were rendered in particularly morbid fashion. She sighed inaudibly and returned to Walker and Josh. "What's the score?" she asked gaily.

The men looked at each other then back at her. "I didn't mean to listen, but it sounded like you were on a call from one of my clients," Walker said evenly, poorly disguising his ambivalence and discomfort.

"Glen Pinsky. He's an English teacher at Trinity . . . but I guess you know that, since you're the boss. So we're sort of on the same page from the get-go, since we both teach similar subjects at private schools. We're meeting at the Met on Friday night, but since you didn't mean to listen, I guess you gathered that."

Josh raised his longneck to Kathryn. "Good for you! I hope it goes great for you. I keep telling our friend here," he gestured toward Walker with the beer bottle, "that permanent bachelorhood is an unnatural state." He looked over at his pal. "Yo! You should invest in *futures*, Mr. Wall Street financial guru!" Walker ignored his friend's admonishment and pretended to be engrossed in the runaway first quarter.

The phone rang again and Kathryn went back to the kitchen to answer it. "Grand Central Station."

"Have you seen today's *Post*?" Eleanor asked.

"No. I don't usually buy it. It's all I can do to keep up with what's in the *Times*."

"Are you busy?"

"Walker and an old friend of his are watching *Monday Night Football*. *I'm* not busy, though. What's up? Is everything okay?"

"Can I come over? Dan and I just had dinner and he's entertaining Johanna, who's been asking for him all day, and I haven't seen daylight since I got up this morning, although I was futzing around with the Brownie Points for part of the afternoon—'til Johanna came home from a play date. I could use the fresh air. Just to remind myself that there's something beyond my apartment."

"I've got news for you . . . you still won't be seeing daylight. But come over if you want. I'll be here. And I've got plenty of herbal tea."

When her younger sister arrived—and good thing it happened to be halftime—Kathryn introduced her to Josh, then drew Eleanor into the kitchen and made them some tea. "Did you really just want to get out of the house for a while, or was there something specific you wanted to tell me?"

Eleanor withdrew a page of newsprint from her purse. "I thought you might want to see Liz Smith's column from today's paper," she said, handing Kathryn the folded page.

Kathryn opened the paper and read the item her sister had marked with a yellow highlighter. She swallowed hard and took a sip of tea, followed by a deep breath. Eleanor came over and put her arm around her older sister, who had turned away to wipe the beginning of a tear. "Will you be okay with this?" Eleanor asked.

"Yeah," Kathryn said softly. "And I wouldn't mind if you read it to Walker. It can't get any worse, so reading it out loud won't change anything. And he might as well know."

"Are you sure?" Eleanor asked. "Or should we wait until Josh goes home?"

"*Monday Night Football* usually becomes Tuesday Morning Football, and you need your rest, so let's bite the bullet. I'm a big girl. Or so I keep telling myself."

The two sisters walked back into the living room

during a commercial break. "Walker, can Ellie read you something?" Kathryn asked him.

He nodded. Eleanor gave her sister another look. Kathryn nodded and waved her hand at the torn page of the newspaper.

"This is today's Liz Smith column," Eleanor began slowly. The men looked like they were wondering why it was being read to them. "You sure you're okay with this, Kitty?" she asked.

"Yes."

Eleanor gave Walker a significant look, then read the news item. " 'What oft-maligned film hunk was noticed nuzzling at Nebuchadnezzar Saturday night with a Bernadette Peters look-alike? Seems he's been squiring young ladies around Gotham in preparation for his next role . . . he's slated to play a hapless romantic who tries his luck with a dating service in Ian Sorensen's satirical comedy, *What's Your Sign?*' " Eleanor folded the paper and looked at Walker with all the malice of a district attorney.

There were a few moments of silence. Josh looked uncomfortable. Walker was very pale. "Oh, hell. I had no idea, Kitty," he said quietly. He got up from the couch and moved to embrace her. She pulled away and went into the kitchen, where he followed. Kathryn put both hands on the counter, turning her back on him.

"Believe me," Walker said softly, reaching out to stroke her hair. "If I'd had any idea what was going on, do you think I would have accepted his application? How do you think it makes *me* look?"

"It's all about you, now, isn't it?" Kathryn scoffed. "You're worried that people won't trust dating services anymore . . . as though we should trust them in the first place."

"I'll make it up to you," Walker offered.

"I had a feeling you'd say that. *Déjà vu* all over again. It's starting to be your litany. But I don't need you to save me. And I *don't* want a 'do-over' match with a *seventh* bachelor. I'm not sure the horses in your stable are stable." She turned around to face him. "If I hadn't had such a positive phone call this evening, I might be more upset than I am." She managed a somewhat triumphant smile. "I have a very good feeling about Glen Pinsky."

"Okay, then," Walker said, "this won't count in the 'making it up to you' department, but let me take you out for ice cream after the game."

"How old do you think I *am*? Isn't that the sort of thing you say to cheer up a seven-year-old?"

Walker grinned and shrugged.

"Hey! On second thought . . . I could use a hot fudge sundae right about now. Or maybe a banana split." Kathryn looked at the clock. "Wait a minute, Bear, it's already pushing midnight and they're just about to get to the two-minute warning—which in my experience of watching this stupid game means there's at least another half hour of play. What ice cream parlor is open at one A.M.?"

He ruffled her hair. "Trust me, Red."

Red?

Chapter
15

At 1:17 A.M., Walker was maniacally wheeling a shopping cart through the nearly empty aisles in the local twenty-four-hour Food Emporium, with Kathryn riding shotgun, her feet perched on the front of the cart and her butt sticking out like some sort of aft-facing figurehead. Walker skidded the cart to a halt in front of the frozen food section. "Pick your poison, Kitty. Any flavor you want. Load up. My treat."

Kathryn hopped off the cart and began to scrutinize the abundant selection before her. "Nothing better than coffee ice cream with hot fudge," she said, grabbing a pint of Häagen-Dazs. "Then again, they *do* make the best chocolate." She tossed a second pint into the cart. "And hot fudge with mint chip really is hard to beat," she added, grabbing the third flavor. "What kind do you like, partner?"

"Cherry vanilla."

"Well, you're in luck, because they just so happen to have . . ." *Thunk.* A fourth flavor joined the rest at the bottom of the shopping wagon. "Have I ever told you my theory about ice cream and calories?"

"Nope," Walker replied.

"Okay. Now bear with me. This is scientifically

proven to be true." Kathryn lifted the pint of chocolate ice cream out of the cart and held it like Carol
Merrill demonstrating a product on *Let's Make a Deal*.
"Chocolate. Dark color, rich flavor. A perfect example
of the highest-calorie ice cream. Vanilla—which we're
not bothering with this trip—has fewer calories. Why?
Lighter color, lighter flavor. Fruit flavors," she said,
holding up the pint of cherry vanilla, "have even fewer
calories than vanilla because the fruit takes up all that
room in the container. And besides, everyone knows that
fruit is dietetic. After all, there are only about sixty calories in an entire basket of strawberries. Now, we get to
the most dietetic flavor of all: coffee, because you actually *burn off* calories as you consume it, due to the caffeine content." Kathryn brandished the coffee ice cream
to prove her point.

Thoroughly charmed, Walker was in stitches. "That is
the silliest, sorriest excuse for chowing down on dessert
that I have ever heard."

In tandem, they rolled the cart into another aisle.
"Some people think paper or plastic is the biggest decision you'll ever have to make in a trip to the supermarket," Walker said, straight-faced. "But actually, it's
wafer or sugar," he added, bringing the cart to a stop in
front of a display of ice cream cones. "Concentrate now.
Our future as roommates depends on your answer." He
hummed the *Jeopardy* theme.

Kathryn gravely studied the boxes. "I think it all depends on the kind of ice cream you're having. For instance, can you imagine having a Carvel softserve in
anything but a wafer cone? I can't. However, for the kind
of ice cream that you need a metal scoop to dish out, it's
got to be sugar cones all the way."

"Yes!!" Walker exclaimed, raising his right hand for a high five. Kathryn's hand met his in a resounding smack. He impulsively gave her a hug.

After selecting three different kinds of fudge, and adding a jar of hot butterscotch for good measure, Walker and Kathryn wheeled their bounty to the produce aisle. Kathryn picked up a box of strawberries. "Ummm, smell these," she giggled, inhaling, then shoving the box at Walker. "We can dip these in the hot fudge. After all, they have only sixty calories for the whole box!"

She giddily plucked an apple from a pyramid-like display and swirled the fruit under his nose.

"Temptress!"

"You wish!" she laughed.

"Wheresoever you are, *there* is Eden," Walker said.

"Hey, I was just reading that line tonight, while you were watching the football game. That book I was reading—the love letters of Mark Twain and his wife—refers to hypothetical diaries Twain wrote of Adam and Eve. They were supposedly highly autobiographical . . . he adored his wife, and the personality he created for Eve and the relationship she has with Adam is modeled on his own marriage. 'Wheresoever she was, there was Eden' was the last line of *Adam's Diary*. It made me cry when I read it, but you probably didn't notice. You and Josh were too busy yelling at those guys on TV while they crunched each other's bones. How did you know that quote?" she asked incredulously.

"I guess *you* didn't notice when I mentioned it in between 'yelling at those guys on TV,' that I seemed to know a factoid or two about Mark Twain. I may love football, but I have read a book or two, missy."

Kathryn snapped a banana from its bunch and brandished it. "Glen Pinsky's got some competition in the Renaissance Man department. You are one continuous string of surprises, mister."

"*Now,* who's 'Flirting with Intent'?"

Before she could come up with a quick reply, Walker enfolded her in his arms and kissed her, full and deeply. Kathryn felt herself respond to his passion with equal intensity. His ardor made her lose all self-control and awareness of their surroundings.

"Stop that!!!"

The amorous pair immediately ended their embrace, startled out of their skins.

They were assailed with, in heavily accented English, "This is not the place for that sort of . . . rivky-pivky!"

Kathryn blinked and looked at their accuser, an elderly woman, barely five-feet tall, with two apples, a pint of almond-flavored nondairy creamer, and a Lean Cuisine in her handheld red plastic basket.

"Hey, lady, what's your problem? Get a life!" Walker said gruffly.

The old woman heaved her shoulders, harrumphed at them, and shuffled toward the checkout line.

"Good thing she didn't catch me squeezing the melons," he added under his breath.

"Why did you do that?" Kathryn asked softly. "Not *that*," she said, nodding in the direction of the retreating senior citizen, "but . . . you know . . ."

Walker gazed into Kathryn's eyes. "Because you looked like you needed it."

"I like the way you think," she murmured. "You know, maybe we shouldn't be too hard on that lady. Did you ever play the game where you see a total stranger and then you make up what they do and you give them an entire existence? You said she needed to get a life. Let's invent one for her."

"Okay," Walker said. "You go first."

"Well . . ." Kathryn began. "Maybe we should really feel sorry for her. After all, she's here all by herself, shopping in the middle of the night. Maybe she's lonely and she can't sleep, and she wanted to be around people, so she went out grocery shopping. It must be so sad to grow old alone. I know *I* would hate it."

Walker began to get into the game. "Maybe she was married for something like fifty years and now she's a widow and she can't fall asleep in a bed without her husband. Every night, she looks over and sees that empty space, the sheets still cool to the touch, deprived of the warmth of his body. So she prowls the produce aisles at night because sleeping alone is too depressing."

"Yeah," Kathryn added, building on Walker's supposition. "And maybe she interrupted our kiss because she goes to the supermarket—a clean, well-lighted place—to forget her pain and her loss of the great love of her life, and we just inadvertently reminded her of what she once had."

"I shouldn't have been so hard on her," Walker said ruefully.

They wheeled their cart to the only checkout line open at that late hour. The elderly lady had carefully placed each of her purchases on the conveyor belt and was watching the price scanner with some trepidation. When she saw Kathryn and Walker approach the counter, she turned back to glare at them.

"That's $5.66," the aqua-smocked cashier told the

woman. The old lady reached for her purse and methodically began to count out the change.

Walker took out his wallet. "It's okay . . . 'LaShawna,'" he said, reading the cashier's nameplate. "It's on me." He looked at the old woman. "I'm sorry I was rude to you. I'm sure you've had a rich and rewarding life. Please accept this as part of my apology."

The elderly shopper turned her face up to look at her benefactor. Her eyes misted over. "*A sheynem dank,*" she whispered softly. "Thank you."

"*Nishtoh far vos,*" Walker replied. "It's nothing. *Zay gezunt.* Have a good night."

"You speak Yiddish?" Kathryn asked, amazed.

"'Just one continuous string of surprises,'" Walker replied, smiling down at her. "With a mother who's a professional Yenta, how could I not know a phrase or two?"

"Damn!" LaShawna said, wiping a tear from her cheek with the back of her hand. She sniffled a little. "That is the nicest thing I ever seen anyone do since I been working here. You're a good person." She tossed a Milky Way bar into their shopping bag. "Y'all have a good night, now. What was that you said to her? '*Gesundheit*'?"

"*Zay gezunt,*" Walker said. "It literally means 'go in good health.'"

"Yeah, well, back at you," LaShawna said, retrieving a crumpled Kleenex from the pocket of her smock.

"That was . . . you are a really special person, Mr. Hart," Kathryn said, slipping her arm through his as they walked back to their high-rise. The night was quiet and still, and from somewhere—perhaps the sparse greenery that dotted Abingdon Square—came the scent of night-blooming jasmine. With a pang as bittersweet as the hot fudge in her grocery bag, Kathryn realized that she was not looking forward to her date with Glen Pinsky with nearly as much vengeful anticipation as she had been just a couple of hours earlier.

Chapter
16

"So what do you do, Valerie?" Lou asked Walker's date. "These getting to know one another things are always kind of awkward. I apologize. Josh and Bear have known each other for dog's years, so I know what it's like to be the new kid on the block." Lou bit into a dim sum. "Does anybody know what's in this one?" she asked the table. Walker shook his head. Lou fed the other half of the Chinese dumpling to her fiancé, as though he were a trained seal, popping it in his mouth.

"Shmmphhff," Josh said definitively, trying to chew the hot dumpling with a modicum of decorum.

"Oh, well then I'll have another one. I like shrimp." Lou snagged another dumpling with her chopsticks. "I just like to know what I'm eating."

"Lou's the same way with swimming. She's one of those people who won't go in the water unless she knows what the bottom's like," Josh said. "So she's more than happy to let Bear and me do the camping thing, and Lou and I hit the spas and resorts, where she can see the bottom of the pool. Of course, Bear will wade in mountain streams only if I promise him there are no sharks. He has a horror of them. Hey, did you hear the one about the lawyer and the sharks . . . 'professional courtesy'?"

Valerie Adams chose to ignore Josh's lawyer joke and delicately wiped the corner of her mouth with one of Tsé Wot's large white linen napkins. "I handle trusts and estates, matrimonials, mostly. Every once in a while I do some business law. With a sprinkling of intellectual property."

"So how did you and Bear meet?" Lou asked, hunting for the soy sauce bottle.

"I'm his mother's lawyer. She's coming back to the States and needs some things handled for her, and she gave me Walker's number to call so he could review some papers that pertain to him."

"So Rushie is planting her tushie stateside again, Bear. Hmmmmm." Josh ate the last of the shrimp dim sum. "Does she want her business back, bro?"

"Later," Walker replied quietly.

Valerie barreled ahead. "She's looking into the possibility of setting up a Web site, and there are some legal ramifications to be explored; at the moment there's no legislation regarding professional matchmaking via the Internet, but there are obvious legal minefields . . ."

"I'm afraid I'm still not very computer literate," Lou said without apology.

"Yeah. She still thinks a MAC platform is one of Ru-Paul's shoes," Josh deadpanned.

"Well, maybe we could use a matrimonial attorney," Lou mentioned, nudging Josh. "We're getting married in April."

"April is the cruelest month," Walker said, *sotto voce*.

"Matrimonials means divorces, not weddings," Valerie said condescendingly.

"I knew that," Lou responded, smiling like the Mona Lisa.

Walker wondered if she was putting Valerie on and bit his tongue. "Lou is a sculptor," he said, changing the subject.

"Sculpt*ress*," Lou corrected. "I do collages and murals, too. That's how Josh and I met. You've heard of the Leo Galleries? That's my honey's family. Of course, you realize I'm only marrying him for his name. I want to be Lou Leo. Such a great name for an *artiste*," she said dryly.

"Lou creates erotica out of household items. Found objects. That sort of thing. She's really quite remarkable," Josh said, patting Lou's cheek.

"Does it bother you when he patronizes you like that?" Valerie asked.

"Why do you think that's patronizing?" Lou asked, smiling enigmatically again. "When this man touches me, an erotic, electric current ripples through every capillary of my body."

"Peking duck, anyone?" Josh interrupted.

"I take it then, you're not a feminist."

"What's a feminist, Val-pal? I've been making a good living since I was fourteen years old, and made *Glamour* magazine's Ten Most Promising College Grads list the year I left art school, got a full scholarship to the Sorbonne for graduate studies, and have never needed to ask anyone, man or woman, for a handout or a leg up." Lou also never needed to raise her voice to someone's challenges.

Like any barracuda lawyer, Valerie refused to accept defeat. "So are you planning to have children?"

"Possibly. I don't think that's something we need to decide right now. I haven't even finished my sweet-and-sour soup."

"Well, are you going to continue to build erotic sculpture with children around the house?"

Lou smiled. "It's not really that erotic. But Josh seems to think so. I guess adults might find it 'suggestive.' It's very tactile." The sculptress turned to Walker and deftly changed the subject. "You're very quiet this evening."

"I'm listening," Walker said laconically. "And thinking."

"I've been this man's best friend for decades. Bear gets really noisy on two occasions," Josh interjected, raising an eyebrow provocatively.

Valerie drew in a quick breath.

"When the Jets are behind . . . and when the Jets are ahead."

All four of them took a sip of water.

"I got a scholarship, too, that I used for law school," Valerie said proudly. "I won a beauty pageant in Louisiana."

Lou looked across the table at the elegant attorney, aware that Walker loved legs that went all the way up. "So you found a way to use your looks to get ahead."

"Ten, fifteen years ago, it was harder for women to get into law schools," Valerie replied, a bit defensively.

The men looked at each other—watching two strong women square off, size each other up. Walker was listening to the stunning brunette on his left and thinking about the dynamic, eccentric, romantic little redhead he'd last seen heading to the Metropolitan Museum of Art to meet Glen Plinsky, dreamboat English Literature teacher. Valerie Adams was the kind of woman Bear had dated for years. Intelligent, no-nonsense, tall, basically gorgeous in that Julie Newmar way.

Valerie looked at Josh and Lou. "I think it's sweet

that you want to get married," she said. "It's such a throwback."

"To what?" Josh asked.

"Well, I don't see as many prenups nowadays, but especially since you aren't sure if or when you want children, it just seems so old-fashioned, and well, *unnecessary* to get married."

"Maybe he just wants a little woman to come home to," Walker said sardonically.

"Well, he can do that without their having to be married."

"And then there will never be a divorce," Walker muttered.

Josh finished chewing. "Call me a hopeless romantic, but I don't think anybody gets married to get divorced. Actually, it was Bear who convinced me not to let Lou go. I can't see *not* spending the rest of my life with her." Josh stroked Lou's cheek. "You know, Valerie's perfect for you, bro. She's as down on marriage as you are."

"Really?" Valerie angled her body so that she was leaning closer to Walker.

Walker shifted his weight away from her ever so slightly. "It's true, I've never seen a happy marriage."

The lawyer flashed him a dazzling smile. "Isn't it easier just to have great sex and then leave, owing each other nothing? And you can see each other whenever you want, with no recriminations, no hard feelings, no acrimony."

"No matrimony," Walker added.

"I just got an idea for my next sculpture," Lou said. "Two boobs peering through a pair of rose-colored glasses." She exchanged a sly look with her fiancé, then turned to the couple seated opposite them. "Frankly, I think you're both delusional. I mean just look at you,

Bear. You claim to be Mr. Permanent Bachelor. In fact you're sending out mixed messages like crazy—to the point of doing stuff that's bad for business—like falling in love with a certain specific client whom you're getting paid to match up with other people—people who *do* want to get married. In other words, people who, according to your antimarriage litany, aren't *you*!"

Valerie and Walker responded almost simultaneously.

"He's what?"

"What are you talking about?"

"Oh, forgive me. I hear things." Lou sipped her green tea daintily. "You've done well for *yourself* though, Bear. Even though this is a first date, you two seem like a perfect match."

Valerie used her chopsticks to push the shredded chicken with cashews around her plate. "Well, it certainly sounds like Walker and I want the same things in the long run. Why should we need to sign a piece of paper? What would it prove? That we might be more in love than people who haven't signed a paper?"

"No. It just proves that you're less gutsy. Life is about taking risks," Lou said quietly, the gauntlet down. "Life is going along for the journey, no matter where it's headed. It's not refusing to get in the car because at some point, you might reach a 'dangerous curve ahead' sign."

"Actually, Bear," Josh cut in. "To me, there's something inherently a bit selfish about people who are so adamantly unwilling to try something—whether it's marriage or sushi."

"Why do you say 'selfish'?" asked the attorney.

"Well, it's a sort of 'my way or the highway' approach to life," Josh responded.

"Well, lawyers never run from a good argument," Valerie laughed. "And it's all in good fun, right? Truce?" She offered her hand across the table to Lou, who gave it a firm handshake.

The check came and both men took their credit cards from their wallets and gave them to the waiter to split the bill in half.

"Not *so* much a feminist," Lou teased Valerie. "If you really practiced what you so vocally preach, you would pay for your own meal."

"Not on a first date, honey," Valerie said triumphantly. "I'm from the South."

Valerie slipped her arm in Walker's as they left the restaurant. In her three-inch heels, she was at least six feet tall, the length of her legs accentuated by the shortness of her mustard-colored Tahari coatdress.

"I've never been to a penthouse," Valerie purred, as she headed toward the corner with Walker, their arms still linked.

"Unfortunately, you're not going to see one tonight either," Walker replied.

Valerie looked very disappointed. "I thought you and I were on the same wavelength."

"We may very well be, but the roof has been leaking and the ceiling needs repairs. And first I had to wait for the cessation of the near-biblical rains we've been having; then I had to call for estimates . . . being a homeowner is like marriage. You've got to fix everything yourself. When you rent, you can just walk away."

Valerie sighed. "So I guess I have to wait until the second date to find out what else besides the New York Jets gets you excited."

Walker nodded. "If you'd like to come over for a brief nightcap, I'm crashing at a friend's house until my place is repaired."

"Well, at least that prolongs the evening somewhat," Valerie said, squeezing his arm. "You are a lot like me."

"How else?"

"I get the feeling that you and I . . . we don't like to owe anyone anything. To be honest, I would hate to have to come home to a man who expected me to put a hot dinner on the table for him every night, even when I'm exhausted. I like a little foot massage, a little pampering myself sometimes."

"Funny you should mention massage. I worked my way through school as a licensed masseur." No sooner had the words escaped his lips than he realized it was a mistake. He hadn't thought his response to be anything more than polite conversation, but Valerie's body language changed immediately.

"My, my." She rolled her head around slowly, a hint to her date to help release the tension in her neck.

Walker hesitated. Watching Valerie in action all evening made him unintentionally focus on everything the leggy brunette was *not*, rather than what she was. Frankly, she was not Kathryn. Still . . . maybe Ms. Adams was better one-on-one. Maybe she was the type whose nerves got the better of her in a group. He'd spend a few minutes alone with her before Kathryn got home from her date with Glen—just a quick drink—then he'd put Valerie in a taxi. "So, are you up for that nightcap? What do you say?" He stroked his jaw, wondering if he were doing the right thing.

"I think . . ." Valerie said, biting her lower lip, and looking up at Walker the way only a truly practiced

Southern belle—lawyer or no lawyer—can, "I think the lady's answer is a most gracious—and grateful—'yes.' "

"Evening, Carlos," Walker said, as he walked into the lobby of his apartment building with the statuesque Valerie on his arm.

"*Buenos noches, Señor Hart.*" The doorman eyed the woman from stiletto heel to perfectly coiffed hair, clearly impressed, but he shot Walker an unforgiving look. After the couple stepped into the elevator, Carlos shook his head and pursed his lips. "Miss Lamb. *Pobrecita.*"

17

The string quintet's musical strains could be heard from the moment Kathryn stepped into the Great Hall of the Metropolitan Museum. There was something so civilized about it. Beautiful music, magnificent art. She scanned the room, looking for the man who might be Glen Pinsky. There were a couple of men who seemed to be waiting for their respective dates, but none of them seemed to fit the profile of the self-effacing English teacher. Kathryn realized that she was expecting a stereotype, from the way Mr. Pinsky had described himself over the phone.

Finally, she spotted someone peering cautiously from behind a large potted plant in the foyer. He was *actually wearing* a red carnation in his lapel. She'd been kidding when she mentioned it on the phone. *Oooh, boy,* Kathryn thought to herself. Glen waved tentatively at her, and then called to her in the same high, reedy voice she recognized from their telephone call.

"Kathryn? Kathryn Lamb?"

She waved across to him, and they met in the center of the Great Hall. He was taller than she had assumed, and much better looking, with very light blond hair, and pale, almost translucent skin, lending him the air of a sickly

Edwardian poet. True to her expectations, Glen was wearing the requisite tweedy jacket with the fawn-colored suede elbow patches; but underneath it, the blue-and-white-striped shirt, and the paisley tie in shades of red and brown made Kathryn want to phone in a 911 to the haberdashery fashion police.

"Glen?" Kathryn shook his hand. He returned it with a surprisingly strong grip, then lifted her hand to his lips and kissed it tenderly. His narrow blond mustache tickled her skin.

She laughed nervously. "How very European."

"Oh, no. I was born in Canada. Toronto, in fact."

He was so literal. "Oh, well. How very . . . Canadian, then!"

Glen didn't smile.

Kathryn shook her curls. "I'm an idiot, what am I thinking? It's a first date, for God's sake. I'm sorry, Glen. I hope we didn't get off on the wrong foot."

"You are a hundred percent forgiven, my dear."

Actually, Glen's manners were kind of quaint. Kathryn sort of liked how he had kissed her hand, the way he called her "my dear"—there was something charmingly retro about it. And he wasn't bad looking at all.

"Well, shall we see the Caravaggios?" Ah, yes. Caravaggio. Glen extended his arm. She gave him an uncomfortable glance, and reluctantly linked her arm through his. He looked at Kathryn admiringly. "Lovely. Simply lovely. I should like to stroll through the medieval exhibits before we boldly venture into the Italian Renaissance."

"Where no man dares to go."

"What?" Glen registered his confusion.

"Oh, nothing," Kathryn said. " 'To boldly go where no man has gone before' or something like that. I think it's from *Star Trek*; my bad paraphrase. I have a . . . friend . . . who's into *Star Trek*, so I've seen a lot of it lately. Never mind."

Glen and Kathryn promenaded through the small, dark rooms of Byzantine madonnas staring forlornly back at them, then through the large hall of the famous Unicorn Tapestries—the ones that weren't on display at the Cloisters uptown—and into the exhibition of Arms and Armor, where lance-wielding knights in hand-hammered plate armor, sword and shield at the ready, threatened to bear down upon them from their lofty perches atop stuffed stallions.

"Oh, yes, I think this is truly your era," Glen said. He slid his arm out from underneath hers and opened his worn leather satchel, removing a small silver camera. "Let me just take a photo of you here." Glen carefully posed Kathryn by the side of one of the charging horsemen. "Look up at him as though he is about to do battle for your honor. Ivanhoe for the brave Rebecca, as it were."

Kathryn winced, but the drama teacher in her decided to make the best of it, so she looked up at the armored figure and acted the part.

"Lovely, simply lovely." Glen snapped the picture.

"I hope your film is fast enough for this light," Kathryn said helpfully. She wasn't quite sure what she had gotten herself into.

"Oh, there's no film in the camera," Glen answered mildly.

God, this man was weird. "No film? Then why did you take a picture?"

"It's digital. It doesn't take film. I develop this and I

can put the pictures on a floppy disk and give it to you, so you can download it onto your computer."

And who else's, Kathryn wondered. "Does this mean you can put my photo on the Internet?" she asked, uncomfortable.

"If I wanted to, I certainly could. But I'd rather not share you."

Damned if I do and damned if I don't. His answer was sort of creepy, but Kathryn decided to give the man the benefit of the doubt. Maybe he was simply eccentric—a harmless sort of weird. After all, a highly respected private school trusted him to teach their kids. Still, she decided not to reassume the medieval arm-linking position when they toured the Caravaggio exhibit.

The rooms were dimly lit, making it difficult to appreciate the painter's mastery of light and shadow known as *chiaroscuro.* "Look!" Kathryn exclaimed. "Did you know his real name was 'Michelangelo'? Michelangelo Merisi da Caravaggio."

"I suppose with a name like that, he was destined to become an artist." Glen took a pair of bifocals from the brown leather satchel and balanced them on the bridge of his nose. He perused the biography of the controversial painter. "Goodness! What a brawler he was. 'He was imprisoned for several assaults, and killed a man over a disputed score in a game of court tennis.' "

Kathryn continued to read. " 'After receiving a pardon from the pope, he was wrongfully arrested and imprisoned for two days. A boat that was to bring him to Rome left without him, taking his belongings. Misfortune, exhaustion, and illness overtook him as he helplessly lay watching the boat depart.' Wow. I wonder why no one has ever made a movie of his life. The Caravaggio biopic, starring—Keanu Reeves."

She and Glen walked through the rooms filled with images of biblical figures, common peasants, and beautiful young men, most of the subjects depicted as tortured souls. Here, right in front of her was "The Sacrifice of Isaac" she had seen in a photo on the Internet. In the painting, the young boy's face was contorted in anguish, his eyes desperate and unbelieving, his twisted body so apparently racked with pain even in anticipation of the plunge of his father's raised, sharpened blade. The angel seemed to be applying brute force to stay Abraham's hand. With a few strokes of his brush Caravaggio had somehow managed to depict the dent made by the pressing of the father's thumb into his son's cheek. It made Kathryn wince. "I look at these paintings, and I feel like I need a drink," she said.

"Then perhaps we should go to the café now, my dear," Glen suggested, offering his arm to her again.

"I think I need something stronger than coffee, after looking at all this anguish. His work is brilliant, but a little goes a long way. It's striking, but smothering . . . very claustrophobic."

"You have quite a vivid imagination, my dear."

Kathryn shrugged. They paused in the Great Hall to listen to the chamber music.

"Ahh. Bach's 'Concerto for Two Violins in D minor.' " Glen closed his eyes and swayed a little to the music.

"I'm impressed. I know very little about classical music. I just know whether or not I like it. I never know who wrote it."

Glen continued to sway to the music, playing air violin. "I studied for twelve years," he said, without opening his eyes. "I wanted to be a concert violinist. But I ended up as an English teacher, nonetheless." He continued sawing the air with his imaginary bow.

"And I am sure that Trinity is a happier place for it."

Glen opened his eyes. "Where do you teach again?"

"Briarcliff. In Riverdale. I try to get a bunch of sophisticated teenagers who think they already know it all to let go and allow themselves to make discoveries about the theater and about themselves. Depending on the annual crop, I have occasionally met with some success."

"I think there is no nobler profession than teaching," Glen said as they headed toward the café. That's what Rick Byron had said, too. Was this the new hot pick-up line? Was there a magazine they all read: this month in *Testosterone*—"How to disarm the schoolmarm."

Kathryn nodded her head. "Unless you count firefighting. But that's what I keep telling my father, who firmly believes that his daughter should do something that makes lots of money. He doesn't share my viewpoint, which is: the nobler the service, the more money it should command."

They were seated at a small table in a quiet corner of the museum café. Kathryn perused the menu. "Well, at least I can get a glass of wine." She looked over at the center of the room. "Didn't there used to be a fountain here? With dancing figures made of bronze, and people threw pennies in the fountain. For luck."

"There was a children's book about that," Glen said, as he looked at the menu.

"*From the Mixed-up Files of Mrs. Basil E. Frankweiler,*" they said in unison, remembering the title at the same instant. "Jamie and Claudia hid out in the Metropolitan Museum and they fished out the pennies and used them to buy food," Kathryn added with glee, the memory of the story coming back to her.

"And they slept in that big red velvet Renaissance bed in the period rooms," Glen chimed in. "Now wouldn't that be fun? Trying that today." He leaned toward Kathryn conspiratorially. "Shall we give it a whirl? I can take pictures, just to prove that we got away with it."

Kathryn hoped that Glen hadn't seen her cringe. She motioned to the waiter and ordered a glass of cabernet sauvignon. "I think some things are better left as fantasies, Glen. Besides, I can't afford to get arrested."

Glen asked for a cappuccino without the steamed milk. "Spoilsport."

Kathryn shrugged. "Been there."

Luckily, Glen assumed she was kidding; thankfully, he didn't pursue the subject. "Well then, what other adventures shall we embark on, milady? What glorious quests can I sally forth on to continue to merit your favor and kind regard?"

She looked at her date, amused. "Oh dear. I'll have to think. I'm not currently aware of any dragons I require you to slay, unless I count Briarcliff's principal."

Kathryn sipped her wine. She wasn't sure what to make of Glen Pinsky, whether he was truly strange, or whether he felt he had to act a part in her presence for whatever reasons. "Did you play with toy soldiers and knights in shining armor when you were a boy?"

"I used to build models of castles and villages. But my therapist has explained where a lot of that comes from. My father was in and out of institutions for paranoid schizophrenia; when he was home, he used to beat us—myself and my mother. He hated me because I was puny and pale." Glen spoke dispassionately, in a detached voice.

Kathryn watched him intently. Glen's childhood seemed to account for a significant portion of his eccentricity.

"My father finally left us when I was ten years old. Walked out of the house for a pack of cigarettes and a quart of milk and never came back. He didn't even smoke. My therapist says that as a result, I developed a fierce drive to protect my mother."

Kathryn quietly sipped her cabernet, listening.

"It's hard for me to meet women I feel I can have a relationship with," Glen continued. "Because, frankly, it's difficult to find someone who could possibly hold a candle to my mother. I still live with her, so it's awkward for me to invite my dates home. They have to be a very understanding sort. I should like you to come home with me and meet my mother, my dear."

Kathryn heard herself saying "I should like that very much," although she wasn't at all sure whether she should. Then she added, "Not this evening, of course. I have a . . . houseguest."

"Perhaps you are right. We should take things slowly."

"There's no rush, is there?"

"No, mother will keep."

"Like you, Glen, I haven't had much luck with the dating scene lately. Actually, I was engaged until I broke it off several months ago."

"Do you want to be married?"

"Well, yes, eventually. That's why I'm not shying away from climbing back onto the horse, but Lance turned out to be as self-absorbed as I initially thought he was."

"Ahh. Lance. *Lancelot*. He really wasn't all that much of a good guy when you come down to it. Why didn't you trust your first instincts, then?"

"At that point, I was so thrilled that *anyone* wanted to marry me, that I saw what I wanted to see. I never thought I could change him. That's usually the biggest mistake we women tend to make—thinking we can change a man by, or after, marrying him. But that wasn't the mistake I made. I was just hoping against hope that there were more facets to Lance than self-absorption and blond highlights. When I found out there weren't, it was a good thing the invitations hadn't been engraved yet."

She finished the glass of wine. "And when it comes to instincts, I'm trying hard not to let my first impressions of people turn into a judgment. Because then I fear I'm not giving people a fair chance."

"And what do your instincts tell you about me?"

Kathryn debated whether or not to tell him the truth—that he was, well—weird. "Let's just say that you already appear to have more facets than Lance."

Glen reached over and took Kathryn's hand in his, then lifted it to his lips again. "Fair enough, fair lady. I should very much enjoy the pleasure of your company on another occasion. In the not-too-distant future, dare I hope? I should like you to come home with me to meet Mother."

Kathryn withdrew her hand, and placing it discreetly in her lap, wiped it with her napkin. "May I call you next week about a date? I need to look in my calendar, and I didn't bring it with me this evening." She knew she was stalling, but she wanted to give herself time to mull over the evening's events, and decide after a few days' hiatus, whether or not she wanted to see Glen again. She deliberately didn't ask for his number. If she did opt to phone him, she could always get it from his dossier at Six in the City . . . or ask Bear to bring it home to her. *Home. Bear.*

Kathryn realized how much she was looking forward to seeing him sprawled out on her sofa, remote firmly in hand. From the outset she'd resisted the idea of his staying with her, but now the arrangement was beginning to fill her with a sense of pleasurable anticipation. Particularly after spending an evening with the eccentric Mr. Pinsky, in the company of morbid artwork, the return home to Walker's comparative normalcy—however fraught the situation was with emotional pitfalls—was infinitely preferable. She would miss the big lug when he eventually moved back up to the penthouse.

Kathryn asked Glen to escort her to the Fifth Avenue bus stop and no farther. He kissed her hand yet again before she boarded the bus; and after Kathryn located a seat, she looked out the window only to see Glen dramatically placing his hand on his heart. Her radar wasn't up to its usual speed. Kathryn couldn't decide if his quirks were charming or just plain creepy. Too bad Eleanor hadn't gone along on the date. She'd always been better at winnowing out the weirdos.

Valerie kicked off her shoes and sank onto Kathryn's plush velvet sofa. "How about that drink, sugar," she asked, slipping slightly into a Southern drawl she hadn't used all evening.

Walker's ears pricked up at the change in Valerie's tone. He wasn't sure whether or not he liked it. He searched through Kathryn's bar and found two sherry glasses, somehow pleased that they weren't crystal—just ordinary glass. Less romantic. He congratulated himself on not knocking anything over. Finding a bottle of Harvey's Bristol Cream, he poured two fingers' worth for each of them, then turned to the sofa to hand Valerie her glass.

What he saw was a trail of clothes: the mustard-colored coatdress, a black lace demi-bra, the sheerest thigh-high nylons draped over one of the lace doilies on the arm of the sofa. He gasped. "Valerie! What the hell do you think you're doing?" He gazed down at the attorney, lying on Kathryn's carpet like a naked Maja, her abundant voluptuousness inviting him to join her.

She stretched out a lithe, pale arm, and beckoned to him with her manicured hand. "So what about that massage I've heard so much about?"

"I don't recall you hearing anything beyond my admission that I've given massages professionally."

"So sue me." She tugged on his leg, trying to bring him down to the floor with her.

Walker struggled to maintain his balance and his composure. "I can't give you a massage, Valerie. My table is upstairs, and it will take too long to bring it down here and set everything up. I'm just a houseguest here, and my friend should be back soon." He gazed at the attorney's spectacular body, and decided he should be awarded purple hearts, blue ribbons, and perhaps the Nobel Prize for Self-Restraint.

Valerie showed no signs of moving. "We can do it on the floor," she suggested seductively. "Just a quickie." She smiled that Ultra-Brite beauty queen smile. "I'm sure you've done *that* before."

Walker stood over her, still between the Devil and the deep blue sea. The attorney was not taking 'no' for an answer, and he made the decision that it would be quicker to get it over with and hustle her out the door, than to prolong his hesitation. "Well, all right, I'll just give your back a quick massage." He searched through Kathryn's linen closet for a flat sheet and brought it out to the living room. "Here, just let me place this on the rug. Roll over for a minute."

The curvaceous brunette complied, rearranging her body to afford Walker the most comprehensive view. Walker put the sheet down on the carpet and asked Valerie to roll back onto it and lie on her stomach. Then he folded the remainder of the sheet over her lower body.

"I'll be just a second," he said, as he loosened, then removed his tie, followed by his blue oxford cloth shirt. "I can't give a massage when I'm dressed like an executive," he said, heading into Kathryn's bathroom to hunt for some oil or lotion. He emerged, bare-chested, with a bottle of delicately scented Body Shop massage lotion.

"I'll be right with you," he advised Valerie uneasily.

"Take your time, honey," his date murmured huskily. "I'm the one who's got all night."

Walker hunted up a CD of relaxing, new-age music and put it on the stereo, then lowered the lights.

He knelt beside Valerie and tried to massage her while still on his knees alongside her body, but he couldn't get proper leverage, and the last thing he wanted to do was work her muscles incorrectly and risk injuring her. She wouldn't have to go far to sue him for malpractice. Against his better judgment, he straddled Valerie's relaxed, prone body, and started to feel for the tension in her upper back, as the matrimonial attorney seemed to melt into his strong hands.

"*Buenos noches,* Carlos," Kathryn said, when she entered her lobby.

"*Buenos noches, pobrecita,*" the doorman responded. Or at least that's what Kathryn thought she heard.

As she approached her door, she heard the strains of a

Windham Hill CD emanating from the stereo. And a couple of groans—or were they moans? She turned the key in the top lock and heard a gasp from the other side of the door. Then she turned the bottom lock and opened the door.

There, lying on the living room floor, was a poor man's Yasmine Bleeth, wearing nothing but Kathryn's damask-patterned bedsheet and a surprised expression. Above her stood Walker Hart, an unflattering shade of crimson spreading from his embarrassed face down his bare chest.

Chapter
18

"Out! Both of you." Kathryn was seething with rage, barely controlling the tears that were about to fall. There was little disguising the hurt and humiliation she felt at seeing her erstwhile roommate in the company of a primarily naked brunette, in *her* apartment, covered in nothing but *her* massage lotion—and *her* sheet, having had every pore and orifice no doubt lovingly tended to by the masterful fingers of Walker Hart. *Shame on me,* Kathryn thought bitterly, *for practically losing my heart to this undeserving son-of-a-bitch!*

Valerie struggled to find her clothes. Kathryn refused to allow the stranger the dignity of getting dressed in private. "Who told you that you could use my bathroom?" Kathryn snapped, as the attorney tried to scuttle in there with her pile of lingerie and coatdress pressed against her statuesque body.

Well, she's not much *better looking than I am,* Kathryn thought in the fleeting moment she allowed herself to compare the invader's body to her own. The brunette had a good six inches of height on her. So, she was leggier, but who cared—unless Walker was a leg man. The tart looked like a low-rent former beauty queen, with a cancer cabana tan and an expensive wardrobe.

"Valerie Adams—Kathryn Lamb," said Walker, in a futile attempt to make polite conversation. "Valerie is an attorney—doing some work for Six in the City—for my mother."

"And I'm sure you gave her all the Six she needed," Kathryn snapped. She picked up Walker's rumpled blue oxford cloth shirt from where it lay puddled on the floor near the corner of the couch. It was still warm. "Out! Both of you—now!" She tried to deliberately rip the shirt. If she couldn't rip Walker's face off, this was the closest she was going to get; but thanks to Ralph Lauren, the fabric refused to give and her moment of melodrama was destroyed.

Walker's companion composed herself as she dressed, albeit with most of her dignity stripped away. A quick shpritz of Ysatis behind each ear, and a third one in her ample cleavage, and the lawyer was ready to depart.

"Call me, sugar," Valerie drawled, bestowing one of those Miss America vaseline-on-the-teeth smiles on Walker, who was trying to remain aloof. Valerie's voice dripped molasses. "We still have some unfinished business. I haven't yet had the chance to thoroughly go over your briefs." She extended her hand to Walker and they exchanged a firm handshake. Then she turned the Southern charm school smile on Kathryn. "You have a good evening," she said, with no trace of a honeyed drawl.

"You're going with her," Kathryn said firmly to Walker, after Valerie had closed the apartment door behind her. She attempted to steer his massive frame toward the door, but he planted his feet.

"Not until we talk through this thing."

"Mr. Hart, there is nothing to talk about. You make me sick. Against my better judgment, I allowed you to stay in my apartment while your roof is being repaired. You make yourself comfortable on my furniture, eat my food, consume my booze, get in my way when I'm getting ready for dates that *you* have set up for me—good GOD! You even crash on my bed, and *sleep* beside me, and tell me how much you want to make love to me— and you have the gall—the audacity—the temerity—to *abuse* everything I have done for you—my space, my *trust*, damnit!" Kathryn flung the blue shirt at Walker, fighting the tears.

He tried to smooth out the wrinkles, sniffed the collar.

"Looking for *her* scent?" Kathryn spat. "Go! Get out! I have nothing else to say to you, unless it's of a professional nature. You owe me two more dates after Glen Pinsky, for a total of six match-ups, since your fix-up with Eddie Benson nearly got me killed. I don't know how many guys looking to settle down are expecting to spend their golden years with a woman who was picked up for soliciting in Hell's Kitchen."

"Can I get a word in edgewise?" Walker asked evenly.

"No. You don't deserve to. What could *possibly* be your excuse for what you did tonight? I feel *violated*, for Chrissakes."

"I didn't think . . ."

"Damn straight, buckaroo. You didn't think."

"I didn't think you'd be home from your date as early as you were."

"So that gives you the right to get laid in *my* apartment, using *my* furniture, *my* music, *my* linens, *my* liquor? You're a piece of work, Walker Hart."

"It was just a massage. In my defense, I wasn't planning to get laid. Besides, you want to find a man to marry, right? And if I recall correctly, since we don't share the same goal, you opted out of getting involved with me for that very reason. That's how this whole thing started."

Kathryn grabbed one of the sherry glasses and took a large swig. It burned her throat. Her fingers were itching to hurl the glass at him, but she would have had to clean up the mess herself. "Now it's *my* fault that you brought that woman here? Is it my fault, too, that I had the lousy timing to walk in on you at a critical moment in the development of your friendship? And don't change the goddamn subject! What whole thing?"

"You and I, Kitty. Us. If we had decided to . . . you know . . . I never would have invited Valerie back to the apartment. But *you* were out on a fix-up with Glen, so—"

"Walker. There *is* no 'us.' And don't you *ever* call me 'Kitty' again! This is *my* apartment, not 'the' apartment. *I* live here. Not you. Not *us*. You are a guest here. Or rather, you were. It's over. You abused your privileges. Now, go." *God, I sound like my mother,* Kathryn thought.

Walker revisited his defense. "You want to get married. That's why you came to Six in the City. Therefore, what *you* do with *your* social life is *my* business, because it is literally my job to find you a husband. I don't want to get married. What *I* do with my social life is my business. I am a professional acquaintance of yours who became a friend."

"You sound like a lawyer. And, buster, you made your social life my business when you brought that 'ho' into

my home. You and your goddamn slutty attorney goddamn deserve each other. *Friends* don't take over other
friends' beds and tell them they want to make love."

"I should hope they do." Walker smiled.

How could he smile at a time like this? What was the
man's problem? "Are you deliberately choosing to be ob-
tuse?" Kathryn challenged. "Bringing your tramp back
to my apartment was wrong. There's no other way
around it. You want to get laid, I don't want to know
about it. Rent a room, for Chrissakes! I don't deserve
what you did to me."

She threw the bedsheet that he and Valerie had used
for the aborted massage. Walker caught it over his arm.

"Wash it," Kathryn said in a low voice. "Now. The
laundry room is open 'til eleven. Or burn that and buy
me a new sheet. Of the same quality. It's a hundred percent cotton, two hundred and fifty threads to the inch.
And when you're finished with the dryer, bring this back
to me, folded neatly. Then get the rest of your stuff and
go back upstairs to your own apartment."

"But the ceiling—"

"I don't care if New York's bravest find your lifeless
body covered in wet plaster tomorrow morning." Kathryn glared at Walker, seething with rage and hatred.

Walker perched his large physique on the arm of the
velvet sofa. "Does this tirade mean you love me?" he
asked quietly.

"What?!"

"If you didn't care about me, you wouldn't be this
upset." He reached out his arms to her, but Kathryn held
her ground on the opposite side of the room. "I'm truly
sorry, honey," he continued. "What I did was really
stupid. I *wasn't* thinking, honestly."

" 'Honey,' " she practically spat. Kathryn waved her hand at him dismissively.

"No. Don't cut me off, Kathryn. It was a thousand percent wrong to bring a woman back here. My brain switched off. I admit it."

"Look, Bear. It isn't that easy. I don't forgive you. I don't want your excuses or lame reasons why you had to rip a strange woman's clothes off on my living room floor."

Walker reached for the other sherry glass and took a sip of the Harvey's. He was trying to appear calm, but he desperately needed the drink, and holding the glass kept his hands still, the better to conceal his anxiety. "What I didn't realize until now—what I didn't see—and I'm going to say this, and then I'll leave—is—based upon the intensity of your reaction to seeing me with Valerie—that you love me . . ." *There, I've said it,* he thought to himself. He was pretty sure he was right, but he still had a knot in his intestines. And he was too chicken to admit to Kathryn that he felt exactly the same way about her. What if she rejected him outright? Better that she acknowledge that she did love him but still refuse to be his lover, than to destroy his theory—and his hopes.

"What you didn't *see?*" Kathryn retorted. "You're myopic. You're seemingly oblivious to your own insensitivity. And I trusted you. You need glasses, buddy, if you can't see what's been going on here. And don't you *dare* put words in my mouth."

"If I had thought that there was more here than mere friendship, I guess what I'm saying is that I wouldn't have brought Valerie back at all."

"I suppose that passionate kiss in the produce aisle the other night was just a friendly gesture on your part as well. You said you thought I 'needed it,' so I guess it was a part of the Walker Hart Community Service Program for Pathetic Redheads." When he didn't respond, Kathryn altered her tack. "I'm going on dates, remember?" she said, trying to keep her voice from betraying her true emotions. "If I were in love with you, then I wouldn't be scouring the city looking for a wonderful, kind, considerate, smart, funny, handsome man to marry."

"Which reminds me," Walker replied. "How was your date with Glen Pinsky?"

Kathryn resented his change of subject, but she was tired of going in circles with him. What was she going to say in response to Walker's statement that she loved him? *Yes, I do, you moron, but you're not remotely interested in the one thing I want more than anything, so I have no choice but to look elsewhere.* If he didn't understand at least the second part of the equation, he was truly denser than she thought him capable of being.

"Glen is a very interesting man," Kathryn said flatly.

"Ohh." Walker reflexively stroked his jaw. He was waiting for Kathryn to elaborate.

"He seems gentle . . . well-read, certainly. We'll see where it goes."

Walker felt a pang of jealousy. He had met Glen, of course, made the bachelor's videotape, and was well acquainted with his file. In fact, he'd re-reviewed its entire contents when Kathryn told him that Glen would be one of her bachelors. What did that undernourished, pale-faced pipsqueak have that *he* didn't?

"Goes?" Walker swallowed, and Kathryn detected his anxiety. "So does that mean you're having a second date?"

"I suppose so." Kathryn smiled like a cat with a bowl

of fresh cream. How else could she torture Walker? "I don't see why not. Perhaps catch a concert, or a movie. He wants to take me home to meet his mother."

Walker's expression changed, his eyes widening, his jaw slacking a bit.

"Well, I know it's a bit odd that the man is probably forty years old and still lives with his mother, but have you seen an English teacher's salary lately?"

Walker frowned.

"What's the matter, Bear? Can't take it that I actually got a nibble, a shot at grabbing the brass ring? On the fourth try, I've gotten past the first date. You should be happy that you may score another successful match."

"Glen told you he lives with his mother?"

"I think so. I mean, he kept talking about how he wanted to take me home to meet her."

"You never saw Glen's videotape, did you?"

"No, I never got the chance. When he phoned and said he was an English teacher and we seemed to have so much in common, I figured I'd found out enough from our telephone conversation. I didn't feel the need to rush over to your office and watch the videotape."

"So you never saw his file, either?"

"You're talking about the papers we filled out when we came in to register, right?"

"Those are the ones. So, Glen said to you that he lives with his mother. Present tense. Lives."

"Yeah, he did. I think. Where are you going with this, Walker? You're beginning to make my skin crawl."

"Glen Pinsky's mother has been dead for six years."

Kathryn felt a wave of nausea run from her throat down to the pit of her stomach and back up again. She lurched forward and ran into the bathroom.

"It's right in his file. I just re-read it on Tuesday. Because I knew he had called you. Kitty?" Walker tentatively stepped toward the bathroom, but Kathryn, who was kneeling in front of the toilet like it was an altar, pushed the door toward him, trying to close it in his face.

Walker spoke softly. "Kitty? Let me in."

"You're not allowed to call me that anymore." She retched, then collapsed onto her bottom, embracing the cool porcelain base of the bowl. Her voice was a stunned whine. "You set me up with Norman fucking Bates!" With great effort, Kathryn pulled herself to her feet, opened her medicine cabinet, let out another pained wail, then sunk back down to the floor.

Walker gently knocked on the closed door. "What's the matter? Is there anything I can do? Besides change that light bulb over the sink?"

"No aspirin and my head is going to explode," came the muffled voice from the other side.

"My mother takes that holistic homeopathic crap and I never get headaches, so I doubt there's any upstairs, but I'll make a deli run and pick some up for you." Kathryn was silent. "Kitty? Is that okay? I'll go get you some aspirin right away. Anything else you need?" he asked with genuine concern.

"No, Bear. I wanna die."

It seemed like an eternity had come and gone between the time Walker left the apartment and when he returned only fifteen minutes later.

Walker gently opened the bathroom door and found Kathryn curled up in the fetal position on the mint green throw rug. "Sorry," he said when she looked up at him expectantly. "I had to buy *these* to get the aspirin." He withdrew a bouquet of snapdragons from behind his back, and fished for the small packet of aspirin in his pocket. "I got a larger bottle, too. Just in case."

Walker's gesture bowled her over, especially since, to the best of her recollection, she'd mentioned her favorite flower to him only once before, and they were in the middle of a fight at the time. What made the act seem so incredible was that not only had he apparently been *listening* to her at the time, but he had actually *heard* her, processed the information, stored it up for future retrieval, and recalled it at a crucial moment. In Kathryn's experience with men, where whatever she said to them always seemed to go in one ear and out the other, this was a legitimate first. If she hadn't been in love with Walker five minutes ago, that little stunt just did the trick.

"Bear . . . that is just about the sweetest thing . . . that's really adorable."

Walker knelt and kissed her forehead. "You looked like you needed something to cheer you up a bit. You deserve more than snapdragons but it was the best I could do right now."

"Well, it worked like gangbusters, you son-of-a-bitch."

"Hey, I thought we'd stop abusing my mother for a while, okay?"

"How can I stay mad at you when you remembered my favorite flowers?" Kathryn groaned.

Talking a washcloth from her towel bar, Walker soaked it in cold water, then sat by Kathryn's side and applied the cold, wet cloth to her forehead and temples. She stretched out her arms, and pressed the pulse points on her wrists against the cold tile floor.

"One of us isn't very good at this," Kathryn whim-pered weakly. "This mating-dating game. This is sup-posed to be your job—at least for the time being—and you set me up with a rock musician who's just looking to shag an American chick and get his green card; a laconic vice squad detective, who—if I could get past his lack of conversational ability and the flying bullets, and over-look my false arrest while in his company—might truly have been a swell guy; a movie star who was using your dating service as research for his next flick—never mind that we are women and not experiments—and now . . . you fix me up with the lovely and talented Glen Pinsky who wants me to meet his mother—who it turns out is no longer on this plane of existence. Thank God, Glen didn't invite me to take a shower at his place!"

Walker reached over to stroke her hair, but this time Kathryn brushed him away. "You've got a great track record, Walker Hart. How much did your mother pay you to run her business into the ground, and are you as suc-cessful with the rest of your clientele as you are with me?"

"I'm very good at what I do," he said somewhat de-fensively. But it sounded hollow. He was not especially happy to be running his mother's business. He was doing it as a favor and couldn't wait for her to reclaim it.

While Kathryn lay more or less inert on the bathroom floor, Walker thought about why he was consistently screwing up Kathryn Lamb's fix-ups. He scrolled through his mind, trying to recall if there had been other clients to whom he had felt something of an attraction. A few names popped into his head, but there hadn't been any-thing like the instant chemical reaction that he'd felt when Kitty had entered his world.

Where the rest of his life was concerned, he was one of the most celebrated businessmen on the planet. Since he had temporarily taken over the management of Six in the City, he had scored on average, one match a month that led to the altar. Not a bad track record, he thought. But with Kathryn he'd let his own curiosity about what it would be like to be with her get in the way of his ability to perform the services for which she had trustingly engaged him. She was right: he didn't want what she wanted—yet he wanted *her*. And that wasn't fair to either of them.

What was he doing to himself, and to her, by letting his desire for an involvement get in the way of everything? Rationally, he knew he couldn't keep her for himself. As much as he wanted to stroke her crazy coppery curls and soothe her fears—and make love to her until they lost their minds—even Kathryn could not drag him before a clergyman or judge to say those dreaded "I do's."

Yet, here he was, sabotaging her chances of happiness. Personal jealousy and professional obligation warred side by side in his brain. He'd have to do better by her, because Kathryn deserved everything she'd ever desired, and then some. Besides, she was paying for it. Literally. Including an additional bachelor to compensate for Kitty's disastrous date with Eddie Benson, Walker had two more tries in which to succeed in finding her a husband. And he would. Then he could add Kathryn Lamb to the list of successful matches achieved by Six in the City.

Oh, goody.

The notion sickened him. He reached down to stroke her unruly auburn curls again. This time, she didn't stop his caress, but she didn't appear to welcome it either. He gently kissed her cheek and left the room.

* * *

Kathryn didn't know how long she'd been lying on the cold bathroom floor, with the small throw rug under her belly. Had she drifted off to sleep for a moment, following her argument with Walker? She'd had only the one glass of cabernet, but the room was now spinning and suddenly she was cold. She shivered and tried to put her jumbled thoughts in order.

Maybe I've been trying too hard. Maybe I'm not giving things enough time. Maybe I'm trying to force square pegs into round holes. She wasn't even exactly sure what she meant, but her myriad thoughts were converging. The hunk was right, damn his myopic eyes. She *did* love Walker Hart, although his behavior this evening was reprehensible, unconscionable, and insensitive. She had allowed him in her bed, to the extent that she hadn't kicked him out that night she'd banished him to her boudoir. Her body, if not her mind, welcomed his physical advances. *Yes*, she wanted to make love with him—desperately— and she had told herself—and him—that she would not do so, for fear he would then break her heart.

Too late. It had happened already, and she'd been given no warning. If she'd known the consequences would end up the same after all, she wouldn't have said 'no' to sleeping with the man! At least she would have gotten to do the fun part, so she'd have some good sex and great memories to go along with the suffering and the pain.

Kathryn had always ridiculed women who had the single-minded determination to get married, leaving perfectly wonderful prospects in the dust, just because those men weren't ready or prepared to make the same commitment. Yet, here she was, doing the same thing for which she'd mocked others. Would it really be so bad to give Walker a chance—in a dating situation, and see if they really had something there—a relationship?

I can't believe *I'm considering this, after his assholic behavior this evening.* With a great effort, Kathryn lifted her head from the floor, her cheek missing the coolness of the tile when she removed it from the hard surface.

"Okay. I'll do it," she groaned. "Forget this marriage thing for a while, Bear. I'm willing to try it your way. You're right. I fell in love with you. So, let's go on a date. Just you and me. Start over again from the top. Take two." Her voice became soft, and she mumbled the words as though resigning herself to her fate.

But Walker had already gone out the door. And all she heard in response to her proposal, was the faint melodic tinkle of her grandmother's wind chimes.

Chapter
19

Walker was fishing in his pocket for his keys when he noticed that something was wrong with the door to the penthouse. It was ajar. He was sure he'd locked it, or at least closed it after he'd last been up there, working out his aggressions—and his frustrated passions—on the baby grand.

"Carlos, is that you?" a voice called from inside. "Oh, good. Someone to help me with my luggage!" The all-too-familiar cadences and the omnipresent smoker's cough made him cringe. He pushed open the door to the accompaniment of a jangling cowbell.

"You like that? I got it in the duty-free. They make them right in Dafydd's hometown. It's the sweetest little village—looks like something right out of Dylan Thomas—with a completely unpronounceable name. I kept telling Dafydd they should 'buy a vowel,' but he didn't know what I was talking about. I guess they don't have *Wheel of Fortune* over in Wales." Rushie, wearing little else but control top panty hose, mules, a pink wonderbra, and a pearl choker and earrings, prattled on without missing a beat or pausing to acknowledge the presence of her son.

"Speaking of which," Walker said edgily. "Where is Daffy Daddy Duck?"

"Dafydd Glendower," corrected the former Mrs. G. "I imagine he went back to the salt mines. Or the coal mines. Ya know—and this is an important lesson in our business—you should never base an entire relationship upon a common medical condition." She took another puff of her pastel-wrapped cigarillo and hacked a little.

"Such as what?" Walker found himself asking, despite his better judgment.

"What else? A cough! But let me tell you, that adorable accent aside, a chain smoker and a coal miner do not eternal happiness ensure."

"So . . . let me guess, Rushie. You're divorced now? How many is it? Eight?"

"At my age, who's counting?" Rushie tossed her son a plushy brown teddy bear dressed in a hand-knitted sweater decorated with the Welsh red lion. "Long story short, things didn't go so well, but the archbishop of Canterbury is a very nice man. We traded baking tips. That's for you, by the way," she added, indicating the toy bear. "In case you're lonely at night. A mother knows these things."

"Whaat?"

"She *intuits*."

"I meant what is this about you and the archbishop of Canterbury playing Martha Stewart?"

"He annulled my marriage, sweetheart. It was all very civil. Or very religious, I suppose. Dafydd and I signed a few papers, His Grace waved that pretty Little Bo-Peep thing and then I told him why his babka isn't coming out of the pan as easily as it should."

"The archbishop of Canterbury eats babka?" Walker couldn't believe he was having this conversation.

"No, of course not. He has to watch his cholesterol and his sugar intake. He serves it to his guests."

Walker needed something alcoholic, big-time. He headed for the refrigerator, climbing over his mother's suitcase. It looked like a bedouin trader's caravan had exploded.

"Yes, there's food in there. You're shocked?" Rushie asked. "That's what they're for. Even a bachelor should keep more than Dom Perignon in the fridge. You never know when someone might want a little nosh, a snack. You had nothing to eat in there. So I picked up a few things. Did you know they have the cutest shop now, over on Bleecker Street? Right next door to the place that sells all those crystal balls and massage oils. It's called Faux Paws. It's darling. They have those fake fur coats that look like a teddy bear died to make them, and just about any garment imaginable in fake snake or leopard spots. It's nice to know that the leopard look is still so timeless," she rattled on, "because I still have my Diane von Furstenberg animal print wrap-dress from the 1980's. Now they call it 'vintage.' Vintage-shmintage. I call it 'old.' By the way, how much did that fancy-shmancy decorator charge us for those?" she asked, pointing a freshly manicured hand at the fourteen-inch cheetah print toss pillows. "They have them at Faux Paws for $39.99 apiece on sale, and I could swear you wouldn't know the difference between these and theirs."

His mother's incessant chatter, entertaining though it was—how did he *ever* manage to miss that Faux emporium she was talking about—was giving him the beginning of a headache. And how did she have the chance to

come home, unpack most of her luggage, and stock a refrigerator in the time it took him to have a dinner date,
Walker wondered. Not only that, the kitchen smelled
like breakfast. Walker retrieved a can of cold beer and returned to the living room popping the top.

Rushie emitted a disapproving moan. "Drink light
beer. You've got the makings of a spare tire there and no
woman wants a man who's high maintenance. You
know, after a certain age, it's much harder to lose the
extra weight."

"I'll drink what I like, *Mom*. And what the hell are
you eating?"

"A cold matzoh brei sandwich. My favorite. How
could you forget?"

"I've worked hard at it. Who else has a mother who
eats sandwiches made from the Jewish equivalent of
cardboard and scrambled eggs? That bun you put the
matzoh brei on looks like a Parker House roll."

"It is." She took another bite of the sandwich. "Speaking of which. It's a good thing you've got a mother with
her nose to the ground." Another bite.

"Yeah, like a truffle hound," Walker muttered under
his breath.

"How was your date with the long-legged shiksa
attorney?"

He shuddered. "She's a barracuda."

"The law is a tough profession for a woman," his
mother countered. "A girl has to be twice as sharp to get
taken half as seriously."

"She's a *Southern* barracuda," Walker added, upping
the stakes.

"So? Every other woman will now look good to you
by comparison."

"What the hell kind of logic is that?"

Rushie surveyed her teeth in her compact for signs of a wayward bit of herb. "It's my trademark 'match-ramonial' psychology." She waved her arm around the living room and seemed to notice for the first time that the apartment was in a shambles.

"This place looks like an ice house. What's with the roof?"

"I told you, Ma, it's been leaking on and off since before you bought the place. Probably since the days of the flood. But you were too busy jetting off to Biarritz or Cardiff or wherever to either notice or care. You always assume that someone else will take care of your messes."

"A nice tone for a son to take. I can't stay here, anyway. I've taken a room at the St. Regis. I just love the King Cole Bar there."

"So what did you come home for, then? Surely not to eat a cold matzoh brei sandwich for old times' sake."

"You think your mother doesn't care about you but she does," Rushie countered. "So, have you met the little redhead yet?" she continued, retrieving an unopened box of Loving Care from her suitcase. "You like this color? It's called 'Pumpkin Pie.' I thought it was very *autumnal*," she added, noticing an unsightly chip on one of her fuchsia lacquered toenails.

The woman could switch gears like a Formula One.

"You know the girl I'm talking about," Rushie said before her son could furnish an answer to either the red-head or the hair dye question. "I sent her to the agency. The redhead. Cute little thing. Lives on the ninth floor."

"Kathryn Lamb." Walker sighed, uncertain where this conversation was going. "Yes, I met her. Not only have I met her, but she's a client."

"Terrific!" Rushie said with the zeal of Dr. Ruth. "She's such a nice girl. A bubbly personality, a cute little figure, all those curls. You just want to give her a good squeeze. And she always seems so lonely. Whenever I see her in the elevator, she has nothing to say about herself. I find myself doing all the talking."

For the briefest of moments, Walker considered sharing everything he knew so far about Kitty Lamb, but thought better of it. Especially given Kathryn's opinion of Rushie. The more his mother stayed away from his personal life, the better chance it stood of remaining his own.

He walked out onto the wraparound terrace for some fresh night air. He needed to escape. Escape Rushie and her endless rattling on. Escape her choking clouds of coral-colored smoke. Escape his current itinerant lifestyle. Escape the business he could barely stand, that he was just keeping warm for his mother. Escape his conflicting feelings for Kathryn Lamb. Escape. He was turning into everything he derided. Escape? Who was it who always ran away from any situation that threatened to be in any way difficult or problematic? Oh, God. He was turning into his mother.

"What the hell time is it?" Kathryn felt like she'd been startled from the sleep of the dead and it took her a few moments to place the source of the reveille. Her doorbell was ringing away, the buzzer gone berserk. Tito hadn't rung up on the intercom to announce a visitor. So, whoever it was must live in the building. It was all too much information to process after a night out with a character out of Edgar Allan Poe and a fight with Walker over sluts and territory . . . and snapdragons! She headed off to brush her teeth and found the bouquet, still wrapped in paper from the Korean deli, on the bathroom floor where she had left it last night. Kathryn let the doorbell chime away and performed her morning ablutions.

"Shut up, already!" she yelled at the closed apartment door. She ran her tongue over her freshly Crest-ed upper teeth. "Bear, if your ceiling caved in and you found yourself sleeping under the open sky, and now you want to come crawling back to me, you're confusing me with someone who cares. So stop giving me a migraine!"

"Kitty, it's *me*," Eleanor yelled from the hallway.

Kathryn undid the chain locks and opened the door. Her younger sister's eyes were swollen and red from crying.

"Oh, my God. What's the matter? Are you okay?"

Eleanor headed straight for the living room, tossed her purse on the velvet sofa and seated herself in the middle of the couch, her feet squarely planted on the floor. That was a key difference between the two of them, Kathryn silently observed. If *she* looked like she'd been crying all night, she would have flung herself into a little ball in the *corner* of the sofa instead.

"I left Johanna with Mommy and Daddy. And I left Dan. For the moment, anyway."

Kathryn looked at her sister incredulously. "You left Dan?"

"I mean, I just left Dan. Don't ever get married."

A stunned silence was all Kathryn could manage. Clearly, Eleanor needed to vent.

"Maybe I should have trusted my first instincts. When we first met, Dan and I took things so slowly at first that I thought I was going backwards. When he first asked me out, I wasn't even sure I thought he was attractive. In fact, I couldn't imagine kissing him. It's not that he grossed me out, or anything. It's just that there weren't exactly bells and whistles. And during the entire length of our first few dates, I kept wondering whether I was dating him just to prove to Mommy and Daddy that I could marry a doctor."

"Well," Kathryn sighed. "I wouldn't look to Mommy and Daddy's marriage as a fine example of wedded bliss."

"Kitty, they've been together for nearly forty years!"

"They have nothing to say to each other!"

"That's *why* they've been together for forty years."

"Be serious," Kathryn said, wrinkling her nose. "They married only half a year after they met; and for five of those months of courtship, they lived across the continent from each other. And, if you dare to risk revisiting our childhood, El, we grew up in a household without much affection. You used to make a run for the camera every anniversary, when Mommy and Daddy actually kissed each other. They've reached some sort of marital stalemate over the decades. And they'll never get divorced because neither one ever had any practice—or knows how—to live alone. So Mommy reads her crime novels while Daddy disappears into simultaneous NFL games. Hell, they don't even discuss the nightly news with one another."

"I read this in *Newsweek*," Eleanor added. "Some psychologist was saying that younger generations are either doomed somehow to repeat the mistakes of their predecessors, or deliberately choose to rebel against their parents' behavior."

Kathryn nodded her head in agreement. "That's what Bear did. He says he's never seen a happy marriage, so he decided to never enter the matrimonial state himself, even under a warrant. I'm the opposite, I suppose. I may never have seen what I consider a happy marriage, while we were kids growing up, but I'm totally convinced that they do exist. Until five minutes ago, I thought you and Dan were living proof of that."

Eleanor gave Kathryn a leveling glance. "I'm here to admit that it's not a twenty-four-hour-a-day picnic, especially when you've got kids. But I hear tell that it *is* possible to have frequent and intelligent conversations with one's husband, and to share common activities and adventures. Just not with *my* husband." She drew a deep breath. "I look at you now, Kitty, and I . . . Actually, I've been thinking about this for the past few days and didn't know whether or how to say anything to you, and then the shit hit the fan at home . . . Look. I see you turning into me and I don't like it."

"What do you mean?"

"You're desperate to get married, like I was. And you could make a mistake. Like I did."

"Whoa!" Kathryn was flabbergasted. "I understand that you guys are fighting right now, but I thought you two had the perfect marriage. It always seemed to me that you two had it all: career, kids, great home—"

"I don't have a career anymore, remember?" Eleanor said, her tone acidic. "I *used to* have a terrific job, on the fast track to wherever I wanted to go, basically, but I bowed to peer pressure. All the thirty-somethings around me were so frazzled and freaked out that they weren't married with kids yet, and that they had to hurry up before their uterine walls shriveled up like dried apricots. I fell along in step and the next thing I knew, I was falling—"

"With a golden parachute," Kathryn interjected.

"Yeah, with a golden parachute, but it couldn't buy me a clue as to what I was doing or why I was really doing it. Dan was proud of the fact that he made enough money so that his wife didn't have to return to her job. And while I was pregnant with Johanna, I thought to myself that I could work from home, maybe even go back to some of my old marketing ideas and see if I could get them off the ground. I've been kicking that notion around for years now and never did anything with it. So, lately, I've revisited Brownie Points and have been putting a lot of time into making the project viable. The prototypes are finally working and I took some samples around the neighborhood. And now there's a specialty store that wants to buy them. One of those gourmet shops that has its own bakery."

"Buy the idea from you or buy the Brownie Points from you?" Kathryn asked.

"We're trying to figure out which makes more sense now. If they buy the concept and the recipe from me, there are legal issues that we haven't covered yet. It may make more sense for the time being for them to buy the actual baked Brownie Points, which also turns my kitchen into a factory—and that isn't exactly what I bargained for either."

"So how does Dan figure into all of this?"

"He doesn't. But he wants to. His point of view is that I can afford not to work; I should stay home and take care of Johanna and the one on the way . . . take care of my health." She rubbed her growing belly.

Kathryn furrowed her brow. "That's noble, I suppose."

"Noble, but selfish, too. When you think about it. You can choose to see his opinion as either chivalric or Cro-Magnon. We just had this huge fight. It's all about *him*.

Instead of being thrilled for my success, he says I'm *emasculating* him by wanting to return to work. It makes him feel . . . I don't know . . . to be the sole breadwinner."

"Isn't there room for compromise here? He can win the bread and let you make the brownies."

"That's not as funny as you think it is, Kitty. It's more than his feeling threatened that in a perfect world I could be the next Mrs. Fields. Dan just doesn't get it that I'm going stir crazy wandering around nine rooms high above Park Avenue with no one but a two-year-old for company most of the day." Eleanor emitted a sigh comprised of one part frustration and three parts exasperation. "*Dan's* not home. *He's* always out. There's always some emergency tummy tuck or eye lift or liposuction he has to go perform."

"And what did he say to that?"

"He said 'where do you think we get the money for our lifestyle?' " Eleanor intoned, goofily mimicking her husband's voice.

"So, Dan wouldn't even discuss it with you like an adult?"

The tension still hadn't left Eleanor's voice. " 'What's to discuss,' he said. He actually chalked up my cabin fever to pregnancy hormones! That's when I accused him of having no bedside manner. I also reminded him that the fact that I once made a respectable income didn't seem to emasculate him when we were dating. Can I have a cup of tea?"

"Maybe you need a hug first." Kathryn reached over and held her younger sister. "Jeez. And I always thought you had it all together." She stroked Eleanor's hair.

Feeling safe, Eleanor finally broke down. "I need time to figure things out," she confessed in a choked voice. "I mean, is this symptomatic of everything that's going on in my marriage? Is it in trouble for real?"

Kathryn kissed her sister on the forehead. "You'll be able to work it out," she soothed.

"When did I lose control?" Eleanor sobbed into Kathryn's velvet tunic.

"Look. I'm not an expert on relationships—obviously—but maybe this isn't the beginning of the end. Maybe, in some sick, twisted, codependent way, the fight with Dan was what you both needed to get a lot of stuff out in the open so you can move on to a healthier place in your marriage. Where you feel more like equal partners."

"In the meantime . . . oh, I forgot to even ask—is Walker still here?"

"He was asked to hit the road last night, as a matter of fact."

"Then if it's not too much trouble, can I stay here for a while? I'm too pissed off at Dan to go back home right now. I sent Johanna's overnight bag to the parental unit, so she's got a few changes of clothes. She'll be thrilled to stay with Nana and Abba for a bit. She's such a smart kid. 'Mommy's having a meltdown,' she said when we were going down in the elevator."

Kathryn shook her head.

"Was that a 'no'?" Eleanor asked, worried.

"No, it was an 'I can't believe what a messed-up past twelve hours it's been.' Yeah, of course you can stay here," Kathryn said, giving her sister a brief shoulder massage. She smoothed her hand over Eleanor's hair and moved toward the kitchen. "Now, I'll make you that cup of tea you asked for."

*   *   *

"You blew it, bro. Big-time." Josh lifted the plastic tarp from Rushie's couch. "Jesus. Kathryn's right. This *is* a boring piece of furniture. I feel like I'm committing some sort of sacrilege here by removing the Saran Wrap. I hope your mother won't be pissed, but this is offending my aesthetic sensibilities."

Walker looked glum, wiggling his toes inside his white sweat socks, his feet propped up on an uncovered corner of the glass and chrome coffee table. "Rushie's got her mind on another form of prophylactic at the moment. She's on a date."

"Talk about getting back on the horse, Bear."

"She's terrified of being alone."

"And you?" Josh cracked open a bottle of Rolling Rock, and looked for a place to deposit the bottle top. "Face it. You're acting like a schmuck! It doesn't take Freud to figure out that you, 'Mr. Loner,' deliberately create situations that will ensure your solitary state. You're a self-fulfilling prophecy. Maybe your mother had something in mind when she took off with Ludovic and left you minding the store."

"You mean apart from maternal and professional irresponsibility?"

"No, bro. Maybe she wanted you to gain some first-hand knowledge of all the work it really takes to make a relationship happen in the first place, and then, to maintain it. Maybe she had a clairvoyant feeling that you would meet a nice girl and fall in love, and want to settle down after all."

"My mother doesn't think in coherent thought patterns, Josh. She's very European in that 'if it feels good do it' kind of way. And forgive me for being dense, but how did we get from Rushie's screwed-up love life to my own?"

"You're kidding, right?"

Walker held out his hand for Josh's trash, and took the crumpled metal cap into the kitchen. "Maybe I've let this thing get way out of hand."

"Bear, I have no idea what went through your brain when you brought a chick you want to bang to the apartment of the woman who, out of the goodness of her heart, and against her better judgment, was giving you a place to crash while your ceiling was being repaired. Kathryn's your client, Bear. And you broke that doctor-patient kind of trust with her. Big-time. Face it. You made a big-ass mistake and you've got to fix it. My advice to you is to keep everything on a strictly professional level for a while."

Walker nodded, trying to convince himself to agree with Josh's suggestion. "Six in the City owes her two more matches."

"So really pull the stops out for her. And if those two don't work out, your contract with her is over, so take it from there."

"There's only one thing that concerns me, Josh. What if she marries one of them?"

"What do you care?" Josh asked provocatively. "You don't want to marry anyone anyway. You'll have another name on the company's success roster." He took a long swallow of beer, and looked at the bottle, chipping at the label with his fingernail before turning to his friend. "Moron." He shook his head.

It seemed like a long time before Walker replied. "Okay . . . Mr. Reverse Psychology. I admit it. I *do* care about Kitty. I messed up big-time and I want to make it up to her . . . and I think I know how to begin." He beamed. It was as though a lightbulb had just gone on above his head. "I'm a man with a plan. Josh, in your grand and glorious experience as a gallery owner and art dealer, do you know how to find any Renaissance Faire-type craftspeople? I need to track down a very unusual *objet d'art.*"

Chapter
20

Bob Barton had knocked so gently on the door to Kathryn's classroom that she wasn't even aware of the principal's presence until he poked his head inside the room. "Can I see you a minute, Ms. Lamb?"

Kathryn excused herself from her ninth graders to speak with Barton in the doorway.

"You've got a . . . visitor," he told her in his customary dull intonation.

"It's kind of a bad time," Kathryn replied. She lowered her voice a notch or two. "I've just started a class and this is sort of, well . . . 'short attention-span-theater,' if you follow me."

Barton didn't. He made a loud throat clearing gesture.

"Can whoever it is wait for forty-five minutes?"

Then she heard the unmistakable squeals of adolescent girls in lust.

"I don't think so . . ." Barton countered blandly. "You see—" He made a "come here" gesture with his hand that was about as frantic a movement as Kathryn had ever seen Briarcliff's principal make, even since her own student days when Jordan O'Keeffe admitted to bestowing the school's clerical staff with a batch of home-made—

and hash-spiked—brownies. "I think you'll want to see this person."

Kathryn noticed a crush of students forming behind the principal's back. She opened the classroom door and the source of the excitement elbowed his way into the room. Kathryn's drama class issued a collective gasp that it would have taken weeks to choreograph to such perfection. When she heard a thudding sound, Kathryn could have sworn that one of her freshmen had actually swooned.

"Ohmigod, it's *him*," Lisette Mars breathed, stupified.

"You certainly know how to make an entrance," Kathryn stammered, trying to maintain her poise. Had she succeeded in convincing Barton in the previous millisecond that she had planned this little interruption all along? Probably not.

Rick Byron entered the classroom, a calculated blend of modesty and cockiness in tight black jeans, a black designer T-shirt and an Armani sport coat. He looked like a Barney's ad. Just inside the door, he gave Kathryn a squeeze and a kiss on the cheek that made a 'mwanh' smacking sound. Catcalls issued from both sides of the open door. Kathryn glared at the now-starstruck Bob Barton and motioned for him to dismiss the attendant throng flanking his rear, and to get the hell out of there.

Before Rick could get too far inside the room, Kathryn pulled him aside. "I've got two words for you," she hissed, trying to look as normal as possible under the circumstances. "Liz Smith."

"Uh . . . yeah," the actor replied, shifting his weight from snakeskin boot to boot. "Look, I'm really sorry about that."

"Is this your idea of making it up to me? Or your manager's? I'm just curious. I mean after all that Cristal, I didn't even think you'd remember any of what you were blathering at dinner. And the paparazzo took a pretty flattering photo of me, so I don't detest you quite as much as I really want to."

"Well, about making it up to you—yes. I mean no. This is my idea. In fact my manager tried to talk me out of it. I really meant what I said to you at Nebuchadnezzar," he whispered. "Coming up here to shoot the breeze with one of your classes wasn't bullshit. And, don't get me wrong . . . although I don't see why you shouldn't . . . I mean from your perspective, it probably looks a bit . . . well."

"You're not too articulate without a script, are you?" Kathryn asked him smugly. She hadn't really had the chance to seethe and now she had the golden opportunity to stand up for herself. And on her turf.

"I really liked you, Miss Kitty—I mean, I still like you . . . it just can't be what—well, you know."

Their heads had been together in conversation long enough for the ninth grade class to start buzzing in whispers behind them.

"What's that cologne you're wearing, by the way?" Kathryn asked the film star.

"Green Irish Tweed. Creed makes it; my manager gets it for me at a little place on Christopher Street. He told me it was Cary Grant's signature fragrance. And since journalists can't resist comparing me to him, calling me the C.G. of the new millennium and all that, I figured I'd give them another reason."

"It's . . . very . . . nice." Kathryn was working overtime to suppress her hormones. Rick's cologne did wonderful things to her libido. But to her surprise, it wasn't

Rick whose bones she was thinking about jumping, but *Bear*, even though it was the movie star's scent that had shifted her pheromones into overdrive.

Kathryn composed herself and turned to face her class. "Well, folks, for those of you who have been on Pluto for the past few years and therefore require an introduction, this is—"

"Rick. Just call me Rick." He lit up the room with the lopsided grin that had gotten him on every magazine cover from *G.Q.* to *Rolling Stone* to, ironically, *Good Housekeeping* in the past seven months.

"Rick is here to talk to you guys about the business."

"Yup. That business they call 'Show.' "

If he didn't stop grinning, those freshmen girls would lose their last brain cells.

"Well, Rick, I'll throw you to the wolves. Who's got a question for Rick?" Every hand shot up. "Andrew?"

Andrew picked at something on his desk and tried to look casual before he got up the gumption to look the celebrity in the eye. "Uh, did you really do Sandra Bullock?"

"Next question," Rick said, his face betraying nothing.

"Uh, yeah, I have a follow-up question."

"Andrew," Kathryn warned with a stern glance at the ninth grader.

"Um, yeah. Is it true that you did Sharon Stone that time she played your stepmom?"

"Andrew! Rick came here to talk about the business. About acting."

"Well, that's what I meant, man. It didn't look like you were acting in your love scenes with her. So, like you're either really good or you were doing her, right?"

Chloe shot her boyfriend a deadly look.

"Okay. Let's *talk* about the *acting* in those scenes," Rick gamely said. "First of all, no matter how sexy a scene looks to you when you're sitting in the movie theater shoveling popcorn into your mouth or making out with your girlfriend, the fact is that we actors are out there, mostly butt-naked, in front of all the crew and all these lights. It's not really that glamorous. Or that sexy. And sometimes you have to contort yourself into some uncomfortable positions that feel really weird or unnatural, but when you see the scene on film, the perspective looks right. Also—and I gotta say this so you don't think all us actors are geniuses—it's the director and the editor and the guys who do the lighting who make us look so good up there." Rick laughed.

Tandy Newman raised her hand. "Do you have any formal acting training?" she asked.

"No, I don't actually. I'm what's considered a 'natural.' At least that's what my agent says."

There was a collective laugh.

Kathryn took that as a nice opportunity to segue. "Well, why don't we show Rick what happens in an acting class, then? Who's ready to put their scenes from *Shrew* on their feet?"

The class was silent as a morgue.

"C'mon, guys, don't be shy," the film star prodded. "I want to see your stuff."

No one took the bait.

"Why don't *you* act for us?" Tandy asked.

"Yeah! You and Ms. Lamb," encouraged Lisette.

"No," Kathryn answered.

"Awww. Why not?" some of the students groaned.

Kathryn cocked her head and gave her class a phony

perky smile. "Because I'm the teacher, that's why. So I get to pick what we do! Rick's never studied acting. He's a *natural*. So he might like to check out the process. Scene study. Text analysis. Let's go! Andrew, Chloe, get your butts up and put the Wooing Scene on its feet."

There was no movement from the two freshmen.

Rick leaned over to Kathryn and whispered something to her. After a moment or two of reluctance, she nodded in agreement. "Okay kids," she began. "You get your wish. But since Rick and I have never practiced the Wooing Scene together—" there were hoots from the class "—this will be a demonstration in cold-reading technique. In how to size up a scene in a millisecond and make bold choices, beat by beat." She went over to her students and retrieved two copies of *The Taming of the Shrew*.

"Now, those of you who are serious about becoming professional actors will at one time or another encounter cold readings when you go to auditions. You won't always be asked to do a monologue that you have practiced and practiced until you know it in your sleep."

"That happens in film all the time," Rick added. "Sometimes you get a really short time to look over a scene, and if it's just a few lines, you have to make a choice about what the character wants, even if you don't know what's going on in the rest of the script. You know, your whole character could be 'I have that call on line two, Mr. Sanders.' Or, if it's a Schwarzenegger film, 'Everybody get down! Now!!' "

"Rick, maybe you could also show the kids how a professional actor does a monologue. Do you have anything memorized that you usually do?"

The movie star shook his head. "I don't do monologues for film auditions. Besides," he added, all boyish charm, "when you're in demand, people just call you—I rarely have to audition for anything. In fact, Harlan Josephson's been on my shit list since he made me audition for *I Know What You Did with the Babysitter!*"

The jaded freshmen's eyes widened at his free and easy use of the expletive in the classroom. Kathryn elected to ignore it.

"C'mon, act with Ms. Lamb," Andrew demanded.

"Are you up for this?" Kathryn asked her guest. What a great anecdote to tell the grandchildren. And it would be a much more PG-rated story than her other brush with Rick Byron's greatness.

The V.F.A. pulled Kathryn to one side of the room. "I'm really up for this cold-reading demo thing, but I'd rather not do *Shakespeare*, if you know what I mean. Leo was great as Romeo, but the Bard isn't exactly my 'for-tay,' " he said, sotto voce.

"Tandy, what else are you working on besides *Shrew*?" Kathryn asked her most precocious preppie.

The ninth grader delved into her knapsack and tossed her teacher a dog-eared script.

"Thank you, Tandy. *The Importance of Being Earnest*. Not Shakespeare, but truly a classic." Kathryn flipped through the script and handed it to Rick, indicated where the proposal scene between Jack and Gwendolen would begin and end.

"This is almost as bad as Shakespeare," the actor muttered, as he glanced through the scene. "But at least this is in English."

Lisette Mars overheard Rick's comment and leaned precariously over the side of her chair to whisper something to Tandy Newman.

"Well, here we have two people in this scene who are mad to marry each other, but because of various conventions, some of them social, some of them fanciful, don't move their courtship along," Kathryn said.

"There are an awful lot of words here," Rick said, as though he'd just discovered penicillin. "I mean in films, you just get right down to it. Cut the hearts and flowers. It's 'baby, are we doing this or what?' "

Kathryn tried hard not to pass judgment on Rick's lack of appreciation of the classics. "What you said might be true of movie dialogue, Rick, but Oscar Wilde's characters prize language. The more they can dazzle people with their wit, especially the object of their affection, the more desirable and attractive they are. Think about the time period in which *Earnest* is set. It's 1895. The Victorian era. These men and women are wearing layers upon layers of constrictive clothing. Corsets. Crinolines. Cravats. They're not exactly gyrating their buffed bodies at Moomba as a way of attracting each other. So the sexiest stuff is happening from the *neck up*. *This*," Kathryn said, as she tapped her temple, "is the most erotic organ. Okay kids, you didn't hear this word in this classroom, so I don't want any irate notes from your parents, but . . . Rick . . . think of the wordplay in this scene as *foreplay*."

The celeb's subsequent epiphany was palpable. "Now I get it!" The class echoed his sentiment in a collective "Ooooooooo," interspersed with a few giggles.

"So, shall we go for it?" Rick nodded his head and they dived into the scene.

" 'Gwendolen, I must get christened at once—I mean we must get married at once. There is no time to be lost.'

Why does this guy say 'christened' when he means 'married?' " Rick muttered to himself, shaking his head.

Kathryn ignored the remark and stayed in character, feigning surprise. " 'Married, Mr. Worthing?' "

" 'Well . . . surely. You know that I love you, and you led me to believe, Miss Fairfax, that you were not absolutely indifferent to me.' "

" 'I adore you. But you haven't proposed to me yet. Nothing has been said at all about marriage. The subject has not even been touched on.' "

" 'Well . . . may I propose to you now?' "

" 'I think it would be an admirable opportunity. And to spare you any possible disappointment, Mr. Worthing, I think it only fair to tell you quite frankly beforehand that I am fully determined to accept you.' " Kathryn thought she was looking at a drowning man. Was it the better part of valor to rescue him now? She could just imagine what her students were thinking.

" 'Gwendolen!' "

" 'Yes, Mr. Worthing, what have you got to say to me?' "

" 'You know what I have got to say to you.' " Rick shoved his left hand in the pocket of his tight jeans.

" 'Yes, but you don't say it.' "

The actor followed the stage direction in the script and got down on his knees.

" 'Gwendolen, will you marry me?' "

Kathryn leaned over to follow the words on the script they had to share. " 'Of course I will, darling. How long you have been about it! I am afraid you have had very little experience in how to propose.' "

"I'm afraid he's had very little experience in how to *cold read*," Tandy whispered across her desk to Lisette, loud enough for Kathryn to hear her. When Kathryn shot her student a dirty look, Tandy shrugged her shoulders as if to say "you know I'm right, Miss Lamb."

" 'My own one,' " Rick said, stumbling over the sentence construction. " 'I have never loved any one in the world but you.' "

" 'Yes, but men often propose for practice . . . What wonderfully blue eyes you have, Ernest! They are quite, quite blue. I hope you will always look at me just like that, especially when there are other people present.' "

Actually, the movie star's eyes *were* that blue, except that Kathryn had to *pretend* she was gazing at her scene partner. Rick's face was buried in the script.

The celebrity was clearly uncomfortable. The natural charisma that had made him a film star and a household name from Saratoga to Seattle was nonexistent. He was stumbling over his lines and couldn't take his eyes off the page to make contact with Kathryn, even in the part of the scene where he was supposed to propose to her.

"Okay," Kathryn sighed, relieved that the ordeal, which turned out to be just as painful for her, had finally ended. "Comments. Questions?"

Tandy Newman's hand was the first one up. "Ms. Lamb, you were using an English accent when you played Gwendolen, but . . . um . . . Rick . . . wasn't. Aren't you supposed to use an English accent when you play an English part?"

"Well," Kathryn began diplomatically. "Certainly the rhythms of this particular play lend themselves to being spoken in British cadences. And the characters are clearly English. It's within the text of the play. But in terms of preparation for an acting role, there is nothing wrong if a performer wants to use his own speech patterns until he, uh, gets a handle on the part; and then he can add the accent once he is—er, comfortable about who his character is . . ."

Rick waved his hand from side to side. "Nah, it's not about that. You see, kids, I'm a movie star, not an actor. My agent says I don't have to use an accent."

Lisette snickered.

Kathryn checked her watch against the clock above the classroom door.

Rick leaned in to Kathryn and whispered something to her. She nodded.

"Okay, kids, I'm going to let you go for the day. You've got a ten-minute gift of time. Don't blow it by acting like noisy jerks in the hallways. And next time, *Shrew* is going on its feet. No weaseling out of it again!"

The class spent the next seven and a half minutes getting Rick's autograph. "Look . . . I wasn't exactly Olivier just now," the actor said, after the students had dispersed. Kathryn waited silently to see where he was going. "Ian and I have been talking, and . . ." He caught Kathryn's quizzical look.

"Ian? I'm supposed to know who you mean when you just say 'Ian'?"

"Oh, you know Ian. Ian *Sorenson*," Rick clarified.

"So, if you said to me, 'oh, you know *Steven*,' I should automatically know you meant Spielberg."

"Well, yeah, actually. So, I learned from my agent—and my manager—that I wasn't exactly Ian's first choice for *What's Your Sign?* In fact, I wasn't even his second, fourth, or forty-seventh. But my BORQ—my Box-Office Recognition Quotient—is higher than any of the guys he wanted to use, so Miramax insisted that I was 'dah man.' And . . ." Rick lowered his voice to a whisper, despite the empty classroom. "What it all boils down to is that Ian lacks faith in my talent. I mean, *What's Your Sign?* isn't exactly *Citizen Kane*, but he thinks I'm, well, a bit . . . shallow. And I was watching you in action this afternoon and I thought you really have a handle on it. You really have your finger on the pulse of, like, how to break down a scene and get to the meat of what's going on without everything coming out boring. So, I wondered if you'd be interested in helping me out."

"How?"

Rick ran his hand through his hair, tousling it. "Be my acting coach on this movie."

Kathryn looked at him incredulously.

"Another thing is that I really don't want anyone to know about this. All on the 'q.t.,' if you get my drift. Well, my manager will know, because he'll be in charge of paying you. What do acting coaches usually get?"

Kathryn was on the verge of responding that she had no idea of the going rate, when something told her to hold her tongue.

"Let's say five hundred dollars an hour. We can work in my suite at the Plaza, or maybe I can come to your place sometime, if it isn't too inconvenient for you. We'll be shooting a lot in the bars all along Second Avenue up in the seventies and eighties. It shouldn't take too long to have my driver zip me downtown to you in the village. Shake?" He held out his hand to Kathryn.

"You've got yourself a deal!" Kathryn was amazed at what had just transpired, especially after their aborted date. And she had been so humiliated when she learned that they had gone out solely because he had been re-searching a role and not because he was really interested in dating her. What a fool she had nearly been. Yet, who had really gotten the upper hand here? Did it matter? She wouldn't even have to take a leave of absence from her teaching job because this little part-time gig would be arranged at their mutual convenience, hers and Rick's.

"Just one more thing," Kathryn said, leveling her gaze at the movie star. "Will I get program credit on the film?"

Rick thought about it for a moment or two. "I'm not the one who can guarantee that, either way. But my people will talk to Harvey—"

"*You* know 'Harvey,' " Kathryn interrupted, laughing.

"And see what can be arranged. It's not gonna say 'Rick's acting coach,' though. I can promise you that. Over my dead body, if you get my drift."

"With snowshoes on, Rick." She thought about their date at Nebuchadnezzar, making out in the restaurant, and their amorous interruptus at the Plaza. "But if you call me a 'Research Assistant,' I may have to kill you."

Chapter
21

For a startling split second, Walker Hart thought he was looking at a mirror image. The man sitting across the desk from him possessed the same sandy blond coloring, the same light eyes—sea green, with occasional shifts to blue, as he spoke passionately on one subject or another. The man's eyes turned blue when he spoke about flying.

"So, you're a professional pilot," Walker said, a bit unnerved, as he glanced at the man's application.

"Twelve years for British Airways," the new client replied, in plummy English tones. "I started as a first officer and advanced to pilot for the Concorde."

Walker thumbed through the new client's notes, written in a round English public schoolboy hand. "So . . . you collect antique cars and motorcycles, and went hot air ballooning with Richard Branson. Pretty impressive."

"Right. That. The ballooning was when Dick was trying to woo me away from B.A. I love the guy, but Virgin couldn't come up with the dosh. I've created a bit of a lifestyle for myself, and I have to support it, you know."

"Dosh?" Walker was confused.

"Ah, yes, two countries divided by a common language. Cash. 'Dosh' means cash."

"So where do you keep all these wheeled vehicles?" Walker asked enviously.

"I can't live in London anymore—couldn't find a place to park." The pilot smiled warmly. "I've got a home in Surrey now. It's not a bad commute to the city, when I have to be there, and I've become something of a country squire, although my passion doesn't run toward the usual horses and hounds. I've got some acreage with a seventeenth-century farmhouse, fully restored. Scads of room out back to indulge my enthusiasm for the antique roadsters."

Walker's stomach hurt. Not only that; he felt like he wasn't on top of his game. His eyes were itching like crazy, which had thrown him off-kilter. Ordinarily, he interviewed his new enrollees after their videos were taped; somehow he and Colin had ended up chatting and now Walker was having to go through his customary process in reverse. He took a deep breath. "Well, Colin, shall we make your videotape, now?"

"No time like the present." Colin nodded and stood up. He was a couple of inches shorter than Walker, which made Walker conscious about his size and bulk for the first time in years. The Englishman was tall and manly, but not overpowering. He seemed to move with surety and grace. Next to him, Walker felt like a middle linebacker suddenly thrown onto a tennis team.

I'm not competing with the guy, Walker reminded himself. He took Colin into the taping room and arranged the stool and the lights.

"Should I take my coat off?" Colin asked, starting to remove his navy blazer.

"No, keep it on," Walker said from behind the camera, waving his hand at the Englishman. "Your shirt is too bright. The white is wreaking havoc with my lights." Walker adjusted his lens. "All right, whenever you're ready, you just give me a nod, and I'll count to three and then turn on the camera. When you see the red light out of the corner of your eye, it means we're taping. Look directly into the lens, not at me, when you speak."

Colin lowered his head and closed his eyes. Then he straightened his posture, and angled his body toward the camera. He nodded his head and Walker began to tape.

"Hello. I'm Colin Fleetwood. I've been a transatlantic pilot for British Air for nearly two decades. Perhaps you've seen me say 'buh-bye' in Bangkok, Zurich, or Heathrow, or on my Concorde route to and from New York. I was born in Wales and got a scholarship to study drama at the Royal Academy of Dramatic Arts, but being an actor seemed too hard, so I became a pilot," he added, tongue slightly in cheek. "I enjoy traveling, old black-and-white movies, and . . ."

Colin started to laugh, midtaping. He waved his hands at Walker. "Sorry, old chap, I was just thinking how frightfully silly and serious this all is. Pardon me, a moment, I think I am about to hiccup." He inhaled deeply, held his breath for a few moments, and swallowed hard. "Ah, well, they say Laurence Olivier used to suffer giggle fits as well. Right. Moving along: I want to meet a lovely lady because I get terribly lonely whenever I fly into New York, which is at least twice a week, and I should like to have a charming companion to share my time . . ." Colin laughed again. "And . . . who knows?" This time, he couldn't stop the laughter.

"I don't mean to be self-mocking, Hart. This is the first time I've ever done anything like this, and I admit, I was a bit anxious about it. I'm afraid I've just provided you with some footage for one of those video blooper shows you Yanks are so fond of. Might we give it another go?"

Walker shook his head and stepped out from behind the camera. "Sorry, fella. That's it. Personally, I think it was terrific. Your tape has good life and energy to it and you show a lot of charm and humor. I've been in this business for a while, and trust me, women prefer this kind of introduction to a man, rather than something that seems stiff or over-rehearsed."

Colin rose from the stool and readjusted the lapels of his blazer. "So, how does this work?"

"Your video will be on file, and my female clients will view it, if your profile interests them. They don't read your entire file—just the single sheet labeled 'profile.' Also, you will have the opportunity to view any female client's tape, and profile sheet, and then phone whomever you think might suit you. And vice versa, of course. Although I've found that most ladies still prefer the man to make the first move."

"Super." Colin extended a tanned hand. "I'm looking forward to meeting 'the woman of my dreams.'" The pilot started to walk toward the door, when a sudden thought caused him to stop in his tracks. "Hart? Might I be able to view a few profiles and tapes while I'm here? I don't expect to be back in New York until Thursday, and I should like to get the ball rolling, if I may."

"It's Six in the City's policy to wait until a new client's credit card payment has been authorized or his check

clears, but in your case, I suppose I can make an excep-
tion, since you're not living here now . . ." Walker was
thinking it over. More bad business practice. He'd always been very careful to wait until he was assured that
the client had the money in the bank before he permitted
him or her to continue the matchmaking process.

"Rip up my personal check and I'll give you my Bar-
claycard instead," Colin offered. "Then you should get a
thumbs-up as soon as you swipe the card." He pulled out
an immaculate looking, wafer-thin black billfold from
the inside pocket of his blazer and handed Walker the
dark blue credit card.

"This will start the process for you that much sooner.
Oddly enough, most people do pay me by check,"
Walker commented. "The ones who give me credit cards
always mention that they're doing it for the free air
miles."

Colin flashed a bright smile, tapping his captain's bars
that were still affixed to his navy lapel. "I guess you can
say that I don't exactly need the miles. I can fly to Tahiti
and back for free as often as I like." He gave a jovial
laugh.

"Well then," Walker said, after Colin's credit card had
been electronically cleared, "I'll set you up in the screening room with a couple of profiles and videos. Follow
me." He led Colin into the next room and seated him in a
comfortable leather chair in front of a console. "I'll pull
some matches for you and be right back."

As he left the screening room, Walker recognized a familiar face sitting in his waiting area. The guest looked
dreadfully awkward. He gave his visitor a cordial hello,
then invited her to step into his private office.

* * *

Get back on the horse, kiddo, Kathryn thought, as she pressed the 'up' button in the lobby of the building where Six in the City had its offices. She rode to the fourth floor, butterflies in her stomach, and took a breath before trying the handle to the suite. She found the door unlocked, and stepped into the empty foyer. "Bear?" The door to the private office was closed, the vertical blinds shuttering the interior from view. Kathryn noticed that the screening room door was wide open, so she poked her head in, looking for Walker.

"Bear?" She saw a big blond man sitting in one of the comfy leather chairs. He swiveled around. "Oh." Kathryn did a double take and caught her breath. "Excuse me . . . I thought you were . . . have you seen a guy around here who looks like . . . you?"

The man stood immediately and walked over to her, extending his hand. "Colin Fleetwood. I'm a new registrant. The gentleman whom I believe you are looking for, is in his office with a young lady. I expect him momentarily."

Kathryn continued to stare at this English arrival. *I have no idea who he is, but I could just listen to him read the phone book.* "Was she a blonde? Brunette?" Kathryn heard herself asking. "Oh, God. Never mind me."

"I believe she had dark hair, if you're that curious."

The closed blinds of Walker's office ensured him total privacy. An icky, anxious sensation made its way through Kathryn's intestines. She suddenly felt flushed and dizzy, as though she might faint at any moment, and immediately diagnosed the root of her agitation: jealousy. She prayed that Walker's visitor wasn't the dreaded Valerie. What was wrong with her? Here she was, talking to a strikingly handsome Englishman, and at the forefront of her mind was the thought that Walker was shuttered away in his office with another woman.

"Are you a friend of Hart's?" Colin asked.

"N-no," she stammered. "I'm a client as well. I came by to request a couple of videos to view."

"Do you have a name?" Colin smiled and the corners of his eyes crinkled. Good God, they were just about the same color as Walker's. Shave off a couple of inches of height, and a few pounds, add a drop-dead English accent, and you had Walker's twin. It was eerie.

"Kathryn Lamb," she said, pulling herself together and shaking the man's hand. His skin felt warm, but dry.

"I'm waiting to view some tapes myself, Kathryn, but if you don't find me too forward, I should like to get to know you. Shall we go for a coffee? I have a feeling I won't be able to do better than you."

Anything to take her mind away from obsessing about Walker's activities. "Why not?" she replied, trying to smile.

The door to Walker's inner sanctum opened, and Kathryn did a double-take when he ushered his guest into the foyer. "What's going on?" she asked her sister, stepping just outside the screening room.

"I wanted to get some advice," Eleanor replied. She looked like she'd been awake all night. Her eyelids were swollen from crying and dark half moons of exhaustion had formed under her eyes.

"You didn't tell me you were coming here."

"I hadn't planned on it. But for some silly reason, I thought that a matchmaker might know something about marriages."

"I tried to tell her it's my mother who's the expert," Walker said, trying to lighten the mood.

"Are you and Dan planning to split for good? I thought it was a temporary separation, just to get your individual heads cleared. Wait . . . you're not a Six in the City client now, are you?"

Eleanor finally managed a genuine smile and a half-hearted laugh. "You must be kidding!"

Kathryn gave her sister a cautionary look, indicating that other clients were within earshot.

"What I meant was . . ." Eleanor said, lowering her voice a notch, "was that I'm not exactly ready to throw in the marital towel. Not yet, anyway." She turned to her host. "Thanks for what you said. It makes a lot of sense. And maybe it *will* make a difference."

Eleanor shook Walker's hand and Kathryn felt a little stab of jealousy. She looked at her kid sister.

"Don't worry. I didn't get all tingly," Eleanor whispered to her. "He's all yours, if you really want him," she added, and headed out the front door of the agency.

Kathryn was on the verge of saying something to Walker to thank him for being so concerned about her family, but she stopped before she could get a word out. His demeanor was all business and he barely nodded in her direction before he spoke to his British double.

"Mr. Fleetwood?" The screening room door opened wider and Walker entered the room. "Kathryn." From the way a muscle in his jaw twitched, Kathryn could tell that he was uncomfortable about seeing her again.

"Mr. Hart," Kathryn said evenly. "I came to see a couple of videos, but Mr. Fleetwood here has invited me for a coffee, so I won't be staying after all."

"Ditto." Colin nodded in assent. "I'm impressed, Hart, if Ms. Lamb is any indication of the caliber of your female clientele."

He called me "Ms." Kathryn thought with a chuckle, recalling how Walker had given her such a hard time about that appellation, the day she taped her own video.

"Well," Walker said, trying to keep his composure. "I guess you don't need to view *these* right now." He waved a stack of three tapes, one of which was marked "Lamb, K." on its black spine.

Kathryn decided to forge ahead and not pursue the root of Walker's unusual behavior. "Well, it seems we're all on the same wavelength. That's *my* tape." She nodded at one of the boxes in Walker's hand.

"Delightful. But I would rather hear all about you in person." Colin motioned for Kathryn to precede him out of the screening room. "Thank you, Hart. It's been a pleasure." The pilot shook Walker's hand again, as he stepped past him into the foyer.

"And I thank you, too, Mr. Hart." Kathryn took the opportunity to shake Walker's hand as well. *Uh-oh.* Much to her chagrin, that *frisson* she had felt every time she and Walker shook hands had not disappeared, despite her new prospects. She turned to Colin. "I'm very glad you decided not to view my tape after all. I started laughing in the middle. I just found it so hard to be serious about this whole video dating business."

"You, too?" Colin held the door for Kathryn as they stepped into the hallway. She turned back to read Walker's expression, but couldn't decipher what was going on past his squint. Walker had been blinking and making all sorts of oddly contorted faces ever since he'd come out of his office. "Are you okay?" she asked Walker solicitously.

"Yeah. Why?" he replied, trying not to rub his eyes. "Look, Mr. Fleetwood, I hate to have to meet and run, but I have some pressing business to attend to, if you don't mind my excusing myself." He turned and headed back to his private office, stopping at the doorway. "Enjoy your date, Ms. Lamb," he said, keeping his back to his clients. He stayed in the doorway until he heard them close the main door of Six in the City behind them.

Walker was trying his damnedest to keep the promise he had made to pull out all the stops in terms of finding Kathryn a husband and to keep things strictly business between the two of them from now on. In fact, Kathryn was the first woman he thought to recommend to the handsome and disgustingly dapper British Air pilot. It was time to go back to treating the business like a business. Time to put aside his personal jumble of conflicting feelings and endeavor to provide his clients with the satisfaction they paid him to deliver. And if he wasn't ready to do that, Josh had suggested an obvious alternative: commit to Kathryn. Otherwise, leave her alone forever.

Walker retreated into his private sanctum. He looked at the boxes of tapes in his hand, fixing his gaze on Kathryn's video. Then he did something he hadn't done since he'd dented his dorm room wall back when he was nineteen. So what if he killed a few more brain cells, or self-inflicted more pain. Closing his eyes, he banged his forehead a few times against his office door.

Chapter
22

It was a perfect day to meander through Central Park. Colin and Kathryn ambled leisurely along Poets' Walk, sharing their life stories and ambitions, finding one another extremely amiable companions. They strolled through the zoo and were just in time to catch the spectacle of the sea lions being fed an afternoon snack. "I always wondered what might happen if one of them refused to perform on command," Colin mused. "You know, a moody, temperamental sort. An iconoclast. They must get sick of singing for their supper day after day."

Kathryn thought of her sister. "Park Avenue matrons do it. Why not Fifth Avenue mammals as well?"

They continued their visit, stopping at one of the cages of the higher primates. "Golden-rumped tamarin," Kathryn remarked, gazing at the animal's naturally bizarre coiffure. "I used to date someone kind of like that."

"Do you mean the crotch scratching?" Colin asked.

"Actually, I was thinking about his playing with the mirror. Look how in love he is with his reflection. And the obsession with his hair. But now that you mention it . . ."

They maintained a steady stream of banter as they left the zoo and headed out of the park, toward Fifth Avenue. Approaching a flower vendor at Fifty-ninth Street, Colin asked Kathryn to select some loose blooms and create her own bouquet. No snapdragons were to be had. The pilot recommended that the white roses, freesia, and Hawaiian orchids be tied with a ribbon, rather than wrapped in paper "like fish and chips." Kathryn selected a length of lavender gingham.

Colin suggested that they stop for an Irish coffee, so they popped across the street to the Oak Bar at the Plaza, which was remarkably quiet at that hour. The coffee was strong and delicious, and on her empty stomach, the whiskey went straight to Kathryn's head. "I feel like I'm playing hookey," she said, tapping the pad of her forefinger on and off the hole at the end of a cocktail straw. "Drinking so early in the day. I probably shouldn't be using this. The plastic may be melting into the coffee. But I'll drink it too fast if I don't sip." *I must sound like an idiot,* she thought as she gazed into Colin's pale eyes, wondering if anything made them turn indigo.

It didn't take long to learn at least one thing that made the pilot ardent. The man positively waxed rhapsodic when he mentioned the freedom he'd felt every time he took off down a runway and each time the Concorde reached mach one. "When I discovered flight, and found that the thrill of taking off into the heavens and actually, physically leaving the nasty little vicissitudes of life behind and exploring the unknown . . . not to mention every desirable tangible location I ever dreamed of . . . earthbound things suddenly became frightfully mundane." Colin smiled and reached for Kathryn's hand. "I hope I don't sound crazy."

"No. Not at all. It's a *good* thing to be passionate."

"Quite."

"Sometimes I feel the same way in my work. It's more than the subject I teach. It's the only way I know how to get kids to explore the unknown and to take chances." She chuckled and ran her finger along the rim of her glass. "By the way, I think you should know this. I'm a shameless Anglophile. I could listen to a British accent all day. To be disgustingly honest, it wouldn't matter *what* you said."

"That's what I love about American women," Colin said, finishing his Irish coffee. "You're so refreshingly candid. You see, it's not in our national character to be so . . ." He searched for the word.

"Pushy? Obnoxious?" Kathryn teased. "Not a bit like you English."

"Forthright." He dabbed at his mouth with the corner of the pink linen napkin. "You Yanks are forthright. But Amen I say to that! I'm Welsh-born, not English, actually . . . so *while* we're being forthright," Colin said with a self-deprecating smile. "I realize that you don't know me from Adam, but if you're willing to test your sense of adventure, I should like to offer you a proposal."

Kathryn's heart skipped a beat or two. "Proposal?"

"I'm usually in New York twice a week on average, but B.A.'s changed our schedule for the next month or so and I shan't be back in New York until a week from Thursday. But then I have a four-day layover here until my next eastbound flight; and I have access to private planes out at Teterboro in New Jersey. I was considering flying down to Anguilla before the hurricane season kicks in. If you have never been to Cap Juluca, you're in for a marvelous treat. I thought, perhaps, you might like to join me."

Kathryn struggled to control her dropping jaw.

"That is, unless you have other plans. I realize of course this is a bit on the fly, so to speak."

"I teach on Friday mornings."

"Can the school find a substitute?"

"To be blunt, I'm not comfortable about asking. I would prefer to teach the class. And to throw caution to the winds a bit more slowly."

"Is that a 'no'?"

"The last time I considered doing something this spontaneous, I blew a month's rent at a Calvin Klein sample sale, and lived to regret it. In your case, Colin, it's not a 'no,' but it's a 'can we wait to leave until sometime around noon?' I'll have my bag packed and I'll be ready to rock and roll, but I have bad feelings about playing real hookey."

"I hope Briarcliff appreciates your loyalty."

"Call me madcap, but I feel a tremendous sense of responsibility toward the kids I teach. Toward my job." Kathryn looked Colin full in the face. "Or maybe it's just guilt. Or bad karma to cut school without death or dismemberment as an excuse."

"I think any man would be very lucky to have a woman like you. I can't imagine why you would need to employ the services of a video dating enterprise."

"Things are not always as simple as they seem at first blush, Colin. Remember the golden-rumped tamarin? Anyway, I could ask the same of you. Why did *you* register with Six in the City?"

"I get very lonely when I come to New York. I'm practically bicoastal, spending half of my life straddling one side or the other of the Atlantic pond. There's so much to offer in New York City. And I haven't met someone to share it with."

"Okay, I'm convinced."

"So does that mean you'll accompany me to Anguilla for the weekend?"

Kathryn grinned, dazed, not sure how much of it was the Cinderella-style offer and how much was the double shot of Jameson's coursing through her veins. "Consider me packed."

"*A*, it's hurricane season in the Caribbean, and *B*, you don't know this guy from Adam. Want some popcorn?"

Kathryn took the bowl from her sister. "That's just what he said. Except he said he wanted to go down to Anguilla before hurricane season began. He's a pilot, Ellie, you'd think he'd know the weather patterns. He's not going to fly us into the eye of a storm or something."

"Still, why should you go so far away with him? What's the rush?" Eleanor brushed some stray popcorn kernels off Kathryn's velvet sofa into her palm. "Start slowly. If he likes beaches so much, go out to Amagansett. Or book a romantic weekend at Gurneys. Think about it. I have to head off to retrieve Johanna from peewee gymnastics. Then I'll take her home to her father. He's actually there now—for a change. Seems Dr. Laura canceled her tummy tuck. Don't worry, I'll be out of your hair when your 'student' arrives."

"You know, Rick wouldn't have minded your being here last week, as long as you had stayed in the bedroom with the door closed during his coaching session. It was when you asked him that stunt-butt question that he got a bit uneasy. I still can't believe you had the gall!" Kathryn sighed, and switched the subject. "Look, this separation must be taking an awful toll on Johanna. On all of you. Has Dan been willing to talk about your issues?"

"Yes, he's been very willing, but we're chasing our tails. He listens to what I have to say, but still maintains that he's right. And so far, he has yet to budge an inch. I feel like I've been living with someone different all this time. Someone other than the man I thought I married. He clearly prefers the more traditional incarnation of me to the me that decided I needed more out of life than diapers and playdates."

"What did Walker say to you, by the way?"

"Just some helpful stuff," Eleanor replied cryptically. "He'll tell you if he wants to."

"I can't believe you're not sharing this with me. Your own sister."

"Don't go trying to guilt me, Kitty. I'm immune to that these days. In fact, I was thinking, once the Brownie Points take off, of writing a self-help book on guilt-free Judaism."

"It would certainly be a best-seller. See you later." Kathryn gave Eleanor a kiss on the cheek and escorted her to the door. *Will I ever get any time to myself,* she wondered. For the past few weeks her apartment had resembled Penn Station on a summer Friday and the tension and strain of having to play hostess, confidante, and coach was wearing her down. A tropical island getaway was starting to look better and better.

Kathryn's doorbell rang just as her session with Rick Byron was winding down. She peered through the keyhole and wasn't sure she liked what she saw.

"Excuse me, I didn't realize you had . . . company,"

Walker said. He noticed that the actor appeared quite comfy on Kathryn's couch, cradling one of her brandy snifters. "I didn't think drinking in midafternoon was quite your style, Ms. Lamb," he said tensely. "But I suppose it's all in the company you keep. I guess you changed your mind about the condom 'issue,' too," he added under his breath.

"Not that any explanation is needed, but—"

"I just dropped in to say hello," the actor interrupted. He threw Kathryn a look that clearly indicated she was not to divulge the reason for his presence, not even to Walker. "Would you excuse us, please?" Rick steered Kathryn out of Walker's eyeline. "You said my manager wasn't sending the payments for the lessons too promptly, so I thought I'd bring today's check over myself. No reason you should have to be put out. It's no reflection on you, by the way. Just so you know. Chaz gets very busy."

"Thanks," Kathryn replied, pocketing the check and escorting Rick back to the living room.

"You look great in those jeans, by the way," the movie star said. "You could be Heather's body double on the set. Well, I don't mean you could be as in getting a job doubling her, I mean you could be, as in you look good enough to—"

Walker coughed.

"Inhaling too much smoke from your mother's cigarillos lately?" Kathryn asked sweetly. She turned to the actor. "So, I'll see you next week, then. Give me a call if you want to schedule something in between. It was really nice this afternoon by the way. You should be very proud of yourself."

"*Ciao, bella.*" Rick gave Kathryn a friendly kiss on the

lips and he was out the door. "Good to see you, fella," he called to Walker as he strode toward the elevator.

Walker remained in the doorway. "Are you going into business for yourself?" he asked.

"Yes, I am, as a matter of fact," Kathryn responded, enjoying playing with him. When she saw the look of genuine consternation on his face, she relented and gave up the game. First, though, she looked down the hallway to her right to see if the gossipy Mrs. Horowitz was about. The homebound woman always kept her door open just a crack so she could hear if anything really juicy was going on in the corridor. "Okay, Bear," she whispered. "I promised I wouldn't spread this around, but I am Rick's acting coach on his current film project."

"I see," Walker said, not quite believing her.

"Well, between the La Perla black net teddy and 'Brünnhilde,' the matron of the holding cell at Midtown North thinking I was a high-rise hooker and the fact that I have notoriously promiscuous gentleman callers up to my apartment in the middle of the day, I could admit to you that I have found that being an expensive call girl was an infinitely more satisfying—not to mention lucrative— profession than teaching high school. It may disappoint you to hear it, however, but it's untrue. And there's tea in those brandy snifters, by the way. They're props for a scene we were working on."

"I notice you didn't invite me in, yet."

"Bear . . . I thought, from your behavior at Six in the City the day I met Colin, that finally we were on the same page where our relationship is concerned. I think we've both realized there can't be any gray area between us. Every time I allow myself to get closer to you again, the more ambivalent I become. You . . . you 'rock my world' . . .

but you're only willing to go so far. And that's not far enough for me. So I keep going back and forth about it, thinking it might be better if we had nothing at all to do with each other, rather than my settling for less when I want so much more."

Walker reached down to the industrially carpeted floor beside him and lifted up a glass pitcher filled with snap-dragons. "If I ever learned anything from Rushie, it's that if I break something, I'm responsible for fixing it."

There was a Mexican standoff at the threshold to Kathryn's apartment, as she and Walker waited to see what would happen next. Kathryn must have remained silent for over a minute while she searched Walker's face for some positive reassurance, for an admission of love on his part, or at the very least, an affirmation or valida-tion of her feelings. Finally, she took the vase from him and headed toward her coffee table. "Oh, all right. Come in," she said, glancing over her shoulder at Walker. It wasn't fair to punish him because he was less forthright about his emotions than she was.

"Check out the pitcher," he said, as excited as a kid with his very first Nintendo.

Kathryn examined the glass. "This is *really* similar to . . . almost the same-shaped branches . . . where did you find this?" she marveled softly.

"Let's just say I have my connections. Okay, you can thank Josh. He knows how to find people in the world of Arts and Crafts."

"This is amazing. Thank you so much!" Kathryn spontaneously threw her arms around Walker and gave him a hug. *So much for my intention to keep him at arm's length,* she thought briefly, before she placed a gentle kiss on his lips, lingering there perhaps a fraction of a second too long.

Walker drew her closer and deepened the kiss. "I'm sorry. I really didn't plan on that happening," he said, pulling away only when breathing had become a necessity. "Believe me, I really didn't. I'm as screwed up as you are over . . . this . . . *thing* between us. But I didn't hear you protesting."

"That's because you were keeping my lips busy." She looked at the flowers. "They're beautiful, Bear. And the pitcher is . . . I don't know how you did that. I know you said you felt responsible for replacing what you broke, but this is way above and beyond the call of duty."

"I wish I could do more."

"So do I, but you lack the tools in your kit to fix what else is broken around here. Now, would you mind leaving, before I lose what little remains of my resolve?"

He waited a moment before responding. "Yup. I guess that's probably a pretty good idea." He set his jaw and gave her one long last look before he strode out of her apartment.

Chapter
23

Kathryn picked up the phone on the second ring. "It's Colin," she mouthed to Eleanor, who was sitting cross-legged on the couch, working on a needlepoint she planned to display in her new baby's room when the time came. "I'm really looking forward to this Anguilla trip," she told him. But there was apprehension in her voice.

Perhaps the pilot sensed her squeamishness. Or perhaps he simply changed his mind about flying down to the Caribbean. "If you won't be too disappointed, I was rather thinking of scooting off to Martha's Vineyard instead," Colin said. "It's the height of fall foliage season, and you really haven't experienced the exquisite beauty of New England at this time of year until you've flown over it in a Cessna 172."

"Whatever you say. Actually, that sounds wonderful, Colin. Even better than Anguilla, in fact. What is a Cessna 172 and where does one get such an aircraft?"

"My connections at Teterboro. I'll arrange to lease one. And I know the most romantic inn in Vineyard Haven. The Tugman House. Ever been there?"

"Nope. I've never been a Vineyard Girl. I'm more of a Hamptons Girl. It's a bit more accessible if, like me, you don't drive."

After they finalized their plans and she hung up with Colin, Kathryn presented the latest romantic getaway option to her sister.

"That's better," she acceded. "But I've got one word for you: Kennedy."

"Which one?" Kathryn asked.

"Take your pick."

"First of all, Colin is a professional, experienced, veteran pilot. If he flies the Concorde for B.A., then he's not exactly JFK Jr. And secondly, stop trying to freak me out with oblique Mary Jo Kopechne references. Chappaquiddick was decades ago, and *Ted* Kennedy was driving an automobile and not flying a plane, anyway."

"I really do wish you well, you know," Eleanor said, stitching in the dots on Curious George's nose. "Chalk it up to sisterly concern. I don't want you flying over the Atlantic with an axe murderer."

Kathryn rolled her eyes.

"Or maybe I'm just feeling a bit envious. It sounds like you're starting to fall for this British guy and the last romantic thing I did was rent a Julia Roberts movie."

"I'll be fine," Kathryn assured her sister. "I'll be just fine."

Kathryn stood on the Teterboro tarmac and gazed at the aircraft Colin had rented for their trip. "I've never been in a plane this small," she said hesitantly as Colin placed her bag into the Cessna. He gave her a boost and she climbed inside. "It is safe, isn't it?"

"Nothing to worry about. These planes are thoroughly inspected every time they go out and come back. And if it's the pilot you're worried about, I've flown everyone from Mick Jagger to Kofi Annan with no complaints."

"Well, Mick might have been wasted and Kofi Annan probably would have been diplomatic about any
misgivings."

"Sister Wendy has been on my aircraft. Does that as-
suage your fears?"

Kathryn decided to kick back and enjoy herself. Once
they were in the air, she was surprised that the flight was
as smooth as it was. It was a little unnerving looking out
the window and down at the water, though. Being aloft
was less scary from an altitude of thirty-three thousand
feet when what you saw below you were fluffy, harmless-
looking clouds. "Are there any peanuts on this flight?
Complimentary drinks?" she teased.

"Not for the pilot, thank you. You're flying Air Fleetwood, not Northwest. There's a chilled split of champagne in my flight bag if you want to start without me.
Otherwise, if you can make it 'til we get to Tugman
House, they make a mean hot toddy."

Kathryn looked out the window as they approached
their destination. "Is it just me, or does Martha's Vineyard look sort of like a lobster claw from up here?"

"No wonder you wanted to come here," Kathryn
remarked, as they rode in a taxi along the Edgartown-
Tisbury Road. "It's glorious!" She unrolled her window
and breathed in the autumn air, a crisp blend of cran-
berry, sea salt, and crackling firewood.

They passed a small white sign. "Hey—Oak Bluffs! Is
that far from where we're staying? Isn't that where
America's oldest carousel is?"

"It's not far at all from Vineyard Haven," Colin told
her. "I should warn you, though. They make you give
back the brass rings."

Kathryn reached over and took Colin's hand. "I'm . . . this is wonderful," she said. "I am very happy to be here." She scooched over in the back seat so she could snuggle next to Colin. "I love this time of year . . . and this setting. Russet and gold and leather and tweed, maple sugar and oatmeal cookies. There are more textures in autumn."

The taxi rounded a bend and turned onto a long driveway bordered by hedges. The driver slowed as he reached the main gate. "This is it," Colin said as they approached the white Queen Anne. "Tugman House. It used to be a private estate. The rooms at the top have a completely panoramic ocean view with a widow's walk and the ones on the ground floor have their own private decks and access to the private beach."

An attendant opened the taxi door for them and unloaded their luggage. Kathryn and Colin were ushered into a spacious, yet cozily furnished lobby. It was the quintessential New England inn. A roaring fire was burning in the stone hearth at one end of the room. Elegant colonial sofas and wing chairs formed comfortable sitting areas around mahogany tables. Off to one side was another table with several daily newspapers and a magazine rack for the guests, offering everything from *Gourmet* to *Popular Mechanics*.

"This is one of our common rooms," the concierge told them in her local accent. "You're welcome to relax here and read one of the newspapers or periodicals, but you also have a mini library in your own room. If you want any other books," the woman gestured to a closed maple door bearing a brass plaque, "the Hawthorne Room is well stocked with classics and best-sellers. You can take a peek in, if you like."

"Thanks." Kathryn grinned. "I'd like to." She opened the door and stuck her head inside. The room was impressively furnished, with a floor-to-ceiling library and two overstuffed couches made even more inviting by enormous tasseled cushions upholstered in silk shantung in bright, autumnal tones of persimmon, saffron, tamarind, marigold, and fuchsia. A sole guest was reading a magazine while sipping a glass of cider.

"If I ever have a nervous breakdown," Kathryn thought, "*this* is where I would want to be sent to recuperate. It would make a hell of a sanitarium."

"Here's your key, Mr. Fleetwood," said the concierge. "You and Mrs. Fleetwood are in the Carriage House. The Winston Room. I'm Edie, in case you need anything."

Kathryn felt a pleasant little shudder at the concierge's unwitting "promotion" of her marital status.

Colin and Kathryn crunched along the gravel path to the Carriage House, accompanied by a young bellhop, a local boy who introduced himself as Damon and told them he was working part-time to help defray college tuition costs.

"This is the best room, actually. At least I like it the best. It's very quiet," the young man told them as he unlocked the door and beckoned them in.

"Wow," Kathryn breathed.

"And this is the oldest piece of furniture at Tugman House," Damon said, indicating the queen-sized, canopied four-poster bed. "It dates from 1795."

"Jeez. Imagine! George Washington literally could have slept here! I mean this is *Martha's* Vineyard . . . get it?" she said giddily. Kathryn took in the rest of the room, including the overstuffed reading chair and matching footstool upholstered in pastoral red toile, the working fireplace, which was already blazing, and the little decorator touches like sterling silver dishes of potpourri and a wicker basket of apples and pears.

"You've got a balcony out here," Damon told them, opening the back door to the room. "And that's your three-hundred-gallon sunken hot tub. No one can see you from the outside, so whatever you might want to do . . ." the young man reddened a bit. "Well, you won't have to worry about peeping Toms." The deck was appointed with both a hammock and a pair of Adirondack chairs, from which there was an unencumbered view of the ocean. "Now, if you go through your private gate here and follow that little walkway, you'll hit the beach. It's Tugman House's own entrance, so you won't have to cross the road."

Colin thanked Damon and handed him a sizable tip.

"Excuse me for a sec," Kathryn said and went to check out the bathroom. It was the size of most Manhattan apartments. The huge clawfoot tub surrounded by votive candles looked old-fashioned but was really a jacuzzi; it would also accommodate both of them with room to spare. The fittings were gold plated. "You'll feel very much at home here," she called out to Colin. "There's a phone in the bathroom. The only other places I've ever seen that were in England! And there's a library in here, too. A bunch of classics, half of which I never got around to reading and always intended to. Louisa May Alcott, Nathaniel Hawthorne . . . hey, you can read to me from *The Scarlet Letter* while we're taking a bubble bath in the hot tub!"

"I'd be happy to inspect the premises as soon as you're through," Colin said, chilling the split of champagne. "Tugman House may seem all simple, quaint neo-colonial charm, but this is a four-star hotel. They'll give you anything you want here . . . fresh fruit, champagne, a massage at any time of day . . ."

Kathryn stepped out of the bathroom in time to catch one of the staff clad in a fisherman knit sweater and jeans knocking on their door.

"Your complimentary hot toddys." New England verbal economy at its apotheosis. He handed them two glass mugs, fragrant and steaming. "I'm Dave, if you need anything. Welcome to Tugman House."

Kathryn reached for her mug. "Colin, did you say a massage? I haven't had one of those since . . ." *Bear.* When she'd jumped off his table the night he sprung her from the holding pen at Midtown North. It was hard to keep him off her mind, including when she had asked Eleanor to check her answering machine for her, in case some other Six in the City bachelors decided to phone. After all, while things seemed to be working swimmingly with Number Five, Walker did owe her a Number Six.

Kathryn remembered the last time she'd seen Walker and how sweet he'd been. His snapdragons had long since died a natural death and the etched glass pitcher was stored in a safe place. Thinking about the kiss they had shared wasn't doing her any good right now. She took a small sip of her hot toddy, savoring the warmth as it coursed down her throat. "This is truly heaven," she said, enraptured.

"We don't use a blended whiskey for our toddys. We use Bushmills purple label instead," Dave told them. He gestured to a small refrigerator tucked into a corner of the enormous room. "Your minibar is fully stocked, but if you don't find your favorite liquor in there, please dial two, and we'll be happy to accommodate you. We also serve Afternoon Tea in the Alcott room in the main house until five-thirty P.M."

"Thanks, mate." Colin handed the staffer a $5 bill.

Kathryn had a strange lurching feeling in her stomach, an anxiety pang about what was supposed to happen next. Did Colin expect her to immediately hop up the cherrywood step unit to the queen-sized bed and make love? For some reason, she wasn't in the mood. All the ingredients were present, yet . . .

The complimentary toddy was evidently not enough of a celebration for the high flyer. Colin popped open his split of Taittinger, poured two champagne flutes and handed Kathryn one, raising his glass to hers. "Cheers, love." He deposited a soft kiss on her lips.

Kathryn sipped the champagne slowly. She closed her eyes and allowed the wine to fizzle on her tongue before swallowing it. "Ummm."

"Are you glad you accepted my invitation?" Colin came up behind her and wrapped his arms around her waist. He nuzzled the back of her neck.

"Yes. Oh, yes." She turned around to face him. "Would you mind terribly if I took a shower and washed my hair? I've never flown in a plane that small before and I think I was so nervous my scalp started sweating." She ran her hand through the tangled mop with limited success. "I'll feel much more human afterwards."

"Not at all, love. I could use a shower as well, but I think I'll pop 'round to the front desk and ask about the fitness center hours. I wouldn't mind working out the knots in my back." Colin took Kathryn in his arms and kissed her nose. "See you in an hour or so." He drained his champagne glass in one long draught, and tossed a sumptuous pine green terrycloth bath sheet over his shoulder. With a grin and a wave, he crunched down the gravel path headed for the main house.

Kathryn surveyed the room, then decided that she had to test the waters. She yanked off her suede boots, rolled up her jeans, and followed the path down from the Carriage House to the private beach. It was pristine and desolate, uninhabited by another living soul until a gull flew overhead, its dinner a captive in its beak. The cool sand, silvery white, cushioned her feet. A crisp breeze wafted across her face and the scent of salt and sea filled the air. The late afternoon sun made geometric patterns of light and shadow on the shore.

She raced down the beach into the gray-blue water, surprised to find it much warmer than she had anticipated. Kathryn stood in the surf watching the gulls dip and soar as she monitored the progress of a dilapidated fishing trawler. Seafood scavengers, all. The play of the water across her ankles and the gently abrasive tug of the sand beneath her feet as it was pulled back into the sea had a tremendously calming influence. It was as though all of her urban anxieties receded along with the tide.

It had been a long week, Walker thought to himself. Ever since he'd rung Kathryn's doorbell to give her the pitcher Josh had helped him track down. And her favorite snapdragons, too. And found her with that vapid excuse for an actor. Walker regretted the day he'd accepted Rick Byron's Six in the City application. At least he hadn't fixed the actor up with anyone else before Eleanor saw the Liz Smith column that blew the star's cover. Kathryn's wounded emotions aside, at least there were no lawsuits, Rushie had said pragmatically.

What had he expected—or wanted—from that little visit to the ninth floor? What he got was an awed thank you, a grateful hug, and a kiss he wished he could forget. So much for the promise to stick to business. Since, in his own words, it was part of his "marketing strategy" to hear from his clients after their first date, he was doubly pained to receive calls from both Kathryn and Colin telling him what a smashing excursion to the zoo they had both had. Irish coffee at the Oak Bar, a stroll along the Poets' Walk in Central Park, and something called a golden-rumped tamarin, which sounded like a cross between an exotic dancer and a Siamese fruit.

Rushie was never home, which was a blessing in and of its own since he couldn't yet return to his Connecticut refuge. Just a few weeks ago, he had agreed to extend his subtenants' lease until the end of the year. Most of his leisure time during the past few days had been spent contacting various contractors to repair the water damage to the penthouse and exorcising his aggressions on the piano.

Valerie had called a couple of times, at first under the guise of a professional call, reminding him that they had unfinished legal business regarding Six in the City that needed prompt attention. During the last call, Walker told her pointedly that his mother was back in town and it was Rushie whom Valerie should be speaking with.

When the lady barracuda phoned again to ask if she could make dinner for him, he flatly, and for the first time in his life, refused a woman's offer of a night of passion. Walker coolly reminded her that the night they'd double-dated with Josh and Lou, she had boasted about *not* being a cook.

He'd even called Eleanor to find out if she had heard anything from Kathryn, but got only the answering machine at her Park Avenue home. Eleanor had at least retrieved the message. She returned his call, but responded that she wasn't at liberty to say anything about her sister.

"Well," he said glumly, "call me if you hear from her." He had just replaced the receiver in its cradle when the phone rang. His heart leapt. *That was quick.*

"Hullo?" It was a woman's voice. Lovely and lilting, with a genteel English accent. "I'm trying to reach something called 'Six in the City.' "

"That's me."

"May I enquire what you are?"

"What am I?" Walker asked, confused.

"Yes. What is 'Six in the City'?"

"It's a dating service, ma'am. A matchmaking service in Manhattan. We make videos of each of our carefully screened clients, who complete a full profile of themselves. And then we endeavor to match up each client with the perfect partner. Five matches, plus the client, makes six in the city."

"I see. And who might *you* be?"

"I am the company's current manager, Walker Hart."

The silence on the other end of the phone seemed interminable. Finally, the woman spoke first, her voice slightly tense, her words slow and deliberate, as though she were addressing the village idiot. "Mr. Hart, my name is Gemma Fleetwood."

Chapter
24

Kathryn thought it was her imagination when she heard the phone ringing. Dripping wet, her hair still coated with a generous slathering of coconut-scented conditioner, she groped for the telephone adjacent to the glass-walled stall shower. Finding she couldn't quite reach the receiver, Kathryn stepped out of the stall and crossed the room, hoping she wouldn't electrocute herself when she answered the phone.

"Hi, Kitty!"

"Ellie, are you all right? You didn't give birth or anything, did you?"

"Not yet. Don't worry. If I had, Dan or Mom would have called you, not me. No, you said that I should let you know if you had any phone calls you might need to deal with."

"Where are you? Is there an emergency?"

"I'm at my place. I figured I'd tell you that this woman called twice since you left for school this morning looking for you. She sounded like the Yenta from upstairs in your building, but the name seemed different so I had no idea whether or not it was something that could wait until you got back to New York."

Kathryn frowned and scrunched up her lips. "What's her name?"

"Ruth—how biblical—wait a minute, I wrote it down here . . . Johanna? Hold on, Kitty, she took the paper. Honey, Mommy doesn't want to play games right now. She's on long distance with Aunt Kittycat. Can I have the paper, sweetie?"

Over the phone, Kathryn could hear the muffled tones of a mother-daughter negotiation worthy of the Geneva Convention.

"Kitty, are you there?"

"I'm still here, El."

"Her name is Ruth Goldfarb. Do you know her?"

Kathryn thought for a moment, as she ran her hands through her hair, trying to detangle two things at once. She was having better luck with her tresses. "The name doesn't ring a bell."

"I thought she might be from Briarcliff. Tell you the truth, her voice also sounded a lot like our old after-school preteen theater director from the Y. Must be a 'type.' "

"Hmm. Did she leave a number?"

"She did, but she also said that she would keep trying to reach you."

"Well, I don't know who she is, but I'll try the number after dinner. We just arrived. I've washed all my Manhattan tensions away in the surf, and the last thing I want to do is deal with the outside world, unless the issue is Armageddon."

"Fair enough. I just thought I'd pass along the information."

"Thanks. It's fine that you did. Give my niece a kiss

and I'll talk to you when I get back. This place is absolute heaven. A sybaritic idyll tucked away on two acres of waterfront on Martha's Vineyard! Does that sound *Travel and Leisure* enough for you? So you all have fun in the nitty gritty city, while I finish my complimentary hot toddy and dry my hair in the sun before it starts to set. The sun—not my hair. Let's see," Kathryn gloated to her sister, "shall I try the Adirondack chair or the hammock?"

"Careful, you could catch a chill at this time of year. It's not July, you know. Seriously, I'm just glad you finally met someone through Six in the City who treats you the way you deserve to be treated," Eleanor said with just a touch of envy in her voice.

"Yeah, yeah. Me, too, actually. Talk to you soon. Love you!" Kathryn, dry by this time, hung up the phone and wrapped herself in the enormous fluffy green Tugman House bathrobe. She grabbed a copy of *Great American Short Stories* from the bathroom minilibrary and the remains of her toddy and went out to their secluded terrace where she installed herself on one of the deck chairs.

The sun was dipping toward the horizon when Colin returned to the room. Kathryn was standing outdoors at the opposite end of the premises, transfixed by nature's light show of cerise, gold, and lavender, when he tiptoed up behind her and combed his tapered fingers through her long curls.

She looked up at him and saluted him with her empty toddy glass. "This is lovely. Truly lovely. I can't thank you enough for bringing me here. The perfect fall weekend. It's what my soul seems to have been crying out for. I really needed to try to forget . . . never mind."

She reached up and cupped her hand behind his neck, pulling him down toward her for a kiss.

When their lips parted, Colin drew back and regarded her with admiration. "I admit that I still know so little about you, but with every hour we spend together, I yearn to know more. And everything I learn about you makes me admire you tremendously."

Kathryn felt herself blush. "Thank you," she replied softly. "I could say the same for you."

The air was silent and still as they both gazed down toward the beach, drinking in the splendor and wonder of the sunset.

"You are everything I have ever wanted in a woman," Colin added, as he reached over to caress Kathryn's soft cheek. "I should like very much to marry you."

It felt like a jolt of electricity.

Kathryn saw her whole life flash before her eyes. Every choice and possibility, past and present, paraded itself through her mind with lightning speed. She took stock of beliefs she had long held, behavior she had equally long desired to change, and what appeared to be the prospect before her of what she so overwhelmingly thought she wanted—the opportunity to make a life with someone. She had hoped that the "someone" would be Walker Hart, but how long was she supposed to wait for him to realize what a catch she was and what a dolt he was being by denying himself a chance to ensure their future mutual happiness? What if he never had that epiphany? Was she supposed to remain single and in a state of semi-requited passion forever?

Colin Fleetwood wasn't Walker, but he was a handsome, successful, charming, generous man with a tremendous amount to offer, not the least of which seemed to be

the desire to marry her. Kathryn heard herself say to
Colin, "Perhaps I *will* accept your offer—in . . . in . . . the
fullness of time." Suddenly, she felt like she was underwater. "Colin, this is all happening incredibly fast for me,
you have to understand. I mean it's amazing, but . . .
we're not in any rush, are we?"

"I don't know whether to ruin my French manicure
wringing your thick neck, or thank my lucky stars that
you have finally met a woman who can have an impact
on your life," said Ruth Goldfarb Hart Haggerty Tobias
Haggerty Aviles de Tournay Glendower, to her son who
was bruising his knuckles raw by sparring with filing
cabinets.

Walker grunted something incomprehensible.

"I know you were mad at me for dumping the business
in your lap, honey, but you didn't have to find ways to
make me come home to salvage it." She waved away the
smoke from her pink cigarette, her chunky gold rings
catching the fluorescent light.

"Frankly, Rushie, it never occurred to me that people
would be dishonest about their intentions when they
register for a dating service." He growled at his mother
and punched the wall. "And what bottle did *that* come
from?" he asked, noticing for the first time that the color
of his mother's hair was somewhere between russet and
aubergine—brighter than usual, even for her.

"You've done it twice already to the same girl. With
that Hollywood boy-toy and now with the pilot. Thank
God there haven't been any other slip-ups with the rest
of the clientele . . . or have there?" Ruth asked, tamping
out the cigarette into an air-filtering ashtray.

"Stop smoking in here, Rushie."

"I'm still your mother, Walker. Don't tell me how to run my life."

"Obviously I haven't done that, or you wouldn't be rivaling Liz Taylor for frequent-flyer miles to honeymoon havens."

"Mickey Rooney has still been married more times than I have—I think—and don't blame me because I made bold choices in life."

Walker looked at his scraped knuckles and decided he hadn't destroyed enough property.

"Stop that!" his mother warned, as she reached for a ballpoint that he was snapping in half. "I've been back from the Catskills for less than twenty-four hours and already I'm cleaning up your messes again. Who called that Lamb girl? *I* did. And after three tries, who convinced her sister to tell me where she was, without setting off bells and whistles? And right now I suggest that you rent yourself a nice midsize that gets good mileage and finish what you started."

She opened a hidden catch on a diamond-studded bracelet and looked at her watch. "Who knows what damage has been done by now? A romantic B and B has a way of turning a girl's head. Especially at this time of year. And while I admit that Martha's Vineyard isn't exactly Anguilla in the exotic-locale department, Kathryn's a New Yorker who probably never gets as far as Amagansett on her schoolteacher's salary, not a blushing virgin who's going to keep her legs closed, for God's sake! We're an accessory to adultery!"

Her antagonism started Walker pacing like a caged animal. "We don't know for sure what's been going on in the bedroom up there." He didn't even want to think about the subject . . . except that once Rushie had raised it, he began to obsess about it. It was making him nuts picturing Kathryn rolling around in a four-poster bed at a romantic inn with anyone other than him. "I told you I would handle it, Rushie. Where do you think I'm *going*?"

"First, I think you're going to Staples to get me a batch of new office supplies," she replied sharply, as a three-hole punch whizzed past her head, practically shattering the door. "Then, I think you're going to Hell in a hand-basket. After that, you're going to the Vineyard before Gemma Fleetwood slaps a bigamy suit on us and Eleanor Lamb Allen—whose husband does the collagen injections and lipos for all the big television stars, by the way—screams 'fraud' to the Better Business Bureau." She mopped her glistening brow. "I should have listened to Mira. She told me this would happen."

"Who the hell is Mira?"

"My astrologer. She saw it. She told me that my business might take a nose dive. That's what the Tarot reading said, too. And the I Ching when she threw it."

Walker was exhausted. He held out his hand to his mother. "Give me one of those awful pink things."

She obliged, lighting the cigarillo for him. "I should have read the signs," she sighed. "Mira was right, but I didn't listen. I didn't read the signs."

"You're full of shit, Rushie."

"Watch your language, and what kind of a son calls his mother by her first name? It's not natural."

"What kind of mother runs off to the south of France with a man half her age and leaves her grown son—who has a lucrative life of his own, mind you—with the business she started, just because she's bored and wants to escape . . . or find herself . . . or get laid. Whatever it was this time."

"If I hadn't gone to Cap Ferrat with Ludovic, I never would have gone to Wales."

"You lost me, Rushie."

"And then I never would have met Dafydd Glendower. And then I never would have met the archbishop of Canterbury. Did I tell you I helped him with his babka?"

"Yes, *Mom*," Walker groaned. He took his mother by the arm and steered her into a chair, then knelt beside her and took her firmly by the shoulders. "Listen, Rushie, as soon as I got the phone call from Gemma Fleetwood, I planned to pull the plug on this matchup. And when I learned where Kathryn and Colin were, I made arrangements to go up to the Vineyard myself, immediately. Contrary to your belief, it was not *your* idea, so don't try to take credit for it."

He drew in a deep breath. "First of all, Rushie, you haven't a clue what it is I really do, when I'm not trying to run the business you keep running away from. You think I don't have a regular job because I haven't been putting in nine-to-five hours punching a clock and being a corporate drone. Do you have any idea how gratifying my career is? To set my own hours, call my own shots, have my name alone open doors all over the world? *The Hart Monitor* is as well known and well respected as *The Wall Street Journal*. I can conduct a conference call on my cell phone while I'm fishing off the Christopher Street pier, barefoot, my jeans rolled up, with an administrative assistant baiting my hook as I dispense financial advice to Fortune 500 CEOs across the country. Do you have *any* idea how swell that is?"

"How 'swell' it is that you're a millionaire and you

want to act like the Huckleberry Finn of the Hudson?"
Rushie interrupted.

"And at this very moment, the reason I'm still down
here in the city is because you're keeping me in this damn
office arguing with you so that you can remind me what
a lousy son I am, which only reminds me what a rotten
mother you've been."

Ruth heaved a melodramatic sigh. "It's always a
mother's fault."

Walker slammed his open hand against the wall.
Rushie jumped, startled. "Mother, I want your promise
not to call Kathryn at the Tugman House, and not to tell
her sister what's going on yet. *I* need to be the one to
tell her about Colin. I will handle the situation from now
on. Alone. Have we got that straight?"

Ruth looked her son full in the face. "You better
handle it, son. Because if you don't, I can be a real ball-
buster. You don't know your mother."

Walker set his face in a grimace. "You're damn right
about that, Rushie. You were never around for me to find
out." He looked at the ridiculous, smoldering, bubblegum-
colored cigarette and crushed it in his palm, then stormed
out of the office, shattering the door as he slammed it behind him.

Kathryn was enjoying a delicious buzz. After a sumptuous late supper at the Fisherman's Rest, Tugman
House's four-star restaurant—ranked number one in the
area by *New England Gourmand and Gastronomy*—
and capped off by the slow enjoyment of a couple of
glasses each of port, Colin suggested that they take a

stroll along the beach in the moonlight to walk off some of the calories they'd consumed.

"That's one of the things I think is so funny about you Brits," Kathryn teased. "No matter where you go, you try to bring the motherland with you. Here we are on *my* territory—the colonists did win the war, you know—and they've got fish and chips on the menu."

Colin squeezed her hand. "At least you know the fish is fresh."

"And you drink like one, too. It must be part of your national character that over the course of an evening you can consume several varieties of alcoholic beverages—that would make any normal person deadly drunk and dizzy—and not appear affected in the slightest. I like a cocktail now and again, don't get me wrong, but it's very hard to keep up with you. Ouch," she said dully when her ankle turned. "Wait. Stop." Kathryn slipped off her pumps. "My stilettos are digging into the sand, and I've got a slipper full of silt." She removed her shoes and dumped out their contents onto the beach. "Join your friends," Kathryn said tipsily to the grains of sand.

She plunked herself down on the beach and gazed heavenward into an indigo sky. "Look!" Kathryn exclaimed. "When have you ever seen so many stars?" She looked over at Colin. "Look who I'm asking. A pilot." She shook her head. "Silly me." Kathryn sat on a dune, her elbows propped up on her knees, her chin resting in her hands, staring at the stars.

"Wouldn't you rather sit on a chaise?" Colin asked solicitously. "We can go back and sit on our deck, if you'd prefer?"

"No, thanks. I'm communing with the constellations. Come join me."

Colin removed his navy blazer and folded it in thirds, carefully draping it over his lap, as he eased himself onto the cool sand in his perfectly pressed linen slacks. "Sorry," he apologized, when he caught Kathryn eyeing him curiously. "It's an old public school habit. My parents couldn't afford more than one uniform. It does seem a bit foolish now, I agree."

"Do you know their names?" Kathryn asked him, looking at the constellations. She leaned her head against Colin's shoulder. His white shirt was crisp and cool.

"Do you?" he asked her.

She shook her head.

"Well, then, young lady: an education." He leaned back and pointed up at the night sky. "That one over there—the one that looks like twin circles? That's 'gluteus maximus.' And the smaller one just off to its right, at oh, about two o'clock? That's 'gluteus minimus.' And the *really* big one—the one that looks like *four* large circles. That's 'gluteus omnibus'!"

"You goof!" Kathryn laughed and gave Colin a punch in the arm. "*I* could have done that. I thought you really knew about the stars."

"I do. That's what we called them at the Royal Academy of Astronomy."

"Tease."

He crossed his heart. "Girl Guide's honor."

"*You* weren't a Girl Guide," she snickered.

"No, but I honored a few."

She chuckled in spite of herself. "Well," she said, wiggling her bare toes in the sand, "at the *American* Astronomical Academy, we called them by different names." She tried to think of something clever, but her imagina-

tion failed her. "But we'll go by your names for tonight.
Let's make a wish on the first ones we saw. You first."

"Can I kiss you," Colin asked gently.

"You have to ask?"

"I try to think of myself as a gentleman." He grew momentarily rueful. "A wish." He closed his eyes. "I wish
that I could be able to give you everything you want,
Kathryn. Everything you deserve and desire."

She rose to her knees and looked at Colin, taking his
face in her hands. His mouth tasted of oysters and port,
sweet and salty and sad. "Why did you say it?" she
asked him.

"What?"

"Your wish," she whispered. "If you say your wish
aloud, it will never come true." If Colin truly could
give her everything she deserved and desired, then she
wouldn't have to work another day in her life and could
instead become a lady of leisure, spending her life shopping and traveling. Oh, well, maybe she didn't "deserve"
all that, anyway. Who does? *Still,* she fantasized . . . *being
married to a pilot . . . the vacations they could take together would be fabulous. With his connections, they'd
be able to visit every exotic locale . . . hey, they could even
run through the alphabet, starting at Anguilla . . . Bali . . .
Capri . . .*

Kathryn looked up at Colin and smiled suggestively.
"Did you notice our sunken bathtub, by the way?"

"Darling, the Romans may have invented baths, but it
took the British to elevate them to an art form." Colin
rose to his feet and brushed the pale sand from his
trouser legs, then carefully shook out each Bally loafer.
As they picked their way up the path toward the Carriage House, their arms wrapped about each other's

waists, Colin noticed a glow coming from the direction of their deck. "Did you leave the light on, Kathryn?" he asked.

"I wasn't even sure where a switch was. Why?" Kathryn gave Colin a puzzled look.

"Hmmm. I imagine the terrace light must go on automatically." Colin gestured for Kathryn to precede him up the steps to the terrace.

The driftwood planks felt cool on her bare feet as she gracefully ascended the small flight of stairs and swung open the door, only to stop dead in her tracks. Colin, a split second behind her, poked his head in the doorway and immediately realized why Kathryn had paused so abruptly.

"Bear!" she cried to the large man seated on the edge of the four poster, coiled and ready to strike. "What the hell are you doing here???"

Chapter
25

Colin and Walker looked at one another: the former a picture of apprehension, the latter a study in agitation. Kathryn wasn't at all sure what was going on. "Bear! Congratulate us!" she blurted out, taking Colin's arm. "We're thinking of getting married!"

"What?!"

Kathryn thought she heard the response in stereo. "What? What do you mean, *what*? What the hell! Hooray for spontaneity! Healthy marriages have been forged on a lot less," she added tipsily. "Don't be all upset, Walker Hart, because you missed your chance by being such a Permanently Shortsighted Bachelor! Forgive me, I'm drunk. No, don't. Hot toddies plus Taittinger plus tawny port equals truth serum. You know, not everyone wants to grow old and lonely and maybe even fat all by themselves."

Walker rose, all six-plus feet of him. "I just hope it's not too late. You haven't done anything stupid, either of you?"

Kathryn didn't like the way that sounded. "What the hell are you talking about, Bear?"

"Fleetwood knows damn well what I mean."

Colin stood just inside the doorway, pale and silent. His expression was one of shock, dismay, and guilt.

"If this is some kind of ridiculous macho showdown, Bear, I'm not impressed. You really know how to ruin a girl's weekend."

"Kathryn, I would like to speak to you outside. Alone."

Kathryn looked back at Colin, the pain in his face evident. "Do you have any idea what this is about?"

Colin sighed resolutely. "Go with him." He gently kissed Kathryn's forehead and unclasped his arm from hers.

"Let's take a walk on the beach." Walker took Kathryn firmly by the hand and led her out of the Carriage House.

"I'm not going to pretend I'm glad to see you, Walker. And I know you didn't 'just happen to be in the neighborhood,' " she spat. "I don't appreciate your spying on me. And when I get back to New York, I'm going to find out how to divorce my sister."

"Don't blame Eleanor," he said as they headed down the path to the surf.

"How else did you find out where I was?"

"Actually, I didn't. My mother did."

"Your mother?"

"Rushie. Ruth Goldfarb. She's back to using her maiden name ever since the archbishop of Canterbury annulled her marriage to Dafydd Glendower. Don't ask. So she returned stateside to reclaim her business. Not a moment too soon, if you ask me."

Kathryn disengaged her hand from Walker. "Listen to me. Once upon a time, what feels like a long, long time ago, we had an arrangement. You were not going to butt into my life. You were going to adhere to the contract I made with Six in the City, and nothing more. We have a strictly business relationship, you and I. And you can both blame and congratulate yourself for that. Bringing a woman home to *my* apartment—"

She felt the tension rising in her throat and became short of breath. "If you can't deal with the fact that I might actually be happy—for once—and accept that you've found me a good match—for a change—then go see a therapist. But, just under the wire, and not a bachelor too soon, you found me someone who actually wants to marry me. So if you can't celebrate with me, then get the hell away!"

"Colin Fleetwood can't marry you, Kathryn." Walker's voice was stern and even, almost parental in tone.

"Don't give me that alpha-male jealousy crap. Did you think that if you came up here and declared your undying love for me, I'd 'see the error of my ways' and call it off with Colin? No thank you, however. Kitty don't play that. I do have some pride left, you know." She increased her stride and headed back to the Carriage House.

"Damnit, I'm serious, you little idiot! I didn't say you *shouldn't* marry Colin. I said you *can't*."

"Ooooooooh . . . 'Little idiot'! That's charming. You *so* know how to talk to a woman. It'll make me fall right into your arms, apologizing profusely for causing you emotional distress, and plight you my troth. Why don't you just beat your chest, grab yourself a fistful of my hair, club me over the head, and drag me back to the Massachusetts mainland? You don't want me, anyway. You just want to win."

"You're not listening to me!" Walker sped up, and in moments he caught up to Kathryn, still plowing full steam ahead up the path. "Which word didn't you understand? You can't marry Colin Fleetwood."

"Don't play semantic games. It's none of your business. It's my life. And Colin's decision," she replied through her teeth.

"Actually, I think his *wife*—Gemma—would have a lot to say about it, too. And so would Viola and Sebastian."

Their rapid-fire barrage of words came to a screeching halt. *Boom. Thud. Silence.*

Her system was shutting down. Every nerve ending pinged and fizzled, causing her body to shake involuntarily. Kathryn's voice trembled. "That's a good one. Tell me another. Like the Mets are gonna win another World Series in my lifetime."

"Colin is already married, Kathryn. It's the truth. I wouldn't joke about that. You're too important to me."

Her world spun with dizzying speed, her vision beginning to blur. "Noooo!" she cried, shattering the night air. She felt her legs give way, her toes no longer strong enough to grip the ground beneath her.

In an instant, Walker was behind her, supporting her weight before she collapsed into the brush. Her arms flailed, trying to push him away, but he held her tight. "Do you want to hit me?"

Kathryn gradually became still, yet remained unable to turn to face him. Her face was streaked with tears. It was taking every bit of her self-control to master her breath and stabilize her shuddering body. She shook her head and tried to speak, but no words would emerge.

Walker tried to lift Kathryn into his arms, but she resisted. "I'll go up there under my own steam, thank you.

I don't want your misplaced chivalry." Her voice was thick and husky, her mouth dry. "Stay outside, Bear. I need to do this alone." With trembling hands she smudged the tears away. Her palms were stained with black rivulets of mascara. Kathryn walked slowly up the steps to the Carriage House, which glowed with a surreal brilliance under the full moon. She stood in the doorway, motionless, raising her eyes to Colin. "Why?" she asked quietly.

Colin, still stunned, looked helpless and beaten.

"At least you look contrite, Colin. I suppose that's something." It was hard to stop her lower lip from quivering.

To compound things, the alcohol she had consumed throughout the evening hit her head and her stomach at the same time. Her voice sounded remote to her own ears—distant—as though everything were happening underwater. "I take it Viola and Sebastian aren't your *cats*."

"I'm afraid not, Kathryn. They're my twins. Seven years old."

"You've got a wife and kids . . . how could you have asked me to marry you? I don't understand," she wept.

Walker entered the room from the deck. "I hate to sound cold about this, but all three of us could be looking at the losing end of expensive lawsuits," he informed them. "If you two had . . . relations . . . Colin could end up in divorce court, with Six in the City and Kitty named as accessories. Not only is Fleetwood here an adulterer, but he was on his way to becoming a bigamist."

Colin realized that he had been missing a piece of the puzzle. "You're jumping the gun, here, Hart. First of all,

Kathryn and I did not do what you're assuming we did, and secondly, I never asked Kathryn to marry me."

Kathryn's tear-stained face contorted. "What?" she asked, incredulous.

Colin shook his head as he began to understand what had happened. "Two countries divided by a common language," he said ruefully. "If you recall our conversation of this afternoon, I said 'I should like very much to marry you.' And when I made my wish upon that star this evening, I expressed the fervent desire to be able to give you everything you deserve."

"I don't get it," she said, the words thick upon her tongue.

"I'm terribly sorry, Kathryn. But I *am* already married, which does not change the fact that I meant every word I said. And were my circumstances different, or altered, I *would* like very much to marry you and to be in a position to provide you with all that you merit."

"Then, why? Why are we here? Why did you register with a dating service?"

Colin sighed and sat on the edge of the bed. "For the past year or so, I have been spending half my time in New York. I wanted to be able to meet a lady with whom to share my time when I am in the States. No less."

"Perhaps you *sought* no *less* than a compatible companion, but it seems to me that you were *hoping* for a lot *more* than that. You kissed me! And you let me kiss you back! On my planet, mutual exchanges of that nature and intensity do not exactly lead the kissee to believe that the kisser's intentions are merely platonic. You had to have been planning to make love with me. The Tugman House does not exactly inspire thoughts of purely congenial affection."

"I admit that I was falling in love with you, Kathryn. Even after so short a time in your company. To answer your question about whether or not we would have ended up having sex, I don't know. I honestly don't know. Can't a man have mixed emotions, be confused, love more than one woman at once?"

Colin's defense sounded hollow; like the lame excuse it was. Kathryn realized in an instant what a fool she had been. Her infatuation for Colin was immediately replaced with a queasiness in her stomach: a manifestation of her newfound disgust for the pilot. "There are commandments, Colin, that several million people actually live by. And it's hard for me to believe that you were totally unsure or undecided about the sex question. You rented one room for the two of us. There's only one bed in here. I came here with you in good faith. If I had known you were married, none of us would be sitting in this room right now."

The pilot was silent.

She looked over at Walker. "You've both betrayed me, as far as I'm concerned. Colin's little sin of omission was a pretty grievous one. When exactly were you planning to tell me that you were already married? I would have been entirely in the dark, had it not been for Walker, who has breached his business contract with me in spectacular fashion by fixing me up with five out of five unsuitable men. I don't even know which of you I dislike more at this moment. I even hate myself for wearing my heart on my sleeve and trusting you both, instead of following my initial instinct never to enroll in a matchmaking service in the first place, and never to fall in love with the inflexible, unattainable, impossibly myopic man who runs it! Aaarrrrrrrghhhhhh!!"

Kathryn collapsed on the bed. "Right now, I'm too ragged to deal with this rationally. Now get out." Each man looked at her as though she were speaking to the other one. "I mean both of you. Get out now."

"Where do you expect us to sleep?" Colin asked.

"The beach . . . that hot tub out there . . . the bowels of Hell. I don't really care. But *I'm* the one who deserves to sleep in this room tonight. It's too late to get off the island. The ferries stopped running hours ago, otherwise I would call a cab and be on the next boat to Woods Hole."

Walker installed himself in one of the armchairs. "Perhaps you should talk to Edie or Dave and see if there's a room available in the main house, Fleetwood. My mother, who is the owner of record for Six in the City, has a thing about men who try to deceive their wives. She's even more of a hard-ass on people of either gender who try to deceive *her*. I've got three women to appease here: my mother, your wife, and Kathryn. I will phone Mrs. Fleetwood and offer to refund your five-hundred-dollar enrollment fee, thanking her in advance for reconsidering her urge to file a long-distance lawsuit naming us as co-conspirators in your adulterous shenanigans. I can only hope that the net result will end up appeasing two-thirds of the women in question."

" 'Pay no attention to that man behind the curtain!' " the supine Kathryn crowed, dramatically waving her right arm. "I don't suppose you've got anything in that metaphorical bag for me, Mr. Wizard," she added ruefully.

"You've made it clear to me more than once that I don't have the tricks in my bag to make everything all better for you, Kitty. Which means that your problem will be the hardest for me to fix," Walker replied softly.

"But it doesn't mean I'm giving up. I'm painfully aware that I owe you big-time. And I know I keep saying that to you. And then I keep screwing up. But I haven't given up trying to find ways to make amends."

Colin zippered up his weekender, shouldered it, and headed for the door. He stopped and turned back, as if to say something to Kathryn and Walker, but no words came. His manner was both resigned and regretful. He tried to smile, but the result was a sort of grimace. Then he nodded his head as if to say good-bye, and left the Carriage House.

After Colin's retreat, Kathryn walked out to the deck and lay in the hammock for a few minutes, but her insides were churning too much for her to feel relaxed by the effect of lying in suspension. "I'm outta here," she announced as she extricated herself from the macramé in an ungainly series of moves. Barelegged, she headed toward the ocean.

"Hey! Kitty, be careful out there!" She looked back toward the cottage to see Walker following her out onto the path.

"Leave me alone, Bear! I need this!" she called as she picked up speed, the sand becoming softer under her feet as she got closer to the water's edge. She ran into the surf, letting out a primal scream before she noticed that Walker was still behind her.

"What are you doing? I want to be alone. I didn't want you to follow me."

"I thought you were trying to drown yourself," Walker replied.

"Nut! I'm a drama teacher, not a drama queen. I was cleansing myself of Colin."

Walker wanted to approach Kathryn and put his arm

around her but knew that it was the wrong time to do so; after her recent tirade she would not be a receptive audience. He wished she could see that he wasn't deliberately messing up her life; in fact, he felt truly dreadful about everything she had been through since she enrolled with Six in the City. Most importantly, he wished there had been something in his emotional "bag of tricks" as Kitty had referred to it, that would enable him to tell her outright that he loved her. He wasn't ever afraid to show his love, but the three little words were so hard for him to say aloud. He'd also been unable to get his mouth around them that night in Kitty's bathroom when she was so doubly devastated: first by discovering him with Valerie, then learning that Glen Pinsky was such a weirdo.

"Do you want to go back to the room for a towel? You'll catch cold," Walker said, looking at Kathryn's bare legs.

"Nope. I'm okay, thanks. I just want to sit out here for a while."

Walker watched her head for slightly higher ground, and seat herself on a bluff, staring at the hematite blackness of the water. "Want company?"

Kathryn shrugged.

"When you're ready, why don't you freshen up and I'll take you to the bar for whatever you want. You can get totally snookered if you desire and I promise not to make fun of you if you start dancing on the table or reproach you in the future with anything you may say while under the influence."

"I'm already totally snookered." Walker was trying so hard to be engaging, it was hard not to give in. Besides, what else did she have to do that evening—sit in the Carriage House all alone, stewing over the mess that was her life and watching *America's Most Wanted*? She stood up and walked down the bluff to Walker, who was waiting for her with his hand outstretched. "Nevertheless, you're right about one thing," she said to him. "I could use a good stiff one right about now."

A pleasant-faced young woman escorted Walker and Kathryn to a quiet corner table in Hadley's, the Tugman House bar, and took their drink order. Except for the large shuttered windows that opened out onto the Atlantic, the rest of the lounge had the air of an upscale old-English pub. Something about the red net covering over the glass candleholders was distinctly New England seacoast, though. The service was both expert and efficient. The waitress rolled a cart over to their table and warmed Walker's glass of Martell X.O. over an open flame before serving it to him, then she took her cart back to the bar.

"To better times," Walker said, clinking his snifter with Kathryn's glass of tawny port.

"Back at ya." It was her first smile in hours. "I have to be honest about this . . . I'm glad you got me out of the clutches of the diabolical Colin in the nick of time. But you didn't really need to drive all the way up here to do it."

She expected a response from Walker and was surprised when she didn't get one. "So I have to ask you," she continued, taking a very large swig of port, "it's a very heroic 'Prince Charming' thing to do—coming up here and all—but at the same time, I was wondering what your primary motives were in tracking me down. Which is it: are you falling in love with me even though you haven't used the *L* word in my presence, or are you just trying to make sure your family business doesn't go belly up?"

Walker rolled the snifter in his hands and watched the legs dribble in capillary-shaped rivulets down the inside of the glass. He wasn't ignoring her. He was thinking.

Kathryn surveyed the room. "This is a *very* pretty place," she remarked. "The whole premises. When I first got here and took a look around, I said that this inn would be a great place to have a nervous breakdown, but I hadn't really meant it literally. Seems like it became a self-fulfilling prophecy. God has no sense of humor sometimes."

"On the contrary," Walker said, as he sipped his cognac. "I think he's got a rather wicked one."

Kathryn took a small sip of her fortified wine. It tasted delicious and she thought she'd wanted it, but the last thing she really needed was another drink. "In that case, here's one of His 'Jewish jokes.' Don't look now, but I think I see your-mother-the-Yenta sitting at the bar romancing a Ricardo Montalban clone."

Chapter
26

Walker's insides seized up. Hoping Kathryn was pulling his leg, he nevertheless turned to face the high stools arranged around the perimeter of the bar, and was appalled to see Rushie flirting her ass off with a smarmy-looking silver fox, a stereotypical aging lothario from lacquered gray pompadour to glinting pinky ring. They could ignore her, but that didn't buy them much time, so Walker bit the bullet and he and Kathryn approached the bar.

"Have a Manhattan, honey," Rushie said to Walker without missing a beat. She noticed that her son was holding Kathryn's hand. "He'd better be doing right by you, sweetheart." She reached out and pinched Kathryn's cheek. "Oh, I'm sorry, did I leave a mark?" she asked, having inadvertently dug her nail into Kathryn's flesh. "This one's a silk wrap, and I'm not used to the length."

"*Mother,* did you follow me?" Walker asked. "After I expressly told you to let me handle things on my own?"

"As the young people say, 'you got a problem with that?' " She lowered her voice and leaned toward Walker. "Actually, I did follow you—to make sure that you handled the Colin Fleetwood debacle—and to preserve my business. I couldn't let word of a mishap like this get out in the matchmaking business or I'd be back in retail, selling *schmatas* on Seventh Avenue. Oh, and by the way," Rushie added, batting her heavily mascara-ed lashes, "meet Gillian." She gestured toward the Montalban clone. "Gil, this is my son the big shot."

Gillian flashed a smile full of perfectly capped teeth that competed with the flash from the diamond stud in his pinky ring. "We're engaged," he said, beaming.

Walker looked at the pair of them, stunned. "I've heard that line already tonight, and now it's twice too many," he said tartly. "It was . . . lovely . . . to meet you," he said to Gillian.

Kathryn, meanwhile, was checking out the other patrons. Walker followed her gaze. "Who does that guy think he is, David Cassidy?" he quipped, looking at the mane of chestnut hair on a gentleman sitting alone with his drink.

"That isn't—no, it couldn't be—" Kathryn said. "Bear, I'll bet you twenty-five dollars that I know that guy. Too well. I'd know that '70s look anywhere. Hey, Lance!" she called out. The man turned around. He gave Kathryn an uncomfortable look and a sheepish wave.

"You know him?" Rushie asked Kathryn.

"Yup, that is—well, that *was* my fiancé, once upon a time."

"What a coincidence. He's on his honeymoon," Rushie said.

They watched as a willowy woman returned to Lance's table from the direction of the restroom. She caught a glimpse of herself in the mirror above the bar, and admired the image reflecting back. Her dark hair was pulled into a tight dancer's bun and she must have weighed about ninety-eight pounds.

"Rushie, is that Talia?" Walker asked his mother.

"Your old Talia? Sure. What's the matter, you don't recognize her? Maybe she's put on a pound or two since you two used to go out, but other than that, she looks just the same. Dances with the Martha Graham Company these days. I fixed the happy couple up. Lance came in as a client after his old fiancée broke off their engagement. I guess that would be you, Kathryn. November will be a year since he came in."

"I think I'm gonna be sick," Kathryn said under her breath. "The man's got a shorter turnaround time than a commuter jet."

Rushie leaned over and spoke in a confidential whisper to Kathryn. "If it makes you feel any better . . . about his hair . . . they're *plugs*." She winked knowingly.

Walker waved his hand to fan away the clouds of smoke that trailed from Rushie's powder blue cigarillo. He blinked several times, then scrunched his eyes shut for a few seconds. "Would you mind terribly if Kitty and I returned to our drinks," he asked Rushie. "We have a lot to talk about this evening." He draped his arm over Kathryn's shoulder and escorted her back to their table. "I wonder if they serve Alka Seltzer here," he muttered. "Oh, well, it all happened long after we broke up and I wasn't even working with Six in the City when Talia enrolled. Obviously she and Lance were removed from the files once they found each other. But I can't say they don't deserve each other," he said to Kathryn. "From what you've said about Lance and from what I know about Talia, they're two of the vainest people in the world."

Kathryn decided to see the humor in the situation. "I think they should honeymoon at Versailles," she giggled. "They'll go nuts in The Hall of Mirrors."

They raised their glasses and clinked a toast. "Here's to narrow escapes," Kathryn proposed. "We're much better off without them."

"Did you ever feel like you were performing in a musical comedy?" Walker asked her. He tapped the top of Kathryn's hand and indicated that she should look over at the entrance to Hadley's.

"What a coincidence!" Eleanor exclaimed as she and Dan made a beeline for Kathryn and Walker.

"Gee, Eleanor, what brings *you* up to this neck of the woods?"

"We thought we'd take a much needed weekend to ourselves," Eleanor told her sister. "Can I grab her for a minute," she asked Walker. Not waiting for an answer, Eleanor steered Kathryn into the ladies' room.

"Oh, tell me this is all a big ol' co-inky-dink," Kathryn said. "Puh-lease."

"Well, I didn't expect to see you sitting with Walker, although I think I covered for it nicely, if I do say so myself. And Dan and I did need some quality time together. When I realized that the Ruth Goldfarb who kept calling you was Rushie-the-Yenta, and once I told her where you'd gone, it occurred to me that you really *could* have gone off for the weekend with some serial killer. So I thought it wouldn't hurt for us to have our romantic getaway here so we could check up on you."

"C'mon, Ellie, don't tell me Tugman House suddenly has all these empty rooms in peak foliage season."

"What planet are you on? When I called this place, a woman named Edie laughed at me and told me they had been booked up for this weekend since March. Colin got in on a cancellation and he's apparently a 'frequent flyer' here. And a big tipper. Edie said they actually do keep a short list of preferred customers who want to be phoned in case there are cancellations on peak weeks. Dan and I are staying in Oak Bluffs. I don't think Rushie has a room. I think she came up here on her own but based on what you've told me about her she'll probably find a man to sponge off of. We know Walker didn't have a reservation; so that just leaves your long-haired ex-fiancé 'George of the Asphalt Jungle,' and since Lance obviously knew he was getting married and going on a honeymoon, odds are that he booked his room well ahead of time."

"I'm glad to know that's sorted out," Kathryn said.

"I just wanted you to know that I was really concerned, Kitty. I'm not going to bust up the rest of your weekend. Besides Dan and I need to get some serious talking done."

After Eleanor rejoined her husband, Kathryn returned to the table to find a second glass of port at her place.

"I thought you might not mind if I ordered you another drink," Walker said warmly.

"No . . . not at all. It's very sweet of you." She didn't have the heart to tell him that she didn't even want to look at another glass of booze right now.

"Is everything all right?" Walker asked her. "You look a little glazed."

"I'm fine. I'm very fine," Kathryn said slowly. It was occurring to her that despite all of Walker's maddening rationalizations and protestations regarding commitment, he had in fact made one to her, albeit in a roundabout way. It wasn't a big thing, but it was a significant one. His counseling Eleanor was an indication that he cared about involving himself in Kathryn's relative's crises. Already, he'd come further than Lance ever had in that respect.

She took a tiny sip of her drink. "There's something else that you've done which is really sweet . . . which you certainly had no need or reason to do, and I want to thank you for it: Eleanor and Dan. I don't know what you said to Ellie because she won't share it with me, but whatever it was got her off my couch and into Dan's Lexus."

"You're wrong about one thing."

Kathryn looked up from her glass, straight into Walker's eyes. "What?"

"That I had no reason to speak with your sister. At first, I thought it was a joke—coming to *me* to ask some serious questions about her marriage. But I had two very good reasons to offer whatever advice I could, if it might be in any way useful to her. First of all, you are tremendously special to me, and upheaval in your family affects you as well as the relatives who are directly involved. And if you're important to me, then by extension so are your sister and her husband."

He drained his glass. "And there's another, smaller reason which is a bit less altruistic. The conversation I had with Eleanor was the first time I've really felt like I was being helpful to a couple in all the time I've been involved with the matchmaking service. It's no secret that I've been very cynical about marriage and about relationships in general. I thought Six in the City was part of the problem, not the solution. So, in many ways, your sister's visit was the kick in the ass I needed to accept the fact that matchmaking—when the ingredients are mixed right—can be a good recipe for happiness. I'm not the one who brought her together with Dan, but if there was anything I could do to help *keep* them together, I was willing to step up to the plate. You should get the credit for it Kitty, not me. You're turning me into a hopeless romantic. Who knew what a gorgeous woman in velvet who bakes gingerbread cats could do to a cynical old financial analyst?"

Blindsided by his declaration, Kathryn struggled to contain her emotions in public. "You're swell, you know that? You're really swell. Thanks," Kathryn said, placing her hand over Walker's. "Let's get our check and get out of here," she whispered. "Before you make me cry in front of our uninvited audience."

Walker and Kathryn were getting up to leave when Eleanor approached them. "I don't know if I ever thanked you properly for bothering to listen to me a couple of weeks ago. You deserve Brownie Points for what you did. So, that said . . ." Eleanor handed Walker a glossy shopping bag. "Dan will just have to suffer without these this weekend. You know what finally made him come around? He tasted them and said it would be wrong of me to deprive New York of such a treat. So, 'wonder of wonders, miracle of miracles,' he's willing to invest in my new venture."

Kathryn beamed and reached out to hug her sister. "Congratulations. I suppose in the long run, you shouldn't be surprised. After all, you were the one who reminded me that the way to a man's heart is through his stomach!"

When Kathryn and Walker returned to the Carriage House, they both made a dash for the bathroom. "Hey, ladies first," Kathryn teased, elbowing Walker out of the way and shutting the door.

"You just went to the bathroom at Hadley's with your sister."

"What you don't know about women could fill a book. We didn't go to the bathroom; we went to the ladies' room. Big difference. Where else could we have a private conversation? If you're that desperate, go use the bushes out by the deck. Just head far enough away from the room."

"That's not why I need to get in there," Walker called to her.

Kathryn washed her hands and opened the door. "Here! It's yours. Jeez, what happened to your eyes? Don't rub them; whatever it is, it'll only make it worse. You were doing that a little in Hadley's, too, but now they're really red. Can I do anything for you?"

"Yeah. Both my right and my left eye offend me, so do me a favor and pluck them out. It's Rushie's cigarette smoke that compounded it, I think." He took his dopp kit out of a nylon overnight bag and dumped a pile of contact lens paraphernalia on the marble shelf by the sink.

"Bear!"

"I finally started piecing together stuff you noticed a few times . . . my klutziness. I always thought I was just accident prone. But then you made that comment about my dancing. And when I broke your glass pitcher, you yelled at me and told me I needed glasses."

"I'm sorry about that. It wasn't very nice of me."

"Apology accepted. I kept thinking about that incident. Even though I knew you were mad at me and lashed out, maybe there was some truth to it. So I actually went to an optometrist and got my eyes checked out. And, *Ms.* Smartypants, you were right. I told the guy I didn't want to wear glasses, so he gave me a prescription for contact lenses; but they're bothering the hell out of me and have been ever since I got them."

"You were making all these weird faces that day I met Colin in your office, but I thought you were just trying to semaphore me with your eyes, or something. It never in a million years would have occurred to me that you were wearing contacts at the time. Wow. Why didn't you tell me before?"

Walker was rummaging through his collection of solution bottles and little plastic contact carrying cases. "I was embarrassed that I never figured it out on my own. I still can't get used to them; it feels like there's something in my eyes."

"There *is* something in your eyes. And, if you don't mind my asking, if the lenses are bothering you so much, how come you haven't taken them out yet?"

Walker squinted at Kathryn and then bent over the sink. "Go away, Kathryn. You don't want to look." He turned on the water and in a series of tentative maneuvers, attempted to take out one of the lenses, clearly squeamish at squeezing his eyeball to get the tiny disk to pop out. "Shit!! Goddamn son of a bitch!" Although Walker had finally conquered his fear, the lens dropped into the sink and started its journey south.

They both reached into the basin to retrieve it; Kathryn thought she had the situation under control. "Hold on, I've got long nails; let me try to scoop it up before it goes down the . . ."

Drain.

"Goddamnit! I can't do this!" Walker aggressively threw the saline bottles into the wastebasket. "I. Am. Not. Meant. To. Wear. Contacts." He sat down on the edge of the tub, defeated.

Kathryn felt unequipped to help him. *Should I give him a hug now,* she wondered. *Or would that be misinterpreted.* She went over and tousled Walker's hair. "Hey, who was it who said 'don't sweat the small stuff'?"

"Someone who never tried to install venetian blinds over his corneas. Besides, don't you know that the response is 'it's *all* small stuff'?"

"They're wrong, Bear. You've done a helluva lot lately . . . and it has not gone unappreciated. Now what about a long hot bath in this wildly decadent jacuzzi? You'll feel much better."

Walker's smile lit up the room. "I'll definitely feel much better if you join me."

"Sneak."

Chapter
27

"C'mon . . . you've heard that expression 'you wash my back and I'll wash yours'?"

"That's *scratch*, Bear." Kathryn looked at Walker. She couldn't help smiling. "Tell you what," Kathryn said. "I'm going to close the door and go out there and slip into something more comfortable. When you're in that tub with bubbles up to your armpits, give a holler and I'll come in and wash your back."

"I guess I'll take what I can get."

Kathryn closed the door to the bathroom and changed her clothes. She read a few more pages of the short story she'd begun earlier until she was satisfied that she'd heard the water running long enough.

"Red Rover, Red Rover, can the redhead come over?" Walker called from the bathroom.

"Ready or not, here I come!" Kathryn opened the door to the bathroom, and was relieved when she saw that Walker had abided by her rules. She hadn't expected him to.

"Hey, hey," he admonished, waving her closer with a soapy arm. "You said you were going to slip into something more comfortable."

"And by that I assume that you inferred that I was going to get naked?"

"Yes, actually. Well . . . I was hoping. No, I didn't think you really would. Why the hell did you pack that for a romantic getaway? I mean, I think the Saints jersey makes you look incredibly hot, but I can't presume to vouch for what Colin might have thought."

Kathryn approached the enormous whirlpool, grabbed a terry washcloth and knelt beside the tub. "Okay, turn around."

"Wait. You're not properly attired." Walker scooped up a poof of bubbles and deposited them on Kathryn's nose.

"Hey, no fair!" She skimmed a handful of the fragrant froth from the top of the tub and paid him back.

Walker splashed some water at her in return. "At least *I'm* dressed for the occasion!"

Kathryn skittered back away from the tub as Walker continued to toss water in her direction. "Hey, stop! You'll flood the bathroom! And you're getting me all wet."

"Then you shouldn't have come in here unless you were naked. This is usually where hotel rooms keep the water," he teased. "Or you should have worn something waterproof."

Kathryn leaned over the side of the tub, took the remaining bubbles from her nose and plopped them between Walker's eyes. She started to splash him playfully.

"Doesn't bother me; I'm already wet," he laughed, grabbing her wrists before she could toss any more water in his face. "Young lady, you're coming in! Resistance is futile!" In a matter of seconds, Kathryn, still wearing her New Orleans Saints jersey—and her underwear—found herself flailing on top of Walker in the whirlpool.

And it felt really good. *Really* good.

He lifted her face to his, and with his thumb, gently wiped away a falling tear.

She was the one who kissed first.

Kathryn's arms encircled Walker's damp neck, clutching, clinging. Her hands groped upwards, grasping his thick hair, massaging his scalp, as her mouth opened wider to admit the insistent intrusion of his tongue. Never before had she been so hungry for a man, never before had she so completely abandoned herself to physical desire, no matter what the consequences.

She slithered over him as they embraced, trying to keep her head above water . . . in every sense. Kathryn felt him hard and firm against her thigh and maneuvered herself over him. It was then that she agreed with Walker that she was entirely overdressed for the occasion. With his help, she sat up in the tub, yanked her sopping Saints shirt over her head and wrestled herself out of her panties, throwing the clothes in a sodden heap on the tile floor. She slid back down in the deep bath until she and Walker were reclining side by side. "Why are you smiling at me like that?" she asked softly.

"Your eyes. They're deep blue."

"So are yours." She threw her leg over his and pulled him back to her, devouring his mouth. He smelled new: sweet and clean, and he tasted of cognac. The slickness of his soapy skin aroused her further. She buried her hands in the soft, mossy hair growing around his nipples while she nibbled gently at his lower lip.

Walker kneaded Kathryn's back, exploring the contours of her slim waist and hips. He cupped her firm rear and drew her closer, closer, until she was again on top of him.

Kathryn pulled her mouth away from Walker's just long enough to beg. "Take me, please," she said huskily. "I want to feel you inside me." She was ready for him—emotionally as well as physically.

He had waited so long for her, had wanted this moment to happen from the minute she walked into his office. Her body welcomed him, matching his rhythm like a longtime lover; his body felt like it was coming home.

Kathryn clung to him with every muscle, hungrily taking in his tongue as it danced in her mouth, caressing it with her own, and greedily arching her hips toward Walker's to bring him deeper and deeper inside her, gripping and releasing him in a sustained rhythm.

His expression was beatific. "How the hell do you do that?"

Kathryn gave him a Mona Lisa smile. "But I didn't know I could do it underwater."

"Are you noisy in bed?" he gasped.

"It depends on the company," she teased hoarsely, then kissed him again.

He found out for himself when she shuddered her climax, surrendering entirely, slickly clinging to his torso, her mouth wide open, her head thrown back. Her hips bucked against his, as Walker thrust with increased intensity. Her nails dug into his back when she felt him release inside her, and he muffled his cries against her damp shoulder.

For a long time they held each other, somewhat suspended by what water remained in the whirlpool, enjoying the little aftershocks of their lovemaking. Walker cradled her head to his chest and tenderly kissed her tangled mop of curls.

"We didn't take full advantage of our surroundings," he whispered, and guided Kathryn's body to one of the water jets. She felt an instant arousal from the pulsing water. "It feels good, doesn't it?" Walker asked softly.

Kathryn nodded, her eyes closed, succumbing to the sensation. "Amazing. It feels . . . truly . . . amazing."

Walker's voice was barely above a whisper. "Open your eyes, Kitty. I want to see your face. And I want you to see mine."

She locked his passion-filled eyes in her gaze, her breath coming in quicker, more intense inhalations. Her lower lip seemed to swell, quivering almost imperceptibly as she relaxed her mouth and felt the surge of warmth spreading through her blood. What an intoxicating sensation it was to watch him watch her . . . and to revel in his awareness—as he took her again—that he was truly the source of her pleasure, manifested by the million and a half sensations coursing through her body and reflecting themselves on her countenance.

Blissed out, minutes later, Kathryn flashed Walker a wicked little smile. "You up for heading out to the deck?" she said dreamily. "We didn't try the hot tub."

Sometime well after midnight, when she found herself drifting off to sleep against his strong, warm body, she pulled away. His arm was draped over her shoulder, drawing her close, keeping her safe. It was too safe, and it felt too good. She remembered the night he'd fallen asleep on her bed and how, after she'd finally decided to join him because it was impossible to get any rest on the couch, they'd awakened nestled like spoons. She recalled

the conversation they'd had weeks ago back in her apartment about making love with one another, as well as her
response—her reasons for refusing to give in to her own
desires. Now that they'd finally had sex, at least she
knew what she'd been denying herself.

And she was well and truly in love with Walker "Bear"
Hart. Among other things, he had rescued her sister's
marriage from the rocks and he had rescued *her* in the
nick of time last night. In fact, Kathryn realized, when she
did the math, in so many ways he'd been rescuing her
pretty much since they'd met. Bear was the one who
found her lost lingerie after her dismal date with Barnaby.
Bear was the man who picked her up from the police
precinct, brought her home and made her feel whole and
human again after the debacle with Eddie Benson. Bear
was the guy who had spent a sleepless night worried
about her being with Rick Byron until the wee hours of
the morning. It was Bear who had eased her pain even
while he told her the truth about Glen Pinsky's macabre
living arrangements. Plus, he seemed to be the first guy
who ever actually paid attention to anything she told
him, as evidenced by his effort to cheer her up by bringing
her a bouquet of her favorite flowers as a little surprise to
go along with the bottle of aspirin she'd requested. Oh
yeah, she mused, smiling to herself. There's the great sex
part. Never underestimate the great sex part.

But when they got back to New York, what would
happen? She would be tempted to cook brunch for him
again. Try very hard not to think about the urban
equivalent of white picket fences or to read aloud the
"Wedding of the Week" column to him, even during a
Jets time-out. He would remind her that he had no in-

terest in forming a permanent attachment, while he lounged on her couch, using her coffee table for an ottoman, shod in silly-looking socks, reading the sports section of the Sunday *Times*, while Gershwin or Porter was playing on the stereo.

Nope.

Step back, take stock, rearrange perspective.

No more mixed messages from men. After a literally exhausting search for a husband, and, yes, well, *despite* all the amazing sex they'd just shared, Kathryn was on the verge of deciding she was better off alone.

Her energy was at half-mast the following morning. After breakfast where Walker picked up the tab for everything, including Tugman House's lodging bill, Colin having beat an early retreat to the airport, Kathryn and Walker tossed their overnight bags in the trunk of Walker's rented car and headed out of town.

"Hold it! You just missed the turn for the ferry," Kathryn said, looking back at the directional sign they'd just driven past.

"Did I?"

"Yes. This causeway is taking us farther away from the Vineyard Haven slip. We're headed toward Oak Bluffs."

"Oh. Gee. So we are."

"You're up to something." Kathryn caught Walker smiling mysteriously. She wasn't sure how to behave with him this morning. He wasn't acting all snuggly and lovey-dovey, so maybe her middle-of-the-night resolution to put some distance between them, despite the intense passion they'd finally shared, was the right decision after all.

As the road became less rural, Walker instructed her to close her eyes.

"Did I ever tell you I hate surprises like this?" Kathryn told him, obeying nonetheless. He made a quick turn into a parking place and brought the engine to a halt.

"Keep 'em closed, now," Walker said. Kathryn heard him get out of the car. A few moments later, he opened the passenger door for her. "Take my hand."

She groped for his hand and he steered her out of the vehicle, gently placing his hand on the top of her head, so she wouldn't injure herself in the process. Walker continued to hold her hand as he led her on a short walk that took them inside a building. The air smelled of peanuts, cotton candy, and artificially buttered popcorn, the scents of a carnival midway. She heard music. "Two, please," Walker said. He placed a small piece of paper in her hand and closed her fingers around it. "Okay you can open your eyes now."

Kathryn did so, and her reaction was one she would always remember. "It's the Flying Horses Carousel!"

Walker beamed at her. "Oldest one operating in the U.S. It dates from the 1870s, about thirty years before the one in Central Park."

She took in the scene, completely delighted, totally in her element. "They don't go up and down," she remarked. "And they're so skinny. And so much smaller than the horses on the Central Park carousel. Someone ought to feed you guys." She reached out to finger the genuine horsehair tail tacked to the wooden rump of one of the ponies. "How did you know about this place?"

"Read about the local attractions coming up here. When I stopped at a filling station for gas, I grabbed a map and read all the stuff printed at the bottom of it. I had the feeling you might need a treat. After last night, I thought you *really* needed it."

"I thought last night *was* the treat!" she replied suggestively. They climbed aboard the horses. Kathryn couldn't help laughing at how Walker's bulk dwarfed the poor wooden animal beneath him. With his long legs reaching the planking, it looked like he was riding in a toddler's plastic car where you have to propel it by walking your feet forward on the floor. Of all the adults on the carousel, Walker looked the silliest. Yet he appeared totally unselfconscious about it. Kathryn admired his pluck.

"Now, this is a proper carousel," Walker said. "This carousel has a brass ring." He stretched out his arm, easily reaching the metal bar that dispensed a series of brass rings, and snagged three in one try.

"Colin was right, though. You have to give them back before you leave," Kathryn said, slightly disappointed, noticing the sign next to the ring dispenser as her horse came around. Being much smaller than Walker, she had a harder time reaching for the rings, but handily grabbed one, although she was trying for two, as her horse passed by the bar. "I don't understand something, though, Bear. Why do people talk about going for the brass ring as though getting it was some monumental achievement? Life should always be this easy." She grinned beatifically. "Nevertheless. I love this!"

By the time the ride was over, Kathryn had a handful of brass rings. Walker had a pocketful. They dutifully returned their prizes to the ring collection box, and Walker bought them a striped cardboard container full of caramel corn. Back outside the Flying Horses building, Kathryn thanked him by jumping on him as though he were her Lindy partner, throwing her legs around his waist. The popcorn went flying into the street.

"You're extremely welcome," Walker laughed. And they were back on the road.

Chapter
28

Once they reached the mainland, following a lovely but otherwise uneventful remainder of the trip home, which included a pit stop at a Friendly's on the New England Thruway, Walker deposited Kathryn on her doorstep, kissed her passionately, refused her offer to step inside and have a drink, and went upstairs to the penthouse to try to repair his emotional circuits.

Three days later, the process was still underway.

"You can't barricade yourself in there, bro," Josh warned over the answering machine. "And if you think you're ignoring your mother, too, try again. She called *me* from Maui to see if you're okay."

Walker pushed a button on his mobile phone and continued to pound passionately away at his piano. "Talk, Josh."

"Pick up the damn receiver, Bear. I hate speakerphone. It's for people with Napoleon complexes, and you're too tall for that."

"Maui? What the hell is my mother doing in Maui? She said she was going to visit my aunt Sheila for a few days."

"That new guy she's engaged to has a timeshare there."

Walker was playing a sweeping romantic ballad—one of his own compositions, through the open receiver.

"Hey! It's next to impossible to hear a word you're saying while you're in the middle of taking out your frustrations on the keyboard."

"I know. And I can barely hear you, too. That's deliberate."

"Bear, if you're not going to talk to anyone about what happened on Martha's Vineyard, then why did you pick up the phone?"

"So you would know I was still alive and well, Josh."

"I know that sound, bro. You're on your third martini this evening, right about now."

"It was stupid and wrong of me to make love with her."

"Why?"

"Because she was in deep emotional pain after the whole Colin debacle. I'm afraid she's thinking I took advantage of that."

"If, after what happened between you, you don't contact her for over a week, you're feeding her fears, bro."

"Well, since you brought it up, that's why I've been staying away. To give us both time to think things over. Josh, you and my mother are standing on the sidelines of my life, coaching it like it's a three-legged potato race back at Camp Saranac. Go away."

"What we have here is a failure to communicate. Fine, then. I'm hanging up, bro." A click, and Josh was gone.

Another sip of his dry martini reminded Walker that he hated to drink alone. "Suits me." He switched off the phone and launched into "Where Is the Life that Late I Led?" from *Kiss Me, Kate*. He looked around the beige apartment, winced at the uncomfortable, impersonal

furniture and expensive paintings that he thought more
properly belonged on the wall of a corporate head-
quarters. The ceiling had been repaired, replastered, and
repainted, but he'd been too lazy and uninterested to
throw away the plastic tarps and clean house. Rushie
had bolted as usual, abrogating all domestic responsibilities, but at least for once she'd taken an active role in
handling a crisis by becoming involved in staging the
"intervention" between Kathryn and Colin. For once,
she'd run *toward* something, rather than away from it.
And if *Rushie* could change . . .

He'd finally come around to accepting the truth—that
his feelings for Kathryn had progressed beyond fascina-
tion and infatuation from the moment she had agreed to
let him crash in her apartment. *I love her,* he admitted
to himself. Now he needed to decide what to do about it.

Having hit upon a plan, it was time to execute it. For
the next few days, he tried to "accidentally" run into her.
He stayed in the building's laundry room baby-sitting his
clothes in case she happened to come down to the basement with her own washing. He scanned the room's bul-
letin board in case she'd lost another article of clothing.
Kathryn had avoided coming into the Six in the City offices and every day he found her predominating his
thoughts, taking his mind away from the matchmaking
business at hand.

On Saturday morning, he donned a T-shirt and running shorts, hopped the subway and jogged from the
Columbus Circle station into Central Park, hoping she
might be at the carousel. His heart lurched when he saw
her with Eleanor and Johanna, buying her niece a pop-
sicle from the vendor stationed adjacent to the merry-
go-round. He realized the women hadn't noticed him

standing about fifteen yards or so away. Should he make his move now? Step forward and make his declaration of love, tell Kathryn he'd been so adamant in his opposition to marriage and commitment that he hadn't realized what he might be missing in letting her get away? His thoughts were more or less in order, but he couldn't seem to articulate them as he practiced what he planned to say to her in his head. He watched, somewhat relieved, as Kathryn and Eleanor entered the tunnel that would lead them toward the zoo. He heard little Johanna call out "Echo . . . o . . . o . . . o" and her mom and aunt join in the game before their voices, and their bodies, faded into the distance.

It had been a week since they'd returned from Martha's Vineyard, and Kathryn had heard nothing from Walker. Her decision to get on with her life without him sucked. So, should she take the bull by the horns and be the first one to make contact, swallow her pride, ask him what was going on? Now, when she wanted to "casually" run into him in the high-rise, their paths weren't crossing. Stopping by his apartment just to chitchat would be a flimsy pretext. Besides, there was always the nagging—and nauseating—notion that he might have some other woman up there. She'd even gone with Eleanor and Johanna to the Central Park carousel on Saturday afternoon, thinking that if she and Walker were on the same wavelength, perhaps he'd make the trip up there. But no such luck.

By Monday, she couldn't put her mind to anything else but thoughts of Walker Hart.

"I don't get it, either," Eleanor sighed, crunching on a

gingerbread maple leaf. "You did nothing wrong, so don't blame yourself."

Kathryn was channeling her anger into cleaning her apartment. "I slept with him," she said, punctuating her speech with the aggressive plumping of an amethyst velvet pillow. "I had promised myself that making love with Bear was the last thing I would do. Not only that, it was my idea. Although it sounds impossible for anyone but a contortionist, I basically jumped him in the whirlpool."

"I thought you said you guys were sort of wrestling by the tub. Whaddya call it? Good clean fun? Maybe you made the right choice, after all. I mean, now maybe he'll realize what he was missing."

"Ellie, I've been *desperately* in love with that man for weeks. I knew he would blow all my circuits, and I was trying my damnedest to make myself believe that he was only a professional acquaintance. But then I learned he was a neighbor. And then he became a roommate. The lines of distinction became harder and harder to keep from blurring."

Kathryn dusted her coffee table with unnecessary vigor. "I ended up thinking of him—constantly—and after a while, whenever I was on one of those matches he arranged for me, I was always wishing it were Walker instead. And now that we've made love, I realize that I gave him what he wanted . . . played by his rules, instead of mine. Sex without commitment was never my intention. I haven't heard one word from him since we got back. That "guy-behavior" is why I decided to play the dating game for keeps in the first place. He's not calling me because, of course, he doesn't want to commit. He was totally aware of what a big deal it was for me to make love with him. I warned him when he first brought up the subject that I wanted him just as badly, but if I gave in, he'd end up breaking my heart eventually and no matter how great the sex between us might be, it wouldn't be worth the pain. So, he knows that if he rings me up and tries to be chatty or pretend that what happened between us was no big thing, despite the fact that part of me is desperate to hear from him, I'll rip his head off. Given that, he's probably wise to stay away from me—from his point of view. But it doesn't make it suck any less."

"He may be going through a reevaluation process, too, Kitty. He's certainly acting insensitive to your fears, but maybe he's upstairs dealing with his own demons. Let's say for the sake of argument, he's realized that he does want to be with you. He's probably scared out of his wits. Don't forget that Bear is a guy who has shied away from commitment for so long—I'm not saying that he's from Mars, but he might be finding himself in an unfamiliar universe and not know what to do about it. By the way, if you rub that table any harder, you'll dent it."

"Maybe *my* reevaluation is leading me in another direction. Who needs the pain, the anguish, and the worry? I've thought of nothing but Bear since we got back from the Vineyard. It's gotten in the way of my living the rest of my life."

"He still owes you one more bachelor, remember?"

Kathryn snorted in disgust. "Sorry, that wasn't very ladylike. I think I'll forfeit the favor, and not exercise my option-to-renew clause from Six in the City. One more bachelor is the last thing I want right now. I've learned a hell of a lot—about men and about myself—so I'll take a pass on what's behind door number six."

Eleanor picked up her leather carcoat. "I'm sorry, too," she told her sister. "I feel at least partially responsible, here. I know I told you the video dating service would be a good idea. And not just to shut up The Yenta."

"It *was* a good idea, El. If you hadn't dared me to walk into Six in the City, I would not have met Walker Hart. I'm angry with myself, because I love him. For one thing, in an odd way—even though you know how territorial I can be—I loved the way he just sort of immediately made himself at home down here. At first I was amused, and there were certainly plenty of times when I resented it. Like his bringing home Valerie the slut. But one of many things that made me fall in love with him was when I realized that he didn't need any special equipment to breathe on my planet."

"So tell him."

"Yet my first instincts ended up being right—that if we made love, I'd live to regret it."

"But when you add up all the things that made you fall for him, was it really a mistake? And it's not exactly like he fended you off when you went for it in the whirlpool. In fact, he pulled you into the bathtub. So maybe he just needs you to say the words first . . . tell him how you feel about him and then he'll open up to you."

Kathryn sighed. "Or not."

"Kitty, what do you really have to lose by admitting you were wrong? That it *wasn't* a bad thing to lose your head and fall in love? You might gain Bear. And of course, even if you don't, you won't end up any more hurt than you are at the moment. Think about it that way. My husband admitted he was wrong and he got me back. And speaking of the man . . . I've got to hustle to meet Dan in Greenpoint. Some client of his knows of an available storefront where I can bake the Brownie Points. My kitchen looks like it exploded and I have twelve dozen to deliver to Toute Sweet on Lexington Avenue before five o'clock."

The sisters embraced and said good-bye. Kathryn locked the door and went to the stereo. The gentle strains of Windham Hill or the Celtic ballads of Loreena McKennitt just weren't going to cut it today. She flipped through her CD collection of Broadway shows. Gershwin, Porter, Sondheim. All wrong for the moment. Where did it go— the album with her new personal anthem that she had been playing for the past week, replacing Gloria Gaynor's "I Will Survive" for those occasions when she needed a kick-ass dose of self-esteem?

They'd been using it for a coaster. Kathryn opened the chartreuse and hot pink plastic "jewel box." She pumped up the volume, so Jim Steinman's "Holding Out for a Hero" blasted through her small apartment, rattling the heirloom teacups in her mahogany breakfront. Kathryn danced wildly around the room, pumping her arms into the air, gyrating her hips, belting out the lyrics. She played the same cut on the CD another half dozen times or so before she decided to let the next song on the soundtrack, a ballad, come on. With a more mellow sound filling the room, she finally heard the insistent sound of her doorbell. Kathryn peeped through the keyhole, then unfastened the deadbolt and turned the two Medeco locks.

He stood at the door, wearing his bright emerald running shorts, barefoot, holding a pint of Rocky Road. "Can I come in?" he asked tentatively.

Kathryn looked at the carton of Baskin-Robbins. "Is this a comment on our relationship, Bear?"

They shared a laugh. "I knew you'd get it. And I figured this was the best way to break the ice again. Cut me some slack here, Kitty. It's taken me over a week to come up with it."

She wanted to let him know everything that had been going on inside her head, but she didn't know where to begin. Maybe starting with small talk would lead to a more serious conversation. "Do you mind if we eat this later?" she asked him. It was his invitation to step inside her apartment. He brought with him the faint aromas of ambergris and musk. "You smell good," she remarked, noticing his fresh shave. "Did you know ambergris originally came from the secretions of sperm whales?"

He shook his head, a bit bemused.

"Oh," she added sweetly, "I thought you might be trying to tell me something else about our relationship."

She shelved the ice cream in the freezer and came back out to the living room, expecting to see Walker making himself comfortable on her freshly vacuumed velvet upholstery, squishing several cushions with his broad back. Instead, he was standing somewhat uncomfortably by her stereo. "I heard you were 'Holding Out for a Hero,' so I thought I'd stop down," he joked. "In fact, I heard it through the door. I've been ringing your bell throughout every one of the five times you replayed the song." He shifted his weight from foot to foot and took a dramatic breath. "Kitty? I've been thinking about what to say to you for some time and I didn't want you to think I was ignoring what happened between us; I just didn't know how to . . . well . . . I've come to a major decision about something . . . something I think you've been right about all along."

Chapter
29

Kathryn felt a thudding sensation in her chest and tried to look casual.

Walker waved his bandaged hand at her; she wondered why she hadn't noticed it when he first came in. Probably because she'd been too busy taking in his physique.

He grinned somewhat sheepishly. "Well, after I nearly sliced off a digit cutting an 'everything bagel' in half, I finally came to the conclusion that you were absolutely right . . . I probably *do* need glasses."

"Wh . . . wha . . . glasses?" Kathryn stammered.

"Yup. I only got the contacts because the one doctor I went to said I needed them. I didn't even get a second opinion. But between that and breaking your vase and nearly turning my kitchen into a scene from a Wes Craven movie just now . . . well, you know what they say."

"Who's 'they'?"

"You know. The people who say these things. My grandfather, for instance. He used to tell me 'when three people tell you you're drunk, lie down.' So, I'm giving in. We've pretty much determined my eyesight isn't perfect—and clearly I can't wear contacts. Kitty, I trust your taste—a whole lot better than I trust my own judgment, in fact. Will you please come with me to get a pair of glasses?"

Glasses. Right. Silly me . . . what was *I thinking?*

"Well, we've got more frames in here than in *Double Indemnity*," chuckled the white-lab-coated technician, a balding, round Englishman with a brush mustache, at the Cohen's Optical on Lexington Avenue. "I'm sure you'll find something you're happy with. Over here," he said, gesturing to a four-tiered display, "we have your designer frames. Your Armani, your Versace, your Laura Biagiotti, your Donna Karan. These are the bigger ticket items and to your right, we have what I like to call the knockoffs. These are our own manufacture; our customers seem to find them extremely satisfactory. Let me know once you've made your frame selection, we'll determine your lens prescription, and your glasses will be ready for you in an hour. Excuse me." The technician left Walker and Kathryn to browse while he regaled another customer with his patter.

"He looks like a muppet," Kathryn whispered to Walker, stifling a giggle. "Remember the one with the round blue head?"

Kathryn pointed to a pair of tortoiseshell frames. "Try these; they've sort of got the color of your hair in there. Oh, good Lord; they're Fendi. Oh, well. As long as they're not made with some endangered species of sea tortoise from the Galapagos . . . though for this price, they should be." She glanced at the little white tag hanging from a string attached to one end of the frames, then squinted a bit to read the tiny gold print engraved on the inside of the ear piece. "Oh, good. Genuine plastic. What a relief."

Walker took the frames from Kathryn and turned them over in his hand. "So, you like these."

"In theory. How about in practice?"

"Okay. Here goes." Walker tried on the frames and looked at Kathryn before checking himself out in the oval mirror on the counter top. "And the verdict is . . . ?"

Kathryn stepped back and took him in. She felt a little catch and release of breath as she appraised Walker's appearance. "You look . . . wonderful . . . actually. Like a very sexy, smart guy. Which is what you are. Check it out for yourself."

Walker regarded his appearance and blushed a little. "You once told me that when Lance did this, it was the kiss of death for your relationship, so I'm reluctant to say anything, but . . ."

"Damn, *you* look good!" They both laughed. "It's okay if *I* say it," Kathryn added. "You look *great*."

"Let's get the muppet over here and tell him it's a sale."

The technician examined Walker's eyes and rendered his verdict. "Your husband is somewhat shortsighted," he told Kathryn, who had watched the procedure with some concern.

"No kidding," she muttered to herself. "If he weren't so shortsighted, he'd actually *be* my husband."

"Shortsighted?" asked Walker, who seemed to have ignored the optometrist's inference that Kathryn was his spouse.

"We say 'shortsighted' back where I come from. Sorry, I've only been over here for a few months. I keep forgetting that it's called 'nearsighted' over here in the States.

When I called a guy 'shortsighted' last week, I nearly got myself pummeled into the next county. All right then, we're done. I'll see you in an hour or so."

Kathryn and Walker left the store and stood outside on the sidewalk, neither one knowing what to say or do next.

Walker chuckled to himself. He was shortsighted, actually, in the American meaning of the word. Kitty had accused him of myopia more than once, as far as his eyesight and their relationship were concerned. And she was totally right on both counts. His inability to see what was right in front of his nose, literally and figuratively, and his protracted reluctance to do anything about it had been ridiculous. He did indeed need to correct his vision. Kathryn had been right about the eyeglasses, his problem in microcosm.

It was time to tell her that she'd also been correct in macrocosm. His view of life as a permanent bachelor was skewed as well. It had been easier to maintain his inflexibility on the issue before Love had come into the picture. Before Kitty Lamb. He valued her opinions, trusted her judgment, admitted she'd been right . . . face it, he needed her. Life without her wasn't nearly as rewarding. He'd almost had the nerve to tell her he loved her the afternoon he'd seen her in Central Park, but he'd chickened out. Today was the day. He'd screwed his courage to the sticking place and gone down to Kathryn's apartment. Although he truly did value her fashion sense, asking her to accompany him to the optometrist was partially an excuse to get together.

Walker found himself standing outside the optician's looking into Kathryn's eyes and hoping to communicate his feelings through telepathy, because once again the words themselves weren't making it past his brain.

"Yes, Bear? Is there something you want to say to me?" Kathryn felt like Gwendolen in *The Importance of Being Earnest*. Walker had an intense, amorous look in his eyes, but his lips weren't moving.

"Look," Kathryn continued. "I've spent the past ten days or so hoping we'd run into each other so that I could admit to you that sleeping together wasn't the mistake I'd expected it to be. In spite of the emotional pain I've been dealing with since then, I wouldn't have missed it for the world . . . because . . . I love you. I fell in love with you weeks ago, I loved you when we made love on Martha's Vineyard, I loved you when we woke up together that morning. And, just as I predicted, you did break my heart by disappearing as soon as we got back to New York. I thought . . . I hoped . . . when you came downstairs to visit me this afternoon that you might tell me you felt the same way."

He was silent, but his eyes were full of expression.

"I mean it *looks* like you're feeling at least a little of what I'm feeling, but if you don't say anything, how can I believe that you really *do* feel the same way? How do I know that you're not just trying to spare me more pain by keeping quiet?" Her voice started to break. "I mean, if you don't *say* the words, then I guess you don't *feel* them." She looked down at the ground and a tear splattered to the pavement. "I'm going home. Enjoy your new glasses. Wear them in good health." She broke into a sob and walked away from him as briskly as she could, resisting the temptation to look back.

*   *   *

A few days later, as Kathryn was passing her local newsstand, she did a double take. Next to the headline for *New York* magazine's cover story on "From First Kiss to Nuptial Bliss: New York's Hottest Matchmaker" was a terrific photo of Walker Hart looking eminently confident and approachable in his tortoiseshell frames. She grabbed three copies of the issue and raced up to Park Avenue.

Eleanor was completing the invitation list for the official debut of her Brownie Points at the Upper East Side's trendiest new bakery, Let Them Eat Cake; the event was the culinary equivalent of a book signing. "Oh, God," she said, having grabbed one copy of the magazine away from her sister. "Listen to the very first sentence of the article: 'One of the hottest selling points about New York's most stylish matchmaking service, Six in the City, is that the manager himself, Walker Hart, is available.' "

"Little do they know his bachelorhood would appear to be permanent." Kathryn sighed heavily. "Did they print *that*?"

The sisters each skimmed a copy of the article in silence. "Guess not." Kathryn concluded. "So much for truth in advertising."

"They give Rushie a lot of ink, too," Eleanor observed. "And it would appear that we're not the only ones to refer to her as a yenta. But clearly, Walker is their poster child. They refer to him as 'the pianist in the penthouse' . . . as opposed to the fiddler on the roof, I guess."

"This is hysterical," Kathryn muttered, reading about Rushie. "They make it seem like her oft-married status gives her more credibility in the field. And I think they left out a Haggerty in this list of surnames. She married the same guy more than once, you know."

"Hey! This is you, Kitty!" The sisters flipped back to page forty-three.

"Whoa! It's that photo with Rick Byron that was taken at Nebuchadnezzar. What kind of a caption is this: 'Two on a Match'? Great. Bear must love this."

"Are you reading this?" Eleanor asked. "The journalist put a spin on it so it makes Six in the City seem even hotter, instead of referring to the incident as the total screw-up that it was. Walker couldn't be having sex with the writer, could he?"

Kathryn winced and got that "icky" feeling in her gut. "Let me see the byline." She flipped back to the beginning of the article. "Nope. Not in this case, anyway. I know who this Bea Friedman woman is; she's fifty-fiveish, extremely heavy, bad perm, bad skin, and most people think she's a lesbian. This is the most complimentary piece she's done on a man in a decade."

"Check out the very end of the story," Eleanor said. "Can I read this to you?"

Kathryn nodded and rested her chin in her hands.

"She asks him 'What about your *own* matches? Has there ever been "one that got away"? Hart lowers his sexy tortoiseshell rims and looks down at me, past the bridge of his perfectly straight nose. "Yes," he says, without a hint of the twinkle he displayed during the rest of our interview. "There certainly was." ' "

Walker's quote in the *New York* magazine article had made Kathryn consider initiating contact with him again. Her best bet was to walk back into Six in the City under the pretext of agreeing to his promise to make things right and give her a sixth fix-up for free. But at the moment, there was something even more immediate to be attended

to, and that was Eleanor's Let Them Eat Cake soirée.
Kathryn combed her closets for something expandable,
as she would no doubt be packing in plenty of free
Brownie Points. After multiple wardrobe changes, she
settled for the all-purpose black leggings and a velvet vest
the color of saffron. Caramel suede over-the-knee boots
and a green devoré scarf completed the look. Checking
her watch, Kathryn realized that she'd never make it to
the party on time via the route she'd originally intended
to take: a crosstown bus and an uptown subway. She'd
have to splurge on a cab.

Thirty minutes later and twelve dollars poorer, Kathryn arrived at the brownie *fête*, which was already in full
swing. Dan seemed to be having a blast playing host at the
bakery. He immediately steered each guest over to the
mouthwatering trays of Brownie Points, proudly pointing
out the eye-catching display card that proclaimed "Half
the fat and twice the fun of donut munchkins!"

Kathryn was in the process of stuffing one of the cakes
in her mouth when she noticed two women next to her
elbowing one another and gesturing in the direction of
the door.

"Ohmigod, it's that guy from *New York* magazine,"
one of them blurted. "And the first thing he'll see is me
with my mouth full." She stuffed her face with the last of
her Brownie Point and tried to discreetly turn away as
she chewed.

Kathryn watched as a bespectacled Walker shook
hands with Dan, who greeted him warmly, and then confidently strode over to the Brownie Points table. The be-
sotted female guest noticeably straightened her posture
and brushed the crumbs from her bosom. Walker picked

up a Brownie Point and leveled it at Eleanor. "Hey, I hear these make you lose weight!"

Eleanor leaned across the display and gave Walker a hug and a kiss on the cheek. "Not only that, they'll make you smarter, your love life will be successful beyond your wildest fantasies, and your first born will be guaranteed to become a doctor."

"But today I have to pay retail, huh?" Walker chuckled.

Kathryn turned around and tried to act calm. "I don't go in for hype. I like Brownie Points because they taste great and are less filling. Just read the sign." It was the first time they'd seen one another since the eyeglass-shopping trip. Her stomach was pumping with butterflies. "Well, Bear, I had a funny feeling you might show up this evening," she lied, looking meaningfully at Eleanor.

"I received an invitation, same as everyone else," Walker said pleasantly.

"You seem to have very little problem communicating with my sister." Kathryn replied. "Too bad it doesn't extend to the other sibling in the family."

"What are you talking about? I think we communicate very well, you and I."

Johanna skirted between them. "Aunt Kittycat, kiss!"

"Of course, jujube." Kathryn interrupted her conversation with Walker and knelt down to greet her little niece.

"Taste!" The toddler thrust a Brownie Point in her aunt's face.

Kathryn took a bite of the cake. "Yummy! Johanna, tell your mommy these are very, very yummy."

Johanna scampered off and Kathryn continued edgily, her volume increasing. "Yeah, right, we communicate terrifically. Except that we only communicate about things that aren't important. I put myself on the line and pour my heart out to you and you look back at me as though I were speaking in Urdu or something."

"Excuse me, could you sign this, please?" The young woman who had recognized Walker from his *New York* magazine cover photo pulled a copy of the periodical from her purse and shoved it under Walker's nose.

"I'm a little busy right now," he replied, somewhat flustered.

"Oops, I thought I had a pen. I'm so embarrassed," she said, fishing through her handbag. "Have you got one?"

Walker flipped back the lapel of his navy blazer and retrieved a ballpoint from his pocket.

"You *should* be embarrassed," Kathryn said loudly. "Can't you see you're interrupting something here?"

The autograph seeker ignored her. Walker signed the cover of the magazine and handed it back to its owner.

"Look, lady, we're trying to have a private conversation!" Kathryn shouted.

"Just one more thing, then. Could you just kiss me, here?" the woman shyly asked Walker, pointing to her cheek.

Walker had lost all patience by this time. "No. Go away!" The woman skittered off to show the precious autograph to her friend. "Good Lord, how pushy can one person be?" Walker muttered to Kathryn.

"I don't know, Bear. Ask your mother," Kathryn said pointedly.

"That was a low blow, Kitty."

"We were talking—before we were so rudely inter-rupted—" Kathryn continued, "about how the only time we seem to manage to communicate with each other is when the stakes are low."

Walker raised his voice. "That is absolute bull. We had mind-blowing sex several times in one night! That's not exactly communication on an 'unimportant' level."

The room suddenly grew quiet. Guests stopped to gawk at the now red-faced participants in the escalating confrontation.

"You're right, it's not. But then I practically rip open my chest, tear out my heart, all red and warm and pas-sionately pulsing, and virtually tie it to my sleeve, and you act like you don't even notice! I tell you I love you and you don't say a goddamn thing?! That's your idea of communication?" Without thinking, Kathryn snatched a Brownie Point from Eleanor's central display table and pelted it at Walker's head. The pointed tip caught him just below the right eye.

"Who decided that the game of love was being played by your rules?" he demanded, ducking to avoid a second chocolate cake missile. He feinted to her left and seized a Brownie Point from the table. "Is that what this is all about? Why does saying the three little words 'I love you' automatically make it so?" He hurled the Brownie Point at Kathryn, hitting her squarely in the chest.

She brushed the crumbs from her bosom and reached for another round of ammunition. "It doesn't. But when somebody tells you they love you, there is usually *some* response. Is my name 'Claire Voyant'? How am I sup-posed to divine what thoughts are zinging around in your head?" Kathryn hurled the Brownie Point like a dart, hitting the breast pocket of Walker's blazer. She grabbed another one, rushed at Walker and smooshed it all over his chin, smearing the chocolate cake down the front of his previously pristine white shirt.

They grappled, each struggling to reach the Brownie Points table while attempting to keep the other from taking more cakes. Walker finally managed to pin Kathryn's hands behind her back and hold them there with his left hand while he reached for a Brownie Point with his right. He snagged two of them and rubbed them into the V-shaped expanse of flesh above her breasts.

"Hey, watch where you're smearing. This vest is velvet. Do you have any idea how much it costs to dry-clean?"

Walker threw open his arms in a gesture of futility and yelled, "What makes you think it's as easy for me to say 'I love you' as it is for you?"

"Because you just said it," Kathryn said, pushing her weight against his. She managed to hook her right leg into the crook behind Walker's left knee, catching him unaware. He lost his balance and they both went crashing to the floor. She rolled on top of him, rubbing cake crumbs into his hair. "What do you have to say about that?"

Walker collected a fistful of bits and pieces of brownie from the floor and dropped them into Kathryn's curls. "First of all, I think you need to know that I did decide to share my feelings for you and even sought you out to tell you what was in my heart. I deliberately went to Central Park to look for you the week after we got back from the Vineyard and saw you by the carousel with Eleanor and Johanna. But I chickened out. When I asked you to ac-

company me to the optician's I had every intention of letting you know how much I care for you, but I just
couldn't get the words out—and not because I didn't feel
them. Kathryn, you didn't grow up in a household where
your mother said 'I love you' as often as she said 'I'm
going to get a manicure.' The most important words in
the world became utterly meaningless, as ephemeral as
her pastel cigarette smoke. When Rushie told a man she
loved him it meant she'd marry him until it was time to
get divorced. When she said those words to me, it was
usually before she left me to grow up on my own while
she embarked on yet another honeymoon excursion. So I
learned that 'I love you' means you'll probably be abandoned before you can ratchet up the courage to say those
words back. It's not what you say when you love someone, Kitty, but what you do."

Kathryn by now had managed to get to her knees and
hobble over to the Brownie Points table. She stocked up
on artillery, then pounced on him again, punctuating her
words with the sweet projectiles. "You're so damn
scared that you're going to lose love that you don't even
try to go for it. Are you afraid to begin because there's a
chance that things might end? Love is about taking risks,
Bear."

The couple had been doing their best to smother one
another with chocolaty crumbs as they tussled on the
floor. In Walker's attempt to roll away from Kathryn's
brownie bombardment, a small beribboned box in a
highly identifiable shade of robin's egg blue fell out of his
jacket pocket and onto the floor.

Kathryn's eyes lit up and she flung herself, breathless,
toward the box. "Been shopping at Tiffany, have we?"
she asked Walker sweetly.

"Not yet," he replied, pushing the box out of her reach.

After a few more thwarted attempts to reach the jewelry box, amid chanted shouts of encouragement from Eleanor's female party guests, Kathryn finally wrested it away from Walker's grasp, by going for his midsection and starting to mercilessly tickle him.

"Stop! Wait!" he said just as she was untying the ribbon. Walker stood up and brushed himself off. They both looked like they'd been mud wrestling. "Hand me that magazine," he told the infatuated autograph seeker. The young woman reluctantly obliged and Walker waved his arms to call everyone's attention to the publication in his hand. "If I might have your attention for a moment or two, please, everybody." The room grew quiet. Kathryn rose and ran a hand through her hair, trying to extract as much of the Brownie Point crumbs as she could.

"It was the journalist's assignment to make me seem like New York's most eligible bachelor. In fact, that's not the case."

There was a flurry of conversation from the intrigued bystanders.

"In fact, that's only a half-truth. I am a bachelor, but I am not eligible."

"No kidding," Kathryn kibbitzed.

"And not for the reason you think, Kitty," Walker replied, addressing her directly. "Folks, the issue of *New York* magazine currently on the newsstands is about to become a collector's item. Because some of the information contained in the magazine's profile of me will soon, I hope, be obsolete. Kitty, you can open that box now."

Kathryn pulled the white ribbon off the Tiffany box and lifted the lid. Nestled inside was a brass ring from the Flying Horses carousel on Martha's Vineyard. She stood, stunned and speechless, looking from the ring to Walker and back again.

"Now, look who can't put emotions into words," he said gently. "See? It happens to the best of us."

The only thing Kathryn finally managed to say was "I can't believe you stole this for me!"

Walker turned to their captive audience. "I told Bea Friedman who wrote the *New York* magazine article that in my own life, there was a woman who had 'gotten away.' Well, she's here now, and I hope she'll stay. Kitty, I know that gold is traditional, but that brass ring is meant to be a temporary stand-in for the real thing, if that's okay with you. You've got a room full of witnesses; I'm publicly hanging up my fear-of-commitment spurs. The idea of spending the rest of my life without you in it beside me is not only a really stupid one, it's entirely unacceptable."

She beamed up at him, tears rolling down her cheeks in silent but happy sobs.

"Oh, and one more thing," Walker added. "I love you, Kitty Lamb."

She ran forward and threw herself in his arms. Who cared if two hundred people saw them kiss and make up?

"I think we need to apologize to Ellie," Kathryn said, after she finally regained her composure.

Walker grimaced. They headed for the central display table where, upon their approach, Eleanor practically threw herself protectively over her remaining wares. He picked up a Brownie Point and noticed Eleanor's look of panic. "Don't worry," he told her, popping it in his mouth. "You're onto something here. I don't recommend them for a food fight, but they taste terrific. These are really spectacular. Open up." He steered the cake toward Kathryn's mouth and fed her the brownie, point first.

"Hold that pose!" Dan snapped a picture.

"You two have just given me an idea," Eleanor said. "Ice them with white fondant, pipe the lower edge, stick a crystal of rock candy through the bottom and I've got Wedding Bells." She grinned like the Cheshire Cat.

"If you don't mind our cutting out early, we've got a lot more communicating to do," Walker said to Eleanor and Dan. "Just one more thing before we go." He removed his checkbook from his inside breast pocket and dated and signed a blank check made out to Eleanor Lamb Allen. "I feel largely responsible for all this . . ." he said indicating the residual effects of the food fight. "Kitty, would you care to join me for dinner? I feel a sudden craving for more substantial fare."

Kathryn turned to her sister and winked.

Eleanor was about to hug her chocolate-cake-coated sister, but thought better of it. She mouthed her reply instead, so Walker wouldn't hear. "Congratulations! And good luck."

They had taken only a few steps outside Let Them Eat Cake when Kathryn stopped walking. "Can I have another hug, please? If you wouldn't mind?"

"My absolute pleasure." Walker enfolded her in his arms, stroked her hair, and held her close.

"This," she said holding him tighter, straining to reach her arms around his broad torso and back, "this feels so beautiful."

Walker lifted her face to his and gently kisse eyelids. "Because it is, sweetheart. What do you say skip the restaurant, go back to your place and hit the showers?"

Chapter
30

Kathryn lit a handful of candles and carefully placed them at strategic locations throughout her bathroom. She drizzled a few droplets of essential oil into a terra cotta burner and lit the flame beneath it. Some Mozart on the stereo completed the mood.

Walker held out his hand to her and led her into the bedroom. A shaft of moonlight found the narrow opening between her rich damask drapes and illuminated the bed, as though lighting the way to perfect ecstasy. He started to carefully unbutton the silken frog closures on her topaz-colored velvet vest. Kathryn was wearing nothing underneath it, and her skin immediately went from cool to warm as she felt his touch. He nuzzled her chest, licking off the remains of the Brownie Points he'd smeared there. The sensation was electrifying.

"Can I undress you, too?" she asked him.

He grinned mischievously. She thrust her hands into his sportcoat pocket. "Were you saving these for a rainy day?" she whispered, pulling out two Brownie Points. She placed them on the dresser, removed his blazer, his chocolate-stained white shirt; then deftly went for his belt buckle. "You're quite accomplished at this," he said impishly. "I especially like the way you . . . ohhh."

Kathryn's hand enveloped him. "I thought that might shut you up." She knelt down, positioning herself at his feet. Her hands cupped and stroked him with feathery dexterity as she took him in her mouth. Kathryn, sensing his urgency, slowed her rhythm, teasing him, her tongue tracing sensuous circles that increased the intensity of his pleasure. As she suckled him she reached for a Brownie Point, crushing it with her hand. She applied the sweet chocolate paste to his skin, enjoying the melange of tastes.

His hands ravaged her hair, massaging her scalp, while she worked him in long, steady strokes. Walker moaned, then eased himself away from Kathryn and raised her to her feet. He slipped his hand underneath the silk triangle of her panties and felt her slickness. "Let's get in the shower," he murmured, as she moaned.

Amid the fragrant steam, they continued their exploration, soaping, teasing, cleansing one another of the smears and crumbs of chocolate. Walker stepped behind Kathryn, rubbing himself against the hollow of her back. He nibbled her neck as he lathered her hair, sending delicious tinglings into her scalp and down her spine.

"What if Eleanor had never had a party this evening?" Kathryn asked softly. "What if you didn't have a way to run into me that was a sure bet? Would I have ended up some lonely old lady in a rocker caring for a dozen stray cats, pining away for the match that might have been, while you played the field for another few decades until your yearnings for succulent young female flesh made you the laughingstock of Manhattan?"

Walker ran his hands through her hair to rinse out the shampoo. "That's the most unflattering portrait of either of us I can imagine."

Kathryn turned to face him. "You didn't answer the question."

"Can I spread soap suds all over your breasts first?"

"Oh, all right. If you must, you must." She wriggled under his gentle touch.

"Today was D-Day," Walker whispered. "The third try is supposed to be the lucky one, and I'd promised myself that no matter the cost, I would tell you how important you are to me and that I don't want to grow older without you. It came at a pretty high cost, too, I might add."

"Yeah." She smiled at him. "I'd all but given up on you."

"That's not the cost I mean," he teased. "I ended up paying for the entire Brownie Points launch party!"

They stepped out of the shower and wrapped one another in enormous fluffy bath sheets, toweling each other dry. Then Walker lifted Kathryn into his arms and deposited her on the bed. He lay down beside her and held her, inhaling her fresh, clean scent.

"Yum. This feels so right," she said, burrowing against him.

"It feels right because it is right and every way with you is the right way," he whispered, darting his tongue in her ear, sending a series of electric shocks coursing through her body.

Her nerve endings were like fireworks, her body felt more and more electrified with every stroke. Kathryn arched her hips up to meet his hand, as he slid his fingers inside her. Wide-eyed, she watched as he tasted her by making a sensual show of licking his finger. She felt his breath on her neck, a rush of warmth against her increasing heat.

His hands began a slow, masterful exploration of her body, heightening her desire for more. Her thighs quivered as he caressed them ever so softly; then he inched up the length of her torso, gently fluttering over her, tracing the contours of her breasts, teasing her nipples to hardness, his touch generating increasingly exhilarating sensations, like the explosions of millions of tiny stars inside her. Everywhere his skilled fingers landed, her skin seemed to come more alive, as though experiencing sensation for the very first time.

He nuzzled the side of her neck, driving her so wild with the intensity of the feeling that she found herself writhing beneath him.

The fervor of Kathryn's desire fueled Walker's ardor. He sought her beautiful mouth, which yielded so sweetly, so fully to his own. Kathryn Lamb was his. Fully. Completely. And he was hers. What an exquisite thing, he thought as his lips made a thorough pilgrimage down Kathryn's body, nibbling, nuzzling, finally burying his face in her sweet softness, teasing and tasting her with his tongue.

Walker took his time, letting his mouth brush over her as she moved rhythmically against him, allowing him to bring her higher and higher until she reached an ecstatic, exquisite plateau.

She felt as though she were floating in some form of divine suspension. Her body shuddered when he entered her. *Welcome home,* she thought. They meshed together as though they were made for one another. The moonglow on his muscled back gave him an almost otherworldly look, like an angel sent to minister to her every need. Her earthly needs. Her every sexual desire. And minister he did. Walker seemed inexhaustible, moving so

slowly at first that she cried out, begging him for more.
"Don't stop . . . please," she heard herself plead. He
obliged, treating her body to a banquet of strokes and
speeds, knowing instinctively how to prolong her rhapsody and how to bring her to gradually increased heights
of sensual gratification.

Walker's release was the most sustained he ever could
remember. And afterward, he held Kathryn in his arms,
their bodies glistening with sweat and sex, their eyes
shining with the light of someone truly fulfilled.

"Did I fall asleep?" Kathryn asked when she looked
back up at Walker and noticed his eyes were wide open.

"It was beautiful," he murmured, meeting her lips.
"You looked so sweet and peaceful. Like a little Pre-
Raphaelite angel."

She snuggled against him. "Thank you."

"For what?"

"Everything."

"You know, according to the terms of your Six in
the City renegotiated contract, I still owe you a sixth
bachelor."

"I'll waive my rights. In case you hadn't already figured that out."

He stroked her head. "I love your hair, Kathryn," he
said, seeming to ignore her remark. "It's so much fun to
play with." Walker ran his fingers through her tangled
tendrils. He shifted his position so he could face her and
they could talk eye to eye. "You see, I took a lot of time
to think things over. But the only thing that makes sense
to me is to follow through with my offer and fix you up
with a sixth eligible man. Someone who really wants to
get married to a beautiful curly-haired red-head; someone who will love and cherish and adore her, and fry

bacon with her on Sunday mornings, and read the Sunday *Times* to her while she bakes gingerbread cookies in whimsical shapes. I want to hear anything you have to say—and I promise I'll remember it. I want to make you laugh every day; I want to hold you when you need to cry and I feel blessed every time you unburden your soul, open your heart, and share your body with me. I love you. There, I said it again. That's twice in one night. Kathryn, I hope your reaction to the brass ring means that you'll give *me* a try as Bachelor Number Six."

Tears of joy welled up once again inside her. "You are one goddamn special guy, Walker Hart. I accept."

His kiss tasted of fire and desire and promise. "You have no idea how hard it was for me to fix you up with all these eligible . . ."

Kathryn arched an eyebrow.

"And not as eligible as they had represented themselves . . . men. Actually, I felt that way from the day you walked into Six in the City; it just took me a long time to come to terms with it. Every night I went to sleep wondering if I was going to lose you to the next guy . . . even when Josh succinctly observed that I didn't even have you to begin with. But in my mind . . . or my ego, I guess, I felt you were mine all along. Josh also said something else to me awhile back . . . about you."

"What was that?" Kathryn whispered, running her hands through Walker's hair.

"He reminded me that I don't have to be like my mother; that I have a choice. I don't have to run away from things; I can run toward them and embrace them. It was an epiphany. It's very easy to avoid commitment if you've never been in love before. Then, I met you, and suddenly, after a lifetime of mocking the idea of matrimony, I had to do some serious soul-searching. All my life, I've been saying one thing and craving another. My aversion to marriage was funneled through the kaleidoscope of Rushie's myriad relationships. I kept running away from anything that might lead me toward commitment because I was using her template when all along, it's what I've really always wanted; I've just been too scared to give voice to it and make it happen . . . but I'm finally ready. In you I've met *my* match."

"You know what this means, don't you, Bear?"

"I do."

Kathryn kissed him deeply. "Damn right, you amazingly wonderful, heart-stoppingly sexy man. It means 'I do.' "

"I said it this evening in front of a room full of strangers and I'll say it again now. The last of the dyed-in-the wool bachelors is freely, happily, decidedly kissing single life good-bye. This is a huge deal for me, you realize? Our love is so important that I'm willing to commit to an admitted shopaholic."

Kathryn stifled a giggle. "I promise not to make too big a dent in your wallet."

Walker deposited kisses on Kathryn's nose, mouth, and chin. He smiled, his eyes sparkling a deep shade of teal. "Let's get dressed; I have something to show you."

She felt herself blush a bit. "I think you already did. Besides," she added, "shouldn't I shower again?"

"I think you smell pretty good right now, actually. Anyway, we're not going far. Just upstairs." He swung his long legs over the side of the bed, stood up and extended his hand to Kathryn, pulling her into a hug.

* * *

"Wha ... what happened to this place?" Kathryn stammered when Walker opened the door to the penthouse and gestured grandly toward the interior. The boring *"brut champenoise"* wall-to-wall broadloom had been replaced with large Oriental carpets in jewel tones. The parquet floor peeking out from underneath the fringed edges of the antique Persian rugs gleamed. Where the butt-ugly "amoeba" glass and chrome table had stood, there was an ebony coffee table with graceful curved edges embellished with stunning cutwork.

"*Now* I understand why one would want Austrian shades," Walker said, raising the soft white swags, exposing the view across the Hudson. The night's full moon illuminated the river so that the swift current seemed like an endless ripple of diamonds flowing southward to the Atlantic. "Finally, they match the décor."

"Why did you do all this, Bear? And by the way, what does your mother think about your redecorating?"

"It's none of her business."

"Isn't this *her* apartment?"

"Not anymore. Rushie is thoroughly convinced that the marriage to Gilligan . . ."

"*Gillian.*"

". . . will last forever. She said this place never felt like home anyway."

"*Quelle surprise.* She was never here."

"So I bought the mortgage from her." Walker seized the opportunity to thoroughly kiss Kathryn's open mouth. "The Connecticut property is still under sublease. And . . ." he added, "I've grown rather accustomed to the view."

Flustered, her heart beating with joy, anticipation, shock, amazement, and other emotions her mind was racing too fast to put a name to it, Kathryn nodded toward the river vista. "You mean the . . ."

Walker turned her face back to meet his. "No, I mean *this* view." His kiss was deep and sweet and full of . . . well, *commitment*.

"And I was thinking," he said slowly, "that your apartment is a bit small . . . for two people . . . so I was wondering if . . . if I 'Kathryn-ized' this place, that you might consider . . . ? And I didn't take down the Warhol yet, but I thought you might want to hang one of your Pre-Raphaelite prints, if you decide to . . . you know . . . move in here. That is, if you like the place."

He led Kathryn to the sofa; the leather monstrosity had been replaced with a handsome couch with over-sized pillows upholstered in a rich paisley textile. "And you wondered what I was doing all that time after we got back from the Vineyard," he teased. "Wait . . . there's something else. Stay there." He poured them each a glass of sherry, then sat down at the piano and started to play.

Kathryn closed her eyes, enjoying the melodic rhapsody.

"If you were expecting The Torykillers, I apologize," he teased. Then Walker started to sing in an impressively professional baritone.

As the last note faded away, Kathryn suddenly realized that he had written the exquisitely gorgeous song just for her. She was completely overwhelmed. "Oh, my God," she breathed. "It's so . . . it's . . . so beautiful." She patted the sofa, grateful for the reassurance that the fur-niture beneath her was solid, because everything else seemed so unreal.

Walker knelt by her side, clasping her hands in his. "Kathryn Lamb, would you—will you—do me the honor of marrying me?"

"Gee, Bear," Kathryn said, happy, happy tears coursing down her cheeks, "it's quite a magnanimous offer. But you see, I'm not so sure I can accept."

He looked completely crestfallen.

Her wicked little smile reassured him immensely. "Simply because . . . I haven't seen what you've done with the *boudoir* yet."

In an instant, she had been scooped up into his arms in a single sweeping motion. They headed for the bedroom, Kathryn's long red curls cascading over Walker's shoulder, their lips fused in an ecstatic give and take of passion and desire.

"*Ms.* Lamb," Walker said huskily, during a brief pause for breath, "we've had this date from the beginning."

Read on for a sneak peek at
REALITY CHECK
The next romantic comedy by
Leslie Carroll

Coming in Spring 2003

Are you perennially single?
Do you want to make $1,000,000.00?
Have your dating experiences been "doozies?"

You could be a contestant on

BAD DATE

The new reality-based TV game show coming to you this fall from the people who brought you last season's hit series "Surviving Temptation."

14 lucky contestants'll share harrowing tales of their hard luck laps on the dating circuit. Our studio audience will vote on who has the worst date of the week. If you're the solo single standing at the end of the season,
YOU WIN ONE MILLION DOLLARS
Plus an all-expense paid trip for two to romantic Paris, the City of Lights.

Auditions March 15 in NYC, Chicago, and L.A.
Phone 1-800-Bad-Date for audition information.

I was the first one to see the ad. It must have been a karma thing, because I never read the *New York Post*. I'm a *Times* kind of gal, and these days I read even that on the Internet. Jem, one of my roommates, buys the *Post* for the horoscopes. You would think a Professor of Communications at a local community college, a grown woman with a Ph.D. on her wall and three pair of Manolo Blahniks (bought retail) in her closet would have more sophisticated journalistic tastes. Not Jem. I know for a fact though, she reads more than the horoscopes. She reads "Page Six" and Cindy Adams' column, too. I tease her to no end about it being a tabloid rag. "It's nothing but gossip columns and ads."

This particular ad made me reconsider.

I'm a sharer, so I thought it would be unfair to Jem and to Nell, my other apartment mate, to leave a gaping gash in the newsprint and smuggle the ad into my room. Besides, it wasn't like I was the only "perennially single" woman in the country, let alone the city, to see it. I was convinced however, deep down in that unknowable way, that the jackpot was mine, though in the great collective unconscious, that was probably the thought shared by every unmarried person in the contiguous forty-eight states within a three thousand mile radius of either coast.

"C'mon you guys, let's audition! I think we're all photogenic enough to be on the show," Nell said I thought that was mighty charitable of her since Nell is perfect. She even has a perfect-sounding name, Anella Avignon. Nell has the naturally straight honey blonde hair that every movie star pays a fortune to have theirs look like on all those awards shows. She's got a metabolism like a tiger shark and never needs to exercise. She's also got a trust fund. Nell is drop-dead-gorgeous and does absolutely ly nothing all day, but since she pays the rent on time, I can't complain. She could easily afford her own apartment but she says she gets lonely and has a horror of ending up like a modern day Miss Havisham, wandering aimlessly for decades around a warren of overdecorated rooms, so she prefers the company of roommates. Nell is also one of the most generous women on the planet. Witness her complimentary remark about all three of us vis-à-vis this *Bad Date* show. Nell is perfect. A perfect blonde goddess. This morning I started to face it. I've got Venus envy.

"Nell, you don't need the million dollars. Why would you humiliate yourself on national television?" Jem asked her.

"Well," Nell said thoughtfully, gazing into the middle distance. "It's something to do. Besides, Daddy's fed up with giving me something for nothing."

Jem and I gasped in tandem. "What?!"

"Does that mean you can't pay your share of the rent?" It was the first thing out of my mouth. "Jeez, Nell, I didn't mean that the way it sounded," I added quickly. "I'm sorry."

"It means I may actually have to get a job," Nell said sadly. "So if I win the million dollars then I can afford to do nothing. And still give half the money to charity if I wanted to." Nell got that "epiphany" look in her blue eyes. "That's what I would do. I'd throw charity balls with it. Dress up in an evening gown, meet rich, great-looking guys, and give a bunch of dough to the Fresh Air Fund or something. I could do that. I'm good at throwing parties. Mummy brought me up to know the difference between beluga and sevruga, and if I can use that skill to benefit inner city kids, I'll be a happy camper."

See, this is why I can't hate Nell. She really is such a generous soul despite the fact that she mentioned the chance to dress to the nines as her primary motivation for giving to charity.

"I've never quite understood how you can do nothing all day and not get bored," I said.

"Well, I do nothing *now*," Nell insisted ""It's only until I find something I really like to do—besides shop and throw parties. I'd rather do nothing than something I don't like. I don't know how *you* can do *that*, Liz," she added, looking straight at me.

"Because some of us don't have daddies who are CEOs of Fortune 500 companies," I sighed. "And because people actually pay me money to write. Even though half the time these days I have zero belief in the product I'm writing the copy for…which makes it a tad hard to promote. And occasionally makes the client a little testy."

"Yeah, well, I can see that," Nell said helpfully.

I used to get a thrill out of coming up with an ad campaign from scratch, writing clever copy that would hook the consumer. Lately, though, I'd been getting my creative kicks by writing a Regency-era novel called *The Rake and the 'Ho'* that takes place in one of Capability Brown's idyllic gardens.

"I feel so soulless now, you guys. When I started writing ad copy, I enjoyed its creative challenges. There was an alchemy to it. Spinning words into gold. Smoke and mirrors. When we developed public service campaigns, it was rewarding to know that my words were reaching other people and perhaps making a difference in their lives. Maybe one more battered wife would seek help. Maybe one more mother would warn one more child about the dangers of ingesting lead paint. But over the past few months, every day I feel more and more like a charlatan. One of our clients—a *very* big account—household name—launched these little computer screens called "The *Intel*ligencer" mounted inside elevators. The screens flash headline news, traffic conditions, weather, sports for the captive audience. A fifteen-word visual bite that changes every five seconds or so. Not even enough time to remember what you read, or enough information to make it truly useful."

"You're on your soapbox, girlfriend. It's just a new form of communication," Jem said. "What's the matter with that?"

"The matter is that I was struck with how useless the product really was. My ad agency is being paid to sell a product that no one needs and no one would have even known they wanted if it hadn't been invented. Complete manipulation of the consumer and a totally useless waste of technology."

"So, if *you* won the contest...?" Jem asked me.

"I'd open my own cutting edge ad agency that specializes in PSAs—smart public service messages for companies with a conscience. A million bucks would pay for the start-up. It would also be the kick in the butt that I need to finish my Ph.D. All I've got left is the dissertation, which I've been procrastinating about for years. If *Dr.* Pemberley is heading up her own agency, it'll add extra clout. Besides, my mother always wanted a doctor in the family."

"Fair enough," Nell said, dog-earing a page in her Victoria's Secret catalogue. "This bathing suit wouldn't make me look fat, guys, would it?"

Jem and I rolled our eyes.

"Honey, it could be down-filled and you wouldn't look fat," Jem answered her.

"Why would *you* enter this contest?" I asked Jem.

Jem may be the most hyper-educated woman I know, but she's finally—after years of psychotherapy—coming to terms with her name. "How can a black woman name her daughter *Jemima*," she used to rant. The true genesis of Jemima's name is that her mother saw the movie version of *Chitty Chitty Bang Bang* when she was pregnant with her and fell in love with the name of the little girl (Jemima) in the story. But Jem claimed that she was stigmatized, traumatized, and every other kind of "tized" for the rest of her life by the appellation.

Jem laughed. "I think it would be a damn kick, that's why. And kind of an interesting experiment to be part of. From a sociological point of view."

"What would you do with the money if you won?" Nell asked her.

"Get out of teaching apathetic college students who are taking my courses merely to satisfy a requirement. Not have to deal with the unwanted sexual advances of a department head who's a self-professed warlock. I'd bank the money so I could afford to teach inner city first graders. Mold their sweet little minds; teach them to read."

"You're incredibly noble," I told her.

"I mean it," Jem said.

And that was how we all decided to shelve our dignity in the name of a commitment to community service and audition for *Bad Date*, the reality game show.